GALACTIC PASSAGES

Planet 6333

D0967410

DEAN & ANSON VARGO

Illustration Consultant
NATALIE VARGO

ISBN 978-1-64079-402-3 (paperback)
ISBN 978-1-64079-403-0 (digital)

Christian Faith Publishing, Inc.
832 Park Avenue
Meadville, PA 16335
www.christianfaithpublishing.com

Printed in the United States of America

Thank you to all my brothers and sisters at the MAC Fire Department, (special recognition to C-shift station 2, 2016), and the Minnesota Air National Guard (special recognition to 148th Chaplain's office), for providing inspiration for the story. Also, thanks to Minnesota State Parks, where the rugged and majestic beauty of Minnesota are highlighted at places like Gooseberry Falls and Tettegouche. I sprinkle the charm of such favorite family places into the story.

Sarah, thanks for your support in allowing me to devote time and resources to this project. Thanks for your keen eye, and knowledge of proper grammar! Abigail, thanks for lending a listening ear, and knowledge of cats in particular! Natalie, your talent for visual details added a unique spice to our story. I enjoyed working on the 7th illustration with you: *Onsan and Oghy: Pair of Swindlers.* Anson, our conversations about the direction of our story will always be treasured memories for me. With your ideas and twists along the way, it's twice as good as it would have been! Finally, I'd like to recognize and thank Shalanda Gilliland, my agent at Christian Faith Publishing. I'm grateful for your patience and kindness throughout the process.

Dean Vargo

Thank all my teachers from Barnum, Minnesota. The teachers who stand out the most for me are Mrs. Audra Richardson and Ms. Kristen Helland. You helped me early during 7th grade, to learn the importance of paying attention to details and expressing myself to others. There are a few "Easter eggs" in this book to represent my friends. Thank you for all providing us with character ideas by simply being who you are! Thank you, Mom, Natalie, and Abby, for providing support for our book. Thank you, Dad, for acknowledging my ideas, so we could present our story to the universe!

Anson Vargo

It was fun working with Dad on the illustrations, thanks Dad! I learned about how the pictures changed from rough drafts to the end of the art process. It was cool how story concepts became art to make the book better. When I told the artist my ideas or changes, they were added into the pictures nicely afterwards. I enjoyed drawing Chase, and creating the 7th picture with Dad.

Natalie Vargo

CONTENTS

ILLUSTRATIONS INDEX

CHAPTER 1

The Haunting Artifact

*Z*zzzttt, *pop, grind!*

An electric blue arc was followed by a spray of blinding golden sparks. The mining shaft supervisor yelled over the chaos, "Hold it, stop the borer before you fry the motor!"

The confused driver looked out the window of his tractor, "What was that?"

"Back outta there. Let's see what you've hit."

The excavator engineer tried to move the machine out of the hole, but the battery had died. He exclaimed, "How can that be?"

"Better replace the power cell," said the supervisor.

"Just did a full check before the shift and replaced it an hour ago. It should've been good until next week's operational test."

The supervisor shook his head, "Faulty unit, obviously."

After they replaced the battery, the operator backed out and the miners inspected the rock. They were astounded by what they saw.

"Impossible!" Their faces were frozen in terror!

"This is beyond my pay grade. We'd better move it up the chain," said the supervisor.

Deep in a dimly lit mining hole, 150 meters beneath the icy crust of a desolate planet called Muudia, a surprising and haunting discovery was made. "Operation supervisor, this is Ned Starkly, mining team 5B chief engineer. We have an unusual finding. Please come down here as soon as possible," pleaded the astonished controller.

Five trillelium miners working the night shift found an engineered structure that couldn't be explained on the lifeless frozen planet. The mining operation on planet Muudia was initiated from Trecon, a planet five solar systems away from their current location, after an accidental discovery of the ore by a misguided, run-away satellite. There had been no evidence of any previous inhabitants there.

Everything on Muudia was ice, rock, and mud. To find remnants of a man-made structure in the ground as they were digging out trillelium ore was an unthinkable proposition to the miners.

The mysterious relic appeared to be a dense metal superstructure beam, measuring roughly four meters high and wide, and 10 meters long, a cage protecting an oval canister in the middle. It was likely manufactured to provide stability and support to the center part but also appeared a smaller part of something substantial, like a superstructure of a ship. Seeds of worry found fertile ground deep within their minds!

The ore-rich planet was at the edge of a quiet galaxy, seemingly an unexplored and uninhabited planet since the Trecons started the mining operations five and a half years prior. The miners realized there was no reasonable explanation for it. It was as though they were being haunted by an alien ghost from a distant past.

Starkly contacted his supervisor, who ordered the team to halt excavation activities and return to the surface until it could be investigated further. Everyone was cleared from the area as the perplexing information slowly climbed the ladder of influence within the camp.

The 5B supervisor skipped a few links in the chain of command and transferred a message to the top. "Muudia operations, this is Thom Johston, 5B supervisor, you need to come down here and see this."

"Please explain what you've got, 5B," replied Major Tallik, a sleepy staff officer. The stout balding major had cloudy, half-opened blue eyes.

Johston wisely didn't want to broadcast their finding over the transmitter. It seemed logical to keep the info tight to the vest. He respectfully replied, "Negative, sir. You'll have to come down here to see this for yourself!"

"Give me 20 minutes," was Tallik's groggy response.

After the major saw the anomaly for himself, he woke the top dog, General Thomas Krevety. Krevety was a hulking man with handsome features and kind dark brown eyes. Black hair was graying along his ears, giving him a distinguished look.

The general set a course of action with a sense of urgency. The next three and a half hours were a buzz of activity around the location, as excavating and scientific experts were brought down to investigate the scene. An order was given to dig the structure up and place it in storage behind a shroud of secrecy.

Every miner and officer who knew about the discovery was placed on an immediate hush order. They reported to a holding area until further notice while management sorted out their options. The thought of such a discovery instilling uncertainty among the mining settlements deeply concerned leadership. Watching fear mingle and grow within the declining souls of the miners was out of the question.

The number of quarantined individuals included the five initial miners; one controller, five excavator and ground-equipment specialists, four scientists, six security, and three command staff—totaling 24 people. It was quite an ordeal organizing equipment covertly to pull the metal object out of the deep crust of the planet.

A lockdown was ordered in section 5B, and Storage Area 2 in Mining Camp 1 (MC1SA2) from the Muudia operations commander. Krevety supervised the quarantine until they could get a handle on the situation. The general immediately appointed his second-in-command, Colonel Ferd Honassen, to the position of acting operations commander.

Miners quarantined from the rest of the camp population meant that others would have to carry more of the workload. It placed another weight on the ankles of sinking morale in the foreboding landscape of the lonely planet. Thus, began a massive conspiracy among the encampments. The rumor mill was the primary source of getting the information out through the masses, regardless of the official word.

Reputations and relationships were the true fuel for how people felt, and Krevety knew he could do little to change that.

General Krevety contacted Trecon mission control to report their new and unusual finding. "Trecon Control, we're in urgent need of assistance down here! We have exhumed a metal structure while mining ore in shaft 5B. The discovery of this fabrication could cause increased unrest within the colonies. As a result, I'm personally overseeing a quarantine operation and will accompany the package to Trecon upon the arrival of my replacement."

He continued his report, "Our trillelium ampules are full, and we have consequently been piling ore on high ground surfaces of the planet due to a recent ground thaw. Increased problems with mud are causing the ore stores and equipment to sink, and flooding is a constant threat in certain areas."

After his report, Krevety was pleasantly surprised to receive an immediate response.

"Understood. A small supply convoy will be underway within the week. We expect a quick turnaround. We'll be sending compact fleets from now on due to the current hazards around Muudia. General Etrod is looking forward to meeting with you, as well as the challenges of building upon your successes."

Krevety was surprised when his message actually got through to Trecon with all the recent interference. Solar flares had made communication to Trecon difficult recently. The general quickly added one last fervent comment, "Highest priority are the sump pumps, potassium iodide, and the cats!"

"Got it general, your req—."

Once again, communication with the home planet was lost. General Krevety knew they were at the crossroads of something big! Trecon control had always believed that they were the first to discover the planet and the precious trillelium ore. They were genuinely confused why Muudia remained uninhabited with masses of valuable metal ore encased within the crust.

There were many questions but no clues to build upon. Why would a past civilization leave such a valuable resource behind? There were planets around the universe who'd gamble bankrupting themselves to have the chance at the wealth that trillelium would bring. Trecon itself invested enormously, betting the endeavor would pay for itself within seven years. The government hoped that afterward they'd be a major economic player throughout their quadrant and the greater universe. The new find could change everything for them.

Trecon control became filled with curiosity and fear about the unknown civilization that no longer had a presence there. Their curiosity went deeper with every new question. Would the mysterious society suddenly come back and want to claim and protect their past investment? Would they find more evidence that would lead them to more antediluvian worlds in the distant corner of the universe?

General Krevety asked Pnoi Nbnok, his lead scientist, to study the object and give him a detailed report as soon as possible.

Nbnok's initial findings offered only more questions. "General, it appears as though these are the remains of a superstructure of a very substantial ship that crash-landed long ago. The only thing odd about that conclusion is the fact that such a sizable structure could descend down over 150 meters deep into the planet's hard crust with no other remnants of the spacecraft." Nbnok took a breath.

"Go on," said the general.

"Breaking through the Muudia ground and not completely disintegrating on impact seems impossible for a gigantic ship crashing at supersonic speeds. It's puzzling we've found nothing else closer to the surface. I don't have a clue. Muudia has been covered with ice so rock solid that it has caused us to pay a heavy toll in maintaining the excavating equipment alone."

Nbnok continued, "If it sank during a period of thaw, as we're in now, we should've found a sizable vessel down there. Somehow this thing penetrated deep into the planet with the outer parts of the ship shattering along the way, while leaving no evidence of charred remains in its path. There should've been a huge defacement at the crash site, but there was nothing. The whole surface of Muudia appeared smooth as a baby's bottom during our first exploratory mission before the mining operations began. The facts just don't add up. An intriguing mystery, for sure."

General Krevety responded, "We'll get you any resources within our power to find the answers, major."

"I won't rest until we solve this riddle, sir!"

CHAPTER 2

Trecon Mining Settlement Timeline

During five years, the Trecons had set up three immense mining camps on the surface of Muudia where the richest veins of trillelium deposits were discovered. The initial confirmation of trillelium deep in the crust of Muudia happened through strange circumstances of an exploratory satellite being thrown off course and into the lonesome solar system in the far reaches of the galaxy. It was as though the planet were gifted to them out of the blue!

Trecon was thrilled to learn of the natural stores of ore within the planet. They invested heavily, assuring there was a rich supply of trillelium ore on Muudia before they acted. Then they capitalized fast. The Trecons nearly over-leveraged themselves establishing a mining settlement in the most abundant area of the planet. Eventually, they built three identical camps above the richest veins of Muudia.

Each camp consisted of a main center vault that functioned like a city center for the settlement, called the Life Dome. The rotunda provided both physical and social sustenance to the miners. Going out from the Life Dome in all directions were thick glass tunnels that led to the underground barracks, equipment storage, and maintenance repair bays. A landing pad and other essential structures filled out the camps.

Constant sounds of the coming and going of miners flowed in and out of the Life Dome; heavy machinery here, a horn honking there, official greetings and informal news flowing through the settlements. A tunnel twice as high and wide led from the equipment bays to the mining operation area to accommodate heavy machinery. Off the mining areas were trillelium storage zones, where the lifeblood of the operation was stockpiled and prepared for loading onto cargo vessels.

Every settlement resembled a small city housing about 500 people including miners, support professionals, and a small security detail of Starlance fighters to protect them. Plans for permanent settlements were in the works in Trecon, as soon as their initial investment paid dividends.

A massive military base was in the 12-year plan, but the project was put on the back burner. Scientists were studying the toxic Muudia mud and finding it to be an inadequate growing medium, so they'd have to ship in food. Every scientific experiment bent on making Muudia a self-sustaining domicile failed.

Most people hated the assignment, but were there for reasons of necessity until they could improve themselves. Mining trillelium ore on Muudia was a thankless job for the mining community; much different than on Trecon where mining taconite and granite was considered a noble occupation and the backbone of their economy. Every miner stuck on the desolate rock habitually fantasized about being back home in the taconite mines where they could go home every day after their shift.

The Muudia mining settlements also included those who wanted to make scientific research or exploration their career choice. Those with greater aspirations joined the mission knowing they needed to put their time in in a place like Muudia to gain rank and status, then it would be on to bigger and better things.

*****

Overall organization seemed to crumble from the top down, starting five solar systems away at Trecon Control. Things were changing so constantly that Trecon Control was always behind on information coming from Muudia. There was a feeling in the camps they were gradually being abandoned. Problems were compounding on one another.

Even on the lifeless planet, they had a growing rodent problem within the settlements. Rats were brought in from Trecon on a supply ship, and were running rampant among the camps. Black droppings greeted the miners daily on the floors and galley tables. They glared at the miners from shadowy places that offered refuge, with red glowing eyes.

They were big, malicious, and becoming increasingly daring! The nasty creatures felt entitled to the stores of food meant for the mining camp workers, and were intent on defending their turf. The greasy sheen on their fur was accentuated by a repugnant odor; foul and sour like rotting garbage. Their claws scraped grotesquely against the cement as they darted across the floors, and they made high-pitched screams at the miners.

Squeak, clatter, shriek!

They were normally shy animals that hid out in holes and dark corners during the day and scavenged at night, but a lack of a natural food source forced them into the open. Lately they came out at mealtime, scurrying under the tables looking for scraps. The disgusting animals occasionally bit miners while they ate. Some people carried small clubs with them, even hitting the elusive creatures occasionally during mealtime.

Cooks and galley workers engineered traps for them, catching dozens. However, the problem wasn't improving because the rat population was steadily increasing. It seemed the rats had breeding habits more intense than wild rabbits!

Mining control knew that rats were a problem that would drive morale down to the absolute rock-bottom. When people were already dealing with the isolation and dense cold of a mining operation, hot chow acted like a buoy for their emotional state. However, when the one remaining pillar of survival was affected, it could create a planetary-wide mindset of depression from which they couldn't recover. Something had to be done.

*****

Meanwhile on Trecon, leadership consulted with a leading biological scientist to find a solution. Tephen Davss was a respected researcher in the frozen forests of Northern Trecon who suggested that the best solution to their problem was the relatively mild-mannered Trecon lynx. The cat fared well in captivity, lived in the cold, and was a voracious hunter. The 40-pound bobcats could roam and hunt the settlements nightly for their provision.

Trecon Mining Control ordered nine of the natural predators to eradicate the rat infestation. Davss was included on the mission manifest to care for the cats. He'd also train the miners to feed and care for the animals once the rat population was eradicated.

*****

The only thread of common sense holding the settlements together was that they were babysitting the most valuable known ore in the universe. Trillelium was an intensely strong metal with a pliant property that provided a high level of protection for deep-space travel and armor for space-combat craft or land-battle vehicles. It got its strength through introducing electron particles into the molten ore just before the cooling process.

The precious metal was a game changer for their economy, a glaring detail that wouldn't be overlooked on Trecon. Control would use all the knowledge at their disposal to solve the mounting concerns.

General Krevety had the difficult job of pushing for constant production while trying to keep morale afloat. It was a tough endeavor even if all the circumstances were right, but Trecon Control did their best to make the tours bearable. They set shorter rotation schedules to make the duty as tolerable as they could. Eight months working in the mining camps, then four months off when they returned to Trecon. The homesick miners had plenty of time and wages to entertain themselves before heading back to Muudia again.

Morale and wellness stations within the mining camps made life somewhat better. Enhanced communication networks were installed for the young miners to keep in touch with friends and family back home.

However, the recent amount of disruptive activity within the tiny solar system blocked contact between Trecon and the Muudia camps. It prompted command to cut off social calls to keep the best lines open for official business. Trecon's lack of quality communication and supplies to the mining settlements lately made the tough job of managing the young miners nearly impossible!

General Krevety was due a replacement even as he was fighting the same feelings of abandonment as his troops.

Then, the relic appeared and Trecon Control was suddenly motivated to help them. Finding the artifact sealed the deal for a prompt return to Trecon. Krevety was pleased the Trecon government agreed with his assessment. They wanted him to accompany it back home to ensure complete security. The general was tired of the daily grind on Muudia. He was looking forward to seeing his replacement, General Etrod, when the convoy arrived.

Mining was becoming increasingly dangerous and complicated by the hour. The Trecons didn't know about the coming seasons there, or the critical timetable they were up against. It was an unsolvable problem set by the solar system itself!

CHAPTER 3

Strange Seasons

N o mining camp ever survived to a second season on planet Muudia. It was a perilous and unstable planet quickly befriended time after time for its valuable resource, just to be abandoned as it battered its unsuspecting inhabitants.

Nominal understanding of the Laurus solar system indicated that mining Muudia was a no-win situation, hardly worth the effort. Complete knowledge of Muudia disclosed her resources were there for the taking, but only during the long winter season.

It was a large dirty-looking ice-capped planet, being named Muudia by the Trecon explorers because it looked like a ball of cloudy dark mud from space. The name was prophetic. Whenever moisture hit the ground during the warming trend, muddy dirt turned to a thick impenetrable mess.

The Trecons were rigging experts with plenty of experience on hills, caverns, and caves. Applying their knowledge in the shafts under the mining settlements was easy for them. Dealing with equipment mishaps in the spur of the moment was no issue. They were a resilient people by nature. The most depressing issue for them on Muudia was the lack of forests, grassy hills, and water as they trudged through the muck! The biggest distress on Muudia was the absence of lakes, not freezing temperatures or radiation. If they could've went ice fishing once a week, a lot of their problems would've been solved!

*****

There was a reason for the fluctuating composition of the planet. Muudia was unusual not because of the path it traveled. An elliptical trek around a star was common for a planet on the outer reaches of its solar system, it was a frozen lonely orb most of the time.

Muudia was an average-sized planet, (40,075 kilometers in circumference). The distance from its sun was a healthy 389.25 million kilometers, (2.6019 in astronomical units, or AU). A unique route took the planet into a gravitational lock between its star, Laurus, (4.379 million kilometers in circumference), and a larger one named Magnus, (1.127 billion kilometers in circumference). Between the two stars was a portal.

The portal between the Laurus and Magnus was slowly ebbing away through the complicated pressures of its location. It was 389.5 million kilometers (2.6036 AU) from Laurus and 778.5 million kilometers (5.2039 AU) from Magnus. Eventually, the two would collide and provide a spectacular display for the rest of the universe!

Laurus and Magnus would be a typical pair of binary stars save for one detail, they weren't inhabitants of the same dimension! The dimensions coexisted through an intense process called tidal capture, being held in place at a precise distance through gravitational binding energy. Neither had the power to engulf the other or pull away into the greater universe.

Everything from physical debris to invisible radiation from the stars was held in place in the ergosphere zones, where gravity was too strong to dissipate into deeper space. It was a volatile area, with each dimension pulling at the other in a fierce, scorching battle! Rocks, ice, and debris from the solar systems approached the portal and were suspended at the apertures, threatening everything around them. The hazard zone became more dangerous as winter ended.

Muudia's elliptical orbital cycle was six years and nine months. Six years of winter were followed by three months each of spring, summer, and autumn spent in the hazard zone. Its course brought the planet through the region like clockwork as winter waned. Mining operations would fail as the planet's orbit moved from winter to spring, qualifying the conditions the Trecons were experiencing. Time and money worked in direct conflict as spring came to an arduous end. Mining camps were destined for destruction during the summer apocalypse!

Every summer season, Muudia orbited into a direct line between Magnus and Laurus. It went through a radiation bath, intensifying conditions and scorching the planet from the inside out! No known living being, structure, or mining shaft could tolerate the deadly conditions.

As Muudia moved through summer and into autumn, the planet gradually turned benign again, as it cleared the portal hazard zone. Dense molten metal cooled as it ran under the mud toward the planet's core once again.

As autumn evolved into winter, the muddy surface hardened until it appeared to be an unexplored planet. In the early winter season, superheated trillelium was ultra-cured through a natural metallurgy process, making the valuable ore ready to mine once again.

*****

Muudia's moon, Pladia, was 15,329 kilometers in circumference. Its magnitude, coupled with Muudia's heavy gravitational pull kept it in orbit around the planet during the portal fray. Pladia was nothing special, just a desolate rock that orbited Muudia once per day.

From spring through autumn, smaller free-floating objects would smash into the moon as it went through the bumpy gravitational zone. Pladia served Muudia like a body guard, bashing away every meteorite in its path. Everything from large rocks to meteorite-sized chunks of ice crashed down like bombs on the moon's surface, due to Pladia's thin atmosphere.

Pladia had many scars to show it was a steadfast companion to Muudia through thick and thin. At first glance it appeared to be only a faithful moon to Muudia. Closer inspection would show evidence of activity on the dead moon rock.

CHAPTER 4

The Secret Scout Base

On the rock moon of Pladia, a technologically advanced outpost ship called *Rockwell III* was stationed. It belonged to the Raihans, an intelligent race located through the portal in an adjoining solar system from the Magnus Galaxy. The Raihans had conducted 18 previous missions using surrogate miners for over 128 years, up to the Trecon 19-128.25 endeavor.

The three most important components of the *Rockwell III* outpost were the advanced communication equipment, dynamism-force bulwark shielding, and meteorite-busting impulse blasts. The shockwaves were invisible to Planet 6333, but protected her well from rocks colliding onto Pladia during the seasonal tempests. The third-generation outpost provided the crew with the utmost advantages over their victims.

Inhabiting the Raihan ship were beings embodying different human sizes and cultures, brought together through the decades by comparable circumstances. *Rockwell III* outpost was there to spy on and purposely affect the communication processes of the mining operations on Planet 6333 (the Raihan tag for Muudia).

The Raihans were intently watching and affecting the Trecon activities from the safety of the Pladia outpost. They endeavored to control everything happening on the surface until they filled their coffers with the labors of the Trecons. The crooked planet meticulously researched and preselected the Trecons, becoming intimate with Treconite procedures before they sent the first ship to Muudia.

Throughout the universe, advanced Raihan scouts were always researching and preparing the next possible victims, ranking them and lining them up on their deceptive conveyer belt of self-indulgence. Unwitting partners like the Trecons did the grunt work and made huge sacrifices, while the Raihans reaped all the benefits!

*****

Over 140 years prior, A Raihan science spacecraft discovered the gravitational portal. For two years, they sent exploratory missions to the radiation zone before they attempted to enter it. They started small, sending experimental probes into the event horizon. The first attempts failed, as they were obliterated by space debris on the Laurus threshold side.

Eventually, the Raihans sent a shielded probe through, which sent back a high-frequency signal to the Magnus side. They used the data and mapped a route through the wormhole that avoided most pitfalls inhabiting both sides of the portal. Although they succeeded, early exploration resulted in the total loss of three ships and crew before they finally charted a fail-safe passageway through.

Afterwards, they explored the Laurus solar system, and were feeling it was a dud until they discovered Planet 6333 and its stores of trillelium. The Raihans were eager to mine the ore, but lost 1,200 people and four mining settlements during their first attempt to permanently settle the volatile planet.

They kept at it and eventually learned of the seasons, developing portable technology to mine trillelium ore on Planet 6333. Lighter and cheaper materials used in early excavation equipment proved troublesome from the beginning. It was too delicate and couldn't hold up on the icy surface of Planet 6333. The feeble machinery was breaking down all the time, sabotaging their missions before the operations could hit a good stride.

Other issues involved human chemistry. Chronic radiation exposure took a heavy toll in physical and psychological reactions. Raihan miners unknowingly surpassed safe threshold limits working in increasingly toxic conditions. The results weren't obvious, like penetrating misery leading to excruciating death; it would have been better for Raihan society in the long run! Systemic contamination eliminated their ability to produce offspring. The details of the problem weren't discovered until it was too late, after they'd performed several full-cycle missions.

The effects of chronic exposure soon ravaged through Raihan, leaving their population in a serious flux. If the symptoms introduced themselves differently, they could have possibly prevented the calamitous consequences through better selection and medical testing procedures. With the inherent genepool dwindling, the Raihans were forced to choose between saving their population and continuing mining operations on the dreadful Planet 6333.

Deep in the halls of the government, intense secret meetings were taking place daily to solve the complex riddle. On the justice scales of their consciousness, the ore outweighed all moral concerns. The sacrifices paid gave the Raihans a feeling of ownership of the portal and planet, and they were determined to keep it! They considered all their options to come up with a viable solution to the problem.

As a society, Raihan would slowly age and become extinct if they continued the blueprint—too high of a price to pay even for such a valuable resource.

A "drawing of straws" system was proposed but quickly voted down. Eventually the sickness would work its way through the entire governing population through time and attrition. What good would all the wealth in the universe be to a dying society?

Another proposal was introduced, but fell apart as rumors circulated. The government considered training and using the lower classes for as long as they could work for payment and setting their next generation free from the burden. There were immediate reactions to the proposal, beginning with rioting in the streets! Many of the lower classes sent their young into the wilderness to become nomads and scavengers to save their bloodlines, rather than send them to toil in radiation on Planet 6333.

The Raihans took in hundreds of thousands of workers every year with no knowledge of the mining operations on Planet 6333. The immigrants made up a large part of Raihan society. Their loyalty went only as far as Raihan's purse strings. Using them for mining on Planet 6333 was quickly voted down, because they'd turn into a risk. It would be impossible to keep the treasure trove planet a secret for long if they did that.

*****

Even the limited amounts of trillelium flowing back to Raihan raised their economic prominence throughout the galaxy during the early years. The unbelievable return on investment meant they wouldn't stop. They were addicted to wealth and power, and would go to great lengths and personal cost to keep it! Raihan invested heavily in ore purification and fabrication factories, and they were paying off.

Their biggest advancements were within the realms of communication and navigation, as they were continually improving ways to solve the treacherous gravitational portal. The two branches of their emerging identity were heavily involved in their solution.

The council explored how they could use their growing strengths to solve their enigma. Finally, a radical idea called the Servitude Directive was proposed. Raihan commitment to evil was born at that critical point in their history!

*****

The first Servitude 01-06.75 Dourcom operation looked vastly different than the 19-128.25 Trecon mission.

The Raihans set up a mining camp as winter began, and 01-06.75 was underway. After two years, when one mining camp was up and running at full potential, they deserted the settlement and lured the small local planet of Dourcom to send miners to the vacated camp. For the Dourcoms, the trial operation was as much about learning and perfecting their system as harvesting trillelium.

The Dourcoms were cautious at first, sending secret scout teams to assure that the camps were unoccupied. The encampment sat vacant for a year before the Dourcom operation finally got started!

The Raihans were frustrated, but their oar was in with the Dourcoms and they couldn't change course. The Dourcoms eventually sent a team of 300 miners to Planet 6333 to conduct operations. They were caught up in the *process* of mining the ore, where mining was an industrial occupation concentrated on *results and product*. Their meticulous attention to every detail paralyzed them, and the victims appeared to the Raihans as senseless and lazy.

The Dourcoms were working with unfamiliar alien hardware, so learning how to use and maintain the existing machinery effectively took another year. They took their time learning every facet of the equipment provided them, with no thought of making it better or inventing their own solutions. They had no imagination or ambition and ended up as scavengers, using only the existing equipment without aspirations of bringing in their own technology to advance the ore production.

The minute they started to produce, major problems arose as equipment broke down.

The Raihans even sent in a secret repair team once, but the Dourcoms never revisited the shaft to discover the fixed excavator. When a mechanism broke, it was left to rust and expire like everything else. After a while, none of the mining equipment worked! The Dourcoms seemed to inhabit the settlements with no idea of what to do next. They finally left the planet when the spring storms began, taking what they could load and leaving only traces of trillelium behind for the Raihans.

The Dourcoms' lack of ambition was a disaster for Raihan goals, but it provided them with a blueprint of what to do in the future. Through the first mission, the Raihans realized they must be more selective in their process, using foresight and advanced scouting to ensure their next inhabitants would be more energetic and ambitious.

Raihan expanded their spying network to the outer reaches of the universe on both sides of the portal, to maximize their return on investment. They couldn't afford to waste another six years!

The Dourcoms taught the Raihans another important lesson. A mining crew should bring in their own equipment and technology, so the mines could get up and running sooner. Then they could be easily repaired by a crew familiar with the machinery.

Although the first few missions were bumpy, eventually the Raihans included the Pladia observation post and softening missions, which eventually made everything work like a well-oiled machine!

CHAPTER 5

Greed Begets Evil

The Raihans perpetrated the unlawful act many times for three reasons: Advanced knowledge of the solar system, superior technology, and visionless compliance of their victims.

Raihan spies combed the universe looking for planets advanced enough to conduct mining operations on Planet 6333, but not well-connected. They used their expertise for scouting and recon operations, eventually drawing their unsuspecting targets through an off-course probe, and intercepting communications. History indicated the Raihans picked their victims well!

They developed a six-phase method of capture and conquer that was calculated down to the minute in harmony with the seasons of Planet 6333.

The first phase was to judiciously pick a planet who'd unwittingly go along with their harvesting program. The history, language, and technology of the planet were studied, so the Raihans had every possible advantage before the process started.

As technology improved, so did the Raihan reach. They perfected leaving an enticing breadcrumb trail leading to Planet 6333. Of the 19 victim planets, 10 came from the Magnus dimension, and nine from the Laurus side.

Phase two was to establish their outpost on the Pladia moon and listen to a victim's communication beginning with the exploratory phase. The *Rockwell III* could cloak itself from physical and technological senses of their prey, whether from passing vessels or unsuspecting inhabitants of the surface of Planet 6333. A communication "splicing parasite" was established and monitored 24 hours a day until mission completion. The parasite disrupted and controlled the network between Planet 6333 and the home planet.

The third phase was to observe and control Planet 6333 while their victims established settlements and mined the abundant deposits of trillelium ore. As the winter season slowly waned, the Raihans gradually stalled communications to slow the supply train to a frustrating standstill.

The Raihans knew the effects that Planet 6333 had on the ergosphere of the portal through measuring the radiation, meteorites, and solar flares trapped as the planet neared its summer season. Planet 6333 wouldn't allow the adverse effects to escape into the system and dissolve, trapping everything in like an envelope. The end of the third phase happened as the portal entered the Hazard-Class-Six stage.

When the planet neared the portal zone and solar flares increased, the universe worked with the Raihans to keep freighters out and trillelium close where they could steal it. The Raihans realized that they were sitting on a ticking time bomb as it pertained to the lethal seasonal changes, so everything had to go like clockwork as winter drew to a close during the third phase. They controlled what happened through following protocol down to the letter.

Phase four was to attack the settlements of Planet 6333 through a "softening mission" during the later stages of Hazard-Class 8. Fake pirate carriers arrived out of nowhere and attacked the camps. The marauders took out defenses, communications, and any spacecraft docked at the mining camps. Every detail of the pirate attack was scrutinized by the Raihans to appear authentic. The ships looked ragged on the outside, but in reality, they were highly advanced craft with every top technology and weaponry afforded them. They needed to look the part of bandits to carry out the Raihan plan. If the inhabitants were attacked by pirates, they would be more likely to see the Raihans as saviors!

The purpose of the softening attacks was not to kill and destroy, only to leave the visual imprint of pirates on their victims and make them vulnerable for what was coming next. The result was devastating for the mining settlements. People were stuck on a remote planet without the ability to communicate with their compatriots in the cosmos or on the surface. Each settlement was alienated to contemplate their future. The unconceivable events left them feeling depressed while radiation wore heavily on their physical bodies.

The interval after the softening was called the "cooling" period. The Raihans left the planet and let nature take its course. Below the settlements the ground continually sank and weakened the resolve of the miners. Meanwhile, the Rockwell crew traveled back to Raihan, where the commander briefed and prepared the harvesting team for the next step.

Phase five was to return during the harvesting mission, in the last weeks of Hazard-Class 8. They dug down to the sunken settlements to pillage everything and everyone from the sites. The fifth phase had to be swift because the planet was becoming more radiated and dangerous every day with summer approaching fast! During the mid-spring season, settlements sank deep into the mud as molten trillelium disintegrated everything in its path while flowing to the surface. Melting ice and debris drove through the planet's atmosphere and pelted the surface with torrential sheets of acidic rain as the planet approached her torrid summer period. By that point, the Raihans were a welcomed sight to the miners!

Phase six, the home planet would send an investigation mission to Planet 6333 on a timetable manipulated by the Raihans. Many ships were destroyed in the impossible conditions of the portal. The Raihans would do nothing to stop a determined fleet while the portal measured a Hazard-Class 10. As autumn turned into winter, most sent rescue and recovery fleets. The reactionary fleet would find what looked like the same untouched planet they encountered six years before.

The discovery would send terror up the ranks. They'd return home carrying a burden they couldn't explain because it was wrapped in an unsolvable riddle. Resources would be tight, and time short, with many stresses closing in and squeezing the victims like a ravenous python! A hopeful future turned to one of uncertainty and fear. The dispirited planet was now at serious risk of losing their political stature, being invaded by adversaries or even civil war.

Most would curse Planet 6333, lay low, and lick their wounds until they were able to remotely recover what they had before. Others were more resilient, and Raihan had a plan to deal with them.

If a victim government pushed the issue or showed signs of an attempt to resettle Planet 6333, Raihan spies were pleased to spread evidence of their weaknesses throughout their quadrant. The victim planet was low-hanging fruit, fragmented and susceptible to attack as a declining body was to a viral sickness. It happened only five times prior. In each instance, the planet became a claimed colony, subordinate to another government.

The six-phase system worked like a charm for the deceitful Raihans. In the higher levels of government, they were constantly evaluating the process, but on the operational level it was important that everyone follow protocol.

CHAPTER 6

Raihan Rockwell III Outpost

The most treacherous and rewarded assignment for the Raihans was the Rockwell outpost on the Pladia moon. A long line of volunteers stepped forward, but a small percentage actually made it through the rigorous selection process. Only the best of the best candidates was chosen to command the *Rockwell III* outpost. It was a hazardous mission, and the Raihans needed their best officers in command.

Many died during outpost missions for various mishaps, but radiation madness scared Raihan leadership the most. The result of the sickness might sour a whole mission. Worse yet, expose the Raihans to the galaxy for what they were!

The most infamous case of radiation madness on the Rockwell outpost affected the 16-108-Yiohhaw Mission, involving Commander Yerb Grolegg. Grolegg's story was what legends were measured up against from then on!

Daine Hertag, a low-level communications officer, went mad and took out five in their sleep in the waning months of the mission. He intended to kill everyone and steal the Rockwell for his own purposes. Commander Grolegg had to fight and terminate Hertag to survive and keep the mission afloat by himself.

If the Mission 16-108 was blown at that point, the Raihans would have lost the element of surprise. The mining settlements could have restored communications with their home planet. The result would have been an entire harvest lost; six years of wasted effort!

The most important leg of the outpost mission was completed by the 16-108 mission commander living in solitude on virtually no sleep. When he was finally relieved during the softening phase, doctors were astounded the man kept his sanity through it all. Dark brown stains covered the walls; dried blood from Hertag's rampage. Rotting corpses were stacked in the corner of a bay and covered with a blanket, threatening to appear every night in Grolegg's nightmares!

Grolegg's lips were cracked, his black hair matted, and his uniform soiled. Despite smelling awful and being severely malnourished, Grolegg emerged from the mission a true hero. He returned to Raihan a rock star, a status that would serve him well for the rest of his life. He later became President Yerb Grolegg.

*****

The Controller of Mission 19-128.25 was Commander Steph Knuddrul, a dependable officer with a sterling military record. He was a brilliant military strategist (only in his own mind), with high arrogance to match. Commander Knuddrul always thought he knew a better way of doing things, regardless of the experience or knowledge of his peers. He rubbed everyone the wrong way with aspirations of incredible wealth and position, which he felt were owed him.

He was calculating, quickly stepping forward for easier assignments with a high probability of success while letting others take the gritty jobs. The commander had a big opinion of his own abilities, stepping on or over others on his way up the Raihan career ladder. Every four months, departing outpost crew members were thankful to be rid of him.

Knuddrul possessed a high IQ, which made him a top competitor throughout his career. He made his superiors look good when it served him, through technical knowledge and a keen ability to retain data. His judgement was trusted by those above him, but he couldn't fain even an inkling of false humility. Knuddrul often questioned leadership decisions in private while praising the same superiors in public. He made sure never to slip up in front of anyone with credibility who could affect his career in a negative way!

In his early forties, the boastful officer was the youngest commander in the history of the Pladia outpost! Knuddrul was well-informed of the rigors of the grueling mission, but also knew he had a clear path to the top when the assignment was finished.

Commander Knuddrul's arrogance sometimes led him away from protocol. He'd freelance occasionally if he figured to gain from a situation. Such was the case with Mission 19-128.25.

The commander was in his stateroom listening to music and meditating on fame and fortune, when he was hailed by a com officer named Dreck Lobart. "Commander Knuddrul, there's a situation in shaft 5B. The miners are sending an urgent message to the surface."

Knuddrul sat up on his bunk and turned down the music. He was a handsome man, with a chiseled frame, rockstar face, and striking brown eyes. In his mind, he was the perfect kind of person for the good fortune accompanied with the position. The commander was irked with Lobart, and didn't want to be bothered.

"How's that different from any other day? More flooding in the shaft, I presume?"

"Apparently they've found something."

"Did they say what?"

"Nothing specific yet. It's moving up the chain of command as we speak."

"Get all the facts before you bother me again, copy?"

"Yes commander." Lobart closed the connection and thought, *I hate working for you!*

After all the information was received, Lobart contacted Knuddrul again, and the commander reviewed the data.

"Send it through," ordered Knuddrul.

The order didn't sit right with Lobart. He knew that Knuddrul wouldn't like it, but he did his duty just the same, "Commander, Planet 6333 will be a Hazard-Class 8 by the time the supply fleet arrives. Protocols say-."

"I know our standard operating procedures Lobart! As commander of this outpost, I also get enough details to see the big picture. You're just a communications officer; follow your orders and keep your mouth closed!"

Lobart's neck became beet red as his blood pressure spiked to the crown of his blond head. The com officer's blue eyes were swamped in disdain for Knuddrul. He choked out his response professionally, "Yes commander, patching it through now."

"Good. Now that we've established who's in charge, there should be no more bumps in the road, right? Let me know when you get a response from Trecon Control."

When the Raihan outpost intercepted the Trecon message about the relic, the decision was made by Commander Knuddrul to allow General Krevety's message to go through to Planet Trecon rather than splicing or blocking it. A devious plan rapidly formed in the commander's warped mind. Knuddrul's spontaneous decision veered the mission off track and put the Trecons in a deadly situation!

During turbulent seasonal changes, the solar system was easy to enter but impossible to escape without proper knowledge, like a fruit fly effortlessly crawling through holes in cellophane to reach apple cider vinegar in a cup, only to discover too late it was doomed. Everything about allowing the Trecon supply mission to go through was wrong, yet Knuddrul ordered it! The critical timetable protocol in Servitude Directive 009 indicated he was simply cutting it too close to allow a supply convoy to safely start a resupply mission.

Knuddrul saw it a different way, however. Allowing the Trecons to send a small supply convoy to Planet 6333 would have the advantage of capturing additional Contributor candidates before they escaped back to Trecon. Trillelium was not the only resource the Raihans took from their harvesting operations; people were also essential to keep their system working. Most important, the Trecons would provide the labor to extract the relic before he took it back by force!

At the end of Mission 19-128.25, Commander Knuddrul would arrive on Raihan like a conquering hero loaded to the rafters with people, trillelium, and the new mystery structure in tow. The government would be most curious about a metal compound that survived the intense radiation and melting processes of countless summer seasons. The artifact would be possibly the greatest scientific discovery in their history! *Perhaps they'll call the new iron Knuddrulium,* he thought. Everyone would benefit from his plan, but mostly Knuddrul.

Despite the slight change, the rest of the 19-128.25 softening mission would proceed as usual without deviation.

CHAPTER 7

Radiation Distress

M ining on Muudia became a risky business for the Trecon colony, just as the solar system affected many others before. The effects of radiation and solar flares were increasingly affecting their lives and equipment. The Trecons were a very resilient people, used to the harsh environment of a home planet that toyed with their lives daily.

Trecon had three oceans and five massive lakes, from where their main diet of fish was taken from year-round. They relied on the water for survival and recreation. They'd fish from boats during their warm season and through thick ice in the cold. Their main lake, Mic Mac, provided many resorts that were busy throughout the year.

The biological hardiness of the Trecons presented them as prime candidates for the Raihans! During the summer, they enjoyed scenic landscapes and hiked root-covered timberland trails among moss-covered rocks and rugged terrain. Trecon youth developed and toned their muscles by climbing foreboding cliffs as children, and digging granite and taconite out of the bristly ground as adults.

In the winter months they'd cross country ski or go on long snowshoe hikes in the forest. Beyond that, there wasn't much enjoyable about the Trecon climate during the winter. The joke was that Trecon had a continuous cold season interrupted by a short summer, where they'd fix the roads again! Because of the intense cold for the majority of the year on Trecon, they'd developed attitude and attire very durable and resistant to the elements of Muudia.

The Trecons were expert riggers and miners. Trecon was rich in granite and taconite ore. Exporting the two was a main source of economy. Mining was a standard way of life for the majority of people who resided outside their capital city of Tettegouche. Whenever other endeavors didn't work out, a young Treconite learned the tough occupation of mining their planet to earn a decent and honorable living.

The Raihan onlookers knew that signs of stress were not unusual for a mining colony at this stage, but it seemed to them the Trecons were on the mild end of the acceptable spectrum of suffering. Living underground was becoming a logical option for the Trecon miners as radiation and acidic rain hit Muudia. There wasn't any scenery to enjoy on the surface anyway!

There were several key dynamics of survivability as radiation levels climbed. Personal health was the biggest factor in resistance. Age and body composition were also important influences associated with recovery. Mental conditioning played an important role. If the will to survive was diminished, there was nothing the Raihans could do to replace it.

Originally, it was within the Raihan parameters to experience a 10 percent loss due to radiation sickness during a harvest. Updated Servitude Directive 009 improvements indicated that losing 5 to 8 percent was acceptable. Advancements in care improved the numbers to 4 percent during the Loehn 18-121.5 mission, and the hardy Trecons were right on par.

*****

The most severe instance of radiation sickness was during Mission 9-60.75. The Rodanes were a race of humanoid creatures with large heads, although slight in build. They were technologically advanced, constantly looking to increase their knowledge of the cosmos. The Rodanes were expert space travelers, flying around the universe in great disk fleets as they explored the heavens. The Rodanes intrigued the Raihans, but the perpetrators miscalculated their hardiness.

They were not as skilled in mining, but advanced enough to keep the trillelium ore running to the surface at an adequate pace when radiation levels were absent during winter. Mission 9-60.75 looked like any other mission mostly, with the Rodanes running ore up at an above-average clip.

As Planet 6333 crept into the portal belt neighborhood and spring approached, things took a deadly turn for them. Despite a slight moderation in the radiation levels during the early spring season, tragedy ensued. The Rodanes weren't physically built to handle the slightest of radiation increases.

The ore production ground to a standstill. They couldn't keep up their pace with fewer workers on the job and more personnel visiting the infirmary. Once the Rodanes reached their radiation threshold limit, they rapidly deteriorated. There was no way for them to continue with their regular underground schedules, so they were not afforded protection of the crust. Radiation sickness set in faster and harder than the Raihans had ever seen it before, because the miners stayed in their aboveground infirmaries and dormitories.

There was so much misery that the Raihans skipped the softening mission and conducted the harvesting operation early, when the planet measured only a Hazard-Class 6. For the first and only time, the Raihans conducted a genuine rescue operation! The unbearable elements of Planet 6333 provided a natural softening operation, saving the Raihans time.

During the harvesting operation, about 50 percent of the Rodanes had expired, scattered bodies were wilted from the inside out. Dead Rodanes littered the mining settlements because no one had the energy to move them. The harvesters couldn't escape the rancid smell of decay in the contaminated settlements. It was a haunting sight for the Raihans, turning the harvest mission into a nightmare!

The living Rodanes were in severe anguish during the operation, unable to recover from illnesses as they received advanced medical oversight and treatment. Between the harvesting operation and the trip back to Raihan, all 1,634 perished, most screaming in excruciating pain as they died!

The effect of the mission on the Raihan medical crews was undeniable. When they realized there was nothing left to be done for the Rodanes, the mission commander ordered the medical bays be evacuated for the physicians on board. The ramps were opened, and the Rodanes were "cleared out" into deep space.

Mission failure and guilt ran rampant within the medical vessels during their voyage home. The acrid smell of suffering and demise couldn't be cleansed from the ships no matter how much they scoured! The medical oversight crews received extensive psych treatment upon their return to Raihan.

Mission 9-60.75 ensured changes in Raihan Planet 6333 policies once again. It was the Rodane Mission that caused them to devote even more resources into medical equipment and care. Because of 9-60.75, the Raihans researched and gained a sterling reputation for medical expertise throughout the universe.

Along with advanced medical knowledge, surveillance and communication technology were refined. The Raihans ensured they could reach farther out to find others more fit to do the hazardous work for them. Eventually, hostages were affected minimally by the radiation, while some populations even flourished!

*****

The most extreme history of health success was the Mihhidites from Mission 14-94.5. They were a penal colony, forced to mine for violent crimes committed on their home planet. Planet Mihhid conducted their mining operations through forcing prisoners to do it through a work-for-freedom plan. They didn't lose a single soul during the mining, softening, or harvesting missions; but 75 Mihhidite superiors and guards didn't survive the first night on Raihan!

The Mihhidites were known around the galaxy as exceptional voyagers, but also as ruthless pirates. What they lacked in technology, they made up for in sheer aggression. They were a warring society, fighting all comers, but mostly they fought each other. Mihhid had a high rate of leadership turnover at the top. When a new government came to power, there were dire consequences for the vanquished, such as forcing them to mine trillelium ore on a desolate planet.

They hailed from the Fromlayan Galaxy, which was relentlessly bathed in radiant solar energy. Planet 6333 offered nothing they couldn't handle. Their bodies were so adept at survival in sour conditions, they were healthy when the Raihans arrived for the harvesting operation. The robust Mihhidites conceded during the Mission 14-94.5 harvesting operation without a fight for one main reason. They'd use the Raihan ships to escape the burning planet, then steal them to create a Mihhidite fleet.

The main difference between the Mihhidites and others in the past was that they welcomed their hostage takers with the intent of eventually overthrowing them. They saw a great opportunity during the journey back to Raihan.

The commander of the 14-94.5 mission saw them as a threat from the very beginning and feared that his life was in danger. Mihhidite Boirt Zalbek established himself as the major threat, dangerous and not to be trusted. The Mihhidites spent the entire journey back to Raihan in shackles. When they arrived on Raihan and were initiated into their reeducation process, a lightbulb went off in the mind of Zalbek the visionary!

Eventually, a partnership formed between the Raihans and Mihhidites, both sides seeing a way to exploit the other equally. The Raihans could offer their new partners immense wealth, freedom, and a legitimate (faux pirate) fleet of their own. The Mihhidites were given dangerous destroyers called

Sharks. The pirates would no longer be outcasts on their own planet, but be paid a respectable sum for their vile services while living it up on Raihan.

The Raihans kept their contract a secret, letting Zalbek and his men do what they did best. Due to their immunity to higher radiation levels, Zalbek and the Mihhidites evolved to play dominant roles within the Raihan softening and harvesting missions. Both sides benefited from the relationship for over three decades.

Increased Mihhidite responsibilities during the softening missions stamped their brand within Raihan society. Boirt Zalbek eventually entrenched himself within secretive levels of the government. As Zalbek gained power and influence, aspirations of Mihhidite aggression and galactic conquest trickled into the Raihan social order!

The Mihhidites were spreading their influence not because of talent, but because they were so difficult to deal with! Once the Mihhidites became involved, others were chased out or left on their own. Throughout the years, Zalbek's vision evolved into pushing a theory of violent Raihan expansionism throughout the universe. He aspired to return to Mihhid and exact revenge on the same people who forced him into the penal colony. Zalbek had the fleet and backing of a military power to do anything he wanted, but enjoyed the good life too much to risk it.

CHAPTER 8

Trecon Supply Convoy

On Trecon, a small supply convoy embarked on a voyage to Muudia. Three large cargo vessels, *Mule 111*, *Mule 302*, and *Mule 357*, left post-haste after Krevety's message to recover the mysterious relic. A small security component consisting of one Bruiser carrier-class ship escorted them. The carrier had a squadron of 10 Starlance fighters, mostly to accompany the fleet loaded with trillelium back to Trecon. There was no need for greater security due to the remoteness of their destination.

Mule 111 was the lead ship in the convoy, having aboard the next mining operations command element, General Etrod (the replacement for General Krevety) and 50 replacement miners and settlers. *Mule 302* had 145 personnel aboard, full of miners and settlers grumbling from day one how the six-man command element on *Mule 111* accounted for an extra 95 people, forcing them to make due with less space. They looked at the *Mule 111* as a luxury ship for the pampered and privileged.

There were only four crew members assigned to *Mule 357*, but that ship was stock full of supplies destined for all three mining camps and the crew was secluded—by no means a picnic! Her crew easily had the most freedom of anyone on the convoy, as long as they didn't mind climbing over crates.

There was a reason for such a small crew. Leadership felt that a ship full of young and dejected miners among fresh supplies increased the possibility of theft, in their attempt to make their upcoming mining tour more tolerable.

The freighters were simply designed ships engineered to haul cargo, devoid of creature comforts. Each Mule had four main cargo bays. Above the forebay was the bridge where a maximum crew of six navigated and operated the Mule's critical systems.

Straight back from the bridge on the main deck were the galley to the left and a small conference room to the right. Between the two was the center star of the ship, a widening hallway with a brass ladder in the center that vertically connected all levels of the Mule. The ladder reached from the lower cargo decks to the rail crane above the fore cargo bay, and finally up to the NAV/COM port and gun turret on the very top of the ship.

The main forebay had a descending ramp for loading large equipment and supplies. There were three aft bays on the middle deck, including two with twin dimensions on the port and starboard sides of the ship. One or both of the opposing bays could be converted to bunk quarters for transient passengers, as with the *Mule 302*. The officers' quarters and infirmary rounded out the main deck of the ship.

In the rear of the ship past the center star on the lower level, the engine room provided full access to critical areas. A small anechoic chamber was carved out between the engine room and corridor on the bottom level. A reinforced center bay included a safe used for storing weapons, currency, or dangerous cargo. On the *Mule 357*, 43 one-year nuclear fission batteries were included for the mining camps in the center bay; to power generators and equipment in the settlements.

The supply convoy was to report first to Muudia MC1SA2 where the *Mule 111* had a specific mission. While the other vessels exchanged passengers and unloaded supplies, the command element planned to meet General Krevety and load the

24 quarantined settlers along with the top-secret relic for the return to Trecon. The mission was to be a quick turnaround.

It was a routine assignment for the Mule navigators and loading the artifact wouldn't slow them down for a minute. This was a military operation, and the well-trained aerospace crews always followed their orders without question. The Trecon officer motto was that you had to take orders before you can give them. There was a great deal of trust among leadership. Devoted attitudes stayed consistent down to the lower ranks. Even the youngest miners were trustworthy despite their annoyance. The Mule crews were eager to show their superiors they had what it took to lead.

Onsan Vorga was exceedingly excited to be captaining his last supply mission to Muudia, and looking forward to continuing his military career to commission as a Starlance fighter pilot. He spent nine long years training on the Mule-class supply ships, one more year than the standard eight-year commitment required. When the supply convoys to Muudia slowed down to a trickle, his commitment was extended as he waited in line to perform his last mission. The simple assignment was to take him to the main mining camp to drop off supplies and pick up ore. *After this final mission, I'll be free of the painfully monotonous supply missions,* he thought.

Vorga didn't care he wasn't commanding the lead ship, only that the mission would fulfill his requirement. He wasn't pleasant to be around to begin with, wanting it over before it started. He settled in nicely, however. Although he was eager to finish the last obligation, Onsan had a deep sense of integrity about him that drew respect from his crew.

He was honest and fair with the copilot and navigator of the vessel. Onsan's colleagues understood his frustration and merely gave him the space he needed until he settled into the mission. His no-nonsense approach was appreciated by his shipmates as they got to know one another.

Onsan headed a crew including copilot CeJarious (CJ) Nrag, veterinarian Tephen Davss, and Milerous Akugis. CJ was an aspiring pilot, and Milerous an entry-level mechanic. They were both in long training programs. CJ was in his sixth year, and the "rookie" Milerous was in his third year.

The military officers were young, taller than average, and in-shape. Each had short brown hair and brown eyes. Looking at them side-by-side in their sharp blue Trecon uniforms, the three could've easily been mistaken for brothers.

Tephen Davss served as the medical and science officer for the journey. He wasn't in the military but from Tettegouche University due to the special aspects of the mission.

Davss was older than the others by far, and cantankerous even on his best days. He mostly kept to himself. The scientist valued data over relationships and it showed. He was allotted the infirmary and more living space than the others.

The civilian was slightly taller, but slumped when he stood. His bad posture and squinty blue eyes were created from years of leaning over a computer screen at the university. He had a thin neck and chest, but his gut protruded out un-proportion-ately with the rest of his frame. His shaggy graying hair fell over his pasty forehead and onto dirty glasses. His sterile gray lab coat was a true representation of his attitude. He seemed to suck out the energy whenever he entered a room.

While the others became a tight crew, Davss hid in his workplace gathering and dissecting scientific information and caring for the animals. He seemed inattentive with his duties or the concerns of his shipmates. He felt he had better things to do than basic ship chores. It didn't take long for Davss to isolate himself from the crew of the *Mule 357*, just as he'd done back at the university.

Onsan eventually saw the bright side of his final oblig-atory mission. He'd been accepted into the Starlance fighter pilot program, and it was just a matter of time until he'd start his dream job! Spending his time wisely learning about the Starlance fighter would be wise rather than sitting mentally idle and harboring a bad attitude. The eight-month journey to Muudia and back meant another good part of a year before he could move on with his life, but he'd be well prepared for the Starlance academy upon return.

The biggest difference between the captain and first officer was that Onsan wanted more than anything to fly the Starlance IV while CJ inspired to be a Bruiser carrier commander. Onsan was serious about a girl, and had many good friends on Trecon. Staying close to home and providing planetary defense from the cockpit of a Starlance fighter was an optimal choice for him.

CJ was right on track within his training time frame, so his initial attitude was opposite to Onsan's. Cruising through the blackness of deep space suited him just fine! CJ had an interest in seeing a broader view of the universe, which he would as a Bruiser commander. He was quiet and wise, preferring not to let petty differences between the two make the trip unbearable. CJ knew Onsan had many good qualities. It was best not to throw everything out because of his partner's frustration.

Although there was agitation between the two officers right away, a level of respect and trust grew after a short while of slugging through their differences.

Milerous was younger and not firmly convicted about his career path, so he initially felt in a position to take sides between the two. He showed his age often by not guarding his thoughts before words came out of his mouth. Milerous was excitable and positive mostly, but his immaturity often led to mood swings as he tried to find his place in the small crew. He wanted to know the reasons they were doing things right away, and wasn't patient enough to learn from experience. He was a doer rather than an intellectual, the polar opposite of Tephen Davss.

The kid was good with his hands, a natural mechanic who understood power-driven and technical systems as they strongly suited his interests. He would have a harder time verbalizing how to fix something than just digging in and doing it. Onsan and CJ could get over his lack of technical language, but Davss seemed unable to overcome his constant annoyance with Milerous.

First impressions and personality differences could wear on the best of people, but the officers were professional, knowing they must count on one another during their trip through deep space to Muudia. Being in cosmic purgatory meant that each had plenty of alone time to study and better themselves. The young trio used their time wisely, investing in their perspective careers.

Onsan spent most of his time furthering his knowledge of the Starlance, space combat manuals, and military conflict theory. CJ spent his downtime mastering the Mule-class ship and poring over navigational charts of the known universe. CJ would serve as lead pilot on the Mule on her next journey to Muudia, and he was looking forward to being the number one on the mission! Milerous was occupied with learning the basics of *Mule 357*, her thruster engines, load capacities and storage procedures, communication and navigation systems, and basic navigational charts.

Despite their differences, there was mutual trust growing on a professional level. On a personal level, the crew grew tighter. There was often mental banter between Onsan and CJ as they debated their views on everything from the meaning of life and taste in women, to which spacecraft career was better. If their conversations got too heated, they'd agree to disagree until the subject came up again.

Onsan and CJ would often bait Milerous on a whim, bringing him into their banter just for amusement! After a while, Onsan and CJ changed their repartee to get Milerous to join the opposing career path than their own as if they were trying to get him off their side. Eventually, Milerous could see when he was being taunted and would just leave the bridge rather than be the brunt of their jokes.

The four officers were not the only living beings aboard the Mule trying to figure each other out. They also contained a load of nine caged cats in the aft starboard bay to address the

rodent problem on Muudia. The cats and the Muudia structure were the two reasons Tephen was brought along on the
journey. Davss had with him a wealth of information from
Tettegouche University meant for Nbnok. He'd accompany the
Mule 111 on the return trip, which made the others glad. He
did the minimum, tending to the animals without an ounce of
compassion.

The cats were Trecon lynxes from a sanctuary near
Tettegouche. They were all orphaned males from separate
litters, being studied by a university for conservation. The
Trecon lynx was a beautiful mid-sized gray cat with pale blue
olive-shaped eyes. They had black puffs of fur ascending up
over the top of their white ears and on the tip of their bobtails.
The felines had a sleek body and long legs descending down to
their large paws with soft pads, which allowed them to sneak
quietly through the leaf-covered wilderness or snowy terrain
undetected.

They thrived in the Northern Trecon wilds, in the harsh-
est environments imaginable. The Trecon lynx looked majestic
in the wild, rarely seen except by trained eyes. They looked
sorely out of place in a cage secured to the hull of a spaceship.
They had an adaptable spirit, however. As long as they were
well-fed, the animals tolerated one another and the crew well.

The ship had three large cages, each containing a trio of
cats destined for different camps. Problems of the complex age
boiled down to a primeval fact, the Trecons had to use hunters
to catch and eat prey.

It appeared after a short time they'd arrive on Muudia with
only eight cats. One cat was obviously the runt of the whole
group, and the others didn't let him forget it. He was continually harassed by the other cats. The poor thing was beat up no
matter who they put him with, and Onsan feared he wouldn't
make it to the settlement. Milerous wanted to free the cat, but
Davss countered they should put it out of its misery.

Hiss, snarl!

Two larger cats had the runt backed in a corner. Whenever he turned to defend himself against a lunging bully, the other would jump on his back! The cage clattered with the action, provoking the other cats to jump around their cages.

Milerous became a fan of the runt. "Look at the little guy, he doesn't stand a chance in there! Can't we rescue the poor thing?"

"Out of the question. These animals aren't pets," chided Davss.

Growl, pounce, merooow!

"Do you have any other suggestions, Tephen?"

The man looked at Milerous, and got a gleam in his eye. Davss tried to look like he was making an educated conclusion. He took off the grimy glasses, and looked silly cleaning them with the tail of his dirty shirt.

The cat had become a situation to put the kid in his place and establish the pecking order. "I'll put him down. It seems cruel, but it'll save him three months of getting mauled every day by the others. He'll cause them to riot and hurt themselves and each other. We may end up with *no cats* if we're not careful!"

Onsan had a life and death choice to make, and he couldn't make both men happy. He didn't like how Davss could take a life so gleefully just to spite a kid. "As captain of the *Mule 357*, my decision is that we let the animal out of the cage and see what happens for a trial period before we destroy it."

Davss raised his voice, "The animal will never be able to adapt to its job of hunting rodents if it becomes a pet."

"Perhaps there are rodents roaming the ship that we're unaware of," Onsan dryly stated. "It happened before, or they wouldn't have the problem on Muudia now."

"There is no evidence of rats, and you know it!"

Onsan's brown eyes bore a hole through the dingy glasses and straight into the scientist's soul, "The cat stays, final decision."

"I'm going to add into my report that you directly went against my wishes!"

Onsan didn't care, Davss was a civilian. "Do what you must Davss."

With that, the vet stormed off the bridge and sulked back to his room. Davss didn't like being overruled by younger people, but Milerous getting his way burned him more than anything.

Milerous let the cat out of the cage to roam the ship and live among them. They named him Chase for no particular reason, other than he would run down the passageways of the ship at full speed, delighted with his new-found freedom. Chase soon cavorted around the ship like he was a king. The crew had to keep him from the other cages, as he tormented the other cats intentionally and worked them into a furious state of jealousy.

Chase ate with the Mule crew during mealtimes and slept in the bunk room on a bed they built for him when he wasn't snuggled up to one of the crew. Shortly after the meeting, the hyperactive cat knocked over a cup of coffee in Tephen's office and was banned for life from the scientist's workspace!

*****

Three months and 20 days into their journey, the supply convoy was hit by a sudden meteorite storm as it approached the outer Muudia deceleration zone. When the fleet entered the invisible furnace at the outer reaches of the hazard zone, they never had a chance! They were subjected to a sudden ionospheric disturbances (SIDs) that rendered their electronic, protective, navigation, and communication systems ineffective. The SIDs hit the unsuspecting fleet with full force, disabling all four vessels on impact. Then came the meteorites!

Meeeerrrooowww!

Onsan was awoken abruptly as Chase jumped on top of him in an ear-splitting hissing fit, just before the storm hit. The instincts of the animal alerted him seconds before the natural ambuscade bombarded the vessel with massive pieces of rock and ice. The cat saved the ship!

The fleet entered the belt and felt it throwing great jagged spears at them! It was on them before the crews could manually maneuver the ships or raise the shields above a normal level, rendering them unable to steer clear or recover.

Bash, wham, boom!

A large ice meteorite scored a direct hit on *Mule 302*, ripping a jagged hole in the hull and disintegrating the ship's oxygen supply in a matter of explosive nanoseconds!

Thud, scrape!

Aboard *Mule 357*, Onsan took the manual controls in just enough time to steer away from a direct hit, but the communications port on the top of the ship was hit and heavily damaged as it was gouged by the meteorite.

"Milerous, man the shields!"

Tephen was on the bridge in an instant, asking, "What can I do to help?"

"Take over the shields so Milerous can get the gun!"

Milerous gave Davss a quick lesson on the secondary shield override, allowing the ship to transfer energy manually to different areas to keep the meteorites at bay. As the override kicked in, it robbed power from less-needed areas of the ship.

Whack, ram, crush!

The Mule shuddered violently, but the shields held and the ship snuck safely through the storm.

The youngest crewmember transitioned from his slumber to their life-or-death ordeal with a calmness about him that preceded his experience and years. He blasted away three meteorites, making a pathway for the ship to squeeze through as Tephen Davss directed the shields to absorb the brunt of the storm until they were clear.

CJ had been in his bunk on the bridge when they'd entered the field. He felt responsible for the catastrophe, "There was no alarm. It was on top of us before I could do anything!"

"I know, CJ." Onsan knew there was nothing CJ could have done differently.

The crew completed a damage assessment on the vessel. Right away, they noticed the hit impaired the ship's communication and left them with no way to connect with the other ships in the convoy. Their awareness of what was happening around them was limited to the bridge viewing area, the dayroom, and the small viewing ports located around the ship.

Mule 111 and *Bruiser 7* were in deep distress as they tried to get through the rock field. *Mule 111* contacted Trecon and informed them they had a visual of *Mule 302* being destroyed and lost communication with *Mule 357*, but had seen it hit by a meteorite just before it lost communication with her. *Bruiser 7* had been heavily damaged, and was turning around for a return trip to Trecon. The war vessel had greater shield protection and made it back through the storm despite substantial damage. The storm was eerily similar to a space battle for the carrier.

The *Bruiser 7* attempted to clear a path for the *Mule 111* without success.

"Mayday, mayday, mayd-. Arrgghh!"

The last communication from *Mule 111* to *Bruiser 7* and Trecon command gave audio proof to them she too was destroyed by a meteorite. Without supplies on board or a convoy to protect, the Bruiser commander's choice to return to Trecon became clear. The carrier set the course and began their trip back to their home planet. *Mule 357* was suddenly on their own with no way to request for help.

CHAPTER 9

Resilient Mule 357

U nknown to anyone, Onsan Vorga and crew successfully guided the *Mule 357* through the meteorite storm. The ship was grazed hard by the meteorite and pelted dozens of times, but it avoided a direct hit. The crew's training enabled them to navigate through the rock belt with no further damage. After the ship had been hit, the Mule's ability to traverse through space was intact, but they were forced to pilot the ship manually.

An advanced diagnostic check confirmed the meteorite struck the ship on the top rear, taking out the communication and navigation module they relied heavily on for interstellar travel. The damage made them blind and invisible!

CJ and Milerous inspected the port while Onsan navigated the '357 through the hazard zone. They were thankful to find the ship's superstructure still intact, but there was a major problem. A small crack formed in the interior of the hull. It could be contained by entering the accessibility hatch to the port and spot-welding the area. Valuable time was ticking away, the crack was weakening by the second! If it led to a tear, they'd be destroyed before they had time to react.

CJ turned to Milerous. "Get up there right away, I'll bring your welding gear."

"Here's your plasma torch." Tephen Davss was on the spot again. He'd assumed it was needed and grabbed the equipment for Milerous. It was a side of him that no one expected; survival was an excellent motivator! CJ and Davss fished the hose up to Milerous as he inspected the damage and prepared to fuse the chink. The weld was completed in 15 minutes, and everyone breathed a little easier. Milerous lowered out of the hatch and also soldered the hatch to form a double barrier.

With the threat contained, the trio returned to the bridge to help Onsan guide the ship. Onsan peeked over his shoulder. "Great job guys!"

"We're on our own getting to Muudia."

The only chance for survival going forward was through old-fashioned star-chart navigation. CJ pulled out the maps and studied the data, relaying their location to Onsan.

The '357 crew had to choose from two paths: They could attempt to navigate back through the worst of the storm to Trecon, or continue on to Muudia.

Turning back meant going through the meteorites again and continuing a three-month trek to Trecon. Having to manually navigate through the treacherous field and through deep space in a wounded ship was a dangerous proposition. Onsan pictured himself returning to a waiting list and not getting another convoy mission for a year, ugh!

On the other hand, they could continue to Muudia, drop off supplies at MC1SA2, load the cargo *Mule 111* had been sent to get, fix their navigation and communication systems on Muudia, then return to Trecon. Arrival on Trecon would elevate the crew's status immediately upon return, and Onsan would be on to the next stage in his career. It was not a selfish concept, because the *Mule 357* held desperately needed supplies meant for Muudia. They'd return with the top-secret cargo from MC1SA2.

Their choice was clear. They'd continue on to the mining settlements on Planet Muudia. Little did they know, their days of being up close and personal with giant revolving space rocks was just beginning. Their temporary lull was over in minutes.

As CJ pored over the computer files and archaic charts, they realized that the meteorite belt was not in the records of past supply convoys. The situation in the atmosphere around Muudia was changing for the worse. They double and triple-checked, ensuring they were following the exact Trecon route that had been in use for six years. "The data is right Onsan. The meteorite field simply didn't appear on our scanners."

"It is like the universe deliberately hid the zone from us. It doesn't make any sense!"

So, they continued to Muudia with their eyes wide open for surrounding dangers. The road was paved for them, but the question was how many more hidden potholes they'd face along the way. The crew didn't realize that the storms resulted from entering the gravitational hazard zone. Soon they'd encounter increased radiation and other cosmic dangers. But they were also oblivious to the greatest danger lurking in the Muudia solar system—the Raihans!

The realization it wasn't just a routine supply mission weighed on their minds, and stress tightened their shoulders as they contemplated the next few weeks in deep space. Two pairs would split watch shifts on the bridge while piloting the vulnerable ship through the fissionable quadrant. Onsan and Davss would be on one shift, and CJ and Milerous on the other. He turned to his fellow officers. "You two get some rest. You'll need to be alert when you return for duty."

Davss sensed that he was the odd man, like the last kid chosen for a team. CJ would have been the scientist's natural choice, because he offered the path of less resistance. He reverted back to his grumpy self. "Wouldn't I be more useful in my lab? The atmospheric monitors probably still work. I coul-."

"No Davss," interrupted Onsan. "Go get your instruments and report right back. You'll stay here with me for the first shift. Two sets of eyes are better than one."

The scientist scoffed at CJ and Milerous and left the bridge.

When Davss was out of earshot Milerous cracked, "Enjoy your shift Onsan!"

As the *Mule 357* neared Muudia, they felt increased anxiety about the dangers loitering outside their spacecraft. The readings of radiation continued to rise incrementally. The amounts were not at a drastic level, but fractional changes provided one more vehicle of stress aboard the ship. When Onsan went above his clearance level and studied the top-secret portion of the mission, he became even more concerned.

Onsan had a growing feeling in his gut that their stop at MC1SA2 would be too complicated for the crew of four to figure out. Unloading their freight was the easy part, but the added pressure of repairing the Mule's NAV/COM system, loading the relic, and boarding 24 miners was compounded by the probable need for another fleet. More hands and minds would be a welcoming sight, but what good would sick miners be? Onsan and Davss contemplated the ramifications.

"With the radiation levels increasing as we get closer to Muudia, what kind of shape will the miners be in when we arrive?"

"I don't know Tephen."

"How is it going to be decided who'll come with us and who'll stay back on the rotting planet? Getting people to stay behind and accept their dark fate without ripping this ship apart will be the biggest challenge of all!"

Davss made a good point. The Mule crew might be in danger of being thrown off their own ship. "I guess we'll find out when we get there."

"Perhaps we should turn back now, while we're ahead."

"That's out of the question Davss. We have a duty to them!" Onsan was frustrated with the slouching scientist, the debate was over.

CHAPTER 10

Softening of the Mining Camps

General Krevety sat in his stateroom and prepared the transition report. His mind wandered as he grew fatigued with the administrative grind. Twenty-three people had become intimately familiar with one another during four months of close quarters at MC1SA2, and would stay together for the next four as well during their voyage home.

The supply fleet would arrive soon enough, and the general was looking forward to leaving the godforsaken place as much as anyone! He'd put on a good face for his subordinates, however. General Etrod would be there shortly, and Krevety could then kick his feet up and decompress during the trip home. Any time now, he thought.

Krevety was an astute and just leader. He knew his junior officers needed genuine leadership experience by the time they commanded others. The general trained his subordinates to decide for themselves, letting them sink or swim and learn. Krevety valued their opinions, and always gave them credit for good ideas.

The general always did what he thought was right, even if it didn't benefit him. He thought about issues from many angles, offering wise solutions that everyone understood, even if they didn't agree with his decision.

He was rapidly approaching a crossroads as it pertained to his military career and private life, at the age where retirement was always tapping him on the shoulder. After the mission he'd take account of his personal life for the first time in years. Krevety would visit his children and grandchildren and take a long vacation with his wife Abigail. The general detested thoughts of retiring and growing old, but he couldn't stop time. He became lost in his thoughts and nodded off in his worn leather desk chair.

Suddenly, Krevety was snapped out of his stupor as the intercom blasted him into the present. "Major Tallik and General Krevety, please come to the control area immediately. The skies are still filled with the orange trails of falling comets, but these gas-blast distortions are unmistakably spacecraft. Nine ships are coming in fast!" As Lieutenant Steben's voice cracked at him over the intercom, Krevety shook his head disapprovingly. The lieutenant seemed to miss the boat yet again. Going up the chain was supposed to be one link at a time, not all the way to the top!

The young officer gained a reputation over the past eight months of jumping to conclusions too quickly. Steben wasn't an essential part of the 24, but the general included him from the beginning, sparing Colonel Honassen from the "pleasure" of working with him.

When Steben alerted Krevety that his presence was requested in the MC1SA2 common area, the general assumed it would be more of the same immaturity. Still, he knew that the lieutenant was laying it on the line to call him like that, so there might be something to it. The tired general sat up and rubbed his temples as if trying to knead out his lethargy, and pulled himself out of his memory-worn chair to investigate.

The excitable lieutenant shrieked during his report over the com, alerting everyone in the building. "The unidentifiable ships aren't answering our attempts at communication."

General Krevety picked up his pace. *Probably a lost fleet that's experiencing com problems. We've had our share recently,* he thought. The longtime diplomat formulated a greeting in his mind as he walked along. He considered the advantages of a give-and-take dialogue. *We'll offer a welcoming greeting, tell the outsiders they may use the landing port until traveling conditions improve again. We'll exchange information and they'll shed some light on the situation the convoy's facing out there. Can't tell them everything on our end. There are stockpiles of ore sitting out in the open. And the relic?*

There was plenty of information that he'd hold close to the vest, but realized for the most part dialogue could benefit them both. The crews could rest while their ships recharged, and the Trecons could discover more about their suddenly populated stellar neighborhood.

Steben was taking command and trying to hail the vessels. "Unidentified craft, this is Trecon Mining Command, please respond."

No reply.

He attempted again, same result.

The ships came into closer view, and Steben discerned that they were likely pirates. The officer called for a preliminary alert launch of the Starlance fighters. "Red alert, launch the fighter squadron!"

The invaders looked like an experienced crew due to their stealth and highly organized formation flying. When the ships gained lower atmosphere, six broke off while the other three headed straight for MC1SA2. The ships appeared first to be in an investigative mode, but a nanosecond after the red alert they changed their posture, as if they could hear Steben's order.

Varoom!

The pirates dived to their prearranged targets!

General Krevety arrived in the operations center. He called, "Red alert, upgrade to level one response. Launch the Starlance fighters!"

"The order was already given, sir," Steben muttered sheepishly.

For once, the general was satisfied with the young officer. "Good work lieutenant! Sound the alarm again with my authorization code!"

Beep wail, beep wail, beep wail!

The sounds of the high-pitched klaxon filled the station, alerting everyone to prepare for battle! The Trecon defenses were light, but well equipped to fend off smaller pirate vessels. The Trecon pilots picked up their pace, but it was too late. Unfortunately for the Trecons, the pilots originally hesitated because Steben wasn't qualified to give such an order. His reputation for being impulsive had factored in.

When the first shots were fired, Krevety knew they were in trouble.

Vwip vwip!

The Mihhidite Sharks made a unique sound as they fired upon the camp. The pirates flew down with great speed, attacking the squadron of Starlance fighters first.

Blast, baboom!

The pirates scored direct hits with intense laser blasts; fire and smoke lit up the landscape! The camp cannons were manned and defense shields raised. It was too little too late.

Krevety sent another message in a threatening tone to the pirates, ordering the ships to vacate their airspace. It was comical to think they'd listen. His harsh voice added bland spice to the chaos, but nothing more!

Vwip vwip!

Kaboom!

Major Tallik reported, "General, our Starlance squadrons aren't launchable. The rescue crews deployed the crash fire trucks to extinguish the flames, but ran out of agent because the pirates are keeping up the pressure!"

After the defenses were down, the Mihhidites took out the communication capabilities with a skilled surgical approach.

"Contact the main camp and see if they can spare any fighters."

"No use sir, our com tower was just destroyed!"

"And I suspect the other camps are experiencing the same problems."

Flash, bwoom!

It was the first time there was evidence of another presence in the lonely quadrant of the universe. Trecon had fallen hook, line, and sinker for the Raihan deception.

With the Starlances destroyed, the camps were left virtually naked against their aggressors. Everything happened too fast for the groggy Trecons to respond. Their limited surface-to-air defenses were inadequate, easily avoided at the distance the pirates were attacking from. The Sharks executed the onslaught with pinpoint accuracy, these guys were good! The camps smoldered as the attack progressed.

Crash, shudder, burst!

Major Tallik bellowed, "We might as well be throwing rocks at them!"

The Trecons were in no position to make demands, and General Krevety knew it. With MC1SA2 smoking and crumbling around him, General Krevety knew they were no longer in a position to resist their aggressors. "Prepare to surrender!" He had no choice.

Tallik shuddered at the thought of surrendering to outlaws. "To pirates, sir?"

As General Krevety watched the ships attack, he realized it was obviously a scripted attack from the beginning. The ships targeted foundational supports around the camp and isolated the trillelium stores. "Those aren't pirates! They knew exactly where to hit us and what to avoid. Unfortunately, we're out of options."

Across Muudia, Mihhidite Sharks methodically blasted away at the paltry defenses of the mining camps. They were well organized in their attack. The Trecons were in dire trouble, grounded and under heavy siege.

The attack seemed to last for ages, but it didn't take the Mihhidites long to finish their work. A unanimous feeling bled through the camps, that the antagonists knew them well.

Krevety reluctantly prepared an official statement of surrender to their new enemy, knowing that fighting to the last man was not the right move.

General Krevety thought the thugs would load the trillelium and be on their way, but the pirates flew off again, just as suddenly as they'd arrived.

The shell-shocked Trecons tried to process the strange circumstances they were involved in, but the situation quickly changed again. Twenty minutes after the attack, as they were assessing damages, the lieutenant noticed another ship in the distance. "One more vessel approaching atmosphere, sir," announced Steben matter-of-factly. Their first reaction was that a warship was coming in to finish the job in a second wave.

General Krevety responded to the situation with a flat order. "Prepare for hand-to-hand combat if they don't accept our terms!"

The pirates would soon raid the camps and they didn't know what to expect. The general checked his laser pistol and prepared for close combat. Weapons were drawn around the soggy smoking camp as best they could, to prepare for a ground assault.

As the spacecraft drew closer, however, Lieutenant Steben recognized it as a Mule-class cargo ship. "It's a Trecon freighter, the bruiser should be coming into view soon!" Everyone from General Krevety down was astonished at the timing. They knew the carrier escort ship would change the odds in their favor, hoping the skies would soon be filled with Starlance fighters. "We could have really used that Bruiser an hour ago!"

"The pirates must have detected our fleet and fled the quadrant!"

As the Mule moved in closer, their hopes were dashed as quickly as they were born. No other ships came into view. The one supply ship was obviously damaged. Why was a Trecon ship coming in to land shortly after the camp had just been wiped out by pirates? It was a surreal experience. There was no precedent set in history that prepared them for what had happened to them during the past hour, and yet this was the next chapter in their strange saga.

As the ship approached, they couldn't hail it because the Mule's communication equipment was inoperable. Krevety concluded that the ship had also been hit by the pirates. The Trecon Mule knew exactly where it was headed, floating down to their position at MC1SA2. As the vessel approached closer, they noticed deep gouges on the top of the freighter and the NAV/COM port sheared clear off the ship!

Neither was in a great position to assist the other, but at least the Trecons had limited capability to gain atmosphere. The sky was quiet as the *Mule 357* eased toward the charred tarmac, but they wouldn't be alone for long!

CHAPTER 11

Mule 357's Impromptu Rescue Mission

The Mule crew observed three vessels in the distance, about 20 kilometers from the planet's surface. The trio were moving away from the smoking camp, presumably to another location. There was no doubt in Onsan's mind the enemy would soon return. "What do you make of it?"

Orange flames and thin columns or bluish-black smoke were accented against the luminous yellow and muted purple hues of the stormy sky. CJ scanned the camp, "Three pirates did that?"

Davss asked, "Where are they going?"

Onsan responded, "They saw us and determined we were the tip of the spear coming to defend the settlement."

"Where are our fighters?" The answer to the question presented itself on the ramp before the words escaped from CJ's mouth.

"We'd better prepare for a fight! It won't take them long to discover we're the only ship." Onsan knew they had nothing more than a slingshot to fight with compared to big guns of the pirate ships, yet he ordered Milerous to man the top cannon.

"Yes, sir," replied Milerous. Adrenaline shot through the kid's body, making his jittery heart jump within his chest! The mission became extreme once again for the crew of *Mule 357*!

The pirates faded off into the horizon. Onsan kept a safe distance until he felt it was safe enough to land at MC1SA2. "Bring us down slow. Look for an intact spot on the landing platform, and watch for survivors and loose debris." CJ nodded and eased the Mule toward the fractured landing pad.

As the Mule circled the camp, her crew observed the aftermath. The settlement was burning in several critical areas where communication towers and defense positions were supposed to be. The Starlance fighters and several other ships were rendered unrecognizable and useless on the landing pad, melting into pitted smoldering metal.

What the '357 crew saw was complete chaos on the ground! In the distance, they saw people fruitlessly trying to repair defenses for the next assault. A small group of security police were frantically trying to access the armory depot to issue weapons to the miners.

The Mule used the established alternating red-and-green light signals to indicate they were in communication distress. The signals were received and returned to the Mule by the ground crew in flashing red, indicating the apron was unsafe. They had no choice, and searched for a spot among blackened junk.

Onsan ordered Milerous to keep watch from the laser cannon position while CJ tried to land the ship. "There's nowhere to land on the pad, but we'll sink to the rafters in that mud!"

"There," pointed Davss.

On the landing platform, a crash fire truck pushed aside a charred pile of wreckage. The empty truck strained against the heap, but managed enough momentum to push it over the edge and into the mud. A tall man jumped out of the crumpled cab and struggled to the platform as the front of the fire truck sunk past its wheels.

The Mule landed and was immediately surrounded by 24 puzzled settlers searching for refuge aboard the *Mule 357*. General Krevety introduced himself as the settlement commander, and conveyed to Onsan everything he needed to know in two seconds, "Sorry, no time to talk. Let's get loaded and I'll brief you in the ship."

"Yes sir. I'll give you our report as well."

Krevety turned to the group, "Load up, take only the basics!"

General Krevety and Onsan formulated a spur-of-the-moment plan as the miners scurried into the spacecraft. They'd shuttle the 24 people to another mining camp and find usable equipment. Then they'd see what they could do when they got there. "We're unable to send a distress signal, because our com system was destroyed in the attack," said General Krevety.

"That makes both of us." They decided the crew would seek help and return for the others when they were able. They had no choice.

"We'll have to shuttle workers, food, and equipment to the least damaged camp and bring everyone there. All we can do is hope for the best." They quickly unloaded smaller supply stores of secondary goods to make room for the 24 extra passengers.

After they unloaded the Mule, everyone's attention shifted to the mysterious alien structure. Loading it was briefly considered, but it was decided by General Krevety that ferrying people to safety was more important. Wasting time loading the relic could cost many people their lives!

At first, Tephen railed raucously against the decision, asserting that the structure was a valuable archetype in the eyes of culture and science. He wasn't alone in his apprehension. Pnoi Nbnok had spent valuable time trying to figure it out and was also against leaving it. He offered, "General, I believe we should consider bringing it. We can load it in five minutes, and it won't take up too much space once it's secured to the side of the hull." Nbnok looked like a parent being asked to leave his beloved child behind!

General Krevety appeared dejected to leave it, but was also wondering if the relic had something to do with the battering of the camp in the first place. The beleaguered general was finished discussing the issue. "There isn't time. The pirates could return at any moment. Everyone on board the vessel now!" Krevety knew it was prudent to get everyone out and consider Trecon's military options at a later time. The relic simply wasn't important any longer!

Davss stomped onto the deck of the Mule and disappeared toward his lab.

The general turned to Tallik, "Set the fuses by the loaders and the relic. That'll keep them busy for a while!"

Tallik ran away, "On it, general!"

The Mule was at MC1SA2 for only 15 minutes, but unfortunately, they were detected by the intruders.

As they launched, Milerous alerted Onsan from the gunner position about a massive ship rapidly approaching their location. The *Rockwell III* was coming in for a closer look. Another new ship; all Krevety could do was shake his head.

The Mule running without communication systems made her somewhat undetectable at first, but it also kept the crew in the dark. They were unsure if the ship was there to secure the structure or attack them. Fortunately, the spacecraft paid them no mind as it floated by.

As the mysterious ship jetted into the distance, the '357 attempted to make a run for it into deep space. CJ hit the thrusters as they attempted to gain altitude. "Easy CJ, take us up slowly. We don't want to draw their attention!" During their ascent, the enemy ship continued along to the planet's surface, away from them.

Could they be in the clear?

For a moment, the Mule crew felt they had given the invaders the slip. Everyone was extremely quiet, as though any sound could be heard by the prowling warship.

Suddenly reality hit! CJ interjected the silence of the bridge with a terrifying observation, "Onsan, er, General, a second ship is out there!"

Onsan's brown eyes flashed with anger. "Engage maximum thrust!"

Pskeeew!

After three minutes, the jig was up. CJ responded, "I'm giving you all we've got, but the vessel is bearing straight for our position!"

As the ship closed the distance, they saw a bewildering sight. They were being followed by a carrier, not a pirate ship. It was the third introduction of a new ship in the last hour.

"That's a flagship vessel!"

The Mule hit the edge of the hazard zone at a dangerous speed. "CJ, slow to half speed and divert all non-critical energy to the shields!" The Mule evaded a giant asteroid and entered the field.

The carrier took a half-hearted shot in their direction, and the Mule evaded.

Shatter, crunch, scrape!

A massive rock disintegrated in front of them, and the jagged remnants crashed against their shields! CJ shook his fist at the carrier. "The ship is toying with us. Why don't they just get it over with?"

Onsan was onto their game. "No. They're only trying to stop our momentum. Continue forward!"

General Krevety watched intently and offered no input. He realized he was out of his element in the Mule, and felt they were in capable hands with Onsan and CJ at the helm.

Onsan felt they had no choice but to escape from the giant war ship by returning to the treacherous rock field they'd recently escaped from. "Our only hope is to lose the carrier in the asteroid belt!"

Milerous blasted a large rock out of their path as another shook the ship from the other side, just missing his position.

Zzzttt!

A red laser passed by so close he could feel a jolt of energy from it pass into his control panel. He felt naked in the gun turret, "This just keeps getting worse!"

The Mule twisted through the arduous zone, dodging meteorites and pushing its limits as they absconded into space.

71

General Krevety decided they'd return to Trecon because they were detected, they had no chance of rescuing anyone else from the encampments. "Keep moving into the field Onsan!"

"Right sir," responded Onsan. "We'll do our best to get through this mess!"

Milerous reported that they were still being followed by the carrier, but it had slowed its pursuit. The laser fire stopped. The hefty warship didn't appear aggressive like before, almost as if they'd given up chasing the Mule. For a moment, the inhabitants of the Trecon ship thought the carrier had lost interest.

Suddenly Milerous noticed several smaller ships exiting the carrier and heading in their direction at eight kilometers, and he yelled their plight to the captain. "Fighters launching, sir!" There was a tone of impending doom in the kid's voice.

*****

The Raihans were confident it would be a short battle. The Vehemence carrier released six Talons against *Mule 357*.

Vzew, screech, roar!

They screamed at their target with a high-pitched ferocity and murderous intentions!

Raihan Talons were a small single-piloted ship sufficiently armed and very nimble in space. They weren't heavily shielded, but made up for any shortages with their speed and agility in battle. They could appear like a swarm of unrelenting mosquitoes, not giving up until they destroyed their target. They were perfectly suited for such a battle!

The Talon pilots were flying their ships to display great skill, a psychological tactic they played on their enemies to win a mental battle even before they fired a shot. The Raihans showed supreme overconfidence, only sending part of their armada to destroy *Mule 357*.

*****

Onsan knew their strategy too well. The fighters would be nimble and dangerous in the rock-strewn surroundings.

72

The crew prepared to protect themselves the best they could. Continuing forward was the only option. The Mule was bigger than the fighters, and the shields would hold for a while if they could continue their outward course. Although the Talons could thrive in the shadow of their carrier, they might struggle as they entered into deep space. Onsan knew it was wishful thinking.

"All experienced hands to the bridge!" Onsan made the order specifically to pull the sulking Tephen Davss out of his stateroom. They needed the Mule's best handlers on the bridge, even the egotistical old scientist. Davss gained experience with the secondary shield override during the storm and there wasn't time to train anyone else in. General Krevety and Major Tallik stayed on the bridge for visual input. The others could only assemble in the cargo bay, belt themselves in, and hope for the best.

"The carrier is holding a distance of 10 kilometers," announced CJ. It appeared the ship was unwilling to chase them into the meteorite cluster.

"Great, we've succeeded with part one of the plan," announced Onsan. "Part two is the real challenge!" Now they could turn their full attention on the six fighters, still an impossible task. The Trecons had never seen a Talon before, and were gravely concerned as they saw the small fighters maneuvering with great speed as they approached.

The single-laser cannon aboard the Mule-class ships weren't meant for defense against faster ships, that's what their Bruiser escorts and legendary Starlance fighters were for. Milerous had practiced firing the cannons once at slow-moving targets during training, but it was just a basic class meant to familiarize him with the ship's turret. He knew that his training and experience blasting meteorites wouldn't be enough. The fighters were so fast that his slow cannon was akin to throwing a punch wearing a blindfold every time. It wasn't impossible to hit them, but luck would have to play a part!

CHAPTER 12

Space Dogfight

"Primary shields at 68 percent," bellowed CJ, as if he knew what Onsan would ask.

Tephen Davss was their only and best option on the secondary shields now. Onsan gave him a pep talk. "This will be different than the storm. They'll be coming fast, just listen for my orders. They'll attack head-on but will also attempt to outflank us to cut off our escape."

"I'll do my best, Captain," responded Tephen as he further oriented himself with the shield controls. Onsan was pleasantly surprised how the Trecon professor pulled himself together and set aside his triviality in the heat of battle. He'd even cleaned his dirty glasses for the occasion!

Onsan instructed Davss, "You'll need to be quick to anticipate their movements, alternating the shield override into our four main quadrants as they approach, port and starboard, front and aft." Tephen showed quite a knack for the manual shields during their previous ordeal, and Onsan knew he was their best option now. "We'll also stay intimate with the meteorites to avoid the big guns of that carrier, in case they show interest again. Keep that in mind."

"Yes Onsan!"

The secondary shield converter was operated manually to protect the ship during a meteorite shower, not an active attack. It would've been enough to save their fellow Mules during their initial journey if manned in time like the '357. One section was charged to high protection while switching the others to low protection. Power was drained from other areas of the ship into the protective sector, like a body shutting down certain areas to save vital organs.

The captain quickly turned away to assist CJ in flight and navigation of the Mule, focusing his full attention on the task at hand. He knew the best way to fight the battle was to continue farther into the meteorite field, hoping to reach deep space on the far side. He gambled that the carrier wouldn't want to follow them off into the rocky clutter should they survive the first wave. The Mule had shield strength to hold the fighters off for a while.

Milerous breathed deep and tried to calm his nervy hands as he prepared to engage the Talons closing at two kilometers. CJ excitedly called out final instructions to Davss as they quickly covered their checklists.

Onsan looked around. *Who am I kidding?* Reality slapped him in the face! Aside from the laser cannon turret on the top of the ship, the side viewing ports, and the bridge; the Mule would be fighting blind.

The Talons raced to 500 meters and worked into a V attack formation, forming a spear at the Trecon vessel. They prepared to take out the Mule with minimal passes then return to their carrier ASAP to exit the hazard zone.

Milerous fired a shot that missed because of the range and swiftness of the Talons. He knew the shot wouldn't hit a target, but he wanted to get a feel for the cannon again and let them know she wasn't a defenseless ship. He fired again to see the recharge time of the gun, 1.5 seconds seemed like an eternity!

The Mule shook hard as her shields sustained a hit on the top of the ship between the damaged NAV/COM port and the laser cannon turret.

"C'mon, bring it!" shouted Milerous in an excited voice as he fired a return shot.

Inside the ship, several passengers were thrown about as the Mule's shields deflected the blast.

Milerous knew that he was in a precarious position due to his gunner location on the ship. The bloodsucker ships had found the scab where the '357 was damaged during the meteorite storm, and would pick on the weakened part until it bled the livable atmosphere out of the spacecraft. The strategy was a brilliant tactic that showed the attentiveness of the attackers.

Vzzt vzzt, bash!

The shields were rapidly draining down to 45 percent as the Talons tried to force her to a slow crawl. The Mule's shields were weakening, only able to protect her for a bit longer.

The gunner thought he'd led a bird enough, but missed the Talon by 50 meters.

"Arrgghh!"

If Milerous couldn't earn a measure of respect for the ship's defenses, the Talon blasts would take their toll and the Mule would collapse into a thunderous burst of energy! As he fired another shot, Milerous realized that they were anticipating his shots and easily outmaneuvering his aim. *I might as well have my eyes closed!*

Bang, thunk!

The ship shook from another blast that hit her dead on the nose. Their tactic was evolving into that of a cat playing with a mouse before he killed it. The Talons seemed to enjoy the occasion of taking out their hapless target. Just seconds into the attack, the Trecons realized there was no way to win. After all they'd been through, it was such a sad ending to the story of *Mule 357*!

Hope was lost for the Trecons. It wouldn't be long, as the shields drained below 25 percent.

What happened next surprised everyone.

Vzzt vzzt, baroom!

Milerous yelled on the intercom, "Did you see that, one of their ships just destroyed another!" Time stood still as everyone involved tried to process what happened. During the limbo, the fighter took a second shot and killed another Talon.

Vzzt, boosh!

"What's he doing?"

In the next second, a front Talon sent a volley that shook the bottom of *Mule 357*, severely shaking the cargo area of the ship where the majority of the passengers were riding.

Vzzt vzzt!

Shudder, bright flash!

That one hurt! There were injuries as the hit threw two passengers through the air and into the side of the metal supply crates.

After the blast, the remaining hostile Talons were distracted by the deserter. There was a great confusion within the attacking force as they tried to compute the surprise attack by their comrade. The Mule continued forward through the confusion, and her shields fought to stabilize.

Milerous got a shot off and destroyed a Talon, whose pilot was obviously distracted by the chaos around him.

Vzew, blam!

"Yeah, how do you like that!"

As the Talon exploded into space dust, everyone collectively realized there were only two hostile warbirds remaining, and survival was a distinct possibility!

General Krevety observed the action from the bridge. The giant man raised his thunderous voice and filled the flight deck with jubilation, "We're going to make it through this yet!"

Milerous roared from the cannon, "Yeah, another one down, two more to go!"

Vzzt vzzt, shatter!

The fighter exploded into a thousand pieces as the mysterious Talon scored another hit!

The last enemy Talon decided it was time to head back to the carrier and align with reinforcements, but it was too little too late for the escaping bird. As the panicky ship attempted to return to the Raihan carrier, it was easily destroyed by the friendly Talon.

The battle lasted seven action-packed minutes from start to finish. Everyone expected a short battle, but the result surprised them!

The Talon flew by, then turned back to *Mule 357* and tipped its wing to the Trecon crew.

Everyone on the bridge saw the gesture. "I think he wants to make friends," stated CJ.

Onsan answered in a bewildered tone, "Stay at the ready Milerous!" He turned to General Krevety. "What should we do now?"

They quickly prepared for another wave of engagement from the carrier. Mysteriously, the Raihan ship didn't move closer or deploy its remaining fighters after the scarred Trecon freighter. "The carrier is turning away!" The Mule continued on its course away from Muudia, with the Talon falling into formation alongside her. The fighter gestured to the bridge again.

Milerous had his cannon trained on the fighter, but there was no aggressiveness about the movements of the craft. The two ships stayed side by side as they drifted farther out away from the dangers of the carrier, but vulnerable in the meteorite belt. After the Talon tipped its wing again, it was obvious the pilot was trying to communicate with the Mule.

Onsan was the captain of the vessel until recently, but he gladly deferred his authority to General Krevety in the unusual situation. It was unprecedented; even the general had never heard of anything like it before! Onsan wasn't shy about offering his opinion to his superior officer. Since the two men had barely met, the discussion was to be as much about feeling each other out as it was about the rank each held.

"General," Onsan began, "If it wasn't for that pilot, we'd be blackened ashes floating around out there! He's clearly trying to establish communication with us. I think we should consider any help as an option going forward."

The general was mentally sorting through the event rolodex files in his mind, reaching for a stitch of professional military education and personal experience to help guide them. His answer to Onsan was filled with the facts of their situation. "The only thing we know, is that we've been attacked by two unknown enemies in a short period of time in a quadrant of the universe uninhabited until two hours ago. Now we've witnessed one of their pilots betray his comrades in the midst of a heated battle when they clearly held the advantage over us."

Krevety was open to suggestions. He ordered Onsan, Major Tallik, and Pnoi Nbnok into the conference room adjoining the bridge to discuss their options where they could speak more freely.

The general began the meeting by stating rigidly, "We're responsible not just for the souls on this ship, but also to ensure our Trecon brethren receive support as soon as possible. There's no way we can survive another attack, and a return trip to Trecon will be treacherous at best. The longer we wait here, the more time it gives our adversaries an opportunity to change their mind and finish us off. Lingering here is the only way to ensure our settlers perish. We're in real trouble, no matter how you look at it." He continued with vigor, "Now, we have an enemy pilot who wants to make our acquaintance. What are your thoughts?"

Onsan provided Krevety with a daring option, "We should open the bay door and let him land. He can surely shed some light on the situation we're in. Our communication capabilities are lost. Perhaps we could use the ship's communicator to contact the colonies or Trecon Control to send reinforcements sooner. At the very least, we could send out a distress call."

General Krevety was intrigued by the suggestion. He turned to Tallik and asked, "What are your thoughts major?"

Major Tallik thought for a moment then offered, "We're in a damaged ship at the mercy of an unknown enemy. We're unable to communicate, and unfit for a long journey to Trecon. Our only ally in this deep space limbo seems to be flying alongside us in an enemy fighter. Now is the time to consider all our options, including our new companion!"

"Very well Captain. Prepare to take the ship into our forward cargo bay," stated General Krevety in a composed manner.

"That ship isn't meant for extended deep-space travel. We'll have to move fast, or the pilot will become the last casualty of the battle," stated Pnoi Nbnok matter-of-factly.

The next course of action was put on hold for the moment. "Noted Nbnok. Speaking of casualties, you and Davss tend to ours," responded the general.

"Yes, sir."

CHAPTER 13

Unanticipated Collaboration

A slow-flashing green-light signal was given from the bridge to the Talon pilot to indicate Trecon amity. The bird tipped its wing in response.

They had one pressing issue: The front bay was packed full of supplies. The crew had to figure out a way to get the fighter ship into the stall without damaging the essential supplies on board. Onsan ordered over the com, "We'll be receiving the ship, so we need to clear the forward bay immediately. We have many things to do. Move the supplies, empty the pressurized observation chamber, and open front bay to outside stratosphere to receive the vessel."

Preparations were hastily made. The Mule front stall could handle the size of the diminutive Talon with plenty of lateral and vertical space to spare. As they assessed the risks of accepting the craft, Onsan's fighter-pilot side kicked in. "A blindfolded child should be able to land it in here," he bantered. "A professional pilot should have no trouble at all!"

Fortunately, the mining replacement parts and repair equipment were loaded in the front of the fore bay by the ramp. The equipment was no longer needed and could be easily discarded off the ship into space. The cumbersome equipment took up roughly half the space of the bay, which would make the job of moving the remaining supplies not as daunting once it was cleared out. The crew could safely work on clearing the bay once the weighty mining equipment was gone.

Milerous sat in the overhead crane, which was a self-contained unit for deep-space maneuvers such as this. It was a unique situation, and Milerous had never been trained on advanced crane operations. It would be a challenge for him to learn as he went along.

He climbed into the crane, and flipped the master switch. *Jerk!*

For a moment, Milerous's chocolate-hued eyes grew wild with terror as the machine came to life and tilted down to face the load.

Creeaak!

The ramp slowly tilted downward until the bay was open to the outside.

Slump!

The crane activated, bringing Milerous down the sloped track. Milerous was simultaneously terrified and filled with wonderment as he worked the rail crane to the edge of the ramp. Being held from eternity by a few bolts and a rail attached to the ship spiked his blood pressure, and made his heart feel like it was beating out of his chest!

He eased the forks under the first crate and unlocked it. "Off you go." Milerous gently moved it off the ramp. He didn't want to tempt fate and go too fast! As he moved to the end of the track, Milerous was relieved that the crane held.

Sigh!

The container floated in suspension once it was outside. Milerous needed to creep outside. As he did, he felt like he was in a bubble that would pop if touched by the smallest rock. They'd found a "soft spot" in the field, but that didn't make him feel less vulnerable! He had to ignore the dangers and concentrate on his work. In the distance he could see a billion stars winking at him through the meteorites. It was strikingly beautiful despite the heart-pounding dangers.

He carefully nudged the crate and it drifted away from the Mule. The first one took the most time, but soon Milerous felt comfortable and in better control of the crane. He picked up the pace as he went along. After 45 minutes, the mining equipment was off loaded, and the ramp was prepared to close once again.

Milerous felt a tremendous sense of accomplishment as the door slowly closed below him!

"Great job Milerous! Now, let's empty the back of the bay by hand."

The bay was normalized, and the crew could work on clearing the rest of the stall. The rear of the chamber was stacked with valuable resources that had to be moved before they were ready to receive the Raihan bird. Receiving a ship was not unusual for a Mule freighter; shuttles were used numerous times before, when the occasion called for it.

It was all hands on deck. Unpacking the cargo to "bite-sized" parcels that could be moved by hand was not a pleasurable experience, but it didn't take long with the determined attitudes of the crew. Everyone including the general worked until their uniforms were soaking wet with sweat.

Pnoi Nbnok and Tephen assisted the injured miners who'd been tossed around during the battle. General Krevety called on the com to Tephen's stateroom and asked the condition of the injured miners. Nbnok answered, "Aside from a concussion and a shoulder that had to be put back into the socket, they'll be okay."

"Good," replied the relieved general. "Let me know of any changes in their conditions."

The plan meant cramped quarters for the crew. After the fighter was loaded, they'd keep tight security around it. The front bay would be off-limits to most of the crew. They'd have to guard the Raihan pilot, so the conference room would be restricted too.

Milerous said their mission had come full-circle; they were headed back to Trecon with an alien artifact, after all!

Stacking the cat's cages to gain space was a challenging job in the time allotted to them. Tephen tranquilized the cats through using a fast-acting gas that would disable them for a few hours, so they could temporarily move them to another area of the ship. They would be cranky for a few minutes after they awoke, but nothing a big meal wouldn't fix.

"Cleaning the cages will be a real hassle," complained Davss, back to his negative self.

Onsan took pleasure in his discomfort. "It's the perfect job for you, Tephen!"

The crew would have to live in shifts, moving through passageways filled with crates and boxes. The more experienced people made bunks on top of the loads. The galley was stuffed half full of supplies, so they'd eat in separate shifts.

As the work neared completion, Krevety, Onsan, and Tallik returned to the bridge to discuss their opinions more freely. General Krevety went along with the impulsive plan because there were no alternatives, but he had a great deal of mistrust about the whole situation. He wanted to treat the pilot as a prisoner of war with useful information that could aid the Trecons in securing their recent losses and rescuing their people.

Trecon command would want to research the fighter and see what they were up against. The pilot would have information about the attack, the military capabilities of his home planet, and the intricacies of the fighter. Krevety knew that Trecon was lagging behind her new enemy, and there wasn't much time to catch up! The attack was an act of war from an unknown people from a strange galaxy, and any information they could get about their new enemy would be valuable to them.

The general prepared many questions for their guest. Did the pilot know about the pirates attacking the mining camps? Why did a flagship carrier attack the Mule? Were these seemingly coincidental events related? Did this have something to do with the artifact found 150 meters below the surface on

Muudia? They would question the pilot with a heavy hand to shed light on the situation.

Krevety also had an opinion of the pilot that added a bitter taste in his mouth. Being a long-standing military man, he looked at this pilot as a deserter, someone not to be trusted in the heat of battle. Was it wise to put their faith in such a person? He could respect an enemy even as he was trying to destroy them, because they were fighting for their comrades. Although the general was grateful to survive a fire ball explosion, he was hesitant to trust someone who'd changed sides in the fight. The pilot must have serious issues to act so irrationally!

Deep down, General Krevety accepted the plan because they needed the Talon radio to communicate with Trecon, a bottom line that couldn't be attained through any other means. He knew the established military procedure about prisoners of war, and they'd follow it to the letter.

Onsan believed the pilot should be treated as an ally. Without his help, they'd all be dead. There had to be more to the situation than a pilot blowing his comrades away just as they were about to dispose of easy prey. They'd have a lot to learn from the pilot. Onsan thought he'd offer honest information freely to them based upon his actions. Weak-minded people rarely desert from the winning side; they do it when victory seems impossible!

Onsan believed the mission was getting more bizarre by the day since the meteorite storm, and this was just the next chapter of their peculiar story. The pilot's actions didn't make sense, it was unlike anything he'd ever heard of before in all his military training. There had to be a deeper reason to help them. It was important to get information out of him, but as an ally rather than an enemy pilot.

Krevety's openness to ideas taught Onsan a lot about leadership. It showed him the wise leader that General Krevety was. The general also realized that his junior officer had brought the Mule vessel through recent events admirably, so he also valued Onsan's instincts. They agreed that any one prescribed way of handling the unique situation was not prudent. They would take a moment-by-moment approach, drawing on each other to assess circumstances as they arose.

Milerous hailed the bridge, "The bay is emptied out and ready, sir."

"Good, we'll be right there."

Krevety, Tallik, and Onsan weaved through the maze of crates and down the ladder to the front cargo hold.

The Talon pilot circled around to a safe distance of 50 meters. When the forward bay was cleared out and prepared to receive the Talon fighter, the Mule eased away from the mining equipment floating around the vessel and gave the Talon a clear approach signal.

Milerous reset the crane and watched from his perch. He looked out into the cluttered cosmos. The equipment and crates floated among the cluttered meteorites. More junk to add to the scene!

"Prepare to receive the fighter craft," ordered General Krevety.

Screech!

The ramp slowly lowered into position.

CJ slowed the forward thrusters and the vessel came to a halt. As the restless crew prepared to board the fighter onto her cargo deck, the Talon swiftly rocketed around and came into position in front of the Mule. Everyone was balled up with a high degree of emotional curiosity. They were now entering uncharted waters, beginning a touch-and-go process of receiving a foreign pilot!

It was soon clear to everyone that the pilot was a master of his ship. The expert flying reassured everyone pressed up against the port windows and air-lock door they'd survive the risky stage of the plan. The Talon pilot skillfully moved the craft into position over the ramp and into the threshold of the bay. Everyone breathed a little easier for the moment, confident that the pilot had done similar maneuvers countless times.

The Talon eased expertly into the landing bay, where the pilot turned off the machine and waited. The ramp was slowly raised into closed position and locked. The atmosphere was normalized with the rest of the ship.

Ssshhh!

The hatch on the Talon slowly opened as steam flowed out of its sides. As the pilot stepped out of the fighter and onto the cargo deck, the door to the airlock was immediately opened and the welcoming squad flooded into the cargo area!

General Krevety approached the pilot with two security officers by his side, their weapons drawn. As they secured the pilot, a second team assembled to "detail" the Talon. The fighter's power and communication abilities were to be immediately disabled by the tech crew to protect them from being tracked or sending messages out to the enemy.

The pilot's helmet was removed, revealing long flowing brown hair cascading over a beautiful woman's shoulders! A pleasant sweet smell of jasmine filled everyone's nostrils as they surrounded her, a welcome surprise for those who'd spent too much time smelling the hourly discharges of man and machine on mining settlements and supply ships!

The lynx walked up and introduced himself to the pilot, purring loudly and nestling himself against her leg. Chase's instincts about her seemed to break the tension and set everyone at ease.

General Krevety was immediately captivated by her soft features and bright blue eyes. She had a distinct exquisiteness, a captivating presence all her own.

CHAPTER 14

Abbsnate Ryderson Etak's Story

The strikingly beautiful woman appeared to be in her mid-forties, of medium height and dark skin.

She was taken immediately into the custody by the security officers and brought into the Mule's small mess area for questioning by General Krevety, Major Tallik, and Onsan. Tallik was involved as a "tiebreaker" in a voting scenario. He had a good reputation for examining the evidence provided before he made a decision. It was the main reason the general had initially chosen him for his command staff.

During the short walk to the mess hall, the crew noticed that the woman displayed a confidence demanding respect and attention, not that of an untrustworthy person who'd just blown up her battle mates. She appeared as though she already knew the drill, anticipated for this to happen, and wanted to move things along quickly so she could communicate her agenda to them!

Abbsnate began her story. "Greetings, I'm Abbsnate Ryderson Etak, or Serlat. Etak is my mother's maiden name. I took it to throw off the Raihans because my father was in charge of the camps. Twenty-four years ago, during Raihan Mission 15-101.25, the Ryderson Omegans fell victim to the same ploy as you. We explored the planet not for wealth, but to save our twin planets and keep our home pristine."

The crew were given a history lesson about the twin planets. The Ryderson Omegans were average-sized dark-skinned humanoids of high intelligence who were great stewards of the land. They wore plain canvas tunics and robes to protect them from the extreme elements of their twin-planet solar system. They were not prone to excess. Every technology they created was to protect themselves or maximize the resources on the planets they explored. They were an intelligent race that immersed itself in scientific knowledge.

In earlier times, they strove to be industrial pioneers, but eventually a focus on sustainability grew that had lasted for centuries. They reached out for resources rather than within. When the RO's discovered Muudia, Abbsnate was a young career-minded researcher who wanted to investigate the universe down to the minutest detail! She had one of the brightest scientific minds on Ryderson Omega. When they found the cache of trillelium ore on lifeless Muudia, they were excited to mine on such a planet where they wouldn't cause harm to its native life.

Abbsnate's father, Serlat, was a scientist well-known for his nurturing touch with the environment and his people. He cared not only about Ryderson Omega, but also the sites they mined throughout their zone of influence. He developed mining equipment to cause minimum damage to the site.

As a young woman Abbsnate was eager to follow in her father's footsteps, being selected when a research team was assembled to identify a solution for purifying the stockpile of ore on-site rather than bringing radiation back to RO. It was challenging work, but she loved it! The team designed an underground system and were in the final stages of development when spring hit and raised the radiation levels.

"We were lulled to sleep by the Raihans, closed off to the dangers of the planet until it was too late!"

"As were we." General Krevety seemed increasingly interested in her story as familiarity added credibility to her version. Abbsnate won over the skeptical Krevety the longer she went, but she had the others from the beginning!

She shed light on the Raihan Servitude Directive 009, where the captives were classified into three specific groups: Class I Contributors, or those who possessed a particular skill set that would help advance Raihan's power and influence (like Abbsnate); Class II Integrators, those who worked necessary jobs and found a new comfortable way of life on Raihan; and Class III Wanderers, those who were contrary to the Raihan ways and refused to be reeducated and rehabilitated.

Once the Ryderson Omegans arrived on Raihan, two things stood out to them. First, no attempt was made by the Raihans to convoy them back to RO, although it was repeatedly requested. They were shut off from the outside world.

Second, gender separation was unusual in a rescue, more typical for a conquering regime. When the women were divided out, they were subjected to different tests from their male counterparts. Were they expecting a child, they'd be immediately separated from the group for indoctrination and prenatal care. Ensuring their brainwashing was effective from the earliest moments was part of Raihan protocol.

The Raihans couldn't afford suspicious individuals reproducing and becoming a growing force of unrest on their planet. They influenced children young, to indoctrinate them into Raihan society. The education of mothers was more persuasive than their counterparts. If they wanted to stay with their child, they'd conform.

When the gender separation started on the medical ships, the writing was on the wall for Serlat. A plan was quickly hatched to Abbsnate by her father before she left with the other women. All it took was a knowing look between the two, given in chaos! Locking eyes from across a bay was the last she'd seen of her father before he was hauled away. "I don't know if he's alive or dead." Abbsnate fought off the emotion and continued.

No one else could know of the plan, or it would put her in danger. She'd find a way for them through false collaboration with the enemy, no matter how long it took! Nobert Serlat realized that an all-out revolt would be fruitless for them in the long run, so he put high hopes in Abbsnate to find a way back home.

Only seven Ryderson Omegans were classified as Contributor candidates, and Abbsnate was the best and brightest of them. Her magnetic disposition and scientific brilliance stood out from the beginning. Fortunately for Abbsnate, the Raihans played right into her hands and took an interest in her from the start.

What aided Abbsnate's cause was that she was a strong individual. While the majority of the Ryderson Omegans bided their time and faced their hurdles together, she was resilient enough to stand alone as a public enemy of her home planet. Being separated from the group was nearly unbearable. But if everyone fought, there'd be no one on the inside to "open the door" for the others when the time was right. Abbsnate had great motivation to see her family again, a resolve to be tested to the limit over the next two and a half decades.

The most important things for her were patience and long-term vision. No one discovered the pact between Abbsnate and her father. It was best, for the safety of everyone involved.

Mission 15-101.25 was concurrently known as the best ore harvesting and worst for assimilation of individuals in the history of harvest operations! The Raihans would review their selection processes once again to see where they went wrong on the human side of things.

Two important facts concerned the Raihans about the Ryderson Omegans. First, their incontestable loyalty to one another; how they'd willingly traded a plush life for hardship. Second, they must keep close tabs on the Integrators and Contributors from the RO group.

Abbsnate knew they'd be watching her closely. Her main objective was to convince the Raihans she was one of them. It was easy for her to pamper herself in the new environment, but it made her feel like a sociopath. After two months of healing and planetary acclimation, she appeared to do well, rolling through the testing with no issues.

Mission 15-101.25 proved there were still basic oversights with Servitude Directive 009 on many sociological levels. The result of Raihan suspicion was that Abbsnate and the others would experience intensive testing during their reeducation process. The examinations confirmed to the Raihans that she was a willing partner and would serve their community faithfully. Abbsnate hid her emotions well, passing the tests and interviews with flying colors. By the end, they were eating out of her hand!

Only 325 RO's were designated for Integrator duty. They were housed in a secured area until they began work in the purification factories, where their numbers declined significantly.

Meanwhile, the majority of RO's were suffering greatly; being visibly hardened against their captors invited misery. The Raihan facade of being rescuers dissipated instantly once the curtain was pulled back. They quickly realized that the Raihan guards didn't care if they died in the purification factory or toiling away in the unforgiving desert wilderness.

There were 53 among the 325 Integrator candidates who started an open revolt in the purification facility. They were charged with collaboration and sent directly to the Base 13 Gallows, the nickname for the main prison complex on Raihan, where they were never heard from again. The Raihans determined the remaining 272 Integrators would be watched closely as they processed the ore and continued through the reeducation process.

The Ryderson Omegans voiced disdain for Abbsnate and the other RO collaborators in public countless times while being put out to pasture. That hurt Abbsnate and her father the most! Many close friends would go to their graves believing she was a traitor. Abbsnate felt a deep pain with the separation, but it was imperative she hide it well. She quickly gained a reputation for her intelligence, testing higher than all but two ever had!

As Abbsnate narrated her story, the crew could see the weighted bond of her countrymen rippling underneath her calm composure.

The RO's fought back both openly and covertly. An underground movement within the Integrators was created shortly after capture, working for revolution. During the first few years, an additional 35 RO Integrators were weeded out and sent to the Gallows.

Raihan's biggest fear was a revolt that would turn their utopia upside down. The closest person in the past to attaining an insurrection was Daine Hertag, a Contributor whose motives were mistaken by the perpetrators. The Raihans misidentified his attempt to take over the Pladia *Rockwell III* outpost as madness caused by radiation and isolation. In reality, he was attempting to take over the station to contact his home planet when he was killed by Grolegg.

After word got back to Raihan, Hertag was secretly regarded as a true hero of the revolution within the ranks of the renegade Integrators. They had to celebrate his memory in silence, though. There were no second chances, an Integrator mole was immediately brought outside the gates to the Base 13 Gallows.

Abbsnate explained how she came to be with them. After the Mihhidite Sharks softened the MC1SA2 sector, the *Rockwell III* inspected the storage area. Commander Knuddrul discovered that the Mule had been there, but the relic remained on Planet 6333. Knuddrul passed the information to Captain Yougsten Brell of the *Vehemence X*, wanting him only to ensure the Mule didn't return for the artifact. He never gave a clear order to the carrier to engage them. Brell independently (with a heavy dose of prodding by Abbsnate) pursued and attacked the Mule freighter. The official attack order was given by Captain Brell and co-signed by his second-in-command, Abbsnate!

Brell trusted Abbsnate fully, and when he didn't dismiss her right away, she knew he was in the palm of her hand! She reasoned with him that most Talon pilots gained combat experience through infrequent surface attacks during softening and harvesting operations. Attacking the Mule was a rare opportunity for newer pilots to gain targeting experience on a moving ship in deep space. What tipped the scales for Captain Brell was they had on board one new Talon II fighter, which had been flight-tested during drills but had never fired on a live target.

Abbsnate knew just how to hook the captain. Bringing home factual statistics on the new fighter in a combat operation would be invaluable. It was against the softening protocol, but Knuddrul was stalling their return anyway. She reasoned the Mule crew was doomed, and the operation would be swift; it would actually be a merciful killing compared to dying slowly of radiation poisoning. Abbsnate used every bit of her persuasive charm on her friend.

Commander Knuddrul had dedicated his full attention to loading the prize onto the outpost ship, so it was decided the simple operation was within the authority of the *Vehemence X* captain. Brell dispatched a quarter of the carrier arsenal to take out the freighter for a "deep-space combat training exercise," for the new-generation Talon II fighter.

Fellow Talon II pilot Ljpoh HNoui spoke in full agreement, excited to test the capabilities of his new fighter. The mission was to quickly destroy the *Mule 357*, then return to the carrier vessel for security escort duty and prepare for their return to Raihan. On the surface, it looked like the live combat mission might take an hour out of their day.

Abbsnate always thought of Brell as a reasonably honorable man despite his elevated position within the despicable Raihan fleet. Her original plan was to utilize their close rapport to petition his help since Brell was actually a captive like her.

Seizing every opportunity to escape weighed continually on her mind during her previous voyages to Planet 6333, but one never materialized. Turning Brell had been her best option, until they observed the damaged Trecon Mule escaping the MC1SA2 rescue site.

The opportunity proved too valuable for her to pass up! Abbsnate couldn't afford to confide in Brell, taking a chance of being called out if she couldn't convince him. Captain Brell was but a simple pawn in her grandiose chess game.

As the pilots strode to their fighters, Abbsnate joked as usual, a normal tactic when calming nerves of younger flyers. Her mouth and mind were on different wavelengths. *Too bad for you*, she thought, *but sacrifices have to be made by everyone for this to work.* They set out to destroy the Trecon Mule with great enthusiasm, but they shouldn't have undertaken a mission of massacre so elatedly!

Abbsnate knew she must destroy the Talon II first, or her mission would go up in flames! The enhanced weapons system on the new fighter meant Abbsnate had to be perfect in her skills to destroy the Talon II before it could retaliate against her. She had to stay in formation until the right moment, then destroy the Talon II on her first shot! Afterward, she'd have to fight the others off before being destroyed. It wouldn't be an easy task, especially because she was inventing her plan as she went along. Abbsnate bet that the green pilots would be confused without a leader, and fortunately she was right.

Following the successful battle, Abbsnate knew the next stage would be important to her immediate survival and long-term strategy as she coasted dependently alongside the Mule.

Two things stood out to her. First, she couldn't survive for long in the Talon as the Mule ship continued deeper into a meteorite field in the throes of Hazard-Class 8 tantrums. They'd be fast approaching the point of no return! If the Trecon vessel didn't accept her soon after the fight, her waning limited life support would terminate, and the real mission would be over before it began.

Second, her decision started a ripple effect that would work its way back to Raihan and throughout the universe on both sides of the portal. Abbsnate knew she had set a time-table for interplanetary war; changing the fates for countless souls because of her actions!

The whole plan was about gambling on events that would bring destruction quickly if things didn't go right. Abbsnate realized that even if everything went perfect and the RO's and Trecons met together in the skies above Raihan, it was still a long shot. The coalition could hold up in space for a while, but it would be fruitless without changes that would begin on the ground and spread into the atmosphere. The most important part of the mission was for the Wanderers and secret rebellion to start a momentum that would snowball among the rest of the Integrators. Establishing a full-scale uprising on the ground was their only hope!

The number of collaborators within the underground resistance wasn't known, nor the number of Integrators who could be turned after they discovered the truth, but it was everyone's best chance! Raihan had stern checks and balances in place among the population to guard against a revolt, so the mission was an uphill climb. Any variance from protocol could cause their house of cards to fall, and there were already two cases of freelancing during Mission 19-128.25 in high-level positions.

Abbsnate knew there was hope for them!

CHAPTER 15

Raihan Reaction

Knuddrul turned irate when the loading of the structure took longer than it should have. The commander's attractive features became twisted. When Knuddrul's foul complexion matched his rotten soul; he appeared ugly, even to his most loyal crewmembers.

The Rockwell crew had nothing to use but pure muscle to load the relic onto the craft. *He* even had to work! Krevety used basic scorched earth strategy as they left, burning all the machinery to a cinder around the relic. The "brilliant military strategist" hadn't considered the Trecons would do such a thing! They finally got it done, trudging thick mud into the Rockwell the whole time.

After two days on the planet's surface, the *Rockwell III* lifted off the surface of Planet 6333. Two days was too much to give up during a season when every minute counted! As they launched into the atmosphere, Knuddrul focused his attention to the *Vehemence X*, and the unauthorized order given by Captain Brell.

Knuddrul wasn't immediately aware of the situation. He'd been too focused on loading the treasured relic before disembarking for Raihan. When he discovered the unsanctioned attack and loss of the Talons, the commander was appalled and driven by anger! The mission commander dissected the possible consequences of what unfolded under his watch.

Although Knuddrul held ultimate responsibility as mission commander, he had a possible reprieve because he hadn't verbalized the attack order to Brell. He knew that the technicality of the fact might be enough to save him upon their return to Raihan. Time was the most precious resource he had to consider. The seasonal clock of Planet 6333 wouldn't wait for him to invent stories to cover his tracks.

As mission commander of the softening operation, he'd lost focus on the greater goal to pursue his own success and glory.

He carefully thought of the wording his official report would include to deflect any blame to Captain Brell:

"While the Rockwell III was focused on securing the mining facilities and loading an invaluable alien artifact, the Vehemence X carrier autonomously committed unnecessary Raihan assets, (including the advanced Talon II fighter), to destroy a damaged supply ship that was not going to make it back to Trecon anyway."

It sounded good to him.

Despite the facts, he reasoned within himself and found several positives in the peculiar situation on Planet 6333. Commander Knuddrul felt that the Mule actually did them a favor without knowing it, through removing the miners and simplifying the situation for him. The rescue operation had saved him the time of fighting them off at MC1SA2.

It was no use; the commander knew he was in trouble.

Knuddrul hailed the carrier. His shaking voice displayed growing displeasure to the crew of the Vehemence as he demanded a report from her captain. "Captain Brell, why did you order that attack?" Knuddrul didn't have the time or patience for anyone acting outside procedure besides himself.

Captain Brell knew the future; with Knuddrul pointing the finger at him and Abbsnate gone, he was left alone to bear the brunt of the consequences. *"I accept full responsibility for the order, commander,"* was Brell's dogged reply. Brell knew it would be a waste of time to point an accusing finger at Abbsnate; she was no longer around to help shoulder the blame. He shuddered and waited for the swift response of the mission commander.

Commander Knuddrul snapped, "Effective immediately, you're relieved of command, Brell. Expect a visit from me soon!"

After the Talon catastrophe, Commander Knuddrul didn't feel it was necessary to freelance from procedure any longer. It wasn't essential to chase the Mule into deeper space, because the inhabitants of the supply vessel would soon die in the hazard zone. With the summer season approaching fast, the Rockwell had to return to Raihan to set the next phase in motion.

The commander thought of Abbsnate and the Trecons with contempt. His Talons would've saved the Mule crew the agony of dying a slower and more painful death, by taking them out quickly. It would've been unwise to send more Raihan pilots knowingly into such peril to accomplish what the solar system would do anyway. Abbsnate's impending death in the radiation bath was better than she deserved. Diabolical thoughts flooded Knuddrul's mind. *May you all live long enough to feel the pain of rotting from the inside out!*

Although losing the Talons was unexpected, it was not unprecedented. A few Talons were lost every mission due to mishaps of inexperienced pilots. Knuddrul knew that Raihan command would be the most upset about losing one of its newest state-of-the-art Talon II fighters.

The incident had twists ever more shocking as the layers were revealed. On the surface it appeared a Talon pilot destroyed her comrades in a case of radiation madness. Unlikely. Talon pilots had to go through extensive training and psychological testing before they were allowed into the program, so radiation madness affecting a pilot was virtually impossible.

Abbsnate was a veteran pilot who'd been through previous harvesting missions with no side effects. She was one of the brightest and most skilled fliers in the Raihan arsenal. She was a highly decorated aeronaut who had performed three missions prior, two harvesting and one softening/escorting mission. Abbsnate volunteered for the mission even though she had completed her space-fighter pilot commitments. She was destined for a promising political career when she gave up flying.

The woman was on top of the world with everything going for her. Abbsnate had always been top of her class, a leader wherever she had been. She had an instinct for protocol, and a charm that disarmed people—a lethal combination for competitors! Most people around Abbsnate grew deeply devoted to her. The government would have to spin the story delicately in public to stem the tide of political conspiracy.

The betrayal of Abbsnate once again brought the Ryderson Omegans to the forefront on Raihan. There was increasing activity within the resistance movement, and the Raihan government would feel a need to know how much they knew or to what level they were involved. They'd round up the RO Integrators for interrogation, and tighten their noose around the Wanderers.

Commander Knuddrul contacted Raihan to inform them that Planet 6333 was softened and ready for the harvesting invasion. There would be consequences upon returning to Raihan, but Knuddrul knew he could spin it to his advantage once Raihan higher command heard of the mysterious structure he housed in the *Rockwell III*. When the Raihans learned of the precious cargo, his ladder to the top would be paved with gold once again!

Captain Brell didn't have the same opportunity to be self-delusional; he'd disregarded protocol and had no ace up his sleeve in the form of surprise cargo. He envisioned eternal incarceration in the notorious Base 13 Gallows. Worse yet, he could be abandoned out with the Wanderers. There was no telling what they would do to a Vehemence captain who'd perpetrated many crimes against them! The utopian way of life was finished for Brell the moment he authorized the combat training mission, regardless of how easy it seemed at the time.

Commander Knuddrul set an immediate course for Raihan, and sent ahead a muddled mission brief to buy himself more time. He had the former captain placed into a holding cell to spend his time contemplating his dreadful fate. The Raihan ships sped toward the gravitational portal with the mining encampments of Planet 6333 smoldering in ruins behind them. The softening fleet would return to Raihan in three days, then prepare for the assault for a week before returning to harvest Muudia.

As they sped through the portal, Commander Knuddrul reflected on the mission. His slanted assessment wasn't steeped in the realization of being two days behind, and losing valuable people and resources during the mission. He reasoned to color the mission with successful overtones.

In Knuddrul's viewpoint, the mission went forward as planned mostly, with only a few setbacks along the way. They'd lost five Talons and a Talon II, but not because of an order *he* gave. Another positive development leaked into his mind. Through the betrayal, the Raihans learned the identity of a major resistance underground spy with powerful governmental potential. Who knew the amount of detailed top-secret information Abbsnate had been leaking for years? Her death would send shock waves through the spy ring. Discovering she was a mole was a great thing for the Raihan government!

A smile actually formed on Knuddrul's face as he realized that a major competitor for top-level positions was no longer in play. Abbsnate wouldn't be clogging the top of everyone's promotion wish lists. In his skewed view, events were coming together and actually increasing his odds of long-term success!

The bottom-line facts were that his mission was still on a positive line. A planet full of terrified miners were experiencing their prescribed cooling period, and the stores were bursting full of trillelium ore just waiting to be loaded. According to the observations by the Mihhidite softening crews from their Shark destroyers, this would be one of the best harvests on record. Knuddrul had maybe the greatest discovery in the history of Raihan aboard his ship; a metal that wasn't melted by centuries of molten trillelium flowing into the bowels of Muudia.

As Commander Knuddrul was preparing his official mission report, he could see many positive possibilities shadowing in his future. He was most thankful to have a scapegoat for the misadventure that happened, and Captain Brell seemed to be a willing participant. Too bad he couldn't claim full credit for uncovering Abbsnate. Regardless, the mission seemed to get better all the time.

CHAPTER 16

Wounded in the Valley of the Shadow of Death

General Krevety had one thing on his mind; the rescue of the miners on Muudia. "We can't leave our comrades to die in agony on the surface. We have to use the transmitter in your ship to contact Trecon Control and have them send help right away."

"That won't do any good, general. Your fleets can't reach them in time." Abbsnate explained the process of the Raihan's harvesting mission. "The Trecon miners will actually be saved from destruction by letting the Raihans continue forward as planned. We have to focus on *our* survival now. Revolution will come soon enough."

As Abbsnate's story unfolded, the crew of the *Mule 357* realized they'd die if they continued on their current course for much longer. Fortunately for them, Abbsnate already knew that and anticipated the next course of action. They had to change their course with a heading back toward Muudia, go through the gravitational portal and pass into the Magnus solar system. The Kremini quadrant was where their destination lay.

Onsan was shocked. "So, you want us to follow the enemy through a wormhole, are you crazy?"

"We can make it, trust me."

"We'll never get through in this heap!"

"We can, there's not much time. If the zone becomes a Hazard-Class 10, then we'll never get through the portal, or out of the meteorite belt!"

General Krevety had to agree with Onsan, but he wanted to hear all the facts. He gave Abbsnate a peculiar look. "Let's listen to what she has to say."

Abbsnate knew what the Raihans were doing. She convinced the crew that the carrier and outpost vessel would be concentrated on returning to Raihan to prepare for the harvesting mission. The Mihhidite Shark crews were intent on beating the Rockwell back to Raihan for some partying and R and R. Once the Mule made it through the portal, the coast would be clear.

General Krevety knew it was the best option. He ordered CJ, "Bring the ship around, and follow her coordinates to the ergosphere."

"Thank you general, you won't regret it!"

Abbsnate detailed the next step in her plan. When they reached the Kremini solar system, they'd head immediately to Planet Kufsiun. Once on the planet they'd go to the Universal Cooperative of Space Vessel Industrialists (UCSVI), in the capital city of Kufsopolis on planet Kufsiun. They'd blend in there easily while their vessel was repaired.

The *Mule 357* council room cringed collectively as they heard of Abbsnate's plan for following the Raihan and Mihhidite ships into the gravitational portal, but the more she explained what she had in mind, their faith grew gradually.

She described the destination to the crew. "Kufsopolis is an industrial megacity, a conglomerate of space-vessel factories and maintenance facilities that is a hub for the entire quadrant of the universe! With thousands of planets represented there, we'll fit right in."

"Good plan, but we still have to make it through the portal in this clunker! Our engines took damage from the battle. And remember, our navigation systems are down."

Abbsnate pulled a tablet out of her jacket. "Gravity will help pull us through. As far as the navigation systems, we can use the Talon's. It'll track the carrier's path, and we can plot our course from the bridge with this com pad. There's a direct link between the fighter and this tablet."

Onsan nodded, and gestured with his hand for her to continue. She was obviously well prepared. He hated putting his life in the hands of a stranger, but it was apparent she knew what she was doing.

Abbsnate continued her narrative. Raihan had strong influences on Kufsiun, but they were covert just like everywhere else. They had no official power to capture the *Mule 357* without Kufsiun approval. There was friction between the two powers, and the Kufsiun government was intent on holding the industrial giant at bay for as long as possible. They did that through heavy taxes and unique laws designed to promote their interests ahead of Raihan's.

Mega corporations down to single bay companies within the UCSVI sold and serviced spacecraft on the planet. Orders from private parties to vast military fleets were taken. Smaller companies also took in and traded used space vessels on the less-corporate side of the city, (which is a nice way of saying the shady side). Security was tight throughout the capital city of Kufsopolis; it had to be because of the wide range of clientele that frequented the planet. A momentary lapse in order could set ruinous events in motion. Power-hungry criminals would rip apart the harmony quickly.

"If the Mule can make it to the industrial city, we can expect to be treated fairly and would receive fair value in return for the bounty of supplies on this ship. Someone will trade your goods for repairing the *Mule 357*. That's your ticket for a return trip to Trecon."

Abbsnate also had a plan to return to Ryderson Omega. She'd trade in her sporty fighter ship for a moderate spacecraft that would safely and efficiently take her to her home planet at a snail's pace. "Good thing we're on the RO side of the portal to begin with, because it'll give me a head start before things get wild!" As for trading in the Talon, it wouldn't be hard to find someone willing to trade a Ferrari for a minivan!

General Krevety objected. "You'll need to find another option. We'll want to study the bird on Trecon to prepare for our assault."

"Got you covered, general!" Abbsnate had all the specs loaded into her mainframe tablet.

"That'll do, please continue."

The only sure thing was that Abbsnate couldn't make it back to RO alone; she'd need a partner to copilot the long journey. General Krevety decided Onsan would go with her to Ryderson Omega. Tallik and Milerous would assist CJ in the Mule.

Onsan cringed.

Krevety smirked. "Tension is good. You'll keep each other in check!" They'd split the remainder of the crew as needed and part from Kufsopolis hoping to meet again as combatant allies in the atmosphere above Raihan.

The plan called for the Mule to shoot back through when the portal event horizon was safe to enter. This would have to be timed perfectly, or it would be a short mission. They all realized the lengths that the Raihans would go to ensuring the secrecy of their industrious Muudia operations.

*****

Suddenly, the meeting on the bridge was interrupted by the visual of a dark and stealthy ship passing within one kilometer of the Mule. The crew assumed a visual only because the pilot of the other spacecraft wanted them to.

The crew felt like a minuscule part of the grand complex universe. The mystic solar system was a busier place than they'd ever realized. The general was sick and tired of new introductions, "This is supposed to be an *empty quadrant!*"

Abbsnate smiled slightly, then grew serious when she strained for a closer look. The classification and identification of the spacecraft was unknown, even to the long-time double agent!

"Here we go again!" CJ stared out of the bridge shield and prepared for evasive maneuvers.

"Davss, report to the bridge. Milerous, man the top cannon," ordered Onsan as they tried to process the new event.

The girl jumped into action, "I'll fly the Talon!"

The ship investigated the Mule at a safe distance of 250 meters. The crew knew that the mysterious craft was inspecting the freighter's damage with great interest. It appeared from the way it flew around that they knew the recent history of the '357. The stealthy ship was the predator and not the prey in any situation they encountered, so it was best not to provoke them through flashing their lights at it.

After the enigmatic ship passed, it sped up to a great rate of speed toward the gravitational portal and quickly disappeared out of sight.

The ship was out of firing range before Milerous reached the cannon, and Abbsnate the bay. Onsan ordered Milerous, "Stay at the ready."

It didn't come back around. The Mule crew determined they weren't in immediate danger, which was evident in the way the ship conducted itself. It could have ended them effortlessly before they even detected it.

The *Mule 357* was vulnerable; the crew were insignificant and unprotected within an arena of cosmic gladiators! The shadow was but one ship that held their lives in its hands and passed on. Perhaps next time they wouldn't be as lucky. The galaxy was also full of natural dangers to avoid, why all the unexpected company? A feeling of nakedness fell over the inhabitants of the '357.

They were sitting ducks in a wounded ship, and they had to keep a low profile until they made it to and from Kufsiun safely. The defenseless feeling would sharpen their senses going forward.

Everyone could see Abbsnate's features drop. She was visibly upset and questioning if the years of planning and fugitive actions were worth it. She'd sacrificed and planned for the moment without having the benefit to consider every step in the complicated process. Even Chase's affability didn't compose her. Abbsnate left the bridge, immersed in despair.

Years of anticipation and planning came down to Abbsnate knowing the right time to strike. She'd put everything on the line, and it seemed to crash down around her at once. She had bottled hope up for so long that she couldn't contain the river of emotion that suddenly ran out of her.

Onsan caught up to Abbsnate, and tried to reassure her they had a viable plan. He reminded her of everything the *Mule 357* crew had been through so far. So many unexpected things had happened, yet they'd made it through by following their instincts. "You made the right choice to come to us!"

"Thank you Onsan," said the woman through watering blue eyes.

The young man's words had little effect on Abbsnate as he tried to comfort her, but she believed what he'd said about the Mule just the same.

Onsan made a pact with fate to make a difference. It was far beyond his earlier career aspirations. He had an opportunity to help Abbsnate and others like her, (including fellow Trecons), to realize their freedom after suffering for so long under Raihan dominion. He'd devote all his abilities to her cause until they either succeeded in this mission, or died trying!

General Krevety later caught up with Abbsnate. He let her know that he'd do everything in his power to get her back to her home and family. She reminded him of his daughter, Gretchen, and he devoted to her cause the rage he'd feel if his daughter was kidnapped in the same situation. Abbsnate was encouraged by the words and actions of her new companions. Their compassion and devotion made her renew her resolute commitment to the impromptu mission.

Her wishes became the crew's desires as they melded into a team. They formed a strong bond, to where they trusted one another and were determined to see the mission through to whatever end lay in store for them!

Abbsnate rested soundly that night. She was physically and emotionally drained by her recent experiences, but she could let her guard down. She felt safe amid the crew despite layers of perilous circumstances. Abbsnate slept like a rock for the first time in decades, with Chase snuggled up and purring beside her.

CHAPTER 17

Returning to Raihan

As the *Rockwell III* and escort carrier set course for Raihan, Commander Knuddrul was concerned with getting the mission back on track. It hadn't been a total disastrous mission by any means, but the last thing he expected was to lose assets unnecessarily. Investigating the loss of Abbsnate to radiation madness and the surrounding circumstances would be top priority for Raihan leadership, so the commander made information gathering a top priority as he tried to put the puzzle together.

They approached the gravitational portal using their pre-scribed route, which would get them through the radiation zone the safest way during the Hazard-Class 8 conditions.

Everyone except Yougsten Brell was amped up for the next step. The subordinates who'd followed orders the whole time had nothing to be concerned about, because they weren't in positions to give direction or make changes. After a few more weeks of intense preparation and execution, they'd be on easy street again on Raihan! There'd be celebrations and considerable leave for the crews involved upon completion of the mission with the stores of trillelium bursting full again.

The Raihan ships entered the ergosphere, and shuddered forcefully as they darted into the event horizon. Tie-dye eruptions climaxed around them in brilliant shades of red, blue, and yellow. The burst of color gradually faded away as they entered the pitch-black midpoint of the portal. They throttled forward through the blackness, raging toward the Magnus exit! Colors invaded the ship once again as Magnus beckoned them forward. After 20 uncomfortable minutes, the two Raihan ships arrived on the other side unscathed.

Commander Knuddrul wanted to assure his bases were covered sufficiently, so he piloted his personal shuttle to the carrier for a face-to-face meeting with Yougsten Brell. First, the senior officers assembled in the main conference room for a fact-finding meeting. Knuddrul felt reassured as they recited to him their version of the story in lockstep fashion. They believed that Captain Brell freelanced from Raihan protocol and acted without authorization from the mission commander. Headquarters would be very interested to know the details, and Brell would pay a painful price for what he knew.

Some felt it was a good day for them. Two of their biggest competitors, Abbsnate and Brell, were taken out in a single action!

So far, so good. A confident smile returned to Knuddrul's handsome face.

The vexed Commander left the meeting to interview Brell in private. Like before, Captain Brell accepted full responsibility. He refused to paint Abbsnate in a negative light. "Like I said before, it was my decision."

"Yes, but I'll need more details to add to my report."

Brell nodded, "No." His blue eyes were watery, red, and puffy. The captain hadn't slept since losing the battle with the Mule.

He had a gut-churning feeling that the commander was covering his tracks. He was already in trouble, so there was no need to hide his contempt for the commander any longer. "I have nothing more to say to you, Knuddrul. I'll give a statement to my appointed counsel."

"Don't worry Brell. You'll have plenty to say when Slae Nodk gets ahold of you!"

Brell shuddered. Nodk was well-known for his imaginative interrogation methods. The captain tried to put on a brave face, but the facade cracked. Still, he refused to give the commander anything useful.

"Very well, have it your way Brell. I'll be adding insubordination to the list of charges!"

Slam, click!

Brell fired a parting shot through the doorway as Knuddrul left the room. "Blaming everything on Abbsnate and me won't clear you!"

Knuddrul tried to ignore the statement as he stepped away.

*****

Within the holding cell, Brell had only morbid thoughts about his future to keep him company. No one came to offer even a shred of support. He was a ghost, experiencing deafening silence from every crew member on the ship. Captain Brell sat on his hard bed and experienced a myriad of emotions.

The guilt of his lost pilots weighed on Brell the most. As a carrier captain, it was within his job description to send Talons into dangerous conditions, but this was different. He'd expanded their role, which cost five lives unnecessarily. Launching the diminutive fighter craft in such a treacherous atmosphere should've been out of the question. The ships were gambling against rouge meteorites and solar flares they weren't equipped to overcome. Their only purpose during the mission was to provide a flagship escort and ensure the *Rockwell III*'s safety during their voyage home. Even if the combat mission would have succeeded, the fact remained that Captain Brell went out of his lane of influence.

His heart burned fully with hatred and resentment for Abbsnate for her betrayal! She'd used him; there was no way around it. He'd cut his teeth with her for the past 10 years, navigating through the politics and self-serving fakes beginning in the officer academy and continuing up the chain. A great deal of admiration and trust had formed between the two as they experienced the ups and downs together. He realized everything she'd ever said to him had the sole purpose of setting him up for a fall!

Brell feared what his future held back home. He clenched his fists as he thought of Knuddrul's smug face. He could sense the commander's sense of relief of having a fall guy. Brell was at rock bottom. He'd been Abbsnate's fool going in, and he'd be Knuddrul's going out!

Meanwhile, in the Rockwell, Knuddrul put a detailed account together. The commander closed the book, feeling confident he would be absolved from any responsibility of the incident. He had the officers of the carrier on his side. Knuddrul even hummed a tune as he typed! His final report included important information about mining camp demographics and the valuable artifact loaded in the Rockwell bay.

After he'd finished his report, Commander Knuddrul entered the supply bay cavorting with a presence of supreme self-assurance. He wanted to inspect the most astonishing contraption the Raihans had ever stolen from Planet 6333! The mysterious metal object was placed in a sealed bay to protect the crew from radiation. Knuddrul peered through the thick glass at his pride and joy, like a proud new father looking through a nursery window. Its construction looked to him like a rib cage protecting a heart. His conclusions were the same as the Trecons.

Whatever it was, the thing had survived an unknown number of summer seasons on Planet 6333. The expert Trecon miners had dug deeper into the crust than any of their predecessors, and pulled out a masterpiece!

President Yerb Grolegg would have to reward him for a job well done and give to him all the benefits that accompanied such an honor.

*****

After being authenticated by another carrier, the vessels passed into the Raihan orbit. Raihan was a large and stunning planet with many striking features, but Knuddrul enjoyed flying over the lush region the most. He made sure his route to Base 13 followed the tropical route despite a slight delay. Knuddrul looked out the bridge shield window at the beautiful sights. As they entered the atmosphere, the commander appreciated the lazy clouds floating over spectacular palm-dotted hills and turquoise waters, and finally set course for Base 13. The two ships arrived, and docked in the early evening as a blaze orange sun was setting over the horizon.

While the crews took the evening to rest, Commander Knuddrul knew he wouldn't be sleeping much that night due to the unusual circumstances of the mission. Preparation for the harvesting operation would begin early the next morning, but Knuddrul had a lot of explaining to do.

As Commander Knuddrul walked down the ramp of the *Rockwell III*, he saw the greeting party waiting for his report. He strutted confidently toward them with the official report tucked tightly under his left arm, offering a salute with his right. He felt prepared to give them a four-point outline detailing the Planet 6333 information, the insubordination of Captain Brell, the betrayal of Abbsnate, and the precious cargo aboard the *Rockwell III*, in that order.

"Commander Knuddrul, why'd you take the scenic route here? we've been waiting all afternoon. You're behind schedule by two and a half days, what were you thinking?"

The commander noticed the intense contempt on the faces of his superiors, which slowed his confident stride. "Sir, I haven't been home for years. I just wanted-."

He was cut off. "We received your report. It looks to be incomplete, and all you can think about is enjoying the scenery. Shocking!"

Knuddrul blushed with embarrassment. "My apologies, sir."

He was nearing 60 hours late in returning, and that was all they cared about. The time he wasted could be the difference that softened the ore to make it non-transportable. Because of him, they hastened their harvesting plans. Time was of the essence in every harvesting mission. Knuddrul knew that stress was the normal setting as they planned for the harvest, but this was ridiculous! He wasn't prepared for the harsh reception he received. In addition, they couldn't have cared less about the relic!

According to Raihan high command, all of his information should be about the upcoming harvesting mission; everything else would put a damper on their goals. His main objective as commander of the Rockwell should've been returning to Planet 6333, period. Any attention paid to unrelated details meant he'd taken his eyes off the ball and put the whole mission in jeopardy!

The structure was unloaded into a hanger dock, where it would soon be brought to the Scientific Center for research. Captain Brell was brought to a holding cell while he awaited his inevitable trial and trip to the Base 13 Gallows.

They'd get answers about the mishaps from him eventually, but preparation for the harvesting mission trumped everything else at the moment. Knuddrul needed to get his head in the game, because the events weren't unfolding like he'd planned!

CHAPTER 18

Dark Embedded Terror

After the softening attacks, the people in the three Trecon mining settlements were in a state of incomprehension! The short-lived attacks weren't complex; the pirates had only stayed long enough to inflict damage on the critical areas of the camps. Afterward, the camp structures sank into the impenetrable mud. Acidic rain storms pounded the planet and melted the mountain ice caps, flooding the settlements.

It wasn't only their structures that were unstable. Colonel Ferd Honassen knew that they had to maintain mental composure if there was any hope of survival.

Honassen assessed the situation surrounding them and saw the communication capabilities were destroyed. He ordered a crew to get the older radios from a storage garage under soggy sludge, perilously close to collapsing. They discovered the pirates had been thorough while destroying of Trecon capabilities. It was becoming hazardous to venture out into the tacky mire for anything!

Honassen's blue eyes were determined, shining like a beacon of hope. "We have to get to those portable radios and create a way to broadcast our situation to Trecon Control. Do you understand?"

Lieutenant Teb Tharly gave the colonel a task size up. Honassen could see the sweat stains soaking through his coveralls. "Yes sir. We're doing our best to stabilize it so we can safely enter, or at least rig it so it doesn't sink farther into the mud. The door is wedged closed."

"You can't cut a hole in the door?"

"Working on that, but it's slow going out there. We'll have to use the ore storage pallets for dunnage to provide a safe work surface for workers and equipment. We'd be sacrificing a fair amount of trillelium."

"I don't care about the ore, Tharly, dump the whole stock-pile if needed!"

"Copy that sir. The way this mud is, we can't move our machines without possibly sliding too close and wrecking the walls. We need to stabilize both tractor and storage unit as we go, or the weight of the mud will pull the building down further. It'll be slow going. May take a few hours, but give me five fresh men and we'll have those radios out!"

Honassen smiled slightly despite the situation. The lieutenant once again let his positive attitude and work ethic shine through! The man was focused on the task at hand and put his fears aside.

"Tharly, do your best! Once again, I don't care if we throw the whole load of trillelium into the mud in the process!"

"Got it colonel," answered a determined Tharly as he left.

Eventually Tharly retrieved the radios. When they tried to call the other camps, silence indicated the others hadn't saved their backup com equipment yet. Maybe they hadn't even thought of getting them. Honassen ordered one radio be used to monitor the channel and call out at the top of every hour. The rest were turned off to conserve the batteries unless they were needed for a specific reason.

*****

The architecture continued sinking into the muddy ground, despite their best efforts to stabilize them. Soon the miners were forced inside the structures as working conditions outside became impossible.

Ttiiisss, hiissss!

Acid rain pelted the metal roofs and provided a drumbeat of death! It poured into the foundations of their buildings, causing them to move.

Rumble, groan!

As temperatures continued to rise, they noticed atmospheric patterns changing constantly around them. Orange and golden meteorite fireballs continued to fall at an increasing rate! Honassen ordered the crews to stay inside, except for dire need. The mining shafts were destroyed as the melting ice surged sludge and water into the chutes. The will to survive sparring against their dooming emotions took a heavy toll on the Trecons, and despair rose in unison with the water levels in the boreholes!

The Trecon settlers were feeling increasingly hopeless about their future. They could feel the buildings sinking further by the hour into the heavy Muudia sludge. Foul smells of all kinds related to sickness and rot accumulated within the settlements as their access to personal-hygienic areas diminished. A feeling of utter hopelessness enveloped the miners. Their world was ending in a muddy, blazing apocalypse!

Colonel Honassen knew that even if Trecon sent a rescue force when the fleet was lost, they wouldn't arrive for another three and a half months. By then, it would be too late. When they'd stopped conducting operations after the attack, everyone left the underground shafts where they were relatively protected. They became constantly exposed to increasing radiation levels. Widespread sickness spread throughout the camps.

All attempts at building stabilization were abandoned. Mud covered up the windows and ports of their buildings. A growing feeling of physical and mental infection spread across the planet!

On top of everything else, a maddening issue of rat bites and flea infestation due to proximity with the animals were becoming an open invitation for denigration and disease.

Darkness and despair surrounded them, seeping like sludge through the walls of the buildings and into their souls; swallowing up every ounce of hope!

The Trecons didn't know it yet, but what they were experiencing was the first step in the Raihan reeducation process. They were slowly losing a sense of reality, making them prime candidates for the harvesting and brainwashing processes coming for them in a short time.

Their helplessness didn't differ from the multitudes of victims before them. The Trecons were acting like typical victims of harvesting, physically and mentally better than most, but not as well as others.

The Raihans knew it was a delicate time to reach them before they did anything rash. Commander Knuddrul's delay at the front end was a gamble that could've cost the lives of weaker-minded people!

CHAPTER 19

Planet Kufsiun and the Universal Cooperative of Space Vessel Industrialists

The *Mule 357* was attempting to travel through the gravitational portal using antiquated navigation techniques. The crew ensured every piece of cargo was locked in, and belted themselves in their seats to prepare for a bumpy ride. Abbsnate was their ace in the hole as she had taken the trip through the portal seven times before. She knew the precise speed and angle they needed to enter the event horizon to come out safe on the other side.

As they approached the portal, everyone had a feeling it would all be over soon either way. They'd need all the skill aboard the ship to make it without breaking into pieces. They passed massive rocks stuck in gravitational limbo, and spectral colors filled the space around them. Dull purple and brass yellow flares surrounded the ship as they navigated to the entry point.

The event horizon looked like a circular blue energy field with white electric arcs emanating from deep inside. Abbsnate assured them it was safe to proceed. It measured only two kilometers in diameter. CJ marveled, "Hard to believe something so small could cause so much trouble!"

Abbsnate shook her head, "Tell me about it. Maintain current speed, here we go."

The first-timers would've liked to take it slow, like dipping their toes in icy cold water to get used to the idea first; instead they had to dive right in and submerge!

Rizzz, rattle!

The ship shook violently as she entered the portal! Pnoi Nbnok monitored and recorded their surroundings as they entered the event horizon. "Faasciinaaatiing." Here they were, locked in a dangerous game of life and death, and all Nbnok could see was the beauty surrounding them! He continued rambling in the peculiar drawl, "Iiif weee maakee iit throoouugh heeree, Iii wiiill waant tooo leeaad aan eexpeediitiioon baack tooo reeseeaarch thiiis plaaace."

Davss responded an annoyed tone, "Iif iiis theee quueestiioon, iiisn't iit?"

CJ taxed the engines to full capacity.

Grooaan!

They tried to break free from the Laurus gravity and advance through to the midpoint with enough momentum to carry them to the Magnus side. Trecon ships weren't built with heavy-duty anti-gravity stabilizers to fight the robust forces of a portal. Pushing a spaceship through the vacuum of space didn't require gravity stabilization beyond what was needed to gain atmosphere.

Bzzzttt!

Sonic waves pounded the ship and provided the illusion of sound. The ship fought on!

"Aaarrgghh! Theee eengiineess aaree goooiing tooo eexploodeee!" CJ was incensed for two reasons. First, they were destroying the ship he'd grown to admire. Second, they'd all die!

The gauges were running into red as the Mule fought for all she was worth against the pulling tide.

Whiiine!

"Dooon't leeet uuup, oor wee wooon't geeet throoouugh theee graaviitaaatiioonaaal puuull of Laauuruus," instructed Abbsnate stridently as she sensed defeat on CJ's countenance.

"Weee'll geet puulleed throouuugh byy Maagnuuus aafteeer theee miidpooiint."

CJ replied excitedly, "Juuust hoopee thhee eenggiiinnees doon't blooow beefoooree thaat haaappeens!"

After 17 minutes battling the forces of gravity at full thrust, the stomach-churning games played tricks within their minds. Time seemed to stretch before their eyes. The ship shook with such ferocity that the main lights cut out at the 20-minute mark.

Craaack!

"Whhhaaat waaas thaaaat?"

"Aaauxiliiaary geeneeraatoor kiickiiing ooon."

The engines held their ground and the *Mule 357* proved she was a fighter! The Mules were built to take a pounding, and the '357 was declaring to everyone her big heart despite the bedlam around them. Her engines continued to whine and convulse as she pushed hard against the yoke trying to pull them back into the Laurus solar system.

The force was diminishing and the ship was slightly gaining speed, but it was hard to tell in their surroundings. The engine temperature gauges were inching their way further toward the point of no return when the automatic cessation system kicked in. The feature was a redundant precaution put into place to salvage the engines before they melted down and were rendered inoperative. It decreased the thrust to manageable levels while they cooled down.

The ship grew dark inside, until a kaleidoscope of color permeated them from every angle. The Mule gave them all she had. At least they weren't being pulled backward toward Laurus!

In a flash, the colors went away, and they spun weightlessly in pitch-black for a moment. It was a temporary relief to not have the forces of gravity pulling on their bodies. Abbsnate voiced her joy with the situation, announcing to the others, "We've made it to the midpoint! The Magnus gravity will pull us through from now on." The slow momentum meant a longer trip through, but presented a unique advantage. Perhaps they'd be able to avoid the giant ice-shards and space boulders that waited to greet them on the other side!

The Mule couldn't generate much power with her tired engines. Still, a longer trip through was better than being pulled back to the Muudia side of the portal!

"Decrease forward thrusters to idle power," ordered Abbsnate as they continued through the eye of the storm in the center of the portal. It was the safe zone they were aiming for. The weary Mule had engineered enough momentum to win the fight against the Laurus gravitational pull, and the crew felt relieved to be halfway through as they floated in the blackness of the midpoint vacuum.

Suddenly, they felt the ship being violently pulled to the starboard side. "Something's wrong," indicated Abbsnate. "We've broken free from the Laurus pull, yet we're caught in another slipstream. Increase to full thrusters again to maintain our course."

"I'll give you all she's got left!" CJ increased to full throttle again, and the ship fought its way back on course.

After a moment, they pulled out of the sudden heaviness and felt the Mule being drawn once again to Magnus. Abbsnate knew that if they attempted to use their main thrusters any longer, they'd speed too fast into the debris field on the Magnus side of the portal, hurling blindly toward certain destruction!

"Decreasing forward thrusters to idle," stated CJ, anticipating the order.

She gave him a thumbs up. "Way different going through on manual controls. The midpoint is more pronounced spring through autumn, but I haven't felt that before. Stay at the ready, we'll be gaining speed again shortly."

Relief turned to terror when Magnus grabbed the '357 with unimaginable power! CJ realized the feeble control they had over their situation. The brief equalization mid-point in the wormhole was quickly overcome by the gravity of the Magnus star.

Onsan sat at the helm of the '357, staring straight ahead into the limited light the ship provided. He was ready to activate the reverse thrusters to avoid any meteorites that would suddenly cross their path! Every second was elongated within the cauldron of mystic black soup, but now all they could do was wait for the next phase.

Meerrrooowww, hiisss!

Chase caterwauled hideously in response to the first half of the portal catching up with his stomach. It was as though he was saying, "Not again!" The cat's cries sounded like a call from beyond the grave in ultra-slow motion. He seemed to express what the entire crew was feeling.

Every moment and movement appeared stretched and slow once again, turning their stomachs into knots as CJ tried to help the Mule to fight against the current. The eternal purgatory was getting to the crew as the ship lurched forward toward the Magnus portal opening. Throttling up at the wrong time for even a moment could've meant instant death! Even Nbnok ceased his scientific outlook and upbeat chatter. It was as if they were free-falling down a pitch-black tunnel, not knowing when they'd hit the bottom.

After a few precarious minutes, colors reappeared on the exterior of the '357. Abbsnate shouted in a painstakingly slow drawl as they neared the exit side of the portal, "Maaan yoooouuur sttaaatiiooonsss aaand geeet reeaady. Weee'ree aaappprooaaching theee Maagnuuus poortaal eexiiit." Due to their increasing speed, she couldn't get the words out fast enough!

Seconds later it was as though time ticked again. They entered a flickering ether that cut through the blackness.

Bang!

The auxiliary lights flickered on but instantly flashed off again as the ship reset itself. Onsan wasn't sure when they lost their electronic power, but the manual controls seemed usable to him if needed. Full engine power wasn't available to them, but it wasn't needed yet anyway as they started through the Magnus exit side.

"Prepare to evade rocks and debris, just as with the entry point," cautioned Abbsnate as they were still getting their bearings.

"On it!" Onsan replied.

Suddenly they appeared to be sucked into the wake of the ships that had traveled through before them! The Magnus gravity took effect on the Mule and dragged it into the solar system with great vigor! The polychromatic mixture of purples and golds flooded the ship once again as they picked up speed.

Abbsnate ordered Onsan, "Reverse thrusters. We have to slow our rate of tempo!"

The ship spun circles at a high rate for what seemed like an eternity before the reverse thrusters took effect and stabilized the Mule.

Pskeeew!

The delayed response from the reverse thrusters was a major cause for concern on the bridge. They needed to investigate the engine issues to discover remaining power, but it was impossible to do in the deadly carnival ride! Once they were through, Onsan and Milerous would attend to engine-thruster repair.

If they could restore half power, they could fight the pull of the star. If not, Magnus could take them in her gravitational death grip and burn them to a cinder with a scorching kiss!

As the rear thrusters slowed the spinning momentum, the best that anyone could do was to stay buckled in and wait for fate to spare them again or pay them back for all of their recent good fortune. Strange thoughts ran heavy through the ship during the next few minutes, as if the universe itself was against them! Perhaps they'd tempted providence too much already anyway, and their time had simply run out.

Click, click, click.

The primary lights abruptly came back on and indicated systems were useable, and the steadfast ship righted itself once again. The engines were tired but would recover to adequate capacity if they weren't pushed again for a while. Once in Kufsopolis, they'd overhaul the broken engines. CJ guided the ship slowly out of the spin and into a stable pattern, narrowly avoiding a big space rock in the process!

Everyone on the bridge remained on full alert to see any debris awaiting them in the Magnus solar system. They were relieved to be through the portal, but too sick to celebrate. After 30 minutes of challenging navigating, Abbsnate oriented them to their surroundings, "We're through the worst of the rocks. Set bearing for 30 degrees starboard at best available speed. We're clear from here to destination."

She continued with their education, "We should be alone for a while, but we'll have to be on the lookout for pirates as we approach Kufsiun. Milerous will need to man the turret at that point, and the Talon will be our final option for protection."

*****

Their destination would be a long journey in the injured Mule.

Cough, sputter!

A 20-day trip in a Raihan freighter took four months in the injured '357. The acute radiation of the hazard zone and portal caught up with the general and veterinarian. They were the oldest by far, and spent the first two months bed-ridden.

Milerous nursed the worn-out engines daily, but he could never restore decent power. He even shut down for a month to do an overhaul, but it did no good. The ship was in decent shape considering what she'd been through, though. The crew had grown quite fond of her!

"No worries," said Abbsnate. "You're not getting back through the wormhole while Planet 6333 is at a Hazard-Class 10, anyway."

Onsan looked at her puzzled, "Planet 6333?"

"Ah yes, I mean Muudia. Two decades of Raihan terminology is hard to forget! The point is, while the planet is close to in-line between Laurus, the portal, and Magnus, you'd never make it anyway. Too dangerous."

Abbsnate used the time to educate the crew about the Magnus dimension and their destination.

Planet Kufsiun was officially a neutral planet, but realistically, they were involved in every conflict in the universe. They'd often supply both sides of a conflict with carriers and starfighters. Money was the big motivator for them, beyond any moral compass. One of their most valued customers was Raihan, which bought and sold ships there frequently. Through their mutual dealings, Kufsiun was always ensured of the most advanced and reliable equipment. In return for a deal on bulk ship prices, Raihan exported technological expertise and apparatus.

Abbsnate cautioned the crew. "Raihan recently received a secretive military order from there, and are conducting testing before starting a refitting process within their entire warship arsenal. There will definitely be Raihan officials milling around there buying, selling, and trading. We'll have to be extremely careful!" Abbsnate knew they must watch their step while on the planet, because things were not always as they appeared.

"We'll attract unwanted attention if we enter the city's corporate district, so we'll conduct our business in the risky independent maintenance sector instead."

They were loaded to the rafters with valuable freight, which was to their advantage. One piece in particular couldn't be overlooked, however. It would be difficult to hide the Talon hidden within her bay. They'd be the talk of Kufsiun if they weren't careful, placing a huge target on their backs on a planet brimming with Raihan merchants and spies.

The ship was barely salvageable. The three main problems with the *Mule 357* were the engines, shields, and missing NAV/COM port—only the most important components of a spacefaring vessel! The engines were unrepairable to full capacity, so they had to be replaced. They could get the crew to where they needed to go, but it was like riding a moped bike on the freeway! The top capacity of the energy shields was 55 percent, meaning they'd be a sitting duck in battle. Once in the city, they could replace the cells easily and get them functioning at 100 percent again. NAV/COM ports were a dime a dozen in a junkyard. They'd shop around and pay extra for a quality unit.

General Krevety saw that things weren't as dire as they could be, assuming the Kufsiuans could deliver like Abbsnate said they could. They had plenty of supplies to trade, plus a fighter that would claim a hefty price on the black market! The four-month trip through deep space occurred without incident. Several supply vessels like themselves were noted off in the distance as they approached the Kufsiun quadrant.

Once, a pirate frigate cruised in for a closer look.

"Prepare for battle!"

Milerous climbed to the turret as Abbsnate jumped into the Talon and readied it for launch. The ragged appearance of the Mule offered no clue to the treasures hidden inside her! The pirates hailed the Mule, and were thrown off when she didn't respond. They simply looked at the freighter and decided it was not worth their effort to rob such a ragged ship.

"That was close!" Onsan sighed.

"Yeah," winked CJ. "She's ugly on the outside, but has a lot of personality."

"No, she's a beautiful lady!"

*****

As they lowered into the Kufsiun atmosphere, they could see the glowing landscape of the polished city off in the distance. They viewed the surroundings and realized that going to the outskirts of the city for repairs held a double-edged sword for them. Sure, they were going to a place where they'd attract less attention. But there was less of a security presence and they'd have to be alert for criminals looking to take advantage of them. Once they landed, they'd stick together and not stray far from their ship.

Abbsnate suggested the Universal Cooperative of Space Vessel Industrialists in a lower-middle-class section of the city. There were plenty of shady dealings there, so it would come down to a gut feeling about who could be trusted. They headed to an area with hundreds of maintenance bays, and used the Talon communicator to pick out a qualified overhaul crew.

Krevety was looking for a crew with a good reputation for doing quality work that wouldn't ask questions. As they sifted through a directory of business owners, they agreed on a particular older gentleman who wasn't too pushy and had a trusting way about him. Llib Esa-erg was the name of the owner. He ran his small shop with his wife Thrasea and son Etan.

The name of the business was the Quality Quasar Repair Company (QQRC), a smaller facility with three repair hangers and only 40 employees.

They agreed to terms with Esa-erg quickly, and were directed toward the bay.

As the ship lowered into the dock, CJ used the red-and-green portable lights to indicate to their greeters that the Mule couldn't communicate. This was not unusual to the workers at QQRC, and they guided the Trecon vessel expertly into the hangar. CJ hovered the Mule down to a smooth landing on the deck of the housing. The hangar doors closed over the Mule, and they were at the mercy of strangers.

It was decided by General Krevety to conceal the bulk of the assets until the time came for payment. Bartering with the QQRC wouldn't be an issue, but security definitely would! They requested a lockdown on the facility while the work was being done.

The lockdown procedure was common in the maintenance business. It was requested over 75 percent of the time. Lockdowns made sense because they kept everyone safer. It'd be harmful for a sozzled maintenance worker shooting his mouth off around town! Criminals raided facilities after discovering unique circumstances, so things were often done under a veil of secrecy.

Ssshhhh!

White steam poured from the *Mule 357* as it depressurized and stabilized to the QQRC hangar. General Krevety, Abbsnate, and Onsan were the first to walk down the ramp to meet with Llib and his son Etan to discuss the needed repairs and negotiate a price. Onsan turned to Abbsnate. "You don't know how great it feels to be on solid ground again!" Aside for a few minutes during the chaotic Muudia rescue, he'd been stuck within the Mule for months on end.

As the trio walked along with the head of the facility, everyone realized that Etan was infatuated with Abbsnate. He'd gaze at her and quickly look away when she returned his glance. Etan wore grimy overalls, with towel-wiped grease on his hands and dirty fingernails. He smelled of fresh oil, dried rocket fuel, and body odor.

Chomp, chew!

Etan looked up in horror, suddenly realizing that noshing on a sandwich with his mouth open was bad manners. He wouldn't have thought twice about before, but in Abbsnate's presence he felt the need to throw it into the nearest garbage can as they walked along!

Llib wanted to be assured of payment before anything else. Experience taught him to get down to business right away. General Krevety had prepared for this. The group strode through the rear cargo holds and inspected the Mule's tradable assets.

"Looks good to me," responded Llib. He was satisfied with the unusual payment in return for the work.

The QQRC owner realized he'd make an enormous profit on this deal, possibly enough to make this his last big negotiation. His wife, Thrasea, had been wanting to retire for years, but they also wanted to help Etan move their business to a more legitimate part of Kufsopolis.

The Mule crew would unload three-quarters of her original supply shipment, more than enough to pay for the repairs. The crew was happy to unload the Mule to gain extra space for their journey home. In return for the goods, the Mule crew would receive quality used equipment and installation. Llib would sell off the supplies to various off-market vendors and make double of a typical job this size! Esa-erg dedicated 10 workers to the ship for three weeks. The contract signed, and work was to begin early the following day.

Early the next morning, General Krevety, Abbsnate, and Onsan boarded a borrowed Pullman craft from Llib and entered Kufsopolis with the plan of finding a party who'd trade a moderate-sized but long-range intergalactic itinerant ship for the Raihan fighter. The Talon was their only bargaining chip remaining, as the majority of the supplies would go to Llib to pay for repairs. They left the Mule well protected, full of Trecons to aid the QQRC workers and guard the Mule from inquiring minds within the hangar.

As the Pullman entered the outskirts of Kufsopolis, they realized they were playing a very dangerous game. First, they had to find a willing business partner to take on responsibility of a Raihan vessel either through purchase or trade. Then they'd arrange a meeting place to swap vessels in a secluded but safe location. It was a leap of faith for everyone involved, the kind of arrangement that would invite the most shadowy characters!

Abbsnate's limited knowledge of the city indicated that the Independent Traders' Union (ITU) was the best option, bridging the gap between governmental red tape and the anything goes nature of criminals on the other end of the spectrum in the Segorlic District. The Independent Traders' Union was a place where hundreds of vendors routinely engaged one another in official and covert government-to-independent contractor deals. There were criminals about, but more of the white-collar variety. The ITU was where Llib would come to liquidate the Trecon supplies.

They landed the Pullman craft on an immense docking port that contained several hundred ships landing and taking off. They noticed a strong security presence amid the bustle of activity.

The cautious crew walked in from the docking port through the ships to the vendors in the crowded marketplace. The trio entered the square with the knowledge they'd be trapped like rats in a maze if anything went wrong!

Suddenly Abbsnate froze, turning white like she had seen a ghost! Their feelings of apprehension came to fruition quickly. As discreetly as she could, Abbsnate ducked behind a post while hoping to remain unnoticed. She pointed out a thin age-bent figure among the crowd, floating around as if he owned the place. The man appeared harmless at first glance. He was older and diminutive, with balding gray hair. He was unbalanced, slouching forward as he made his way through the throng. He had on a dark suit, and an expensive black light-weight cape that flowed with every step.

"Meet Kimn Oghy, high-level spy for the Raihans."

"He looks frail to me," said Onsan. "Let's just lure him into a dark corner and knock him over the head. Then we can go about our business of buying a ship."

"No. We can use him."

Abbsnate knew Oghy well. Officially, he was there to provide boots on the ground for the Raihan government. Privately, Oghy was on an advanced recruiting mission to pick out victims for future harvesting plots on Planet 6333. Oghy was acting like he was well-connected in the place, breezing at a slow pace in and out of vendors with a supreme air of self-assurance.

As they shuffled away, Abbsnate asked Onsan, "What's your size?"

"What, why?"

"I've got a plan." She was adapting fast to the on-the-fly scheming.

Down the street, they found an elaborate clothing shop and planned to part with most of their show money.

"What can I do for you?" The stout shop owner was bored. By the look of the three, they had little to spend.

"Our friend here has to dress for an important occasion. We want to look at your best suit."

"I'm sorry, we're closing up soon. There's another shop-." The owner stopped cold when he saw the wad of cash in Krevety's hand!

"I guess we can stay open a bit longer." He spun toward the back room, almost losing his artificial hair in the process. "Freida!"

His wife peeked around the corner and he motioned to her. She was a thin, cultured woman who yearned to look down her nose at them. "Yes Neil?"

"We've got important customers!"

After half an hour, Onsan was dressed and ready. The shop owner offered to tailor the suit, but they couldn't wait. Wearing the off-the-rack size made Onsan look and feel more out-of-place.

"These shoes are going to give me blisters!"

They spent most of their limited funds on an attire fit for a braggadocious big shot. The suit nearly broke them until Abbsnate used her charm with the owner and got them a deal. They also purchased two robes for Abbsnate and Krevety.

Onsan got dressed in the expensive ensemble and feigned a presence of superiority. After they left, he looked at the copper-sequined suit and smirked at Abbsnate. "I look absurd in this thing."

"C'mon Onsan, take this seriously!"

"Okay, I'll try my best."

He had a long way to go to feel comfortable, but unfortunately it was a short walk to Oghy. They'd have all gotten a good laugh if the situation was different, because Onsan was right, he looked ridiculous!

*****

Oghy would be a valuable asset to an attacking force, and they couldn't let him get away! Abbsnate knew that advanced infiltrators often worked alone and had plenty of resources available to them. A quick strategy was made to capture Oghy. They'd pose as a potential Raihan "client." General Krevety would be the most logical person to pose as a government official, but due to his status on Trecon Oghy would identify him immediately. The spy would recognize Abbsnate the second he saw her!

Onsan was the only logical person of the three to lure him in. They'd have to entice him to a secluded area by the shipping docks before making their move. When the timing was right and they were out of sight, they'd snatch Oghy and bring him back to the QQRC.

They'd request an hour of alone time with the Mule, then bring the spy back to the ship under the noses of the workers and place him under constant guard until they left Kufsiun.

It was decided that Onsan would pose as a swaggering doyen from a distant system. He'd have to be an obnoxious braggart about his planet's wealth while being vague enough that Oghy couldn't look right through him and see the truth. They'd try to lure him in like a big lunker on Mic Mac Lake!

The extraordinary mission was growing once again.

CHAPTER 20

The Harvesting Operation on Planet 6333

As Commander Knuddrul led the harvesting fleet, he felt on top of the world despite the chastisement he'd received. The fleet broke from Raihan's atmosphere with Knuddrul's mind wandering from the task at hand once again. His defiant attitude against leadership was displayed in his countenance like a road sign. He looked over his shoulder and eyed Commander Ohoef from the 17-114.75 Tisdin mission, sent along to babysit him. Ohoef's presence annoyed them both!

During the softening operation, things would've proceeded without trouble if the commander hadn't been preoccupied with his rabbit-trail agenda, a fact that wasn't lost on Ohoef. The former mission commander was selected merely because he was in the wrong place at the wrong time! Ohoef was there to oversee the mission as an "advisor." He'd be paid handsomely for his time, but Planet 6333 was the last place he wanted to be with summer approaching. He watched Knuddrul's every move intently.

"Set course for the portal," ordered Knuddrul. The harvesting mission was the commander's chance to catapult himself past the controversy of the softening mission and straight into the political spotlight. He believed that leadership would come to appreciate the treasure he'd brought home to them once things slowed down. Knuddrul's superiors had chastised him after the softening operation, telling him to refocus on completing the mission. However, in Knuddrul's mind, the hardest part of his mission was over, and the angry directors wouldn't hold power over him much longer.

Satisfied, he turned his attention over to the task at hand. Knuddrul was confident things were back on schedule on Planet 6333. By the time they reached the planet, the mining camp personnel would be decrepit and begging for their ticket out of there! As long as the Raihan harvesters stayed on track they'd be out and back in twelve days, plenty of time to get out of dodge before the malaise of late spring.

Commander Knuddrul knew the target people, and calculated the Trecons would be fine. He was the expert and still had the final say if anything unexpected cropped up.

*****

"Status Report," ordered the commander to the man at the com panel.

Dreck Lobart responded, "Communication still dead from the camps. The zone is currently a Hazard-Class 8, but atmospheric conditions indicate we're approaching a H-Class 10 within 24 hours. We're running low on time, commander!"

"Slow to half speed, divert the power to the shields," ordered Knuddrul to the navigator as the fleet entered the atmosphere of Planet 6333. The commander turned and gave Lobart a nasty look. The low-ranking officer didn't have to point out the fact that they were behind schedule with Ohoef around to soak it in. "Just do your job Lobart, I'll let you know if I need your advice!"

The communication officer's fair skin turned pink again, out of sheer pleasure of seeing Knuddrul squirm! The man's blue eyes twinkled, "Yes sir." Lobart smiled to himself. *Ha!* He'd thrown in the jab knowing Knuddrul could do nothing about it. The com officer enjoyed seeing the arrogant man squirm under the watchful eyes of Ohoef!

Rumble, whoosh!

Planet 6333 was going through typical seasonal tempests. The conditions rocked the Raihan fleet back and forth as it neared the planet's surface, but the bulwark held firm against the fray. The chaotic scene was old hat for the Raihans, but it was still rough going. They were prepared for the tough sledding; past mission experience held them resolute as they drove forward with the operation. The storms were anything but typical to the terrified Trecon victims down in the mining camps. The Raihan raiders' broader understanding gave them the upper hand.

"Disperse the fleet," ordered the smug commander as they descended into the atmosphere above Planet 6333.

Three groups of ships veered away from the main fleet and prepared for their final descent. Commander Knuddrul gave the fleet a final visual inspection from his vantage point, then asked each group for a personnel accountability report (PAR) to ensure they were all accounted for and ready to begin the mission. Each section commander got a PAR report from every ship within their group to ensure there were no last-minute problems to be ironed out. There were rarely issues, but it was procedure.

The receiver crackled as each group responded with 100% PAR accountability. Knuddrul responded with an order as he sneered at Ohoef. "Commence fleet separation procedures, and begin harvesting operation."

The Raihan fleet broke up, with each fragment setting course for their predetermined settlement. Commander Knuddrul's vessel stayed in the upper atmosphere with an escort of warships, where he could provide oversight and quickly respond to any unusual situations. The commander located his ship nearest to Mining Camp Two Operations Control, where the Trecon's leadership was located. It was the most likely area for trouble to crop up.

The harvesting crew had only days to finish the important assignment and get back through the portal. Lobart was right, there was no time to waste! Everything Knuddrul did moving forward was exactly according to the harvesting procedure. He knew there could be no more complications with Ohoef around. If anything else went wrong, there was no one left to be the goat!

As the groups lowered their ships into position, they collectively prepared for what they'd find as they breached the mining facilities. The healthier the miners were, the more likely they were to defend themselves and fight the process. The harvesting crew had standing orders to get the healthiest on board first. They were instructed not to waste time assisting people too sick to help themselves until everyone else was secured aboard the ships.

As the fleets surveyed the damage, they observed crumbled structures half sunken in toxic mud. The Trecons marked the inhabited buildings through a daily struggle for survival. Signs of life were abundant, with evidence of early efforts to fortify corners of structures, and paths leading away from the buildings for daily rounds of refuse disposal. The Treconite will to survive was strong despite their desperate circumstances, but they might as well have left a bull's-eye for the Mihhidite harvesters!

Knuddrul was pleased when the reports came in. Everything was on schedule. He shot Ohoef a look that said, *I told you so!*

Knowing where everyone was made it easier for the Mihhidite foot soldiers to swiftly enter the buildings and overwhelm the debilitated miners. The Raihan vessels decelerated into place above the Trecon mining structures and deployed their leeches. The leeches were large cables that provided an anchored footing for the massive ships. Afterward, cylindrical tubes called stingers were lowered at an angle from the ships. Stingers were portable tunnels for the Mihhidites to gain access to the structures and escort prisoners back onto their ships.

The terrified Trecons couldn't see what was happening above them. First, they heard the loud roar of the ships, then felt a great shuddering as the leeches were dropped onto place above them.

Rumble, crash, crunch!

The stingers drove hard through the roofs of the structures!

An order was given in the darkness, "The pirates are back, grab your weapons!" It was wishful thinking, because the guns had been lost in the pitch-blackness for a week.

In stepped the Mihhidites through the darkness, yelling orders and confusing the dazed Trecons. "Up! Get on your feet now! Move!" The Mihhidites were on top of the miners before they could process what was happening to them. "There's no need to fear us, we're taking you to safety."

"What, where are we going?"

The questions were ignored. "Coast is clear, disable your infrared cameras!" Each soldier hit a switch that simultaneously turned off their night vision and illuminated bright light-emitting diode (LED) lights directly into the faces of the Trecons. Coming in through the darkness and initiating their lights disarmed and confused the Trecons to avoid a fight. It worked perfectly for them.

"Aarrgghh!"

The lights burned the eyes of the Trecons. A miner asked, "Who are you?"

"No time to explain. C'mon, single file, not a safe place to be at the moment!" The Mihhidites corralled the Trecons toward the cylindrical ramps.

As the Trecons adjusted their eyes, they got a better look at the Mihhidites. The harvesters were dressed in black and gray camouflage battle dress uniforms (BDU's), with flat black helmets and black steel-toed leather boots. Their helmets were shielded with dark lenses. An infrared camera extended above their eyes and away from their shield of vision when they weren't needed. LED lights attached on each temple on the dome activated with the flick of a switch. Their short-barreled rifles (SBRs) also had a bright light affixed to them.

"Please hold on a second," said a settlement worker, reaching for his bag.

The Trecon was grabbed by the arm and shoved toward the ramp. "Leave it. Do what you're told and keep moving!"

The soldiers had been on the other side of the operations before as victims. They effortlessly overcame their feelings of culpability with a twisted perspective they were helping the miners in their journey to realizing a better life. They were just aggressive enough to ensure that the prisoners would do nothing to put either party in danger. They reported a target secure when it was emptied of prisoners, and quickly moved to the next.

Unbearable conditions mixed with the lack of time combined to put the Trecons out of commission. With such an imposing force breaking through so quickly, even the robust Trecons didn't put up much of a fight!

An underlying sense of doom turned into a collective feeling of relief as the miners willingly walked up the ramps to the Raihan vessels. Within a short while, the Trecons were safely within the bright confines of the medical ships, shielding their eyes from the lights as they were led along. The Trecons were being evaluated by their captors from the beginning, for a range of characteristics that would determine each person's future.

Once they were all in custody, the doctors were kind to their captives. "We heard your distress call and are here to help you," lied a Raihan officer through intercom systems on the medical vessels.

The overseers were pleased to report that everyone was in relatively good health. There were no losses, which pleased Knuddrul greatly. After three hours, the commander got the message he'd been waiting for. The executive officer was happy to report, "Commander Knuddrul, all present or accounted for." The miners welcomed the sterile smells of the medical vessels, it was ecstasy compared to the putrid environments they were evacuating!

The Mihhidites were slightly disappointed at the ease of the operation, and viewed peacefully escorting victims as a waste of their natural talents! Once the Mihhidites got all the Trecons loaded up on the medical ships, they returned to the troop transports and prepared for a welcomed journey home.

In other areas around the settlements, large conveyor ships hovered over the trillelium stores and collected the ore with speed and efficiency. Salvageable mining equipment was gathered for study within the Research and Development wing of the Scientific Center. The mining expertise of the Trecons came fully into light, as the Raihan ships were packed to the rafters with trillelium ore. They weren't able to take it all! Knuddrul's chest puffed out with pride.

Once the teams lifted off the planet's surface, Commander Knuddrul requested a PAR report as they joined the larger fleet.

"Taskforce 1 has PAR,"

"Taskforce 2 has PAR,"

"Taskforce 3 has PAR."

"Harvesting fleet, mission accomplished. Good job! Prepare to set course for portal."

CHAPTER 21

Playing a Player

The three confidantes returned to the ITU marketplace with Onsan dressed like a copper-hued emissary, but feeling very foolish inside right down to his pointed shoes! Abbsnate and Krevety did the best they could to get him acting the part in 30 minutes. They had to return before Oghy left the marketplace! The spy had an abundance of Raihan information they suddenly had access to should they capture him.

Onsan was quickly brought up to speed with how to act political to someone who wasn't looking too closely. Oghy's first impression was the key, so Onsan used his imagination to look and sound like the right kind of bait. He was directed to act arrogant and injudicious, opening his mouth before thinking too much about what he said.

"That shouldn't be too much of a stretch," Abbsnate bantered.

The young Trecon officer was supposedly from the Fetulas System, looking for an agent who could get him the best deal on a moderate order of 10 cargo vessels to upgrade their aging fleet. Onsan was loud and brash, doing his best to look under the influence of overconfidence.

Being from Trecon, Onsan knew enough about the mining industry to keep himself clear of suspicion for a while. He was as prepared as possible after his quick makeover. Abbsnate spotted Oghy and pointed Onsan in the right direction.

"There he is, straight ahead." Abbsnate whispered.

Oghy was conversing with a tall man and woman, his aged neck craning toward the sky.

"Got him in my sights." It was showtime!

Onsan scanned a leisurely route to his target, not wanting to appear suspicious by making a direct line to the spy. As he walked through the marketplace of the UTI, Onsan experienced a carnival-type atmosphere. Music, loud negotiations, and the smell of exotic food stimulated Onsan's senses and masked his nerves somewhat. The Trecon performer rehearsed the shallow story in his mind as he got a refreshment and sauntered through the vendors in the open market. His shiny suit attracted suiters like moths to a flame.

A strange-looking man made a direct path to Onsan. "Hey bub, what are you looking for? I can hook you up for a price." The man opened his jacket to reveal stolen watches. Onsan had a feeling that something was off, and looked behind him to find another man attempting to pick his pocket.

"Buzz off!" The team of crooks disappeared quickly into the crowd.

Onsan moved on to a promoter, who was drumming up interest for a prizefight. *Now this is interesting*, he thought.

For 10 minutes, Onsan listened to the man from the fringes of the crowd as Oghy worked his way toward them.

When Onsan noticed Oghy passing by, the promoter saw he was losing interest and closed in.

"Do you have a ticket?"

"Er, yes."

"Who you got in the fight?"

"Um, the champ, of course!"

"How much?"

"I'll get back to you."

Onsan put up his hand to the man and walked away. Now he was slightly behind Oghy. He worked hard to stay up with the spy through the crowd. When Oghy stopped to talk to a woman, Onsan eased by him, stopped at a vacant storefront, and peered in the window. *Nobody will sabotage me this time!*

Abbsnate was getting frustrated as she watched him. "Why is he slow-playing Oghy like this. He's alone, now's the time to strike. Get in there!"

"I hope he knows what he's doing," Krevety said, but he wasn't so sure.

As Oghy walked past, Onsan came out of the shadows of a building, he picked up his volume and verbalized his "pickup line", one he hoped would make the big fish bite. He acted as though he was conversing with a passing vendor.

"Got a fleet of three mining transports coming off the line next week. I'm here to inspect them. I can do that in *two hours*. What I really want to inspect is the nightlife around here!"

The irritated vendor gave Onsan an exasperated look. "What are you talking about?"

"Any good clubs around here?"

The annoyed man continued his path to a preordained business destination with a puzzled look on his face. "Leave me alone!"

Onsan knew he'd caused a scene. He kept walking to avoid stopping right in front of the Raihan spy. He followed after the vendor, calling, "Okay, so I'll talk to you later then?"

The poor man rushed to get away from Onsan like he feared getting mugged! Onsan felt awkward because he was sticking out like a sore thumb!

Luckily, Oghy came over to rescue him. "You're in the wrong place for nightlife. If you head downtown to the Scrofula District, you can find plenty of amusement. Just be careful." Then he added, "What are you mining, son?"

Oghy had taken the bait! "Granite and taconite," Onsan answered, sticking with what he knew.

After they discussed mining for a few minutes, Onsan felt the conversation quickly going over his head as it led into the financial and investment realm.

Kimn Oghy salivated as he looked at Onsan, thinking the young man was the perfect prey for the Raihans. There were alarms of disbelief going through his head, but not for reasons of personal safety. Oghy smelled a rat. *If this big-headed doyen has the resources he's claiming, he'd be in another part of town rather than poking around the ITU.*

It had been Oghy's experience that a purchasing assemblage traveled together and not alone. *A "big shot"' such as this should have a security team around him!* But it was obvious this young gentleman knew a lot about mining, so Oghy looked further into the lead.

To everyone's surprise, Oghy extended his hand and invited Onsan for a business conversation over dinner. The kid gave the old man a firm handshake, and Oghy winced slightly in pain. Oghy was intrigued when Onsan waved his two companions off, as one would to bodyguards. *Perhaps he is who he claims, just raw*, Oghy thought.

Onsan's security detail saluted back from under their matching hooded gray robes. They looked as though they were guarding him from a distance, because they actually were. If anything went wrong, they were prepared for a fight!

The situation appeared safe to Oghy. He was intrigued by the young envoy and needed to learn more about where he came from. It seemed like an easy hustle to the spy. *I have another meeting in three hours, but I can spare an hour to investigate the lead. The kid seems pleasant enough to be around!*

The initial part of the plan worked so well it caught Onsan off guard for the moment. He had to hold his composure or the plan would fail before it gained any footing. Although Onsan knew the mining industry well, if he had to talk for over 10 minutes about his home in the Fetulas System, his story would unravel fast!

During an hour-long dinner, Mule-sized holes would appear in his story! If Oghy realized he was being scammed, he'd immediately alert the authorities and the whole mission would be thrown into pandemonium. The trio would have to escape and would likely go down fighting. All of their work would be for nothing. The pressure was mounting in Onsan's mind!

Getting the spy to the outer reaches of the marketplace would be a good start. Fortunately for Onsan, under-the-table dealings were an everyday occurrence there. Some parties within the ITU didn't want unwanted eyes and ears around to hear their plans. Scheming Onsan fit in well! Thinking on his feet, he suggested they retire to his ship to discuss the specifics of his planet's financial capabilities.

The spy agreed, he'd soon know if it was a good lead or a waste of Raihan's time. As they proceeded through dark alleyways and shops toward the docking port, Oghy put a bony hand on the young man's back as they walked along, and Onsan cringed inside. Oghy was comfortable in the sleazy setting. Onsan wasn't.

Abbsnate and Krevety continued to follow at a distance. It was of no concern to Oghy. There were hundreds of people coming and going from their ships, inspecting cargo and conducting business as they walked along.

They finally arrived at the docking station. It was dark, but the tarmac was full of white, red, and green indicator lights. Marshallers used orange wands to direct ships into tight spaces. Azure and golden rocket exhaust streaked through the sky towards the stratosphere, as ships shot away from the city at hypersonic speeds.

Crank, pound, wrench!

The sound of busy crews loading, unloading, and making mechanical adjustments filled the air. Looking around, Onsan counted 16 security sentries in white uniforms walking about ensuring peaceful transactions. Despite the noise, everything was orderly, like the ticking of a clock. If anything went wrong, they'd stick out fast.

Once they entered the ship, Onsan would have to act fast to secure the prisoner. The first crack at the crazy scheme would be their only one. The stakes were high and raising by the second!

Onsan did his best to deflect the attention off his anxiety. "What services can you provide for me, er, us?"

Oghy answered, "I don't want to get into specifics out here while rambling through the crowded port-landing area. Patience my boy!"

Onsan was satisfied when the conversation tapered into silence. Something repeated in the back of his mind like a riddle. When they approached the older Pullman ship, Oghy would see right through him, because there was no way a prince would travel along in such a wreck!

As they approached the ragged ship, Oghy immediately diagnosed the problem according to his understanding. He assumed the young man was humiliated to host such an important guest in a rented Pullman. Governments often made their representatives travel with limited funds. Onsan obviously substituted transportation for fancy suits and nightlife. Things were looking better all the time. *Here's an easy target!* He reassured Onsan it was not the first time he met incognito in such a place.

As it turned out, all of Onsan's nervousness and facial expressions were a perfect cover, because Oghy thought they were due to embarrassment. It put him at ease. Oghy may have suspected Onsan if he was calm and measured about the situation. Only hardened criminals made suspicious under-the-table financial deals without a care in the world. As they neared the ship, Onsan knew that he only had to keep up the game for another few minutes until they boarded.

Oghy suggested they meet in *his* ship for their meeting instead. "I have a full bar, and we can order dinner in. The Likuo steaks here are to die for!"

"Sounds good to me, Mr. Oghy!" Onsan's thoughts reflected a different sentiment. *If you only knew!*

A thought was running through Oghy's head when he offered to host the young grandee. He didn't want to spend one moment in another dingy ship. He'd graduated from such practices. Conducting the meeting on his home turf afforded him a definite advantage over Onsan. Why lower himself when he could learn all he needed to know in the comfort of his vessel? Oghy had gotten used to living lavishly and had made a practice of holding meetings in the boardroom in his medium-sized Stellarstream luxury ship. He could serve drinks in a disarming atmosphere where facts flowed freely while the details of his meetings were transmitted and secretly recorded for research.

The unexpected turn was a sudden advantage to the three companions, but only if Onsan could subdue Oghy before he was on to their scheme. As the pair entered the Stellarstream, Onsan was impressed by the lush interior. The mid-sized spaceship showed Oghy had an ego the size of Planet Trecon! When they reached the boardroom, Onsan couldn't believe his eyes. Plush purple chairs surrounded a rich-grained heavy wood table. *A criminal gets to ride in style, while I trudge along in the Mule 357!*

A bar sat off to the side, with hundreds of bottles of spirits from all over the universe ranging in size and color. "I'll order the steaks."

Onsan froze. He realized he was broke! "On second thought, I'm not hungry. Let's just get down to business."

"Don't be silly! Tell you what, I'll treat!" *It's the least I can do for valuable information!* Sinister plans ran through the old man's bald head. He smiled at Onsan, and deep grooves of satisfaction formed on his face.

Oghy called in the order, then asked the kid what he wanted to drink.

Onsan made the fatal mistake of asking for a Trecon specialty. "Yes, do you have a red Orgoric wine?" *Now you did it, blockhead!*

Right away, Onsan tried to change his choice, but he was unfamiliar with anything else. In the back of his mind he knew it was too late, and his cover unraveled fast!

The pieces were being put in place in the old spy's mind as he figured out what to do next. He continued his way over to the bar, but not as casual as before. Body language from both men visually changed from cordial to guarded, as each planned their next move. The tension in the room became thick enough to cut with a knife!

Onsan knew he couldn't gamble that Oghy hadn't caught his mistake. There may be a weapon or an alarm behind the bar. He jumped on Oghy and tried to hold him down, but was instantly taken back by the spy's strength and quickness. He caught a bony elbow in the face for his trouble.

The rage swelled up, and Onsan socked Oghy in the stomach. "Get down!"

"Ooof!" The old man gasped for air as Onsan brought him down.

Tumble, crash!

"Stay still!"

The spy tried to yell, "Help!" He was still recovering from Onsan's blow, and barely had air to get the word out.

Onsan grunted, "Be quiet," as if the spy would listen to him! He grabbed wildly at Oghy's wrists.

"You'll be sorry young Treconite!" With a last-ditch effort, Oghy strained just enough to hit an alarm button just before he was subdued by Onsan.

Bleep bleep bleep!

Onsan quickly turned off the alarm, but it was too late! A flashing red light joined the audible alarm to alert the guards of the emergency. Security personnel rushed to the ship with their weapons drawn to investigate!

General Krevety and Abbsnate prepared for a fight, drawing their laser pistols up under their robes.

Meanwhile, Onsan had knocked Oghy out, tied his hands, and put him under the table for safe keeping.

It appeared to be the standoff that would end their mission! Abbsnate and General Krevety squared off with the two security personnel in front of the ship.

What happened next was unexpected. A comical scene played out as Onsan stumbled out of the ship, bottle in hand, appearing drunk out of his mind. He explained to the guards that he'd fallen onto the bar and bumped the security button as he staggered to get back to his feet. The wet stain on his expensive copper-colored suit seemed to fit the story to a tee. Onsan stumbled toward the sentries, and offered them a drink while pushing small tumblers into their hands. "Sorry for your trouble occifers! Can I offer you an refreshmen-, er, a drink?"

"Of course not!" The officer held out his arm to keep Onsan and his green alcohol away from his pressed white uniform.

The Trecon took another swig and winced as the hard grog burned his throat.

"Ahem, cough!"

The security guards stood their ground and shook aside his offer while attempting to appear fierce and professional. His act wasn't funny to them, they'd seen it too often!

Onsan invited them in with a cordial tone, "I won't tell. No one will know."

Burrp!

"Just a few minutes and one drink. We'll create old times to catch up on later!"

Belch!

Krevety glared at his young accomplice. *You're pouring it on thick, aren't you Onsan!*

A call came in on their radios, *"What seems to be the trouble over there? Do you require assistance?"*

There was a tense moment for General Krevety and Abbsnate before the main sentinel replied, "Everything is under control. No assistance needed." The sentry started to give Onsan a lecture, then realized it was pointless in his drunken condition.

He turned to Abbsnate and General Krevety. "Keep better tabs on your master. We're sick of wasting our time with false alarms like this. Next time, he'll dry out for a night in jail!" With that, they looked at one another, then at Onsan disgustedly.

Abbsnate snatched the bottle from Onsan's hand, "Yes officer, I understand."

The sentries shook their heads as they turned and walked away to continue their patrol. They didn't even ask for identification! Apparently, they were used to annoying merchants making fools of themselves. Abbsnate and Krevety were stunned.

Krevety turned to Onsan, impressed with his acting abilities "How'd you do that?"

Onsan slurred, "Do what?" He wasn't acting! Onsan explained as best he could through garbled words. He'd grabbed the nearest bottle, which was the infamous neon green-colored Uiguyian Alcoolisées. Onsan spilled it all over himself and drank half the bottle before he went outside, to look authentic. The only problem was that he'd grabbed the strongest drink behind the bar, and his cover quickly became real!

As General Krevety dragged Onsan back into the ship, he found great humor in their situation. The fact that Onsan was affected by the alcohol so quickly had clouded his nerves and vocabulary, giving credibility to his story! He became violently sick and stumbled to the bathroom. They'd love to give him a few hours to recover, but Onsan said Oghy's alarm had signaled two Raihan companions who were trying repeatedly to contact him. "They'll be arriving soon, so we'd better jet out of here!"

The crew didn't have time to waste. Abbsnate and Krevety helped Onsan get settled into Oghy's ship, and she set a course for the QQRC. The general turned and headed for the Pullman.

As the luxury ship launched off the ship port, a delivery man arrived at their spot on the pad pedaling a tricycle with two steak dinners loaded in his basket. He looked up into the sky in disgust at the Stellarstream drifting away against the skyline. "You forgot your meals!"

"For them," called Krevety, pointing to the two officers. "For your trouble!"

"Thanks!" They returned, took the parcels and walked away.

The general disappeared into the lot full of ships toward the Pullman, leaving the delivery man alone.

"But what about my tip?"

CHAPTER 22

Bringing Home the Bounty of Planet 6333

As the Raihan fleet pulled from the Muudia orbit, the storms of spring were drawing to a close, and the scorching summer season was imminent.

The tempests caused by melting ice masses were being evaporated before they hit the atmosphere. A big picture perspective allowed the Raihans to see the planet glow as golden streamers smashed her without mercy. Visible fissures of steam broke from the crust and shot upward. The planet seemed to scream with agony as she was hit by the exceptional haymakers doled out by her surroundings!

Planet 6333 was in the last stage of Raihan's Hazard-Class 8 ranking; soon it would be unsuitable for safe passage. The colors were changing before their eyes from mud rust to a fiery red tinted with silver, as molten trillelium rivers manifested on the surface. The Pladia moon protected Planet 6333 the best it could, taking a pounding from incoming debris. Those who had taken this journey before were standing next to the first-timers in awe of the scene. Incredibly, it was business as usual for the planet. She'd continue her scalding bath for the next three months, then begin a gradual cooling process for the long winter in deep space.

The fleet left orbit with occasional shuddering from massive space rocks deflecting against their shields. Everything happening around them added to the credibility of the Raihan version of it being a rescue rather than an abduction. Knuddrul breathed a sigh of relief as they entered the comparative safety of the portal entrance. Everything had gone right as expected. The mission was looking more successful by the minute to Commander Knuddrul, regardless of Commander Ohoef's presence.

The Trecons were shackled to beds and told it was for their own safety, which was believable. Like the planet, they were going through their own set of physical and psychological storms. They didn't know it, but they were experiencing another step in the Raihan reeducation process.

Raihan officers would watch and learn, bringing back a wealth of information. Trecon methods of tool hardening allowed their equipment to stand up well to the elements of Planet 6333. Research and Development would appreciate the delivery. Trecon military structure and mining techniques would take their place among the long line of others who'd given their best to further Raihan influence across the galaxy!

Colonel Honassen watched the overseers closely and sensed something was amiss. On the surface the Raihans were caring professionals, administering potassium iodide for radiation sickness and a listening ear for varying levels of psychological issues. From the first moments, Honassen noticed a subtle attempt to segregate the Trecons by gender and occupation. As the ships reached orbit, it was like a game of musical beds for the miners.

The colonel observed the situation happening around him and noticed that the liberators appeared to be increasingly less compassionate and more calculating. As Honassen rubbed his ankle under the shackle, he considered the logic of being chained to a bed "for his own protection" while the medical observers milled freely around them. He watched as the Trecons were only spoken to when information was needed.

The medical observers would hold conversations with each other while grabbing and probing the patients like dumb animals. The Trecons were being treated more like livestock than people with the intellectual ability to communicate. Finally, the colonel had enough and spoke to an attendant, "What's our destination, and how long are we going to be shackled here?"

The observer looked at him for a moment then turned away without quantifying his question with a response.

"Excuse me?"

Honassen saw the attendant walk over to another observer and have a discussion, looking in his direction and gesturing several times. The colonel was a quick study in situational awareness, and the body language of the onlookers greatly concerned him as they walked back toward him.

A tall man with dark red hair and a beard approached Honassen. The inquisitor took a small tablet from the pocket of his white lab coat, and prepared to load facts from the colonel. "Feeling better I see. What's your classification?"

"What?"

"Your job, what do you do?"

"I'm an excavator operator. Why are we in chains?"

They walked away. Honassen felt he should keep his rank and position close to the vest until he had a better understanding of the situation. The colonel's instincts were right, the medics were intently searching for collective information from the Trecons. It was too late. Honassen's demanding tone had given him away as a leader.

When the aides returned, they answered Colonel Honassen's question with questions of their own, "Are you in charge here? Where is General Krevety?"

"How should I know, I work the night shift. He's all over the place. General Krevety was in Mining Camp 2, last I knew. It takes time for information to flow down to me."

Honassen's internal alarms were going off! He was one of the few with information about Krevety. Why were the Raihans so curious about the Trecon leader? The colonel knew he had to slow play them while he tried to acquire information.

"Excavator operator, huh?"

"Yeah, I live and work 75 meters underground. That's why I'm so pale."

"I see."

The controllers were classifying the Trecons for pre-selection and purification for when they returned to Raihan. The process had played out many times, and the group of Trecons would be no different. Everyone was told that returning to their home planet wasn't possible because the journey through the storm was too dangerous. After what they'd been through, it wasn't a stretch for them to believe!

The Raihan goal of the first selection was to learn the level of home planet loyalty and resistance to the Raihan philosophy within the prisoners. It was typical for a high percentage of people to believe the Raihan propaganda fed to them. Once a candidate showed their hand, they were selected to be brainwashed or separated from the others, thus the musical beds.

Education level and technical expertise were major factors of the pre-selection method. Possible Contributors were weeded out and given an opportunity to skip the ore purification process and begin their adjustment immediately.

The Integrator candidates would purify the ore and be rewarded in the end as a well-paid, productive member of Raihan society.

Defiant Wanderers were taken out of the bay and brought directly to holding cells. They'd be watched with an eagle eye, because they openly fought Raihan doctrine and tried to influence others. When they returned from the harvesting mission, ground transports would load the Wanderers and drop them off in the desert with minimal resources. From there, they'd figure things out for themselves or die.

The future was already mapped out for the majority of the Trecons. Most would become Integrators, where they'd be immediately transported to the purification factories upon return. Life in the factories consisted of nothing more than following the ore pellets through a purification operation to cleanse it of impurities and radiation gained during the spring season of Planet 6333. The ore would once again be melted into a molten temperature, filtered, and cooled again before it was finally brought through a dyeing and stamping sector. Refined trillelium blocks were loaded onto crates and distributed to safe storage before they headed to various lock-safe locations throughout Raihan.

The tasks for the captive workers wasn't complicated. They transferred mineral and ran automated equipment to move it through the process. Most miners needed little training to run the equipment. The menial responsibilities weren't meant to task the Integrator candidates heavily, but to safeguard Raihan wealth while assessing the physical health and mental stability of each individual. It was the perfect setup, and the Trecons were progressing through the program nicely!

Throughout the process, the Raihans followed a stringent medical protocol, monitoring the Integrator candidates for trace amounts of radiation. The Trecons were vibrant compared to past subjects. The few too sick to work in the factory would be taken to the infirmary to begin potassium iodide therapy. They'd return to the assignment once they were nursed back to health. If they were physically unable but thought to be loyal, they'd be transferred to a research hospital where they were given experimental medicine to improve their condition.

Once the Trecons finished their assignment, the Raihans would keep their part of the bargain. They'd be compensated well at the conclusion the purification process. When the workers experienced what the Raihan life offered (beauty, lifestyle, and luxury); the captors were confident the new Integrators would decide it was a life they'd grow to love! The wardens gambled the settlers would have fresh in their minds how Trecon Command forgot about them and left them to die on an apocalyptic planet. They trusted the Trecons would be proud to call Raihan home, just as multitudes had before them.

The Raihan observers were trying to figure out where Honassen fit on the spectrum.

CHAPTER 23

Criminal Undercurrents Abound

Abbsnate and her two incapacitated passengers headed for the QQRC. Onsan was awoken as the Stellarstream craft lurched upward during launch. She was learning the controls on the fly, and it showed! Onsan rechecked the knots and moved Oghy to a chair where he could keep an eye on him.

"Let me go, I'll pay you."

"Not a chance!"

"You don't seriously think you can get away with this, do you? They're following us as we speak."

"Thank you, great point. I don't want to hear your voice any more than necessary!" After he gagged the hostage, Onsan inspected the vessel to look for homing devices. As he was fumbling around, something buried in the back of the shelf under the bar caught his eye. He reached in and found a small satchel.

"Mmuum, rrhh, ummm!"

Oghy was irate when Onsan found the bag, trying to scold him with his mouth gagged.

"What do we have here?" When Onsan opened it, he found 23 four-carat-sized diamonds, the most brilliant rocks he could've ever imagined! In shock, Onsan brought the bag to Abbsnate.

"Look what I found when I was looking for a transmitter."

157

"I'm not surprised. He's a Raihan spy after all."

"We can pay cash for two new luxury ships with this, and still not put a dent in our cache."

"And put a target on our backs. You don't just buy ships with diamonds without drawing unwanted attention." She looked him up and down, "A prince should know that!"

"Huh?"

Abbsnate laughed at him and pointed at the greenish stain. "Look, you've ruined a good suit!"

They'd soon report the find up the chain to General Krevety. The untraceable gems ensured a larger Raihan force than they'd expected on the planet, obviously meant for an under-the-table payoff between Raihan and another government. What arrogance Oghy had, to fly around with such a treasure unsecured!

In the Pullman, General Krevety dusted off his piloting skills as he followed the Stellarstream back to the QQRC. The general mulled over the two additional assets they hadn't planned on, the spy with a wealth of information and a luxury long-range spacecraft that would travel nicely back to Ryderson Omega. Besides the Trecon supplies left over in the Mule, they had quite a bounty for badly needed bargaining chips to get them off Kufsiun and on their way quickly.

General Krevety sent a message to the QQRC, indicating a rush be put on the Mule. "We need to complete the order in two days, and also would like to rent an additional bay ASAP!"

Llib answered, "We have our work cut out for us, but we'll get it done." He doubled the workers on the Mule while another crew cleared out additional space for the Stellarstream.

As their situation became more complicated, Krevety knew he must convince the QQRC staff to collaborate with them. After they returned to the shop with the luxury ship, Llib would have a choice to make. Everyone associated with the QQRC would pay a devastating price for harboring kidnappers of an important ally and staunch financial supporter of

Kufsiun. General Krevety felt responsible for making everyone involved aware of what they were getting themselves into.

In return for their work, Krevety would hand over all the remaining stores for payment. During the process, the veil of confidentiality would likely be lifted on the QQRC, and Llib's family would be in great danger. Oghy was known as an important Raihan ambassador, and the industrial planet would invest many resources to save him and capture his abductors.

As Krevety docked the Pullman, something appeared amiss right away. The atmosphere in the hangar was full of tension. A greeting party waited impatiently for him to land. "Sir, we have a big problem!" Major Tallik informed the general of an incident at the QQRC during their absence.

A recent hire at the QQRC was caught sneaking aboard the Mule cargo bay, looking through the supplies. He'd been caught red handed by Milerous, who was turning wrenches with the workers.

"A worker named Drake Bloddard has seen the Talon!"

"How did this happen?"

"We had the ship under strict surveillance, but he snuck in through a small doorway in the bay during dinnertime."

The young man wouldn't have been caught if Milerous hadn't been looking for a lost tool in the engine room. The cats were pestered when they saw Bloddard wasn't there to feed them, and wailed piercingly. The racket drew Milerous back in to investigate. Milerous scuffled with Bloddard and called for his Trecon countrymen to help subdue the wiry man.

Initially, there was tension between the QQRC owner and the Mule crew. After it was confirmed Llib had nothing to do with the breach, they questioned Bloddard to see his motives and assure he wasn't another Raihan spy.

Bloddard was only a small-time crook, looking to break into one of the major crime families headed by a boss named Cyve Overlord. The Overlord crime family put a yoke on many down-and-out young people. Overlord made them work for him until their "debts" were repaid back to him; which was never! Underlings were sacrificed by the hundreds with no feelings of remorse, because there were always more coming down the dingy conveyor belt of life on Kufsiun.

The young man was an easy target for the Overlord faction. He was a person without a real home, looking for acceptance. Bloddard was a shady character, hired against Llib's wishes only because Etan felt compassion for him and wanted to help the young man establish himself. He was from the neighboring Clectraec Galaxy, coming over as a supply-ship worker a year earlier. Bloddard was marooned after his boss refused to pay him and skipped town. He had no motive other than to be an informant and gain further standing in the criminal underground of Kufsopolis. Ultimately, Bloddard wanted to gain revenge against the cargo captain Hule Debarg for leaving him in such a predicament.

General Krevety and Major Tallik discussed their next move. "We can't charge him officially, but we can't let him go because he knows too much," stated General Krevety. "Where is he?"

"He's being detained under guard in the main office. I'll have him brought up," said the annoyed major.

"What about Llib?"

"He knows everything, but won't cause us trouble. He just wants to finish the job, get paid, sell his business, and retire." It was a positive spark in a bad situation. Llib was obviously still on board with them, because he hadn't turned them into the authorities. The owner of the QQRC was beside himself with anger as he looked at Bloddard and saw his family business crumbling to the ground beneath him. His vote was to end Bloddard!

After the bay was ready and the Stellarstream arrived, General Krevety turned his attention to Oghy. QQRC crews began work on the spacecraft immediately upon landing in the hangar, quickly "scrubbing" it of known tracking and identifying devices. They'd learned from past experiences not to ask questions.

Onsan quietly showed the general the stash he'd found. After the diamonds were secured, Oghy was brought into the office and prodded for answers. The old man was obstinate toward everyone, enjoying having them on their heels with vague responses. In his mind, he knew he had the upper hand, and it was only a matter of time until he'd be rescued.

"I'm not going to tell you anything! You've offended people in the highest reaches of both the Raihan and Kufsiun governments. There's no escape for you now. You should surrender to the authorities and get it over with." Oghy was brash and demanding in response to their inquiries about the jewels. It was apparent right away that the spy would be a hard nut to crack.

"Not a chance Oghy. You're the criminal here, not us!"

"If you let me go now, I'll give you a two-day head start before letting the powers that be know what happened."

In his devious mind, Oghy knew they must let him go eventually. He was supposed to check in with Raihan that evening, and he was already a few hours late. The authorities were probably on their way to the QQRC as they spoke!

He'd be free in a few days, with evidence of being kidnapped and held against his will. The spy would use the situation to his advantage. The devious man was already devising a plan to hawk the diamonds and escape to the outer reaches of the universe. Two days would be plenty of time to set his plan into motion!

The old spy wasn't fooling anyone. General Krevety knew that Oghy would have witnesses to his crime hunted and exterminated in a minute without holding up his end of the bargain. Gaining from the situation seemed to be a challenge that Oghy enjoyed pursuing! The old man provoked them again, "Or we could sell the jewels and split the money."

"We have everything right now. Why would we split our share with you? That's just bad business!"

Krevety thought more about their convoluted situation. Oghy was deliberately stalling to give his contacts more time to rescue him. The diamonds were likely a bribe for a government that would soon come searching for their prize. A luxury ship, missing high-ranking official, and treasure trove of diamonds on the loose wouldn't be kept a secret for long!

They needed to find a different angle to escape the planet undetected. The QQRC was in one of the shadiest districts of Kufsopolis, one that would soon crawl with Kufsiun riot police and military looking for the lost ship. Two days was the maximum time for the crew to escape before the authorities came crashing down on them!

The general could see they were at a stalemate and time was running too short to keep wasting on the conceited old spy. The wise general's thoughts drifted again to the young thief. Krevety conferred with his crew.

Onsan once again displayed wisdom beyond his years. "We have to look at the prospects of our situation, not just the negatives. If we play this right, we can use it all to our advantage. We've an enormous amount of wealth at our disposal. Bloddard has connections within the criminal underworld here, and just a portion of that money could be used to pay them off to run interference for us until we can get off this planet. As for Bloddard, he's pretty resourceful. We can use him to help us. He knows if we leave him here, he's a dead man. The criminals will turn him in eventually to receive a reward to get the government off their back, or terminate him as a witness."

General Krevety was genuinely intrigued. "Bring him in," he dryly stated.

From the start, Bloddard was trying his best to act defiant and tough as the general pressed him for information. The slender kid was shaking uncontrollably as he tried to stand his ground, "You can't do anything to me. I expect to be paid handsomely to keep quiet."

Major Tallik broke in, "How long do you expect to stay safe here in Kufsopolis, knowing what you know?"

"Overlord will promote me for sure."

Krevety looked into his eyes, "No son, he'll use you and spit you out. That's what he does."

No answer. Bloddard's look of defiance cracked slightly as Etan and Abbsnate entered the room, however. Etan had been the one person willing to show enough confidence in Bloddard to give him a job. Bloddard had broken that trust; and shame was etched into his features. The hardened young man was breaking down.

"Let me at him," said Etan with grim determination on his face.

Onsan grabbed Etan by the arm and whispered, "Hold on a second, please."

Krevety looked intensely at the young man, then laid the situation out on the table for him. No information was withheld, save for the number diamonds found. The general took a page out of Onsan's book as he addressed Bloddard with a "good cop" approach. "This could be a win-win for both of us. We could use the diamonds to pay off your debt to Overlord and get us all out of here safely."

Suddenly, Drake Bloddard's remaining false sense of machismo evaporated, as if he saw the light. He was just a scared kid making threats he couldn't back up, and he wasn't fooling anyone including himself anymore!

He looked sheepishly at Etan, "What would you like me to do, General?"

"Take me with you to meet Cyve Overlord."

Everyone in the room looked at their leader as if he'd lost his mind! Krevety saw the expressions, and had the kid brought out of the room for a minute.

Tallik spoke up. "General, you'd be putting yourself in grave danger. I advise against it. If Overlord turned you in, he'd receive a handsome reward!"

Krevety proposed his plan, "I'm going to bring him four of the diamonds, one to pay off the kid's debt for helping us, and the other three for his assistance. The four diamonds will increase his wealth significantly, and he'll help us again for the other diamonds at a later time. The diamonds we leave here are our insurance policy."

"You've got guts, general!"

Krevety, Onsan, and Bloddard left shortly afterward for the Overlord compound in the Pullman. When they arrived, Onsan stayed with the ship as the other two entered the facility. Two gangsters stared menacingly at Onsan, and walked over. They looked ragged because outside guards were low level guys. Onsan sat sheepishly, trying to avoid their glares.

One guard tried to act tough. "Hey. Nice suit!"

Onsan looked down and realized he was still dressed in the outrageous metallic outfit. "Here, you can have it. Free of charge!"

"Really? Um, don't you want to fight me for it?"

"Nope."

Onsan stripped it off down to his boxers, and handed the getup to the man, right down to the pointy shoes. He grabbed Krevety's expensive robe and tossed it to the other.

The two walked away, satisfied they'd bullied a terrified man out of his clothes. In reality, Onsan was glad to be rid of it. He'd forgotten to change in all the commotion. Onsan grabbed his uniform from the back seat, and got dressed.

A few awkward minutes passed, and all three men avoided eye contact with each other.

Finally, Onsan stuck his head through the window. "By the way, you're going to want to have that dry-cleaned!"

"Ok. Um, thanks, I guess!"

As Krevety and Bloddard walked into Overlord's headquarters, Krevety's body language said he wasn't in awe or intimidated by his surroundings. A burly escort took them to an elaborate office that dripped of legitimacy and importance. A guard said Cyve Overlord was in a meeting, but General Krevety insisted they see him immediately. He handed the brawny man one diamond to present to Overlord.

Shortly afterward, three shady-looking fellows left the office with annoyance written on their faces. Krevety and Bloddard were led in.

The gangster sent his underlings out of the office. Overlord waved at Krevety, "Step forward."

Overlord wasn't dressed extravagantly like Krevety pictured he'd be. He had on a silky brown business suit with light blue pinstripes, a cream-colored shirt with a solid blue tie, and simple black shoes. His blond hair was clean-cut on the sides, and slightly longer in the back. He had a muscular frame, but wasn't bulky. Furtive blue eyes shone from under his handsome brow, looking amused and deadly.

Overlord was a tall man, but it wasn't his size that intimidated others. He was patient and calculating. Everyone knew he went nowhere, or requested others without a purpose. His time was important to him. General Krevety was on shaky ground. Showing up out of nowhere and demanding a meeting with the man was unheard of.

"Drake Bloddard, what are you doing here, taking of my precious time?" Looking at General Krevety, he said, "And who is this?"

The general didn't take to Overlord's threatening overtones. He was tall enough to stand eye to eye with Overlord. "My name is Krevety. You saw one diamond, Overlord. We have three more with us, two as a down payment and one to pay off the kid's debt."

"Continue," said Overlord.

"We'll meet in deep space once we're safely on our way, and you'll receive 18 more jewels just like that. Time isn't our friend, though."

"I have checked the diamond. It is authentic and very valuable. But I am curious how you came across it."

The general knew he would get further showing the crime boss the respect of honesty. "It's a government payoff between the Raihans and an unknown government. I can't tell you any more than that, but we have someone in our custody at the Quality Quasar Repair Company who knows all the details!"

Overlord looked intently at Krevety. "I will want to talk to this party. I need to know all of the angles to keep myself protected. Tell me what you want me to do for you."

"We need to know what the Kufsiun government knows with regard to us. You'll set up a diversion and help us escape in two days."

Overlord looked surprised at the minimal request, "You are going to pay me the equivalent of 350 million credits for such a tranquil task? This doesn't compute!"

"We came upon our wealth by accident, but we've bigger aspirations once we get off this planet. Being that they are completely untraceable and safe, you have nothing to lose."

Cyve Overlord's features flashed red. "Not true. There are always risks! I will be the judge of that. I am just supposed to trust you because you walk in here with four diamonds and a lackey of mine who would do anything to get off this planet and away from me. I need to check this out for myself. You will leave the kid here as collateral, and you will get him back alive when you pay me in full after your escape."

Bloddard's thin face went instantly pale as he stood there, feeling like a dead man.

General Krevety didn't like where it was going. "The kid isn't going to be hurt, he's already gained you 10 years of wealth in 20 minutes!"

Overlord returned to his threatening tone. "We made a deal. He will not be hurt if you hold up your end of the bargain. Now Drake Bloddard's life and freedom are worth 18 four-carat diamonds, much more than it was before! Time is wasting. I will want to talk to your prisoner in the QQRC. We will take my Stellarstream."

Their ride together back to the QQRC was uncomfortably quiet as the two powerful men had little in common and nothing to say to each other.

*****

When Oghy saw Cyve Overlord walk in with General Krevety, he turned ghostly white. He knew Overlord's reputation, and he feared what was about to happen to him at the hands of the sadistic criminal. Overlord knew vaguely about Oghy, but didn't seem overly impressed by the old man or the government he represented. "You need to tell me where you got those diamonds, or you will never see the light of day again!"

Oghy had no doubt that Overlord meant it. He sang in full detail, as if he was racing a clock of pain and disfigurement.

"The diamonds are an investment, really. I honestly don't know where they came from. They were delivered to me by a courier yesterday morning, to be transferred last evening at the Independent Traders' Union, where there would be safety in ambiguity for both sides."

The spy continued, "The jewels were a secretive payoff from the Raihan government to the Hrejweoi government, so they'd accept the higher Raihan bid to install our navigation and communication equipment on their next carrier fleet order. Our bid is always comparable to the Kufsiun bid, but they are able to undercut ours in the end because we're not a full manufacturing partner here."

He took a breath, "Kufsiun manufacturing law states that a minimum bid of 10,000 units has to be first accepted in order for a planet to build facilities here and get a bigger piece of the pie. We could never compete here because we have to account for the extra cost of transporting our finished equipment from Raihan. With this untraceable payment, we could tip the balance and be able to gain a foothold on this planet. We'd begin manufacturing and storing our finished products here to sell at a truly competitive price."

The gangster nodded, "It makes sense to me!"

General Krevety almost smirked as the petrified Oghy loosed his tongue for Overlord. He didn't like either of them, but he was sure he liked the twisted spy markedly less than the faction leader! At least he knew where Cyve Overlord stood on things.

Oghy was sweating profusely as he explained high finance and secret government dealings.

"On the surface, the Hrejweois would be paying an extraordinary amount, but in reality, they'd be buying our equipment at a huge discount after the diamonds. Gaining the bid will greatly enhance Raihan's influence in this part of the galaxy. Being allowed to expand our capital investments here would also ensure we receive preferential treatment for our needs at a discounted price."

"And they call me a criminal!" Cyve Overlord continued his interrogation, "What is the temperament and capabilities of the Hrejweois?"

"They can be belligerent, but also have the option of not securing the Raihan bid. They can accept the Kufsiun bid immediately, or put a hold on the process until Raihan sends a subsequent bribe."

Overlord smugly adjusted his tie and turned up his gallows charm. "You know I cannot allow you to stay here and live!"

With that, the crime boss turned and abruptly walked out of the room followed by General Krevety. The two unlikely partners spent a few more hours together going over specifics of their collaboration, including making sure the QQRC workers would be safeguarded from the Kufsiun authorities for long enough to escape into anonymity.

As Cyve Overlord boarded his Stellarstream to leave the QQRC, he shouted over his shoulder, "I will talk to you soon, General."

Krevety simply raised his right arm and gave a quick wave, then returned to check on the progress of his Mule freighter. A Stellarstream landing at the QQRC was akin to bringing a Rolls Royce to a small-town mom-and-pop service station. *Two* Stellarstreams landing at the QQRC in a day was a major cause of concern that their cover would be blown. Because one ship was Cyve Overlord's, watching eyes knew they'd better keep the information to themselves!

CHAPTER 24

Lifting a Spy and Escaping Kufsiun

Retrofitting the Mule and clearing the Stellarstream of Raihan tracking equipment became priority number one at the QQRC! Abbsnate had the ship disinfected from the peculiar incense smell. Years of lavishness had made Oghy accustomed to being surrounded by strange aromas, but they gave her a headache!

For the Trecon leader, another issue moved to the forefront. General Krevety knew that Kufsiun was no longer a safe place for Llib, Thrasea, or Etan Esa-erg as owners of the QQRC. Their mechanics could hide fairly easily, working for one of the nameless shipping corporations and vanishing in a matter of days. As owners of QQRC, the Esa-ergs had a higher profile within the city. They couldn't hide within the lower industrial shantytowns of Kufsopolis.

With all their assets tied up in the QQRC, the Esa-ergs would lose everything! They'd be hunted by Raihan spies, Overlord's lackeys, and Kufsiun authorities relentlessly. There was no hope for a safe or profitable future on the planet any longer.

The Kufsopolis authorities were motivated to keep their capital city clean of high-profile crime. They couldn't fix every little misdeed that happened within the slums of their city, but the Oghy kidnapping had to be dealt with directly and severely before the media made everyone afraid of their own shadow! The abduction would paint a new picture of lawlessness in the capital. Word would get out, damaging their reputation as the manufacturing and business epicenter for the galaxy.

The Raihan régime would use their leverage to their full advantage. The Kufsiun government would receive immense political pressure until the situation was resolved. The Raihans had plenty to gain by muddying the water for the Kufsiuans. They'd use their influence to accomplish economic ambitions through blackmail if necessary. For the Raihans, another motivation was lurking beneath the diplomatic reasons for resolving the problem quickly. They were horrified with the thought of a top spy floating in the deep reaches of space!

General Krevety had all the factors in his mind as he and his team approached Llib. Krevety began, "If we don't take you with us, your family will never be safe for the remainder of your days. Your business and source of revenue will be destroyed at best. At worst, you'll be imprisoned by the Raihan or Kufsiun governments, given questions that you don't have the answers to."

Llib responded, "I'm a law-abiding citizen, but I helped you because you have more integrity about you than anyone I've ever met. It comes out of your pores! Your story is too unusual to not be true. I realized from the beginning that I was playing with fire. Doing the right thing is better than making it rich being a cheat. Whatever comes my way is deserved I guess, but I'd like to leave my family out of it. Maybe I could leave for a while and come back."

Krevety was straight with Llib, "I'm afraid they'd pay for your crimes. You don't know who you're dealing with."

"We've put all our resources into this place for the last 30 years to provide a better life for our family. However, the taxes keep going up, and we'll never be able to improve our status or move our business to a better section of the city, because the government always stacks the chips against us. If you can compensate us for our business, and help me talk my wife into it, I'd be happy to accompany you out of here! I wish that you could find room to bring along my top mechanic and lifelong friend Hebel Greten, and protect my employees on the way out."

The general was relieved, "We can bring your friend, and taking care of your employees was always part of the deal."

Llib wondered aloud, "Where are we going?"

Abbsnate replied, "You'll be coming to Ryderson Omega with me. When we arrive, you'll be compensated for the QQRC and be given the Stellarstream as additional reward for help-ing us out. You can either retire or continue your occupation where you'll be safe until the end of your days. Please sell your business and come with us!"

"Who'd be crazy enough to buy it now?"

General Krevety broke in like he couldn't wait, "I will!" The beaming general offered Llib the remaining diamond, and the owner's dark brown eyes grew as big as saucers.

He smiled and amply stated, "Sold! But how am I going to tell Thrasea about this?" It was fitting that Llib and Thrasea journey with Abbsnate and Onsan in the luxurious Stellarstream to Ryderson Omega. They'd worked hard their whole lives without a break.

Everyone looked at the woman in the group, trusting Abbsnate could reason with Thrasea.

"What about Etan?"

"He'll need to come with us to tend to our ship. Our mechanic is good, but he's young and untrained on the specif-ics of your engines."

Etan, Hebel Greten, Bloddard, and Oghy would accom-pany the rest of the Mule crew back to Trecon. Etan and Greten would team up as master mechanics, assuring their hasty QQRC repairs held up during the long journey home. Upon their return through the portal for the invasion, the pair would continue on to Ryderson Omega in a neutral ship. The plan gave them a good balance of people on both vessels. Oghy would be monitored and interrogated during the return trip to Trecon.

Onsan was glad to be rid of the cluttered Mule for the first time in months. The Stellarstream was a luxury vessel built for eight, so fitting four inside would feel like a boundless extravagance to him. Chase would occupy the Stellarstream back to Ryderson Omega with the crew. He couldn't stand being more than an arm's length away from Abbsnate for even a minute, and Krevety wouldn't chance months of his heartbroken moans echoing in their eardrums!

Chase seemed to get a vibe of affection between Etan and Abbsnate, and might have attacked the mechanic in his sleep if he'd been included on the freighter. The lynx didn't like competing for Abbsnate's affection with anyone, let alone a greasy mechanic!

Llib was too excited to explain everything to his wife when he returned home. He burst into the house, and tried to hurry Thrasea off into the Stellarstream without enough time to think or prepare.

"Thrasea, pack up fast, we're going on an extended vacation! I sold the QQRC, but we have to leave now! By the way, pack our treasured belongings, and leave everything else behind!"

The confused woman couldn't process what her husband was saying. "What, that's great news! So, you want to celebrate? What a nice surprise! Can't we just go out for a nice dinner? I have a spa appointment tomorrow, we'll have to go afterwards. If I cancel now, it'll cost us extra."

"No. Hurry, please!"

"I want to look good for our vacation!"

"Forget about your appointment. We have to go now! We have two hours to pack. And we're not ever coming back, so they can overcharge you all they want for the missed appointment!"

Although he was doing it for Thrasea's safety, the fact was lost on her as she lit into him.

"Two hours! Not coming back! What's gotten into you? We've too many friends and memories here to just drop and leave everything we've built together. There's no way I'll be ready in two hours!"

"We don't have much time, dear."

"You'll have to go without me!"

It was a rational response. Leaving for a trip without weeks to plan and pack was unfathomable to her.

Llib was speechless, and turned to Abbsnate in desperation. She used her natural comforting influence and diplomatic skills to disarm Thrasea.

She calmly stated, "Hello, I'm Abbsnate."

Thrasea looked at Etan. "Wow, you're *both* full of surprises, aren't you!"

Etan grew red in the face, "No mom, er, she's not with me."

"Well, that's too bad, she seems really nice." Thrasea took Abbsnate's hand in hers. "Can you believe these guys?"

"Llib is right, you have to leave. I'll help you. We can get a lot done in two hours together. Take only your dearest keepsakes, everything else will be provided for you. You can't tell your friends anything. We have to keep them innocent, or they could face real danger!"

"Really, what's this about?"

"This is your chance of a lifetime. You're going to love the beaches of Ryderson!"

"Really?"

Thrasea never had a daughter, and the two men in her life were rough around the edges. She appreciated the feminine touch. Thrasea quickly realized it was for the best, wiped away her tears, and led Abbsnate into their house by the hand to pack.

Thrasea was always looking forward to traveling after Llib retired. Now she'd get her wish, only in a different way than she expected!

Etan further cemented his admiration for Abbsnate during the moment, and thought of her fondly as he and his father returned to the QQRC to resume work on the Mule.

*****

The Stellarstream was finished swiftly, and preparations were made for a hasty departure.

The two crews considered meeting together to exchange information or supplies, but it was deemed too dangerous. If all went as planned, the next time they'd meet would be in a raging battle above Raihan. Etan hugged them goodbye as they loaded the Stellarstream. "See you soon, I love you!"

At the inconspicuous time of midnight, the Stellarstream lifted off into the upper atmosphere of Kufsiun and set course for Ryderson Omega.

The general knew their plan hinged on a tightrope! Everything Krevety was participating in went against him to the core. He was a pro-government guy being forced to act like a back-alley crook, but he had no choice. The crew was infinitely outnumbered in a strange dimension. In their situation, criminals were the only ones who could be trusted!

The agreement was for Overlord to bribe an official to get evidence about the impending raid. Overlord routinely bought and sold information within corrupt corners of the Kufsopolis government and police headquarters. Officials and constabularies often appreciated and consumed the services offered by the crime lords. Whenever the authorities rooted out an infiltrator within their organization, Overlord easily found another participant.

Trust was famished in Kufsopolis, but the Trecons had no choice. Krevety paid Cyve Overlord five times more already what he would have received from the Kufsiun officials for information, but he couldn't be sure the crafty rogue wouldn't play both sides. The diamonds were an insurance policy, but only until Overlord possessed them. After that, all bets were off!

Early the next morning it appeared as though the general's risky plan to trust Cyve Overlord might work. Krevety knew the Stellarstream crew must have gotten through the net, or they'd have been raided already!

As the final repairs were being completed on the '357, word quickly spread throughout the Universal Cooperative of Space Vessel Industrialists that a government raid was imminent within the next few hours. Word about the impending blitz found accommodating channels throughout the slums of Kufsopolis. Everyone was scrambling to make hasty arrangements. Shady citizens spread the word to anyone who'd listen, presuming if they warned their fellow inhabitants this time, next time the information would flow back to them.

In the uneasy community where people were trying to con one another around every turn, they were always united against the governing authorities! As word spread like wildfire, nature took its course and transients prepared to move. Everyone had a feeling of safety in numbers. Cargo was hastily loaded and unloaded; the quay looked like Christmas morning under the tree! Scavengers would have a field day scouring the docks after the melee. Overlord assured people knew about the raid minutes after it was ordered, giving everyone a few hours' head start. The chaos on the dockyard worked to the great advantage of the *Mule 357* fugitives held up at the QQRC.

The Mule took only basic necessities needed for survival in deep space and emptied everything else out in the bay, safe from the rummagers on the street. Crates were hastily loaded onto Pullmans and ragged craft before the QQRC workers vacated the bay. The Talon craft was left on the deck of the Mule, to be taken back to Trecon for military training on the Raihan starfighter capabilities.

CJ turned to Milerous and crossed his fingers, "Here we go, the moment of truth!"

Rumble, rrrr, whoosh!

Etan smiled and gave CJ a thumbs up. "Sounds great, doesn't it!"

The *Mule 357* headed for the atmosphere, relieved to be along with hundreds of other ships escaping the raid!

"Every ship is ordered to land immediately for inspection. If you continue, we'll shoot you out of the sky!" It was an empty threat and everyone knew it. Kufsiun authorities were looking for Oghy's Stellarstream, but there were no luxury ships

among the disheveled fleet. Abbsnate and Onsan were well on their way to Ryderson Omega.

The Kufsiun orders continued, *"Come about!"*

The *Mule 357* was camouflaged well enough among the other heaps fleeing into space. The engines were completed and humming at maximum capability. Although the cosmetics of the ship indicated it looked like a spotted pig in cheap makeup, she was a functional vessel now, 40 percent more powerful than ever before.

The retrofitted Mule would use every ounce of the extra power to get to the ergosphere in days rather than months! Krevety knew their best shot to get to the portal in one piece was if the enemy didn't consider it a real option for them. With Muudia ending its summer season, the gravitational pull was still at its strongest. The Raihans had no interest in the deadly zone at the moment, they'd take their time getting there. However, it would be a race to stay ahead of the Raihan spies roaming the Kufsiun quadrant!

The Mule had a head start on their pursuers, but couldn't afford delays because they had a schedule to keep. Meeting Cyve Overlord to trade Drake Bloddard for the 18 diamonds remained the biggest hurdle for the Trecon crew before they entered the portal zone. They couldn't waste much time. If Overlord stalled or backed out on his part of the bargain, they'd be sitting ducks!

The *Mule 357* looked different from the one that left months ago in the supply convoy, but it was mechanically sound and hermetically sealed. Hebel Greten had to scour the reputable scrap heaps in their area to find a suitable engine replacement. Junkyards were the thriving circuit in the underbelly of the city. Usable parts were continually stripped from ships and sold at a bargain price.

The engine mounted on the Mule was from a Tendentan cargo ship. Although the Tendentan ships were roughly three times larger than the Mules, the engines were only slightly bigger in size than the Trecon units because Tendentan freighters used more of them to power their massive vessels through space. The Tendentan engine was only a half meter taller and one meter wider, allowing for a relatively easy conversion to fit the Trecon Mule! The new engine was mounted with great expertise and welded firmly into place. The extra size of the engine in the rear of the spacecraft required Etan to weld scimitar fins on the front of the spacecraft to compensate for the increased thrust during takeoff and better control during spaceflight.

They replaced the shield originator, and NAV/COM port on the top rear of the ship. If they got through the autumn storms of the Muudia portal in one piece, they'd require precise navigation equipment. Ironically, they used older Raihan technology, because it was the best! Since Raihan was a major trade partner with Kufsiun, their used technology was abundant there. The NAV/COM unit was 25 percent smaller, but 50 percent more powerful than Trecon equipment. Scientists would break down the port for improvements if they returned home.

While installing superior "guts" in the Mule, the QQRC had no time to make it look good on the outside. They ground down the welds for aerodynamic purposes, but that was it. Llib joked, "I'm embarrassed. Don't tell anyone where the work was done, because the QQRC has a reputation to keep!"

In reality they were top-notch mechanics and craftsmen, mending the Mule with expert precision. At the QQRC, they were going for performance, not for looks, and the enhanced Trecon ship was a performance machine!

VICTIM PLANET   RAIHAN HARVESTING TIMELINE   ORIGIN DIMENSION

MAGNUS   LAURUS

Trecon	19-128.25
Loehn	18-121.5
Tisdin	17-114.75
Yiohhaw	16-108
Ryderson Omega	15-101.25
Mihhid	14-94.5
Biiobn	13-87.75
Ciews	12-81
Sroh	11-74.25
Beu	10-67.5
Rodane	9-60.75
Steeva	8-54
Whowuiri	7-47.25
Nibil	6-40.5
Quenond	5-33.75
Mibiip	4-27
Pibci	3-20.25
Wononh	2-13.5
Dourcom	1-06.75

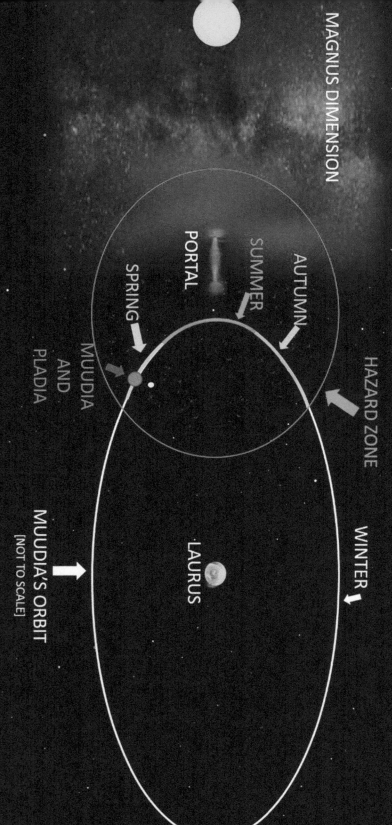

MAGNUS DIMENSION

PORTAL

SUMMER

AUTUMN

SPRING

HAZARD ZONE

MUUDIA
AND
PLADIA

WINTER

LAURUS DIMENSION

MUUDIA'S ORBIT
[NOT TO SCALE]

LAURUS

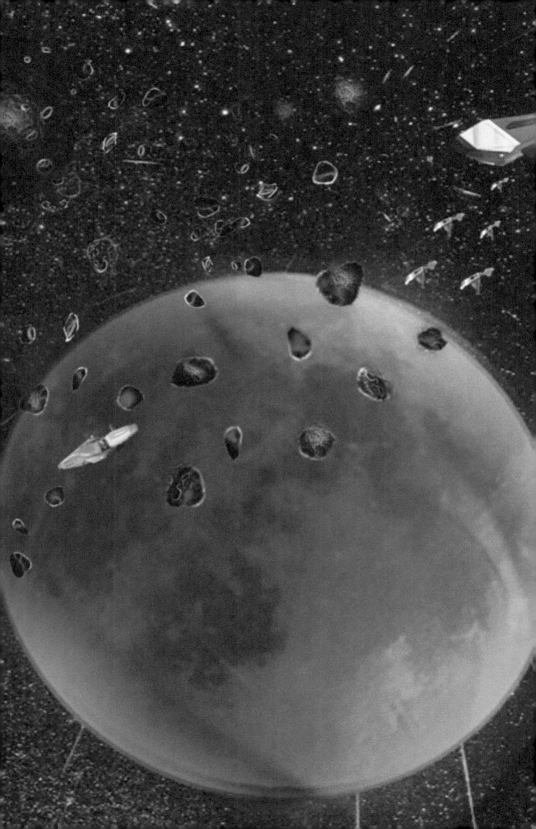

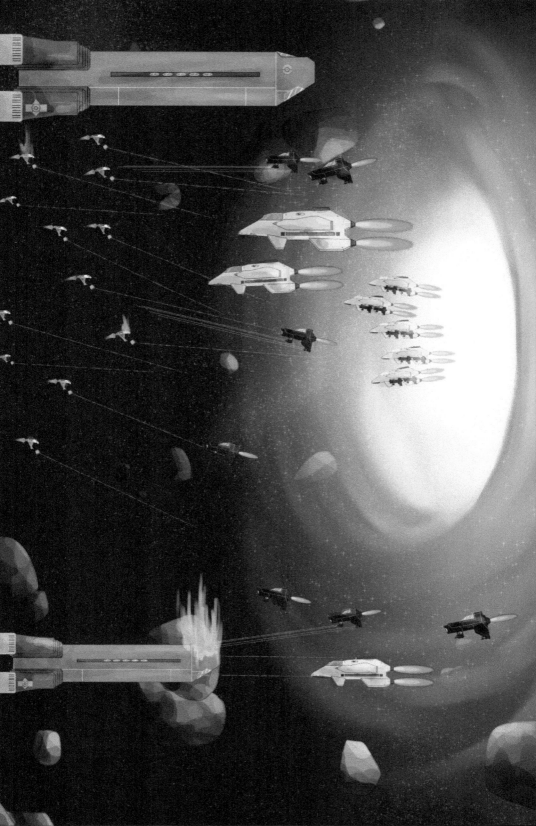

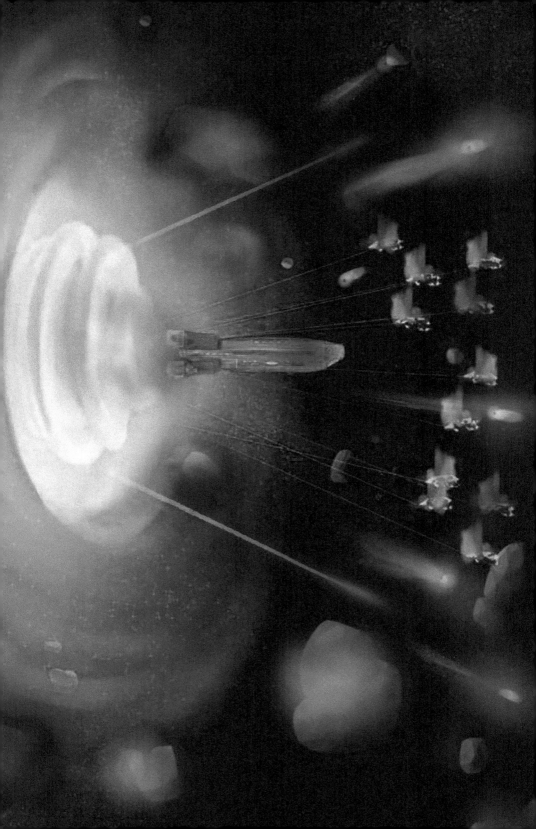

DATA ANALYSIS:

ENTRY TIMELINE

RAIHAN HAZARD CLASS

H-CLASS 10 SUMMER

H-CLASS 8

H-CLASS 6

H-CLASS 4

H-CLASS 2

H-CLASS 0 WINTER

ORBITAL PATH

PORTAL ANATOMY

ERGOSPHERE

EVENT HORTIZON

RAIHAN SOFTENING FLEET

SONARIAN ESSENCE

MULE 357

RAIHAN HARVEST FLEET

REPAIRED MULE 357

TRECON INVASION FLEET

SONARIAN DOCKERS

V-357

SPACECRAFT FORTIFICATION FACTORS

SEASONAL ATMOSPHERIC CONDITIONS:
*RADIATION
*SOLAR FLARES
*METEORITE FIELD

VESSEL CAPACITY:
*NAVIGATION / COMMUNICATION
*SHIELDS
*ENGINES

CHAPTER 25

Two Separate Paths Home

Aboard the luxurious Stellarstream vessel the crew traveled in comfort and style, which only days before would had exceeded their wildest dreams and financial abilities! It was a wise choice for the Stellarstream to depart early. They'd have looked absurdly out of place lifting off with the dilapidated smuggler and cargo ships during the raid. The Kufsiuans would've spotted them easily.

As they sped along deeper into lonely space, it was evident to them they were flying under the radar of the Kufsiun and Raihan network. Time became a blur, and the small ship offered little privacy.

One day Onsan joined Abbsnate on the flight deck, preparing to take his shift flying the craft.

"You're finally awake, sunshine?"

"It's morning?"

Mereoow!

Chase stood up on the copilot's seat, arched his back and stretched. He'd spent the night accompanying Abbsnate during her shift. The cat wouldn't stray far from her side wherever she went.

Meeoowr? Is that bacon?

Chase looked at Abbsnate as if to ask permission to eat after pulling such a "rough" night shift with her.

"Go on, I'll be right behind you."

He jumped down and pranced toward the galley. Chase acted as though they had finally found luxury suitable for him!

They looked out into the reaching expanse. Onsan was optimistic, as usual. "All's quiet out there, I think we're in the clear."

"Don't be so sure, Onsan. We'll hear from the Raihans before we reach the RO system. Count on it. Their net will be spreading by the minute, and we must slip through it as discreetly as possible."

Llib peeked in. "Good morning. Thrasea has whipped up some hot breakfast. You'd better hurry before it gets cold." His features turned serious. "Thrasea had a rough night. She's awfully worried about Etan, we both are. Couldn't you contact him just for 30 seconds so we can hear his voice and know he's okay?"

Before Abbsnate could answer Llib, a distress signal was heard over the Stellarstream intercom, *"Mayday, Mayday, Mayday, this is the Tsajn vessel Oyh. We are experiencing total engine loss and need immediate assistance. Mayday, Mayday, Mayday, this is the Tsajn vessel Oyh. We're experiencing total engine loss and need immediate assistance."*

"Don't acknowledge that signal," exclaimed Abbsnate to no one in particular. "It's a trap. Even if it isn't, what are we going to do to help them from this ship? It would be like sending someone in your copper suit to turn wrenches on an engine!"

Her suspicion was validated a few minutes later.

"Mayday, we're under pirate att—. Aaaaggghhh!"

Mihhidite Sharks forced the Tsajn vessel to call a false mayday, then destroyed them when they tried to come clean. The Tsajn crew were sacrificed, but now everyone knew they couldn't afford to give away their position to help the crew. The Tsajns were simply in the wrong place at the wrong time. Like a fly getting caught in a spider's web, they were dead either way.

Thrasea commented, "But they were innocent!"

"We'd be floating debris right beside them if we answered. We have to concentrate on our mission."

Thrasea knew Abbsnate was right but still felt an awful churning in her stomach. While treacherous situations were becoming old hat for Onsan and Abbsnate, the Esa-ergs were greenhorns militarily speaking. They were growing more concerned about Etan by the minute. Nothing was a sure thing going forward, and feelings of uncertainty rubbed on the raw nerves of the older couple. They needed to learn to mobilize blind faith that Etan was alive and well.

The crew were fighting an uphill battle, even if everything went right. Abbsnate knew all they had concerning the Mule crew was a belief in the abilities and instincts of General Krevety, CJ, and the rest. She didn't want to fill Llib and Thrasea with false hope. She'd also learned that sometimes silence was better as people worked through their concerns.

Abbsnate verbalized her thoughts audibly, "Continue current course in com-silence. The Mule wouldn't answer us anyway."

She knew the Mule mission could go either way. Had the Raihans anticipated Krevety's next move or just covered their bases, the '357 was doomed to run into a Raihan blockade as she approached the event horizon of the portal. If that was the case, the Ryderson Omegans would have to spend valuable time and resources looking for another ally to join against Raihan, and the ROyale solar system would soon be under siege.

There was another possibility. Abbsnate knew Raihan attention was focused on the harvest. They might be content to let the Hazard-Class 8 gales subside to H-Class 6 before proceeding through to find the Mule. The Raihans knew they had the ships to outrun the freighter. If that was the case, Raihan arrogance would give the Mule a small window of opportunity to get through the treacherous wormhole. She hoped the

Raihans would once again overlook the heart of the old Trecon beast.

*****

On the Mule, someone was coming back to his old form after staring death in the face in the form of Cyve Overlord. "You won't get away with this. This bucket won't make it through the portal in one piece again. We'll all die," bellowed Oghy to his guards, who stood undeterred around him.

They'd been pre-warned of his scheming ways, and just looked at him menacingly. Oghy was secured to a firm wooden bench, and the seat bit sharply into his skin. His muscles were achy and cramping, and his head was pounding from lack of sleep. The stress of his situation was constant as he tried to barter a way out.

"Come here son, I've got an offer for you. How much money can you imagine? I'll double it!" The Trecon looked straight ahead.

Oghy'd been coddled by the Kufsiuans for years, to the point he let his guard down through a feeling of invulnerability. But he suddenly found himself in a bad situation. As the '357 escaped further into the outer atmosphere, the other ships thinned out until they were alone in deep space headed for the coordinates of the Muudia portal. The realization was sinking in, but Oghy continued scheming his next move as though he still had an ounce of influence left. He kept talking with his guards until one of the three promptly left, only to return a few minutes later with General Krevety.

Milerous announced, "Hostile ship rapidly approaching sir!"

"Bring him with me," ordered Krevety.

Everyone shuddered because the ship was a Mihhidite Shark and they weren't at their prearranged meeting point with Cyve Overlord yet.

"Trecon freighter, throttle down your engines to idle. Discontinue your progress, or we'll blow you into dust!"

General Krevety ordered, "Red alert, raise shields to maximum power. Continue course straight ahead." He knew they must hold off the attackers as he contemplated their next move.

As Oghy was escorted through the door of the bridge, Krevety perceived an involuntary attempt to guard the ring he was wearing. "Take off his ring and bring it to me," ordered the general.

"No!" The old spy wrestled away from the sentries the best he could, trying to keep his shackled hands away from them.

"Hold still old man!" The guard twisted Oghy's wrist until he had to expose his finger while his partner worked the ring off. Looking closely, a faint blinking light was lit under the emerald stone.

"Looks like a micro-transmitter, sir."

"Put it in the safe for now!"

The Shark was the only Raihan ally close enough to receive Oghy's distress signal, and intercepted the *Mule 357* on their way to the portal. The diamonds were the worst-kept secret in the galaxy, which was to the Trecon's advantage! Krevety knew the Mihhidites wouldn't destroy the Mule with the rocks on board.

"Status report."

"One small fleet approaching fast at 2,000 kilometers, another about a day behind us." answered CJ.

The Mihhidites were rapidly losing patience because their plan was to destroy the Mule and be gone by the time the other Raihan ships arrived.

Oghy hollered, "Too late, they've found us. You can't wriggle out of this!"

A big smile on the general's face made the Raihan cringe, as if Oghy knew he'd been had. "Yet another oversight you are guilty of, Oghy. Your "friends" don't want to rescue you or destroy us just yet. You realize that they'll steal the diamonds and kill you, don't you? Saving you would only blow their cover! I'm curious to know how you see this ending for you?"

Krevety turned to CJ, "Reduce engine speed to idle, divert all power to the shields."

"General?"

"They'll want to negotiate for the jewels before destroying our vessel. We have plenty of time to stall them, at least while our shields hold."

The Mule slowed to idle speed. The general knew that help was on the way. Trying to escape would also put distance between them and Overlord, delaying their rescue further. Krevety was tempting fate, because the tactic also gave the Raihan rescue fleet time to close distance. It was a dangerous game Krevety was playing, but he knew they had no choice.

The pirates appeared confused by the bold tactic. The Shark blasted away at the Mule!

Vwip vwip!

Flash, shake!

Clearly, they were warning shots. The Mihhidites were trying to formulate a plan to board the Trecon vessel and steal the diamonds.

"Hold steady," ordered General Krevety.

"They're trying to hail us sir," CJ said.

"Ignore 'em!"

Milerous lined up the Shark in his sights.

Fzzeeww, bonk!

The Mule's laser blast bounced harmlessly off the Shark. They didn't have time to upgrade the cannon in Kufsopolis. Milerous fired numerous times, but realized it was a useless effort against the heavy shielding of the Shark. It was like trying to cut down a white pine with a butter knife!

The '357 refused to communicate with the pirate craft, and after a while the Mihhidites quit trying to call. Whenever the pirates tried to maneuver close, the Mule evaded them. Gradually, the Mihhidites intensified their attacks, trying their best to walk the delicate tightrope of disabling the freighter but not destroying it. With their shields wearing down, Krevety knew the timetable was short. The impatient Mihhidites were rocking the ship harder with every blast!

Vwip, crash, shudder!

Major Tallik naturally slipped into his advising role, "They'll want to board us, sir. Maybe they'll negotiate for the diamonds. If we give them Oghy, perhaps they'd let us go. After all, their main objective is the diamonds, and ours is the portal."

The general stared straight through Tallik, causing a chill to go down his spine. "Major, there's no scenario where we'd do that! Our final destination is no longer a secret at this point. If by chance the Mihhidites showed us mercy, Cyve Overlord will take pleasure in tearing us limb from limb when he arrives! We have no option but to hold steady."

A dreary silence permeated through the Mule, which was only interrupted by the violent shaking as her weakened shields absorbed another Mihhidite blast. *Everyone* involved in the attack were running out of time!

Vwip vwip, tremble!

After what seemed like an eternity, Cyve Overlord's voice broke through the silence, *"Why would they want to steal or destroy my diamonds?"* With that, three heavily armed ships similar in size to the '357 appeared on the horizon, screaming for their location.

"Yes!"

The three war vessels flew in against the Shark with guns blazing, forcing it to break away from the Mule. The Mihhidites were not ones to back away from a fight, but they knew this was a lost cause with their reinforcements still eight hours out. Oghy looked on in horror as his cavalry turned tail and fled! They attempted to outrun the Overlord ships, but were pursued.

Once away from the Mule, the three predators blasted away at the escaping ship. In the distance, they could see the single ship trying gallantly to fight off the trio. When its shields were worn down enough, one shot blasted a hole in the bridge!

Kaaboom, bright glow!

The Raihan ship flashed bright red orange before disappearing into a million pieces! Cyve Overlord put his ruthlessness on full display, showing everyone why he was the most feared underboss in Kufsiun. Krevety was right. Had the Mule surrendered to the Mihhidites, Overlord would've showed no mercy toward them.

Cyve Overlord was impressed with the determination of General Krevety as he hailed the ship, *"Well done, General! Come about and prepare to be boarded."*

Despite being outgunned, General Krevety had made a deal with the gangster and wanted to ensure he held up his end of the bargain to the end. He asked, "Cyve Overlord, do you have Drake Bloddard on board your vessel?"

"Yes, and I trust you have my 18 diamonds."

"Don't you mean—." Oghy was muffled before he finished the sentence.

Throughout the situation, the spy had been virtually forgotten about on the bridge. The old man was attempting to feed the crime boss information about five additional diamonds that might free him, not knowing Krevety had already paid Overlord four diamonds. The spy could've put a wrench in the whole operation. It was a dangerous game of roulette the Trecon leader was playing with Cyve Overlord, and he didn't need Oghy ruining his plan.

Once Overlord had the remaining diamonds, he'd have many dreadful options available to him. He could take the jewels for himself then go back on his word and destroy everyone, or disable them and receive the reward. Overlord had the situational understanding and firepower to easily accomplish such diabolical goals. He said again, *"Trecon Mule, prepare your freighter to be boarded by my craft."*

General Krevety gave Oghy a look that could kill, then turned back to the com and demanded, "Let me hear Drake Bloddard's voice first."

"You are awfully arduous for someone who has no power over the situation," responded Cyve Overlord demonstratively. *"But I can respect that."*

"General Krevety, I'm here and being treated well enough," said Bloddard.

Overlord's destroyers surrounded the '357. An uneasy feeling of unknown fate came over the entire crew as Overlords transport detached and approached. They were at the mercy of one of the most dangerous criminals in the universe!

General Krevety and Major Tallik walked through the portal lock with their package in hand toward Cyve Overlord and Drake Bloddard. As the door hissed open, General Krevety stood firmly in his tracks, not wanting to cross the threshold with the diamonds.

Cyve Overlord stepped into the Trecon ship with Bloddard, and the wise general held out the satchel for the head thug to see. As Drake Bloddard stepped behind the Trecon crew members, Krevety threw him the bag. Cyve Overlord opened the bag, counted the diamonds, and turned away. He shouted over his shoulder, "It was nice doing business with you, General."

As Overlord's ship distanced away from the Mule, everyone on board collectively held their breath to see what his next move would be. The moment of truth had arrived. Overlord's ships could turn all their firepower on the Mule and blast them into oblivion in a matter of microseconds!

The gangster's ship stayed in place for a few minutes after loading the transport, as if contemplating their next move. The Trecon contingent sighed as the vessel slowly moved away and joined the other two. The three ships came into a tight formation and were suddenly joined by three others. The boss wanted to ensure proper security for his journey back to the industrial planet! Cyve Overlord wasn't one to take any chances without superior backup, and he knew they might encounter hostiles on their indirect route back to Kufsiun.

Overlord said his version of a final goodbye, *"You are on your own now, General."* The fleet rocketed out of sight toward Kufsiun.

The Mule's attention turned to their new boarder. Bloddard looked in good condition for someone who'd been fearing for his life for the past few days. "Welcome to the *Mule 357*," said Major Tallik. The general steamed past them with an irritable look on his face and headed for the galley.

There'd be plenty of time to welcome the kid to the crew, but he had a Raihan spy to deal with. As Krevety stepped into the galley, Oghy's features dropped because he'd been foiled in his attempt to gain the loyalty of Cyve Overlord. The general emphatically stated, "You're going to serve a purpose here during our trip back to Trecon, but you're not authorized to talk to anyone but me or my immediate staff."

He added matter-of-factly, "I have countless questions for you and plan to get to the bottom of your influence as well as the crimes committed by the Raihan government. If you wish to speak to your actions or the Raihan procedures of subjugating other cultures, then I'll listen. Otherwise, your words are unwelcome!"

The next day, Oghy continued an attempt at dialogue with his guards. Krevety had enough of him at that point and put him in the bay between the two cages of Trecon lynxes.

"Enjoy your new home!" The cats were cantankerous from being cramped in the cages for months. Oghy was told that the wildcats would rip off his arm if he wasn't careful. From that point on, he spent his focus staying clear of the cages rather than trying to bribe the guards. The worst part for Oghy was the temperature of the bay. The Trecon lynxes didn't do well in warmer temperatures, so the crew kept them just cold enough where fog formed during exhalation.

Oghy was miserable. He knew he couldn't bribe his guards, and his physical condition was worsening by the minute. He cooperated quickly. In the end, Oghy was easy to break!

General Krevety's goal was to receive an abundance of detailed information from Oghy during the journey. Learning about Raihan espionage practices throughout the universe would be increasingly beneficial to them the longer the war went. Oghy proved to be a valuable resource for the Trecon interrogation team. He appreciated being brought to warmer areas of the ship, away from the cats for questioning!

Oghy had plenty of information to give. He'd participated in three softening and four harvesting operations in the distant past. He didn't want a life in the spotlight as he attained rank, but preferred to live well in a solitary setting so he opted out of the mission commander path. Once he retired from active military service, Oghy was trained as a spy and sent to the outer reaches of the galaxy to troll for unwitting recruits for the Raihan missions. He enjoyed the wealth and privilege of his position, but most of all he savored the freedom of his life as a spy.

The information Oghy provided the Trecons was not as up-to-date as Abbsnate's, but valuable nonetheless. He provided insight on high-level Raihan tactics and motives she didn't have access to.

Oghy also gave valuable information about the seasonal patterns of Muudia, including the effects of ionizing radiation on technology and the body, and their solutions. "We'll all die if you try to take this junker through before winter sets in!"

CHAPTER 26

The Paucity of the Wanderers

As the Trecons entered their next step toward reeducation, the Wanderers prepared for the new crop of arrivals at the end of the cycle. Their settlements were shabby, they lived in mud huts, weathered-thin tents, and even caves. Wanderer population consisted of aging men and women for the most part. The Raihans never wanted to risk increasing the population of detractors on their planet, so they followed strict protocol with young Wanderers just as they did with everything else.

Everyone was registered when they were brought to the camps. people under 45 had to report to the medical evaluators once every three months afterward, coinciding with the camps receiving their trifling ration of supplies to fight over. If one person failed to report, there were no rations for anyone!

If a woman was discovered to be expectant with child, she was taken away from the settlements to give birth. Mothers were confined in a controlled suburb among the Mihhidites, and strictly monitored as servants. They had no rights, and paid heavy consequences if they were caught teaching their children about the history of their home planet. They had a spotlight on them from the beginning.

Since young children say things they shouldn't all the time in public, it was easy for the mothers to be observed and reported by the Mihhidite oppressors. The slightest hint of detraction and they were separated from each other; the parents were sent to the Base 13 Gallows and the child to an institution.

Word eventually got through to Nobert Serlat through secret channels, and he instructed parents to change their way of thinking if they were transported out of the settlements. They could still advance the cause, but not directly to their children.

Sometimes, kids never met their parents, as with the orphan Strider Willstreak, whose parents hailed from planet Yiohhaw, captured during Mission 16-108. Strider was tall and wiry, but slightly uncoordinated because of a recent growth spirt. The kid had sparkling blue eyes and untidy brown hair. He was intelligent in his own way, although socially awkward. Strider was the kind of kid any parent would be proud to have.

Strider's mother, Helete Willstreak, died in childbirth. His father, Bodak Willstreak, was deemed too dangerous to accompany his family into Raihan society. In cases like Strider, the child was institutionalized from day one, with a fast track to becoming a Contributor.

*****

Bodak Willstreak never found out about Helete or the whereabouts of his son. The lack of information intensified his hatred for the Raihans, but he was powerless to do anything about it within the Wanderer settlements. He'd have caused trouble with his fighting spirit if his brother Rander wasn't around to keep him in check.

Bodak would say, "We're getting stronger, now's the time to strike!"

"Be patient brother, Serlat promises soon!"

"We're still relatively young and so are others, but we won't stay this way forever."

Rander smiled. "I don't feel so youthful anymore. My 43-year-old bones are aching every day, and gray hairs are invading the brown!"

The attempt at humor went over Bodak's head. "Right, imagine how some of the others feel. We should move before everyone has to attack the gates with walkers!"

Rander reminded him, "Our time for revenge will come brother, but not now. We have to bide our time playing the Raihan game like the other Wanderers."

"I can't take it anymore! My family goes to bed under the same stars every night, yet I'm stuck here in limbo."

"Trust the process Bodak, please."

*****

The Raihans kept the Wanderers alive for one reason. If they eliminated them, word would eventually get back to their planetary kin and potentially cause trouble in the civilized areas of the planet. The regime wasn't foolish enough to ignore there was an underground network of Integrator spies working against them who'd turn over the evidence and start a civil war. No one knew the full picture of Wanderer desolation except the government and the Mihhidites who dropped off supplies and performed sweeps. Leadership muddied the facts, telling the population that the Wanderers always had the option to return to society and contribute.

Wanderer settlements consisted of people growing older by the day; dead to society just as the native migrants were. They struck the most fear into the hearts and minds of the Raihan officials. They were the dangerous ones who never gave up their homegrown values for the easy life on the wealthy planet. The Raihan government villainized the Wanderers as much as possible.

The Raihans tried to get the Wanderer clans to destroy one another through fighting over the diminutive resources they doled out. A shipment would be dropped off, and the newest and strongest would fight the other clans off to take the food for themselves. Eventually the others would unite against the strong to steal food, weakening the newbies and bringing them down to their same miserable level of reliance. Policies of fear, exclusion, and resource baiting worked for many years. By all accounts, they continued to succeed.

The evil strategies of the Raihans lost their edge the day the Ryderson Omegans entered the equation. When the RO's didn't fight for their rations, they caused quite a stir among the other camps! Where others saw only desolation, the RO's found opportunity.

They used intrinsic instincts to woo the land. Natural root vegetables growing in the rocky crevasses were evident from the first day. Deer and small game provided a constant flow of meat. They stored fresh water from the planet's natural underground watercourses, despite the reservoir built by the Raihans to divert it from their area.

Among the other settlements, contention quickly turned to curiosity about the new arrivals. The RO's didn't intend to make changes through displaying force, which had been typical. Serlat knew the only way they could increase their strength was to teach the other settlements to rely on one another.

The Ryderson Omegans displayed strength through kindness and consideration, looking at their fellow hostages as associates rather than competitors. They'd even leave food and fresh water by the other camps. Curiosity sprouted like silver-green cacti in the dry ground! How were the newbies surviving and thriving so well shortly after arriving there?

Infantile relationships developed into trust, and feelings of hope and independence grew despite their situation. The improving living conditions caused the Wanderer settlements to collaborate rather than war with one another as they were set up to do. Serlat's presence even convinced the elusive Raihan nomads to coexist in peace!

The Wanderer settlements learned from the Ryderson Omegans to work the stingy land. Eventually, they had enough resources to sustain themselves. A stroll through the camps would reveal the savory smell of rotisserie rabbit, fresh bread, roasted vegetables, and fresh spring water to wash it down.

The Wanderers were becoming a population of like-minded people, but Serlat also knew the importance of keeping up the appearances. Most of their energy and resources were devoted to fooling the Raihans. Despite all their technology, the Raihans were blind to the daily lives of the Wanderers. Counting on the often drunken Mihhidites to inspect the camps was the biggest downfall of the government plan.

No one wanted to be there, but at least they were familiar with one another. Whenever a new crop of Wanderers arrived, they were true detractors; planetary kin forced into the wilderness because of their yearning for independence. The settlements didn't have to worry about being infiltrated by spies. If the Raihans tried to infiltrate a mole into their midst, they'd be discovered and dispatched by the others in short order. *"Hey, you're not with us. Get him!"*

The Raihans strove to keep everyone but the Mihhidites away from the camps. They gathered data through long-range satellite imagery and drone surveillance that was unreliable through the dense desert caves. Mechanical monitoring was scheduled, and military sweeps were more a threat than a reality. Wanderers could see the Mihhidites coming for 50 kilometers in the skies above the dusty range, so they had plenty of time to cover up the tracks of their advancements.

Wanderer deception techniques worked because the predictable frequency of the Raihan sweeps and food drops never changed. The protocol of the Raihans made them predictable, their biggest strength was also their greatest weakness! They could only get a partial view of what was happening in the settlements; like trying to watch a game through a distorted screen.

Every group brought strengths to the table for the greater good. Stealthy Loehn (Mission 18-121.5) scout teams were sent out at night, finding hollows along the route to civilization to store food and weapons. They stowed the processed Raihan food in cool caves along the route to civilization, then sealed them for future use. They'd lost an appetite for Raihan junk food and preferred the fresh food taken from the land, but the stuff would have to do when they invaded.

Training exercises in hand-to-hand combat appeared to be fighting from afar. Biiobn (Mission 13-87.75) martial arts were simple but deadly effective, manageable for the older population. Because of the aging bodies of the Wanderers, there were a lot of aches and pains within the camps after combat training workouts. They were staying in shape for their mission though, and the painful progress felt good!

Everyone contributed to the resiliency and fighting capability of the Wanderers, even after death. They'd place their deceased in adjoining caves for safe keeping, then scatter them as "battlefield casualties" to present visual evidence of conflict among the Wanderer factions. Artsy Ciews (Mission 12-81) attended to every detail to make the scenes look realistic. When the drones flew over, everything seemed as it had before!

Information was the main currency, but it was also scarce. Serlat knew they'd eventually need weapons to defend themselves. He requested blaster pistols through the scouts to the underground resistance. The message got through, because every so often one or two small laser guns were dropped with a food shipment. Scouts brought backed seemly information, but sometimes one wouldn't return from their nightly mission. Serlat shuddered to think of their fate.

The most common messages were sketchy because they were written quickly and stuffed into the load by panicky hands. Sometimes the Wanderers would go for months without a message from inside Rochest, and Serlat knew that an Integrator spy was caught and would never be heard from again. In such cases, the underground resistance had to look for another hole in Raihan security measures to open communication lines again.

It took a lot of time and effort to yield a minor result back in society, but Serlat knew patience was the key to their success. In reality, the Wanderers had little power except their daily survival. Their collaboration with the Integrators could only go so far. Despite their growing independence, the needle was always in the red for them. One unmistakable fact known to the Raihans was the aging population of the Wanderers. Even though they were becoming more self-sufficient every day, they were still battling an enemy that no one has ever beaten—Time!

Serlat knew that as every day, month, and year went by, their chances of ever leaving the forsaken place were diminishing. He couldn't hide it from the Wanderers, no matter how much they learned to nurture the land.

Sometimes, a message with important information came back that gave him hope. One day on a drop, he received a treasure trove of information, a message like none other in the past! Details about an upcoming siege were patchy, but they were a sign of hope.

"Greetings. Information indicates that through an act of significant betrayal, Raihan is going to be attacked soon by an unknown enemy. Two months from now, give or take. You are to send a large diversionary force to Base 13, and a smaller one with all your weapons to Com-Facility 12, the closest communication outpost to your camps. The com station can be accessed to send a temporary message into deep space, calling for everyone affected by the Raihans in the past to bear arms and join the assault. The Wanderers should attack the outpost and provide time for fellow freedom fighters inside to gain control of the outpost and send the dispatch. Out."

Nobert Serlat got a faraway look in his eyes, wondering if Abbsnate had suffered for her part in the plot. He knew in his heart she was involved, and that made him proud. He was optimistic about the message, but also suspicious because the dispatch came from a new source. When the scribbled coordinates of the outpost were confirmed by the Loehn scouts, Serlat felt better about it.

Serlat gathered the leaders together that night to read the letter under firelight. Afterward, he looked over the burning coals an announced, "Preparation for our marches will begin tomorrow. Now is when our training will pay off. The clock is ticking and there's no time to waste!"

Bodak jumped up from his seat by the blaze orange camp-fire and clutched his brother, "Yes!"

CHAPTER 27

Ryderson Omega

As the Stellarstream entered closer to the ROyale solar system, Abbsnate knew their final stretch could be the most dangerous. Mihhidite pirates were likely roaming around, hoping to intersect the Stellarstream as she attempted to break through. Onsan and Abbsnate knew they might have to sprint to the safe zone with Sharks in tow.

Fortunately, the luxury Stellarstream had radar-cloaking and top-of-the-line engines designed for interstellar travel. They'd be in dire trouble if they were boxed in by the Mihhidites, but the pirates were spread too thin to close in on them. Abbsnate knew the Raihan tactics. She navigated the ship around traps.

Everyone breathed a sigh of relief as they entered the safety of the ROyal solar system! The three who'd never been to Ryderson Omega marveled at the beauty of the sun and the two planets.

Onsan looked at his friend. "Wow, this is paradise! You left here to go to *Muudia*, of all places?'"

"I was a lot younger then, Onsan."

Abbsnate gave them a brief history lesson of the solar system. "Ryderson Omega is a twin-planet alignment, each orbiting our blue sun ROyale, sharing the orbit around her from opposite sides. The two planets are situated alone within our small and tranquil solar system. They share a very similar mass and atmospheric composition. On the surface, they're vastly different from each other."

Llib asked, "Which one is our new home located on?"

"Ryderson. You'll love it! It's a bountiful planet with attractive landmasses and vast oceans. It has the temperature and humidity of a mild tropical rainforest. Vegetation thrives there, providing an abundance of food for both planets."

"What's the difference between the two?"

"Omega is a planet of vast wilderness, widespread mountain ranges, and rocky desert. She's impressive and beautiful in her own way, with rivers of sparkling water running down from the mountains, the cleanest in the galaxy! With one abundant in freshwater and the other in fertile soil, our two planets are bound to each other in a fraternal sort of way."

"Like lovers from the start, right?" Thrasea asked with a smile.

Abbsnate shook her head no. "Competition naturally arises from two entities existing in such a close proximity. In ancient days, we grew contentious with each other. Our two planets were always involved in civil clashes to the point of war. Things came to a head when an outside force sided with Omega against Ryderson. With Ryderson on the brink of destruction, it was discovered that the invading force would soon conquer Omega as well, with the purpose of over-industrializing us both. Nothing would be able to stop the invaders if we didn't work together to solve the crisis. We had to realize the error of our conflictual thinking before it was too late!" She paused for a breath.

"Go on," said Thrasea, mesmerized by Abbsnate's story.

"Ryderson and Omega banded together to force out the third party. Since those days, we've treated the entire solar system as home, calling it by the combined names of the two inhabiting planets—Ryderson and Omega. We consider our system the same as others do a single planet."

"How do you get along?"

"There's equal representation within the government, and the capital city is rotated back and forth between the two planets every three years. The only way to distinguish between individuals from Ryderson Omega is that our middle name reflects our planet of birth."

As the Stellarstream approached Ryderson, they were contacted from planetary command. "Unidentified spacecraft, state your origin and the purpose of your visit."

Abbsnate replied expertly, as if she'd left home just last week. "Stellarstream craft on Ryderson Point requesting permission to cross through to planet at coordinates 232.2 and on to Base Alpha 230." Abbsnate knew well that ships typically didn't just fly to the borders of a military base and be let in easy. She was expecting opposition to her request.

"Stellarstream, this is Ryderson Point. Hold short, wait for escort at 232.2."

A wave of emotion shook her voice and betrayed her as she excitedly repeated her instructions back. "Copy, Ryderson Point. Holding short at 232.2, waiting for escort!" Onsan detected tears in Abbsnate's blue eyes despite her attempt to remain professional.

As the Stellarstream circled around to wait for the approaching escorts, they marveled at the beauty of Ryderson. Azure oceans the same color as Abbsnate's eyes and lush green land masses greeted them.

Shortly afterward, a greeting party of three Trinity fighters approached the Stellarstream. They were an intimidating sight for the guests on board, although they were assured by Abbsnate that the Trinitys were not apt to be trigger-happy with an unarmed ship. "Stellarstream, Ryderson Point, follow lead ship to port dock."

"Ryderson Point, Stellarstream following lead ship to port dock," replied Abbsnate assertively. As they orbited closer, she was overcome by the sight of home. They followed the escorts, and the planet displayed her beauty to the crew.

RO had learned lessons from the civil wars of ancient days, and things were different now. There were industrial centers on the planets, but not nearly to the scale of other planets like Kufsiun or even Trecon. The Ryderson Omegans used only what they needed and didn't immerse themselves in excess.

The inhabitants of the sister planets revered them to where everything natural that wasn't essential for survival remained untouched. Everything about the place indicated peace and tranquility.

*****

When Abbsnate took Llib and Thrasea to their new home, their features indicated they could be happy for the rest of their days, as soon as they were joined by Etan. Llib and Thrasea couldn't believe their eyes as they toured Ryderson.

Living on Kufsiun for so long had rubbed such scenes from their minds. They'd taken virtual trips to tropical locations, but everything was gray compared to the real thing! Llib had continued working well past his prime, but they'd decided it was necessary to move Etan to a better area of Kufsiun. In reality, they were trapped with hope of only making things slightly better for their son. Any hope of seeing Etan marry and starting a family were choked out among the industrial fumes. Thrasea saw the way Etan looked at the girl. If he safely returned to her planet, there was hope!

The Esa-ergs' new home was a bungalow on the beach on the eastern shore of the Ohfo Ocean, where a bright blue sunrise would greet them every morning. Despite all the beauty there, there was one individual among them making life miserable for everyone.

Mmrreeeoooww!

Chase was left with the couple while Abbsnate conducted her briefings on Omega with Onsan by her side. The cat needed a cold climate to survive, and the warmth of Ryderson was virtually intolerable to him. He would've lived in an oven, however, if Abbsnate was with him! The combination of the warm weather and the absence of his lovely master was too much for him to bear. The only thing that would stop his whimpering for a moment was the abundance of fresh fish to eat. After he scarfed down a meal, he'd immediately go back to his whimpering fits.

Thrasea said, "I'd rather be facing the consequences back on Kufsiun than being here in paradise having to listen to the cat all day long!"

"I have to agree with you,' Llib said covering his ears. "I haven't heard barely a wave since we've arrived."

Abbsnate finally sent a crew to Ryderson to retrieve Chase. This made all three individuals very happy. The cooler weather and presence of Abbsnate made life grand for Chase once again. Llib and Thrasea could enjoy their retirement as much as possible under the circumstances.

*****

There was trouble brewing in paradise. Abbsnate knew that the Ryderson Omegan way of life was threatened, and they must soon confront the Raihans to save it. Abbsnate felt it was best to keep information of the pending assault at the forefront of her mind. She spent the majority of her time briefing the RO generals of the strengths and weaknesses of the Raihan capabilities.

Raihan was like a bully on the playground who intimidated others with her size and bark. In reality, she was slow and weak if attacked the right way. The juggernaut wouldn't know how to react when someone forced her hand in battle. Although Raihan enjoyed an advantage of overwhelming numbers, she'd never been strengthened through the fires of real life-and-death battles. Abbsnate knew the Trecon and RO pilots were battle-tested with superior equipment.

Abbsnate stayed on the Omegan base and didn't return to Ryderson after the first two days. She didn't take the time to visit her home because she had to educate the Ryderson

Omegans to prepare for their assault. Onsan tried to get her to take a few days to visit home but wasn't successful.

"Come on, Abbsnate, your mother would love to see you. She has the right to know you're alive and safe, and you deserve to see her as well!"

In her mind, there were two reasons for her not visiting her mother. "My mother already presumes I'm dead. I don't want to put her through the emotional roller coaster of a reunion, just to leave again on the eve of a major battle!" She knew that duty called her back to Raihan, and going home would only fill her mind with thoughts and emotions she shouldn't deal with right then.

"Also, there are many others here who've missed their families, even Llib and Thrasea are suffering. Why should I be allowed to see my mother again while there are others who may never see theirs again? It might breed discontent among other Ryderson Omegans toward my family."

She didn't have all the information. Abbsnate wouldn't give people false hope that their families may be returning home. She wasn't sure who'd survived and who had died in the Wandering wilderness over the past 24 years. Showing up without definite answers could do more harm than good for her planetary kin. Abbsnate knew the decision to avoid her mother would be one she'd struggle with for the rest of her life.

CHAPTER 28

Back Through the Storms to Trecon

The *Mule 357* looked ragged as they approached the gravitational portal, but mechanically it was running beyond its original potential. The shields were recovering quickly from the recent attack, and were recovered to 85 percent. General Krevety was concerned. "There are still three Raihan warships approaching 45 minutes out. We can't wait for the shields to come up to 100 percent. We'll have to take our chances with what we have. Set course for the event horizon."

Etan assured Krevety that they'd be recovered by the time they arrived at the portal. "We have a reliable shield alternator. You can't beat Raihan technology!" The engines were running like new, purring loudly as a Trecon lynx.

The NAV/COM replacement meant the trip through the portal would be equally bumpy but less hazardous. They'd be able to input their route electronically and fly through at a greater speed. Although the faster shoot time would play havoc on their stomachs, the pain would be over sooner. There'd be more Raihan attention coming soon, so they had to get back through the portal ASAP.

Wobble, sway!

The ergosphere was treacherous. Magnetic storms, SIDs, and radiation were teaming together to eradicate them at any moment!

"Here we go again," bellowed CJ as the '357 entered the portal threshold. When the ship reached the portal entrance, detector indications confirmed the Raihan vessels ended their pursuit.

Milerous ecstatically yelled, "The fleet is turning away from the ergosphere!" Abbsnate's instincts were right, the Raihans had no stomach for entering the portal zone in Hazard-Class 8. The mule crew would soon be reminded of why.

Convulse, glow!

As the Mule navigated through the asteroids in the portal mouth, everyone who'd been there was preparing for the sickening trip. First-timers Etan Esa-erg and Hebel Greten had no clue what they were in for.

Shimmer, shake!

The ship handled their journey through the portal better than before. It shook and shuddered the same going in, experienced the weightlessness of the middle, and took a significant less amount of time exiting out the other side. The engines and shields worked well, but the exterior effects on the bodies of the passengers was much worse than before.

No one was prepared for the increase of radiation that had built up in the ergosphere during the summer season. Five and a half months of Muudia going through the hazard zone and keeping everything in took its toll on the exit route. The Trecon biological systems had been resilient before, but the intensification toyed relentlessly with their bodies.

The hardest hit among everyone on board were the eldest; General Krevety, Oghy, Davss, and Hebel Greten. Effects of a non-lethal dose of four gray (Gy) of ionizing radiation caused their reactions to worsen compared to the others. The four elder statesmen on the ship suffered greatly from the symptoms of fever, headaches, nausea, and dehydration.

As the Mule navigated through the meteorites on its way around Muudia, the four had no choice but to lie down and suffer. Davss was the most qualified medic but had gained most of his experience at the university with animals. He went constantly between the other three, caring for them as best he could despite being sick himself. Davss spent two days administering the potassium iodide medication, and additional diethylenetriamine pentaacetic acid traded for on the black market on Kufsiun. They'd thought ahead and acquired it in anticipation of the journey through the hazard zone.

Although the medication appeared to have positive indicators right away, recovery was a slow process. Caring for them was messy. For medical ease, all four were put on disposable cots in relative proximity of one another. Drake Bloddard was recruited to keep the room clean. He acquired an intimate relationship with rubber gloves, mop, and a bucket! He was thankful to be there, and took it all in stride.

One thing tore at the general beyond his physical condition. He hated to look over at the Raihan spy during the ordeal. It was important to keep Oghy healthy, but a cot away from him was too close. Every time he glimpsed at Oghy, his stomach tightened, and he immediately felt worse. The feeling was mutual for Oghy.

CJ took the helm as captain on the way back to Trecon. The three *Mule 357* officers were given field promotions early on by General Krevety. CJ was on the bridge of the freighter through many harrowing adventures, and showed keen instincts and great ability through them all. His experiences in the past months made him infinitely more qualified than the training he'd receive back home.

Being promoted in the middle of a mission would move Onsan to the front of the line for training as a Starlance fighter when he returned, a distinction General Krevety felt he earned through their travels together. Milerous was recognized for his bravery manning the top cannon during the Mule's battles. No one would question their ability or Krevety's decision to promote them. General Krevety hoped the three would survive so they could experience the benefits of their new ranks.

Etan was useful as master mechanic, but the long trip was wearing on him. He was looking forward to his new home where he'd join his parents in exile on Ryderson Omega. The best part was that he'd be close to Abbsnate. Their destinations could have been on the ruins of Mihib, but it wouldn't have mattered if she was there! Etan split his time on the trip between maintaining the replacement engine and learning everything he could about Trecon ships to be an asset to them during their return trip to Raihan.

He'd been a mechanic for many years, learning from his father about hundreds of different ships' engines and mechanical systems. Reading the manuals didn't come second nature to him because he'd learned more by doing than seeing. Fortunately for Etan, there were computer simulators aboard the Mule where he could explore and reassemble every kind of Trecon engine and system. He enjoyed spending his time in the simulator and picked up on things fast.

Drake Bloddard acted like Milerous's shadow, learning everything he could from the young Trecon officer. There was still a lot of tension coming from Etan, who felt betrayed by the young man after he tried to blackmail them at the QQRC. It would take a while for Bloddard to build up Etan's trust again, but the others accepted him relatively quickly. Bloddard became a jack of all trades, doing odd jobs from feeding the lynxes to cleaning the ship. It felt good to be part of something bigger than himself, and he seemed to have a growing sense of self-worth every day.

The Mule traveled in tech silence during their journey back to Trecon. This time it was by choice. With Mihhidite Sharks and Raihan spies lurking around the edges of the Laurus galaxy, a distress signal from them would alert the enemy. Just before entering Trecon territory, a well-timed dispatch meant the cavalry would arrive promptly.

The Trecons broke out their charts once again and deceive the techies' through tried and true old-school methods. Knowing the enemy would be patrolling the outer reaches, Krevety and CJ decided it would be best to exit the Laurus solar system before the shortest distance back to Trecon in the Yidgo quadrant, which would add another three weeks to their journey.

Going out of the way gave the Mule crew one main advantage. The militants would be unsure if they made it safely through the turmoil of the hazard zone. It was unlikely they'd encounter the Raihans or Mihhidites roaming the area, because they'd be setting up blockades elsewhere. Once they crossed into Trecon's system, they'd stay in com silence until they were in range of their comrades. Response would be short. If the enemy attacked a Mule so close to Trecon, a patrol would arrive in minutes and they'd be shot on sight!

General Krevety got right to work after he recovered. He uploaded a recorded message from Abbsnate as his staff prepared a briefing for Trecon Control.

Whirr, glow!

The recording of Abbsnate came to life.

"Good day general. If you're watching this, it means you've made it through the portal. As you know, we'll be counting heavily on the underground resistance during the assault. However, I'm not sure how many there are. My best estimation is between 8,000 and 15,000 people. There are also perhaps 3,000 able-bodied Wanderers. The hope is that the number will increase a hundredfold after the truth gets out that we were all lied to and coerced to build up the Raihan domain."

Abbsnate told of Raihan's military capabilities, and the location of their main bases. Krevety was astounded at the size of Raihan's military might. He hoped that they could fracture the loyalty of the shipped-in mercenaries.

"I'll lead a small fleet into the heart of Rochest, their capital city. Between the assistance we get from the ground and our siege in space, it'll be our best shot for a short war. I've included some specifics of Rochest, according to my experiences. I can't give you a specific blueprint of the city. They're the most guarded secrets on the planet! If I were ever caught snooping around the wrong places, they'd have sent me to the Base 13 Gallows, no questions asked."

"Heartless," said CJ.

Krevety looked at him, "No doubt. There's an undercurrent of fear controlling the population. The invasion isn't going to be a picnic!"

The girl continued, *"Rochest is 5,000 square kilometers. Picture the capital city like a bullseye. The outer ring consists of the Integrators, and the middle ring has the Contributors. The goal of my fleet will be to reach the center of the bullseye, where the native Raihans reside. There is mingling between the three rings, but only when necessary. Although I've never been inside the walls, I've been underneath the inner circle many times."*

Tap, tap, tap!

Tallik's fingers were firing rapidly on the keyboard, transferring the data into the Trecon system for distance calibration.

"In the exact center of the city is a 400 square kilometer lake with an enormous island in the middle. Integrators and Contributors are able to take an underground tram to the island to visit the cultural and spiritual icon of the Raihans known as the Monument. Six tracks connect the park with the outside of the city. The tracks go underground in the Contributor section, and emerge outside a wall before going over the lake to Monument Island Park. It doesn't matter what route you take, they all provide a restricted view of the Raihan section."

"The Monument is 18 stories of different cultures influential to Raihan history and power. The foundation of the icon looks shabby because it represents the Dourcoms. As it works up to the sky, various cultures are represented based upon the wealth they've brought to the planet. Those who aren't educated think it's beautiful, but to me it was always sickening. The icon is added to every six and a half years, if you know what I mean."

Tallik looked up from his work, "They won't get away with it this time!"

"Soon the tourist trains from the outer rings will be replaced by construction cars for a season, and they'll add another story to the monument. They use trains to bring in the building materials, because they'd never fly anything in. There's a no-fly

zone above Rochest. They take no chances. That's why Rochest remains a mystery. I've included a crude map, but it's the best I could do from the view on Monument Island."

"The 19th story of the icon will be to represent Trecon, unless we can stop them. It'll be adorned with Trecon art, technology, and history. On the walls will be an official tribute to those who the Raihans couldn't save. In reality, it's for those who lost their lives doing Raihan's bidding through harvesting the trillelium ore. I've visited the 15th floor many times, where my father's name is etched into the museum wall. I know in my heart that he's still alive, though."

The footage showed Abbsnate staring blankly into the screen, but the projection was enough to pacify Etan. He was captured by her image, and didn't take in a single detail from her mouth as she spoke.

"The island is a national park, adorned with statues and fountains over perfectly manicured grass. It's a destination point, one of the 20 wonders of the galaxy. I knew the place well, but only because I was trying to get a view of the city to build my rudimentary blueprint. I had to be careful, and submitted everything to memory rather than chance getting caught writing things down."

She concluded, *"Looking out from the island, the golden glass towers of Rochest shimmer in the sun. One area looks slightly out of place amidst the shimmering skyline. I believe that's where the governmental section is. If we can make it there during the chaos, we can win the war. Good luck, and Godspeed!"*

Whirr, fade!

*****

Waiting until the last possible minute to contact Trecon Control gave Pnoi Nbnok extra time to study the frequency of Oghy's ring in the anechoic chamber of the ship. If they could pinpoint the frequency before they arrived home, the spies roaming free on Trecon would be captured before they could transmit important information about the impending invasion back to Raihan. The timetable and other data about the assault would be safe.

The transmitter ring was safely contained in the double-insulated anechoic chamber of the ship. The test chambers were encrusted in anti-absorbent slate. They were originally meant as temporary fixes to study and test contaminants trapped in material from Muudia. As radiation levels and connected health concerns were rising within the mining settlements, the chambers were added to the Mules to conduct tests on the ore before it was loaded. If the radiation levels were deemed safe enough after testing, they could ship the minerals.

Trecon control wasn't keen on bringing ships full of polluted material back home and contaminating their planet. Inserting the small testing labs into the Mules was their provisional solution while they pursued a long-term answer. The anechoic chamber on the Mule was small, with just enough room for two observers to squeeze in around their equipment.

Nbnok and Tephen got familiar with each other as they studied the spy ring. The compartment was double-fortified and adequate in every way to provide superior shielding to prevent the ring from sending a readable transmission to the lurking Mihhidites. Still, they took no chances with security. The main door was to be open and shut just long enough for Nbnok and Tephen to enter and exit. Although most everyone on board were to be trusted, the door was secured and guarded for everyone's safety.

CHAPTER 29

Trecon Selection and Reeducation on Raihan

The number of Trecons captured during the operation was 1,037, all in shell-shock and recovering slowly from their two-week ordeal of terror and darkness. They were improving steadily, learning of their surroundings. The miners were strapped down onto beds in giant bays of the Raihan medical overwatch vessels. Doctors and other officers were walking around and checking on them.

They wondered why they were restrained even though they were too weak to fight. Some Trecons were conversing with one another and the medics who cared for them, trying to figure out what was happening. The confused Trecons reacted in various ways, ranging from yelling and fighting the restraints to calculatingly observing and trying to get a handle on their situation.

The chaos was normal for the Raihan observers, they'd seen it numerous times. If a patient fought too much, they were given a sedative to avoid a mass panic among the others while everyone was told it was for their own good. Their health seemed to improve from the radiation sickness, but hunger raged deep inside their bellies. As they entered the ergosphere of the portal, the detainees realized why the restraints might be a good thing as the vessels shook brutally back and forth!

Shudder, lurch!

The Trecons quickly realized that eating wouldn't have been advised in their weakened condition. Their stomachs couldn't have held in sustenance during the coarse trip through. The Raihans knew all too well that temporary hunger was better than a vomitus mess to clean up!

When they arrived safely on the Magnus side of the portal, food was brought in and placed on large tables in the room, and the medical overseers excused themselves. The restraints were mechanically loosened.

As the Trecons stirred toward the food and attempted orientation, a giant screen lowered from the ceiling behind the food tables and began the first Raihan brainwashing session. The message was an indoctrination into the situation the settlers found themselves. It started with an explanation of how they got there, then painted a picture with bright optimistic tones. Their fortunes had changed for the better!

President Grolegg looked sharp in his dark suit and red tie. Lively blue eyes contrasted his jet-black hair. As the president spoke, a surge of his supreme self-confidence filled the auditorium. Grolegg held all the cards, but would share the secrets of success with the Trecons if they got with the program.

"Good day to every one of you. I am President Yerb Grolegg of the Raihan Republic, and today each of you will begin a new journey to fulfillment and happiness. Your enemies have been vanquished! You are safe now. When we found you, you were refugees, attacked by pirates and written off as dead by your home planet. Your former government didn't prioritize your rescue, in the process deeming you no longer essential to their plans."

The crowd stirred, "What?"

"Yeah, that's right, where was Trecon Control when we needed them?"

'No, I'm sure there's an explanation for it!"

The message continued. *"We heard your distress calls and came to your rescue as soon as we were able. We arrived there with our best resources to save you from certain destruction on Planet 6333. We risked our lives to save you! Don't be afraid. We restrained you without food for your own protection while traveling through the portal. I'm sure you are now aware of the reasons."*

"He's right, they did risk their lives!"

The president continued, *"Your days of toiling on distant planets for the enrichment of others are over. You now have the opportunity to be valued as a part of a greater society. Your skills will be appreciated, utilized, and you'll be compensated fully. Our best wish for you is to assist you into reaching your full potential with us! You'll each be given a choice, based on your abilities, to contribute to our culture at your personal level. You bring a unique value to us, and we'll reward you greatly for it. Enough for now. Please enjoy the meal we've set out for you!"*

The crowd stirred.

Grolegg's speech indicated two things right away to Colonel Honassen. Their captors no longer thought of them as agents of Trecon society. The Raihans were intent on breaking down the fabric of teamwork as Grolegg imbedded individuality and personal success into the pep talk.

Hunger panged in Colonel Honassen and he was reluctant to eat food offered by the Raihans, but he had a significant choice to make. In the colonel's mind, there were two options. He could circulate an order to not eat, which was within his right to do as the top-ranking Trecon officer aboard. It would be the ultimate litmus test for others to display their loyalty. To do that would be to beg for trouble. Panic could find a tranquil home in an empty stomach! Honassen realized this action could drive a wedge between them immediately. He knew it was too risky in their current subservient position.

The better option would be a wait-and-see approach. This course was to take in sustenance, restore strength, and wait for the right time to communicate or act. The whole situation reminded the colonel of a scenario back in basic officer school when they were tested to find their physical, emotional, and mental limits. *Game on!*

It was an obvious attempt by the Raihans to test the quality of the Trecon ranks. Leadership appeared to be strong for the moment on the ship. They were galvanized behind Honassen, as they threw glances in his direction to determine their next move. The colonel stood up.

It became obvious to the Raihans in the bay that the miners were looking for Colonel Honassen to bless their actions before they advanced toward the buffet. Normally as a leader, he waited for everyone else in his party to take their portion before he received his. This situation was different, however. He had to think of their physical well-being first and make it his top priority.

Honassen made his way through the crowd to the table. It was a silent order for everyone to eat and take care of themselves. As he passed by them, the Trecons made their way to the banquet set before them.

On the tables was a meal fit for a king! The sight and smell of the delectable varieties of fish stood out most to them. The aroma of fresh baked walleye garnished with lemon was more than they could take. The sweet smell of the meat was mildly hypnotic to the Trecons, lessening the grief of their recent experiences.

It was as if the Raihan crew had the delicacy flown in fresh from Trecon that morning. They had fish meals in the settlements that vaguely reminded them of the Trecon walleye, but months of being frozen had taken its toll on the flavor of the meat. The fish presented to them by the Raihans tasted like it was pulled out of Mic Mac Lake 15 minutes before, and cooked just for them.

Smoky smells of fresh sausage and double-smoked bacon added to the excitement of the feast. There were fresh exotic fruits, steamed vegetables, and pastries of every kind to fit the fancies of the Trecons. Six varieties of freshly-ground coffee delighted them from the beverage table. For those who'd been, it was like staying in an expensive Northshore resort.

Everything tasted as good as it smelled to them. It was a joyous dance of celebration for their taste buds! The fish was firm and flaky and the sausage not overly greasy. Everything was cooked to perfection. There was plenty of food, and they could eat their fill. The only thing missing from this feast for some was alcohol, but it wasn't included for obvious reasons in their weakened condition.

Colonel Honassen knew that the reverence for leadership on his vessel may differ vastly from other ships in the "rescue" fleet. His spacecraft contained the command team and the most experienced crew. The colonel's instincts were right, unfortunately. On the other medical vessels, the Raihan rhetoric was being swallowed up like vintage wine as they gorged themselves and reveled in their new fortune!

The Raihans watched their hostages through security cameras. Honassen drew particular attention. "Excavator operator, huh?"

*****

Once the Trecons arrived on Raihan, they were immediately taken to a secret base and submitted for medical evaluation, pre-selection, and the start of their reeducation process. Many watchful eyes were on the new entrants!

Upon arriving at the base, they were separated based on gender and initial observations on the medical overwatch spacecraft. The Raihans used the pre-selection process to choose those of exceptional aptitudes and questionable loyalty, to plug into their utopian society. It seemed the Raihans already knew who the formal and informal leaders were as they unloaded the medical ships on the base tarmac.

Right away, Colonel Honassen was separated from his command council and brought into a chamber with 22 others. Along with Honassen, the group included the senior doctors and scientists from the settlements. The group sat in a tiered auditorium in plush brown leather high-back chairs. Grolegg greeted them once again. This time the Raihan politician addressed them in person behind a podium flanked by two sentries on each side. The president was direct and vile in person. His threatening blue eyes scanned the crowd for dissent.

"Greetings once again, and welcome to Raihan. You're here because you have the talent to succeed in the highest positions of our society. Your knowledge and experience are coveted here! You've been selected to be leaders within our culture, and will be given many benefits to compensate for the loss of status on your home world. You've arrived on our planet with the opportunity to be molded into our society. You're welcomed to stay and become a Contributor to our great culture."

Then came a veiled threat. "However, the choice is up to you. We've risked much to bring you out of danger and into safety. You're no longer leaders here, but peers and itinerant guests under our government. If you attempt to assume a leadership role here against us, we'll be forced to prioritize the safety of our citizens against you! If you choose to rebel further, you will, through your insolent choices, be counted as an enemy rather than a refugee. If you choose that route, you and your unmanageable comrades will go through a harsher process of orientation."

President Grolegg looked at his audience intently, almost daring them to make a move. The colonel made up his mind before the speech ended, but realized the danger in standing up and walking out of the room. He gave a short glance around the room and realized the others had also stayed in their seats.

Once again, they'd followed their leader and collectively employed a wait-and-see approach. President Grolegg scanned the audience and stopped cold when his eyes met Honassen's in an icy stare.

Grolegg made it clear he'd remove Honassen's control, and wouldn't give him the chance to become a Contributor until he broke the man. What the president didn't know, however, was that being with the others sweating away in the ore purification factory would suit the colonel just fine!

Colonel Honassen was sent with the majority of the hostages to the ore-purification factory. He was precariously close to becoming a Wanderer, despite having said few words!

The ore was waiting for them when the Trecon Integrator candidates arrived. They were escorted off the ship by their Mihhidite guards and marched toward a structure that seemed to block out the evening sun. As they strode side by side, Honassen felt like they were being marched to a prisoner-of-war camp. When they entered the factory, it towered threateningly above them and offered a tangible feeling of intimidation.

It was fear-provoking for the Trecons, but the place offered a different sentiment for the Raihans. It was an embarrassment to some of the new politicians, and many wanted it gone. The factory was old and crude, a monstrosity that looked out of place on the pristine surface of Raihan. Leaving it on the planet had many advantages recognized by the old guard. It was kept in service because of its effectiveness. Cosmetic issues were the biggest problems with the factory, but operationally it ran perfectly.

Honassen looked up in awe as he walked among the shadows of the monstrosity, fearing he'd never see Trecon again.

CHAPTER 30

Rapid Fall and Speedy Trial for Commander Knuddrul

Meanwhile, Commander Knuddrul was taken from quarantine and summoned to the high court. A 10-day-quarantine was protocol for harvesters, so everything felt like it was proceeding as normal. His power-hungry state of narcissism left him unable to grasp his predicament. Knuddrul first thought he was being summoned for a promotion.

His features were visibly sunken when he realized what he was actually facing! Reality settled in as he was stripped of his uniform and put in chains for interrogation. Mihhidite guards enjoyed roughing up the arrogant man. Knuddrul had kicked others down the rungs from him for years. Now it was their turn!

During the preliminary court martial procedures, three main circumstances from his time as commander came back to haunt him. First, he'd withheld information about the mysterious alien structure found by the Trecons, and against procedure allowed them to send a convoy too late into the winter season. That erroneous decision led to losing six Talons, along with the opportunity for Abbsnate to betray the Raihans.

Next, the structure was transmitting to an unknown location, possibly putting the planet in danger! The Scientific Center was using its best resources to decipher and find the destination of the signal before it was too late.

Finally, video evidence from the Stellarstream confrontation between Onsan and Oghy was displayed for him, confirming the Mule had escaped their predicament.

All the problems found themselves firmly planted on Knuddrul's doorstep. His secrecy and self-delusions of rapid political ascension hadn't only put the softening and harvesting missions in jeopardy, but also brought Raihan on the brink of intergalactic war with the Trecons and Ryderson Omegans!

Knuddrul was immediately imprisoned, and a trial date was set. All his dreams of ascending to high government came crashing down on him. Knuddrul's predicament finally sank in. He wasn't only going to be stripped of fame and position; he was going to prison for life.

There was no way for Knuddrul to redeem himself for the grave mistakes, and he knew it. The physical and psychological consequences of his actions weighed on him like a ton of bricks, and he wanted to die. Knuddrul lost his appetite and soon looked like a skeleton. He was eventually forced to receive nourishment through artificial means.

It was important for the government to have a fall guy! He'd have to survive until everyone on Raihan could see who'd put them in danger. They'd want to know that he received severe punishment for his actions. The government needed to set an example.

The former commander was put under heavy guard to ensure he didn't hurt himself. His body was in such a state of stress from fatigue and radiation exposure caused by the artifact, that his trial would have to be expedited and broadcast later. Greater Raihan society had bigger concerns at the moment, as they prepared for war.

Soon Knuddrul learned the case brought against him. Among the official charges, the most serious were manslaugh-

ter, endangerment, espionage, blatant disregard for procedure, misuse of Raihan resources under his command, and
failure to disclose full information while in command. Many
lesser charges compounded on top of those, but there was no
point in pursuing any more of them.

Through his actions, Knuddrul put himself ahead of the
entire planet of Raihan. The top officials were taking a self-righ-
teous position, quite a contradiction for a society based on
trickery and repression!

The quick pretrial session was over in two days, and
Knuddrul was escorted to rot in confinement while the Raihans
decided what to do with him next. He was taken out periodi-
cally for recorded interrogation because Raihan leadership
wanted to get every stitch of information they could about the
Trecons before he died or they were attacked. Knuddrul was
questioned as an enemy, rather than a former officer in charge
of an important operation for Raihan advancement.

Knuddrul was kept in dark solitary confinement within
the Base 13 Gallows, with no outside information coming into
his cell. He was given simple meals three times a day and only
water to drink. They took every measure of control from him,
not even allowing him to starve himself. He was tortured if the
food wasn't eaten.

The man was called Prisoner 19-128.25 after the Trecon
mission; rather than the rank and name like a traditional
court-martial proceeding. Although he had no contact with
the outside world, it was apparent to Knuddrul he was quickly
viewed as the opposite person he had hoped to be.

His trial was short and concise because his guilt was predetermined. He was too weak to walk far distances or stand
under his own power, so he was wheeled into the courtroom
for the proceedings.

The official charges against him were read. *"Prisoner
19-128.25 openly invited death and destruction not just of his
crew, but on the greater Raihan society through his blatant disregard for his position as commander. Prisoner 19-128.25 was*

in position on the Rockwell outpost to uphold the Raihan proce-
dures, yet he was the greatest miscreant in the entire structure
of his command."

A demanding judge looked down at the broken man. "How do you plead to these charges?"

"Guilty."

Prisoner 19-128.25 had no excuses for his decisions as commander, and he offered no official defense. He was proven guilty on all counts in a record two-day trial. Prisoner 19-128.25 was officially stripped of his Raihan citizenship and returned to the Base 13 Gallows where he would be left to rot!

All the precautions to keep him alive were observed, to ensure he'd continue to suffer for as long as possible. The Raihans had a distinct way of punishment through leaving people to survive under harsh circumstances, as they did to the Wanderers. Giving prisoners a quick death wasn't in their DNA; they felt that extreme suffering was a deterrent and a consequence.

As Prisoner 19-128.25 entered his new and final home, the smell of his dank cell penetrated his nostrils with mildew that stung as he breathed in the moist air. After a while, he'd grow accustomed to the revolting smell, but his lungs would pay the price the longer he stayed in the environment. The damp cement seemed to permeate Prisoner 19-128.25's skin and chilled him to the bone. The sound of water dripping from a cracked pipe in the ceiling of his cell provided a rhythmic drumbeat to his pitiful new existence.

Rather than being viewed as the greatest hero in Raihan history, Prisoner 19-128.25 quickly descended into the rank of the number one enemy of all time!

CHAPTER 31

Building Up Defenses for the Assault on Raihan

On Trecon and Ryderson Omega, rapid preparations were being made for the invasion of Raihan. The allies realized that an immediate strike was their best option for victory against superior forces. They also needed to build their planetary defenses for a Raihan attack, should their invasion plan fail.

Advanced reconnaissance on the Raihans indicated that they must combine their resources for the attack, but the chips were stacked greatly against them. The Wanderers and underground resistance were unpredictable assets, so the two partners would have to plan on doing the heavy lifting until they gained momentum. Raihan was the most powerful planet in the universe, and she'd use all her resources to ensure swift defeat for her enemies!

General Krevety and Abbsnate made a daring timetable that would give them their best chance against the Raihans. Separately, winning a war against Raihan was an impossible task. Together, it was still a treacherous mountain to climb!

*****

On the twin planets of Ryderson and Omega, building a war fleet was a delicate proposition. The RO's had to protect themselves from hostiles all around their small system. With machines of war, they didn't mess around!

Their best assault ship was the Trinity fighter. It was a grand craft, with superior ability for extended-reach attacks. On the flight deck, pilot and wing gunner sat side by side, where they could operate the fighter and still have face-to-face contact with each other. Behind the flight deck was a small living area for the three crew members, with a ladder and hatch up to the third crew position.

The Trinity bird had rapid-fire blasters on each wing tip and a secret weapon like none other in the galaxy! A double hind-cannon turret sat up high in the aft of the vessel. It provided a unique and superior vantage point for offense and defense, for both individual and formation purposes. The bird's powerful side-by-side twin engines allowed for surprising maneuverability for a craft of its size.

The Ryderson Omegans used the Trinity spacecraft in five-ship squadrons, utilizing a diamond formation with three vessels beside one another and one each on top and bottom of the middle ship. The middle fighter in the diamond was the squad leader, with the hind-cannon mainly protecting the rear flank of the squadron. The hind-cannons on the outside ships protected the left and right flanks from passing sweep attacks. The middle-upper and lower ships could use their vantage point to target the enemy as needed. To command a Trinity squadron, a pilot had to endure years of training and combat experience.

When they were in tight formation, Trinity squadrons were an unstoppable force. They had an iron will, and firepower to succeed against greater numbers!

Trinity fighters weren't contained in carriers, but were spacious for their crew of three and equipped for deep-space travel. Rather than carriers, the RO fleet employed 250 massive Titán cruisers to fight alongside the Trinitys and Trecon fleet. The powerful ships were used primarily for defense, patrolling the edges of the ROyale system in pairs.

Every set of defenders gave one of their team to the Raihan assault. They provided all they could for the fight. Any more would leave them short-handed if the Raihans invaded the RO system. There were many enemies still lurking, waiting for an opportunity to attack RO.

The formidable Titáns gave and took a pounding. Each had 120 plasma laser cannons distributed evenly around the warship. One Titán could stand on its own in battle for quite a while, until reinforcements arrived. They'd slug their way through the Raihan gauntlet, and arrive to provide support in space and on land.

Each Titán cruiser held 48 black-clad paratroopers called spiders, that descended to the surface in four free-falling Falcon gliders. When they reached a defense point or enemy planet, the cruisers descended in tandem teams toward a land battle. The pair would launch four Falcons apiece, 96 spider operatives total, at 20 kilometers above the surface. The pair of Titáns covered the Falcons with supreme firepower as they descended to the ground.

The spiders jumped from the Falcon gliders at an altitude of 8,200 meters from the battlefield. The last spider off the glider engaged a short-phase rocket motor that activated the seek and destroy capabilities of the Falcon. The Falcons spread out into an octagon formation, controlled by an operator on each Titán, under the direction of the tandem leader.

Each glider launched a javelin projectile with an energy convertor 70 meters from the ground. The rods were minimally energized and connected together to the other shafts through electric magnetism.

The energized area between the rods looked like a spider's web from the air as it fell.

The lead operator gained control of the octagon web after the spikes were locked together, and guided it to the ground.

In a matter of seconds, the spears burrowed the lightning rods into the landscape. Many webs could lock together to cover a massive area, scatter apart to take out hidden enemy positions, or form a protective ring around isolated comrades on the ground.

The spider operatives stayed inside the ring of gliders for protection as they fell. They used their tactical suits to stay in the atmosphere behind the buckler shielding of the Falcons until the web landed.

Ffffft, thud, bzzzzt!

The eight lightning rods energized, pulsating 200 milliamps of electricity between them. Nothing was spared as the grid-net of electrical current fried every circuit within a 16-hectare landing area! Enemy soldiers had to drop their blasters and evacuate war machines to avoid shocks and burns.

If webs were connected together to cover a larger area, the lethal energy force on the battlefield increased exponentially. The number of connected webs was proportionate to the size and strength of the enemy on the surface.

The spiders would wait for the field to de-energize and drop in as a group, landing in the safe zone created by the energy web. The spider troopers were a lethal force, ready for action, but often the battle was over before they hit the ground!

Since the webs were also meant for their planetary defense, the RO's wanted to disturb the land as little as possible. Except for scorched plant life, they accomplished their mission of leave no trace.

Traveling through deep space in Trinitys and Titán cruisers gave the RO's a nimble fleet, but the Raihans couldn't afford for them to arrive unscathed. RO command was sure Raihan had special plans for them.

*****

The newly acquainted Trinity crew desperately needed to build trust with one another in a short while. Abbsnate knew Onsan would be coming along with her into battle, so she needed to test his skills. "Onsan, jump in the gunner seat," ordered Abbsnate.

"I thought you'd never ask!"

She could sense him salivating on the inside while trying to hold a calm exterior. "We have a lot of training to do if you're to accompany me on the assault."

"Copy, I'm green-to-go!"

The hind-cannon gunner, Torek Dysen, was unsure of the newly formed crew; which included a Ryderson Omegan gone for 24 years and a Trecon who'd never seen a Trinity before!

A hind-gunner had to have total trust in their crew because they were out on an island when the battle began. Once they broke from deep space to attack position, they were locked away from the rest of the ship in their bubble. Hind-cannoneers were often the best target for the enemy. If they were hit, the Trinity pilots were instructed to detach the globe if it hindered the flying ability or mission of the ship.

They climbed into the Trinity and Abbsnate recited the checklist, "Systems check."

Torek announced, "Hind-cannon settings normal, ready. 360-degree horizontal-circumferential capacity and 75-degree vertical range operational. Weapons systems activated."

"All systems normal, ready for take-off," responded Onsan confidently.

"Increase throttles to lift off," Abbsnate ordered.

Onsan flipped the switch and eased the Trinity off the deck.

Rooaar!

The twin engines came to life and the Trinity lifted off the platform.

Throughout the next three weeks, the crew flew twelve intense training missions. First, they learned the ship and all its intricacies as a team, then they flew with a squadron, practicing the command position in the famous Ryderson Omegan diamond formation.

From early on, Onsan displayed a confidence and natural ability that put his two companions at ease with going into battle with him!

*****

Another dimension and a few galaxies away, the Trecons were arriving home. The reconditioned Mule entered the Trecon quadrant, and General Krevety opened the com lines for the first time, "Trecon Control, *Mule 357* requesting authorization to enter Trecon airspace. An escort would be appreciated!"

Immediately, Krevety could sense the distinct confusion in their response. *"Repeat message, Mule vessel, unable to read,"* said the startled controller in a stalling manner.

"Trecon Control, this is General Krevety, commander of Muudia mining operations. *Mule 357* requesting an escort into Trecon airspace."

There was a long pause on the other end, then disorderly and inaudible communication as the controller struggled to get a superior to the bridge. *"Please stand by. Hold your current position, Mule 357,"* came the long-awaited response. Trecon Control was not in a joking mood.

After about 10 minutes, a bewildered but direct response came from the Trecon Control night supervisor, *"Unidentified vessel, this is Major Fren Yarrek. Mule 357 was reported lost over six months ago. Stand fast."*

Krevety was very specific. He slowed his speech considerably the third time, "Major Yarrek, this is General Krevety, Muudia MOC (mining operations commander) in the Trecon supply ship *Mule 357*. We're arriving under unusual circumstances. Get me your commander at once!"

"We're sending a military escort to meet you. Any sudden moves will be your last!"

"Stop wasting time with threats, I need to talk to your superior, now, or you'll suffer the consequences!" General

Krevety was tiring of the games and pulled rank, which he hated to do.

Yarrek needed to cover his bases, if it *was* a general on the other line. *"Yes general."*

The sheepish answer indicated they were finally making progress. "Good!"

After 10 minutes, an irritated voice of an officer who'd been sleeping answered the com, *"This is General Beanne Hekerstine, Trecon Control commander. State your identity and request again!"*

General Krevety smiled. He and Beanne Hekerstine were close friends from back in their officer academy days. If he could pick one person to meet him, it would be Beanne!

As Krevety responded, he was almost giddy at the picture of the disheveled general in his robe trying to sort through his sleepy thoughts to strategize his next move. "Beanne, this is Tom Krevety. It's great to hear your voice! We're returning from the Muudia mission in the retrofitted *Mule 357*. We've been in deep space and on the run from Mihhidite pirates for months now. Would be nice to have a cup on Trecon soil once again. We've got a lot to talk about. Are you ready for one doozy of a story?"

The tone in Hekerstine's voice changed from skepticism to relief and anticipation. *"Of course, Tom. I'll put the coffee on."*

Shortly afterward, a pair of Starlance fighter craft approached the Mule and dipped their wings in a sort of salute to the reliable supply freighter and her honorable crew. After 30 minutes, Krevety was face-to-face with his friend Beanne, who offered him a steaming cup of coffee.

General Hekerstine filled Krevety in on the happenings on Trecon since their last contact. The supply convoy was feared a total loss. Hope for safe return of the carrier was rapidly fading. They hadn't been heard from since they were attacked by a fleet of Sharks. The only way to confirm their fears was to send another fleet into the hazardous zone. Communication with the "camps" had continued, where Trecon Control was being told by the MOC to stay away due to intense solar storms on the planet.

Control was gearing up to send an investigative fleet to the Pladia solar system again, but were strongly discouraged from the settlements. "Funny thing, I thought I communicated with you from the camp yesterday! The message was patchy, but I sensed it was from the interference. Come to think of it, something wasn't right. You seemed like an emotionless robot. Thought you were just down in the dumps about being stuck there."

"You were tricked my friend. We all were!" General Krevety explained that they were canned messages sent by the Raihans.

Krevety assured his friend that travel to Muudia was perilous, but not impossible. In fact, they'd have to return there soon. Their goal reached far beyond the riches of the planet and through a portal on the other side; and their very survival hinged on success! Rather than an investigative team, they needed to build and send an invasion fleet to recover their losses and rescue their miners from a powerful planet named Raihan.

General Krevety spent countless hours with Oghy, squeezing him of information. Since Trecon was still in the harvesting cycle, the planet was infested with spies sending and receiving encrypted high-frequency information to Raihan. Trecons would have to act fast to diffuse and counteract their sabotaging efforts. Although Oghy didn't know names or locations of his fellow spies, he divulged trade secrets that would make them easier to locate.

Their usage of code words and frequencies made them easy targets if one knew where to look, and the transmitter rings would give them away during intensified credential checks. Nbnok and Davss had derived the originating frequency signal from the ring. If the rings were still being used by infiltrators, they'd know what to look for. By reversing the signal, they identified five spies right away and conducted unified raids in the port city of Gooseberry Rapids.

The Raihans had disguised themselves as merchant traders in the industrial port. The authorities easily detained three moles in their homes. The other two were suddenly concerned with self-preservation, and were captured together in a cargo ship trying to escape into the atmosphere.

*****

The Trecons geared up for war. They activated the best fighter craft and pilots in the galaxy! Leadership took inventory of their war assets. They were able to spare 250 Bruiser carriers and still leave the planet with a strong defense, meaning 2,500 Starlance fighters would be included in the fleet.

Each carrier held 100 Trecon marines, which would be brought to the planet's surface by four Boulder troop carriers housed within the hulls of the Bruisers. The Boulder carriers were boxy and slow, so Brawler escorts would have to clear a path to the planet's surface before they were launched. Krevety knew that 25,000 marines were a small force for the mission, but it was the best they could do under the circumstances.

The Starlance fighters would stay loaded on the Bruisers until they were safely through the portal, then exit the carriers for combat operations. Brawler destroyers and Boxer frigates would provide agile cover fire for the carriers until the fighters could launch into battle.

Trecon pilots would make their mark in the war for sure, flying one of the most feared warships in the galaxy! The Starlance was a durable craft with dual reciprocating blasters on each wing. Her electronic weapons system was accurate to within 15 centimeters of a target at 10 kilometers.

In the nose of the fighter was a rotating dome called the auto-bastion. As the Starlance banked, the dome leaned into the turn and projected a heavy-duty frontal shield that gave it protection. The extra shielding afforded maximum protection for head-on assaults. The unique design of the shielding allowed the spacecraft to attack larger warships head-on with a minimal fear of reprisal, then cover for one another during temporary retreat before the next round of attacks.

One engine provided exceptional thrust, which allowed the space fighter to zoom out of range after their frontal barrage, climbing and diving at sharp accelerating angles. She was a first-rate ship, but what made her great were the well-trained Starlance fighter pilots! Starlance pilots were subjected to an intense training program, even before being allowed into the cockpit!

The Trecons were well-known for their patience in training and preparation. The situation was no different, even in their shortened period of preparing their fleet. They studied the Talon fighter intently, striving to become masters of it in a short while. They took it out for training sorties around the clock with their best pilots, learning the capabilities and limitations of the diminutive fighter.

Trecon leadership knew a greater understanding of the strengths and limitations of the Raihan fighter was required for success against the larger fleet. Simulated dogfights between the Talon and Starlance racked up hours fast, as leadership gained valuable data. To their amazement, the fighter held up well despite the demands placed on her.

They pushed the Talon hard until traces of system overheating were evident after 75 hours of heavy continuous usage. Without proper tools or replacement parts to repair her, the Talon was decommissioned. The tests offered welcomed data they'd use to Trecon advantage! If the coalition could hold out for three days, they might gain the upper hand in the atmospheric war.

CHAPTER 32

The Wanderers and the Underground Resistance

The Wanderers had few resources to fight with, but they'd cause havoc and sabotage as best they could.

Serlat's "army" slowly started an advance toward the Raihan main Base 13 with 2000 under gunned but determined insurgents; visitant Wanderers and native Raihan nomads trooping side by side toward conflict. With the primary communication of the Wanderers being from underground resistance Integrators who feared being caught, Serlat didn't know if they were preparing for an assault or just going for a long pilgrimage through the wasteland to meet their final fate at the hands of the vicious Mihhidites. The outcasts had no choice but to act on vague information.

Bodak was excited to be on the move. His dark brown hair bounced with every step as he talked with Rander. "Finally, we get to see our debt paid in Raihan blood!"

"Easy brother," cautioned Rander. "Many things have to work out perfectly before we can do a victory dance. Look around. This doesn't look like an army. We look like we should be standing in a soup line!"

All around them, people were dressed in cast-off clothes. The brothers wore matching blue mechanic's coveralls and worn black flak vests. Rander insisted they look alike, so they could look out for each other on the battlefield.

"I'm going to play an important part in the end, you'll see!"

Rander nodded and walked ahead. Sweat was already pooling on his neck, and running down his back. It would be a long trek, and he needed a break from Bodak.

The ragtag group started marching toward their objectives, moving by night to avoid detection for as long as possible. They were physically famished, but their spirits were fueled by hope as they migrated toward Base 13. Eventually, they split into two smaller groups. One consisted of 500, led by Ranard Ryderson Reud, (nicknamed RRR), to attack the communication outpost. The other group of 1,500 led by Serlat, was to provide a diversion at Base 13. "Farewell Ranard, Godspeed on your journey. I hope to see you safe again on the other side, whatever this turns out to be!"

"You as well comrade. We've persevered much together. Let's take our freedom back!"

Serlat wanted to be in the fighting group, but arthritis in his knees would have made him a liability on the battlefield.

The two factions parted ways where the desert rose into craggy foothills. RRR's younger group climbed toward the communication facility, and Serlat's stayed on the flat ground toward Base 13.

The main objective of both groups was to help the underground overtake the outpost long enough to send an impulse message to a friendly fleet in deep space. RRR's group took all the weapons with them, leaving the Base 13 group in a perilous position. The Wanderer militia scattered during the day to prevent detection as best they could. They knew that chances of reaching their targets undetected was small, but they had to try.

They hoped that by the time they were noticed, the Raihans would have more to worry about than a small group of hungry Wanderers knocking on their doorstep. Nobert Serlat knew his neck was on the line as the unquestionable leader of the Wanderer resistance, no matter how the invasion ended. Their timing had to be close. If they arrived to the "party" before their space partners, they'd be in serious trouble!

Serlat knew they needed to have a cover story so they weren't left hanging in the wind. If he were blamed for the insurrection, then at least his followers might be returned to the wilderness to fight another day. He decided they'd stage a protest march against their current living conditions, demanding larger portions of food and more frequent supply drops from the Mihhidite patrols. Hopefully the riot cover story would protect everyone involved on the inside if they failed, but Serlat knew it was unlikely because of the invasion.

There'd been two riots in the distant past. Both times leadership were captured easily while the main force was pushed back into the wilderness, only to see their rations decreased for two months. In both cases the leaders were never seen again. The first riots were highly unorganized, with the factions fighting among themselves along the way.

Serlat hoped that the fighter escorts would arrive swiftly and provide them adequate cover. There was a lot weighing on his mind as they made their way closer to the Raihan civilization under a star-filled sky. He thought of Abbsnate, and wondered which star she was closest to. She was out there somewhere thinking of him, he was sure of it!

The mass traveled hungry and light during the day to keep up appearances and give credibility to their supposed grievances. At night, they ate better and collected weapons from stashes placed on the dedicated route. Night may have been good for their bellies; but the majority were freezing in the open desert in threadbare rags.

Serlat ran their camps cold so they didn't draw the attention that dozens of large fires would have demanded. He was a leader of high integrity, ensuring he suffered the same hardships as everyone else. This endeared Serlat to his ragged army; they'd march through a brick wall for him if they had to!

The information assured them it was the best time in history for the united Wanderers to act. Serlat had no idea if the spy who'd delivered the information had slipped detection, or was going through unimaginable tortures within the Base 13 Gallows at that very moment to pay for activities of treason. He wouldn't let the informant suffer for nothing!

As the leader, Serlat had to consider many factors. He'd chose to act, but had pressing concerns weighing on him. Had the authorities simply got wind of the resistance plans and staged an elaborate deception to cut off the head of the resistance? There was a possibility that the information was a trap; staged to draw out revolutionary Integrators within, and crush a Wanderers rebellion growing in strength and numbers!

Many things could go wrong, but they were beyond the point of no return. Serlat was prepared to abort the mission in an instant and give himself up at the first sign of Raihan deception. He knew that the uprising was his greatest challenge as a leader. If the Raihans weren't on to him as the Wanderer leader, they would be now! He came to peace with the fact he'd most likely be taken away to a solitary place where his torture and death couldn't influence others if the uprising wasn't successful.

*****

The Raihans were never secure of the alliances of their citizens due to the makeup of their population. They ensured eyes and ears were constantly monitoring the inhabitants for signs of revolt. They encouraged Integrators to spy on one another. A reward system implemented that compensated Integrators for information leading to the capture of spies within their ranks. Mostly, the Integrators felt they were merely being good citizens within a neighborhood crime-watch system. Integrators loyal to Raihan didn't like others messing up a good thing for them.

As a precautionary measure, administration conducted random psychological testing and interviews to detect political and demographic trends that might lead to cracks and rot within their contented society. They placed Contributor spies within the ranks to report any words or actions that weren't consistent with Raihan values. Mihhidite secret police raided Integrator suspects with the same consistency and brutality that had them gaining power within the highest levels of government!

The Integrators had every freedom imaginable, but if they were brought to order they'd lose it all. They'd have to explain their whereabouts and actions down to the minutest detail at the drop of a hat. If an Integrator was caught doing anything questionable, they'd be subjected to intense interrogation at the Base 13 Gallows.

A battered Integrator would be released into prison only after the authorities were satisfied they could glean no more information from them! Once a prisoner entered the grimy halls of the Gallows, they'd never feel the sun on their skin again. Most of the Integrator spies held up. Whenever unscheduled raids happened on the Wanderer settlements, Serlat knew an Integrator had given in to torture.

In charge of the disturbing Base 13 Gallows was Slae Nodk, an evil Mihhidite who enjoyed dishing out punishment in his role as the lead inquisitor. He was short in stature with a burning Napoleon complex that fueled his cruelty. Like the other Mihhidite pirates and secret police, Nodk and his crew were revolutionizing the Raihan position of violence and aggression throughout Raihan reach!

All Mihhidites enjoyed their violent dirty work for Raihan, but none more than Slae Nodk! His only mission in life was to get every piece of useful information from a prisoner before he allowed them to die miserably. He was well compensated for his sadistic imagination, given full authority of the Base 13 Gallows from a government that replaced compassion with "out of sight, out of mind."

Nodk's horrible tactics had recently cracked Prisoner 19-128.25 like so many others before him. Prisoner 19-128.25

wasn't hard to break, depression made him easy to push over the edge.

The evil man was accompanied in power at the prison by another sadistic Mihhidite, Lorri Freolj. She was the female counterpart to Nodk, managing the female wing of the Base 13 Gallows. Her prisoners included Wanderer mothers who'd been taken from the wastelands to have their children, then charged as Wanderer informants. The Raihans couldn't have the Wanderer mothers spreading word about the true living conditions in the wastelands, nor could they allow them back into Wanderer society telling the others about secrets within the walls.

Although Freolj was not as cruel as Nodk, being under her watch was no picnic. Her preferred method of misery was hard labor rather than torture. A Wanderer mother accused of treason was given no trial or time to recover from emotional trauma. They were forced to work twelve hours a day under close watch in the fields of the agricultural center, harvesting food for the population.

Worst of all for the mothers was being separated from their children, which was of no concern to Freolj. Once a child hit four years of age, they were admitted into the academy, and the two would be permanently disconnected anyway. The greatest hope that kept the mothers alive were the dreams of seeing their children again!

As the invasion neared, a big fish was delivered to Nodk.

Shortly after Serlat received the message about the communication facility, Doctor Hetle Orbne got caught because he cancelled an appointment in his office with no solid alibi. The doctor knew about the incoming invasion, but hadn't sent the dispatch directly. The fact was, the Raihans didn't know about the message. Orbne's only crime was asking his patients too many questions!

Through his position as a military physician, Orbne had direct access to data at the tip of the spear. His job was to give physicals to the Talon pilots. One month before the softening mission, he'd connected with Abbsnate. Afterward, the rumor had gotten around about a defection and mishap during the softening mission. No names were given, but when she didn't check in, Orbne knew Abbsnate was involved.

A short while later, when the demand for his services increased due to the immense number of Talon pilots needed, Orbne assumed that Abbsnate had succeeded in whatever she was up to, and an invasion was imminent. His mind went back and forth between excitement and worry. He feared for her safety. *Stay safe my friend, I hope to see you again!*

After a slip of the tongue from several sources, Orbne knew it was time to get a message to the Wanderers. He channeled the sketchy details to his secret contact. His information indicated an imminent attack on Raihan in about two months' time. The Wanderers would attack Com-Facility 12, the closest to them. It was one of many signal amplifiers that encircled the planet to enhance export communication capability. Com-Facility 12 was in the middle of nowhere where its signal could be powerfully transmitted free of potential interference within urban areas.

If the Wanderers could disable the facility temporarily, their inside partners would take care of the rest. A distress message would make the efforts of the invaders fruitful as they tried to organize a league of planets against the Raihans. Dr. Orbne had been under suspicion for some time at the point of his capture, and had a feeling he'd be caught. He was arrested and sent to the Base 13 Gallows, where he'd never see another day of freedom if it were up to the Mihhidite jailers.

Minutes after entering the prison, Orbne was brought before the Commandant Slae Nodk, who called for the new prisoner immediately upon his arrival. The Mihhidite was ecstatic to have a Contributor connected with the underground resistance. Contributors had more access to information. Nodk was sure he'd make the dominoes fall starting with Orbne, and crush the resistance once and for all!

Hetle Orbne was a small man with dark skin, dusky brown eyes, and a receding hairline. The stature and gentle nature of the doctor amused the cruel Mihhidites. They tossed him against the walls, drug him when he tripped, and shoved him forward when he got back up to his feet. By the time Orbne was brought before Nodk, he was scraped, bruised, and bloodied. The doc had a look of horror on his scratched face.

Once the weary doctor was brought in, Nodk began his regular speech with a sadistic smile. Orbne could smell the sickening stench of body odor emanating from Nodk as he talked. The Mihhidite purposely performed a strenuous workout to get his stink glands going before he talked to the prisoners. He wanted every aspect of their experience to be as miserable as possible. As he leaned in toward the prisoner, his yellowing unbrushed teeth and malodorous breath had an overwhelming smell of garlic and onions mixed with stagnant mud puddle water.

"Welcome home, Hetle Orbne! I want to make your stay as comfortable as possible," he sarcastically hissed. "We have much to talk about, so you'll be seeing a lot of me as we get to know each other!" Nodk moved nose to nose with Orbne. "You see, you have information that I want, and I always get what I want in the end! I'm a professional, like you. If you open up and give me information, I'll go easier on you. However, if you prove to be stubborn, you'll be in constant pain without a moment's rest. Either way doesn't matter to me!"

In Nodk's mind, Orbne would be tortured repeatedly until he told them names of fellow underground resistance Contributors and Integrators, and any other information he knew. In the underground, the resistance agents knew very few fellow collaborators for that reason. They reported to one leader and didn't know specifics of one another for protection of everyone upon capture. Most of the time, a resistance member knew little other than the code name and location of their group leader. The sites changed every week.

Orbne was slightly comforted that he really didn't have any information that Nodk could use. Dr. Orbne tried to bluff a brave face, but his profuse sweating gave away his true feelings of terror.

"I have nothing to say to you!"

The detainee knew that his life was basically over, and he had to concentrate on keeping his senses for the prescribed time while his contact covered their tracks or defected to the Wanderers.

The doctor had a wealth of information about specifics of his captive planet, but that was all. It wasn't a crime to be knowledgeable about official Raihan history. He knew everything the Raihans put out, but dug deeper and read between the lines. Orbne spent his time researching the higher classes of the Raihan society; those ultimately responsible for tricking others into mining the ore rather than putting their own necks and bloodlines in harm's way. The end goal for the resistance was that the Raihans be convicted and tried for their long-standing crimes.

Wallop, riinng!

A blow to the side of the head quickly brought Orbne back to the present.

Smash!

Nodk worked himself up, and punched Orbne in the nose.

"You'll have plenty to say soon," Nodk retorted to the man with blood trickling down from his nose into his mouth. "You'll be begging me to tell me what you know!"

Slae Nodk was not one to wait because he felt it would give the prisoner a false sense of power over the situation. He ordered Orbne be brought to his personal interrogation chamber immediately. It was a race against time to crush the underground resistance!

*****

In the outskirts of Rochest, the government tightened the noose on the underground resistance following the doctor's

255

capture. Fana Tobor had avoided suspicion somehow, even after her partner Hetle Orbne had been taken into custody. Word going out was suspended until things cooled down. The underground didn't want the Raihans to look closer out into the wilderness and destroy the Wanderer militia.

Tobor spent every day looking over her shoulder and waiting for her inevitable capture. Her last mission was passing a written note through a side gate to a supply carrier, weeks before Orbne's capture. Tobor knew she may be under close surveillance, but had to get the latest information out before she pulled out of the game completely.

With the message, Fana Tobor had essentially launched the underground assault operation! After the message was out, she stuck strictly to her schedule, not deviating from it for so much as to meet a friend for a spontaneous dinner.

Tobor feared for the fate of her friend Hetle Orbne. She didn't want to waste his sacrifice or inadvertently lead the Raihans to the underequipped Wanderers.

CHAPTER 33

Formidable Raihan Prepares Defenses for Attack

As rumors of war spread throughout the galaxy, nearby governments were curious who was foolish enough to attempt such a feat as to attack the brute in her own backyard! Raihan was viewed by their neighbors like a giant bully walking around an elementary playground during recess. The Raihans had 700 Vengeance destroyers, 350 Vehemence carriers, and close to 20,000 Talons waiting in orbit for anyone who dared to attack them; plus hundreds of ships in the surrounding systems and a giant fleet of Mihhidite Sharks at their disposal!

The Raihans were supremely confident as they prepared for the siege, knowing they outmatched the Trecons and Ryderson Omegans by sheer number. They knew it would be a challenge for the aggressors to reach Raihan in the first place, because there was quite a gauntlet to get through first. They had a special plan in store for each ally.

The Trecons were the weak link, not respected by Raihan military leadership like the Ryderson Omegans because of their convoluted path to Raihan. There were many cosmic dangers associated with the portal that would give the Trecons anguish before they continued on their mission. Magnetic storms, solar flares, meteorite fields, and excess radiation would play havoc with the electronics of the Trecon fleet and test their resolve even before they reached the event horizon of the Laurus portal!

They'd be tested once again when they emerged through the Magnus exit, even before their first encounter with a Raihan vessel! The conditions had already taken out a Trecon supply fleet, and the invasion force would be flying the same treacherous path as the doomed convoy had. The Trecons would feel the effects of radiation sickness and vertigo as they exited the portal. They'd be prime targets for the Raihan armada as they attempted to exit and gain enough composure to continue their assault path.

The Raihans sent a decent group to the mouth of the portal, but not an overwhelming fleet because they didn't feel it was necessary. Raihan leadership presumed the Trecons would lose many ships attempting to throttle their large fleet through the portal if they could delay the first group through for just a few minutes. The meteorite field at the exit was so tight, having more than 25 Raihan warships in the area would've been a waste of resources. They'd simply wait in the ergosphere, where it'd be like shooting fish in a barrel!

The Trecon ships would have to come through a few at a time with no cover, where Raihans would be waiting on the other side to blast them into eternity, providing they didn't hit an asteroid or run into the backs of one another trying to exit the portal! The orders of the "welcoming committee" were to inflict transitory damage as the Trecons passed through. The natural bottleneck of the portal zone meant the Raihans could inflict great damage simply by firing a heavy barrage of laser fire into the fray. They knew the Trecons couldn't stay and fight because they had to clear the way for the next wave of ships coming through the portal.

The orders of the fleet were to hold at the ergosphere and wait for the wounded Trecons to return, then join the pursuing Raihans to finish them as they attempted to escape back through.

A different strategy was employed for the Ryderson Omegans. The Raihans would have to provide a more formidable gauntlet for them to clear before they reached Raihan. Ryderson Omega was closer with more accessibility to Raihan, so they would be dealt with more viciously than the distant Trecons.

Eyes around the galaxy would see a skirmish between two highly respected governments, which wasn't unusual. The Raihans would have to represent themselves well! President Grolegg knew they had to destroy and colonize the twin planets to keep them from getting the facts out. Winners of wars get to fill the history books with their version of the truth.

Raihan leadership had two large fleets hunting the Ryderson Omegan armada as they entered their quadrant of the galaxy. Nearly 2,000 Mihhidite Shark destroyers led by Boirt Zalbek would survey the area to rigidly oppose the RO's. A massive flagship Raihan fleet was also in the quadrant hunting them. The main purpose of the first fleet to encounter the RO's was to block and stall them for as long as possible, until the second one arrived to finish them off.

Even if the RO's survived, the Raihans were confident the Trecon fleet would be destroyed. With word of the Trecons retreating, any remaining Ryderson Omegans would have to decide if it was worth it to face the brunt of Raihan wrath alone. They'd likely retreat and head for the safety of the ROyale solar system.

After the initial battle was well in hand, the Mihhidite Sharks would separate and set course for the edge of the ROyale solar system, where they'd report their findings and wait for Raihan comrades to arrive with a gargantuan invading fleet! Should any RO's survive, they'd run headlong into a Mihhidite ambush and be put out of commission once and for all! It was the same hammer-and-anvil approach that the Raihans were planning to use against the retreating Trecons.

There'd be no quarter granted to the Ryderson Omegan fleet as they fled; they'd have to serve as an example for anyone else senseless enough to attack the Raihans! In the mind of President Grolegg, the divide and-conquer method was their best option. They held the initiative and were about to lay the hammer down on the forces that dared attack them!

If the allies arrived on Raihan, they'd find a ready and waiting force waiting for them! She had 20 bases encompassing her, with main Base 13 billeted by a large military force of 210,000 soldiers protecting her capital, main scientific and government centers. Every possible scenario was scripted and prepared for; the Raihans had a feeling of invulnerability as they prepared to defend themselves against the intruders.

The defending Talon pilots would look to their left and right to see the cosmos filled with thousands of their comrades. The Raihans knew the allies would put up a tough fight, but also didn't have the numbers to compete with them in the long run. The intruders would simply wear down to the superior numbers of the Talons buzzing around them.

The Talon space fighters were small single-piloted crafts, nimble and deadly in numbers. They had a single engine in the back and dual blasters affixed to their wing tips designed to provide rapid fire and wear down shields enough to eventually destroy their target. They were diminutive, ultra-responsive machines. Group maneuverability made them a challenge to destroy. Talons worked together in a single unit of thousands to provide an organized and never-ending rotation of fighters.

They attacked directly then dove off to outflank their opponent before circling back and restarting the cycle. Their level of training was not like the Starlance or Trinity pilots. Rather, they were taught to be a small part of a large machine. If they did their job, they'd ultimately succeed in their goals. There was never meant to be freelancing with a Talon pilot in a space battle. Everyone was to focus on keeping and holding their position within the formation. Their tactics were hypnotic, no one thought about the larger objective of the mission.

There was a logical explanation for their strategy. There were so many Talon pilots it would have been impossible to ensure quality training for everyone. Instead, they were taught to fly the craft and attack in one particular formation. They attacked an adversary in tight, unrelenting waves of consistency, wearing down enemy pilots to the point of exhaustion!

The Raihan strategists decided they wouldn't send a large fleet into deep space or enter the chaos of the portal to meet their foe, but slowly nick them so they'd be bleeding to death by the time they reached the superior forces of Raihan nestled deep within the borders of the Poeihf Solar System. There, the sapped attackers would face the largest fleet at their strongest! Within the halls of Rochest, President Grolegg thought the war would reach a conclusion before the raiding fleets arrived to face the final impact of Raihan's mighty blows.

The Raihans would wipe their enemies out quickly. Then they'd send invading forces to the weakened planets in accordance with their latest goal, the Reaper Initiative!

CHAPTER 34

Allies Racing to the Doorstep of Raihan

The allies used a game plan of their own for the formidable mammoth of Raihan. At a glance, the Raihans appeared invincible. However, Abbsnate knew their secret: Raihan was long on military capacity and equipment but short on tactical experience.

The allied forces knew the chips were stacked against them. The Raihans would be running interference at every turn, so an unwavering trust in their vision would need to be held unchanged. Despite the uncertainties, they had a solid blueprint in place. Courage, self-control, wisdom, and justice were the cornerstones for victory for the allies!

Once the coalition combined fleets, they'd be safer and stronger than they were apart, so Raihan would do everything within their power to deal with them separately. Setting a specific coordinate and time was necessary for them to continue on and pursue their goal of a realistic victory.

The allies were counting heavily on each other to do their part to make the plan work. They employed warships and pilots vastly superior to the Raihans, so it was not an impossible mission for them. Theirs wasn't a perfect plan, but it was all they had considering the circumstances.

Abbsnate assured them that the Raihans were a one-trick pony. The defenders were no match for them, if they could just hold out long enough to rattle their confidence. Allied pilot wings weren't merely handed out like they were on Raihan, but had to be earned time and time again in training and battle!

The majority of encounters the Raihan aeronauts gained was through limited roles in softening and harvesting operations on Planet 6333, firing at minimal defensive targets. Raihan warships were window dressing, as the Mihhidites did most of the dirty work. The Raihan pilots relied on strict protocol to see them through situations. Things were different in the chaos of battle! Getting fired upon for the first time by experienced pilots would make a difference. Quick-wit reactions in the bedlam of dogfights was the difference between winning and losing the war.

The Trecons had less-recent combat experience than the Ryderson Omegans, their latest battles being in the Iug Wars nearly a decade before, but their tough military and the advanced technical training was second to none. Their invading fleet of 250 Bruiser carriers, 200 Brawler destroyers, and 25 Boxer frigates were large and shielded enough to safely get through the wormhole, yet nimble enough to handle themselves in the bottleneck battle on the far side. Once they made it through the portal, they'd unleash their legendary Starlance fighters to give them the needed push into deep space to their meeting point and on to Raihan. They wanted to be there fighting the Raihans and feared nothing!

Each Bruiser carrier was loaded with a cache of ten Starlance fighters, fearless and aggressive masters of their machines. Most fighters carried no bombs, nor were they accompanied by traditional bombers. Bombers weren't nimble enough to evade the overwhelming numerical odds of the defenders, and would be easy targets for destruction. The selected bomb-carrying Starlances had a specific purpose, to join Abbsnate's special fleet and conduct risky strikes on the governmental centers in the Raihan capital of Rochest.

The bulk of the allied assaults would be more sweeping self-defense than surgical, ultimately counting on support from within the Raihan Integrator ranks to achieve victory. There were many innocents on Raihan who'd been brainwashed throughout the years. Indiscriminate bombing raids would be counterproductive to their goals.

At the helm within the lead command vessel was CJ, recently promoted to Bruiser captain because of his ability and experiences. CJ earned the honor to pilot Krevety's ship because he'd navigated the Mule through the portal, and showed competency on the bridge during many intense situations. Within the lead Bruiser were Major Tallik, Milerous, Etan Esa-erg, Pnoi Nbnok, and Hebel Greten among others. Etan didn't feel right about going to Ryderson like they'd originally planned. He wanted to be fighting alongside his friends.

Krevety had gotten sick each time through the hazard zone, and couldn't afford the same result during an attack. He voted down the offer to have someone else lead the attack. He knew more about the circumstances than anyone else, so he was the right choice.

The warships were fortified with more robust shielding and radiation protection than the Mules, but the fleet took extra precautions just the same. Each ship was retrofitted with large anechoic chambers, and every crewmember had to spend eight hours a day in them. It was a crude way of dealing with the problem, but also the best solution. As they navigated through the hazard zone, the method proved successful.

*****

The fleet gave Muudia a wide berth on their way to the portal entrance, but they could see the planet in the distance going through its glowing makeover in the portal zone. The suffering world was in its early autumn season as they entered the ergosphere. The region was less dangerous than before, but Abbsnate assured them that going through the deathtrap zone in the final weeks of H-Class 8 conditions would be no picnic!

CJ addressed Krevety. "We'll proceed through on your command, general."

General Krevety gave the order to the fleet over the intercom, "Red alert. Battle stations. Starlance pilots, strap into your fighters and prepare to launch when we come out the other side. Complete your checklists. Report back when ready."

A bustle of activity filled the warships as preparations were made for battle. The fleet slowed at the edge of the meteorite-filled event horizon and prepared to send the lead ships into the abyss.

After six minutes, nearly all the sections had checked in.

Tallik reported from the fighter bay, *"Starlance pilots all green to go, sir!"*

"Set the coordinates to stay clear of the Magnus meteorite field, and raise shields to 100 percent. Be sure to leave a frequency trail for the others to follow," ordered CJ as they prepared to go through the portal.

"Everything is set, engines are ready," called Milerous from the engineering room after he'd ensured the calibrations a second time. *Much different than the first few times going through in the Mule,* he thought.

CJ turned to Krevety, "Prepared and ready to launch, sir."

General Krevety ordered, "Then lead the way captain, begin our assault!"

"Throttle ahead at two thirds speed."

Milerous responded with an excited, rickety voice. *"No turning back now!"*

Rumble, roar!

The ships thundered to life and the first group initiated the attack!

Three Bruisers, two destroyers, and a frigate launched themselves into the event horizon. Everyone was in awe as they were treated to the spectacle of color playing out before their eyes. Once they hit the "sweet spot," CJ increased to full throttle to counteract the Laurus gravity gripping at the vessel as it sped into a kaleidoscope of purples, yellows, and reds toward the middle vacuum point.

As they continued on through the midpoint, Milerous expertly throttled down and let inertia take them to where Magnus beckoned them forward again. Being a target for a few seconds was a better option than screaming through and getting destroyed by a meteor at the mouth of the exit!

As the Trecon group exited, they were surrounded by flashes of bright red and brass yellow—some of the streaks being natural effects of the portal, and others from lasers by the Raihan warships waiting for them!

Fzzzeeew, fzzzeeew!

The Raihans blasted away at the Trecon invasion fleet!

Crush, bash!

Massive bully rocks waited to greet them with pounding fists as the Trecons fought to gain their bearing!

Heave!

fzzzeeew, boom!

Their stomachs felt queasy, and many succumbed to the urge to throw up into garbage cans. The Trecon ships struggled to orientate themselves forward under heavy fire. Meteorites and ice were suspended about them in a radiated soup of death!

They evaded debris cluttering the mouth of the exit as best they could, which slowed their escape into deep space where they could maneuver, evade, and fight back. CJ had been through the portal and back, so his input had been a significant part to their invasion plan. He knew they needed to exit at a sharp angle as soon as possible. He leaned on the controls with all his weight!

"Move!"

Boom, shudder!

Krevety ignored the feeling in his stomach and announced as calmly as he was able, "We need to push through and make way for the next group!"

Fighting the Raihans and navigating the meteorite field in the ergosphere was only part of the equation. Each wave was to enter through at a prescribed time of two minutes. They needed to continue forward quickly. If they were delayed, the leading ships would be rear-ended by their comrades.

"Turn back, abort mission immediately! Perilous conditions Magnus side of portal! Abort! Abort! Abort!"

"Arghh, nooo!"

The Raihans were sending propaganda interference through the portal, and intense screams filled the loudspeakers of the Trecon ships!

Krevety called his tech commander, "Dach, are you hearing that?"

Commander Bryn Dach hailed the fleet from his Boxer. *"On it general! Changing our com frequency immediately. New message to fleet is to disregard the messages and continue through!"*

Raihan diversionary tactics were powerful, so the invasion fleet included the Boxers to send and receive authenticated information among the allies. The frigates also orchestrated the Starlance attacks through constant contact with squadron leaders within a group. Dach's tech warriors worked diligently to stop the false transmissions. The next batch ignored the Raihans and slugged their way through the portal!

*****

On the other side of the galaxy, the Ryderson Omegan fleet rocketed toward their deep-space meeting point with the Trecons.

The Trinity trio got well-acquainted within the hull of their craft during their journey. They had an easy and uneventful trip until they approached the edge of the Poeihf solar system, where they encountered a large fleet of Mihhidite Sharks intent on blocking their way as they entered the Raihan quadrant.

Torek Dysen left his seat behind Abbsnate and Onsan. He stated, "Battle positions. Here we go, let's take them out!" He climbed the loft ladder to his hind-cannon position and closed the hatch.

"I'll shake your hands after we get through this!"

"Affirmative, stay safe Torek."

Onsan closed the adjoining hatch from the cockpit, as he'd been trained to. A moment later, Dysen called on the intercom, "Horizontal-circumferential capacity and vertical range fully functional. Hind-cannon locked and loaded!" After spending a few weeks' time traveling through lonely deep space in confined conditions, the crew was eager to see action.

"Separate into attack formation," ordered Abbsnate. "Let's take it to them!"

A group of five Trinitys were virtually impenetrable as they could attack and defend simultaneously in their patented diamond formation. Onsan's heart was pounding through his chest as they rocketed into their position in the shadow of a Titán. He had always dreamed of being a Starlance pilot, but this was to be his first taste of actual combat!

The Ryderson Omegan fleet raced in to confront their enemies with an aggression the Mihhidites had never experienced before.

Vzzt vzzt, boom!

The Mihhidites were used to being the bullies, not the targets! The Sharks looked apprehensive from the start, firing laser blasts into the fray prematurely, sorely missing their mark. The erratic display was comical to the Ryderson Omegans; it was as if they didn't need to raise their shields against the shaken pirates!

Vzzt vzzt!

Bright flash, splinter!

The RO fleet rapidly became elusive as each squadron separated and prepared for battle. The Mihhidites couldn't seem to hit the broadside of a barn as they quickly realized their usual intimidation factor had been reversed. The RO fleet were not merchant ships or surprised miners—they were the real deal!

Roar, bzzzttt, crush!!

The Titáns rumbled into action, blasting at the Sharks with a merciless barrage of firepower! Each Titán cruiser fired all 120 cannons toward the shaken pirates, disabling scores in a matter of seconds!

BOOM BOOM BOOM BOOM BOOM!

As the RO fleet viciously attacked their enemy, it was quickly established that the Mihhidites were no match for the fierce armada of the Ryderson Omegans. Within the first minute of battle, 125 pirate Sharks were exploding into glowing ashes, and others were attempting to turn about in retreat.

Crunch, spark, kaboom!

Two ships crashed into each other as they tried to evacuate the fight, and were quickly destroyed by an advancing RO Trinity squadron. The 2,000 Mihhidite Sharks parted for the RO fleet like the Red Sea for Moses, turning tail and running after a few minutes of ineffective harassment! The "tough" Mihhidites were fierce when they had a distinct advantage, but it was clear who the superior pilots were in the encounter!

Torek Dysen used his vantage point and confirmed, *"The Mihhidite Sharks are in full retreat. They aren't coming back for another round. They've failed miserably in their attempt to stop us."*

Kohgg Ufi, the commander in the lead Titán, hailed Abbsnate's ship. *"The Mihhidites aren't retreating. They're waiting for the Raihan fleet to come into range. They're trying to trap us."*

*****

In the lead Shark, Ufi's suspicion was confirmed. Boirt Zalbek had never experienced a beat-down like they'd just received. He decided it was best to let the RO fleet pass, match their speed, and meet up with the Raihan fleet where they'd come together and destroy the enemy. He altered the Raihan plan out of self-preservation, and his disobedience gave the RO's a sliver of opportunity.

"The dispatch has been sent, General Zalbek. Our sister fleet is approaching from the neighboring system at 75,000 kilometers."

"Excellent. Fall back. There's no reason to sacrifice ourselves. We'll stick to them like glue from 200 kilometers, and wait for our partners to arrive."

*****

During the next eight hours, the Mihhidites followed as close as they dared. The Ryderson Omegans knew their plot, but couldn't stop and finish the fight. Soon the bad news came as expected to the RO fleet.

Commander Ufi hailed Abbsnate from his Titán, *"Trinity commander. A Raihan flagship fleet is approaching our starboard side and trying to flank us at 8,000 kilometers. If you take the 3,600 Trinity fighters and forge ahead port, you're nimble enough to skirt around the battle. We'll turn about and fight the Mihhidite fleet so they don't follow you."*

"But you don't have enough firepower to stand alone against them both. We could take them out here and now if we fought them together!"

"We'd only be playing into their hands. Getting bogged down here would be disastrous. Remember the bigger picture and follow your orders. You're to meet the Trecons and attack Raihan. Don't worry about us, we can handle ourselves."

"Yes commander."

Abbsnate knew the colossal Titáns were powerful and hoped Ufi could hold out, but knew the disadvantage was likely too great. She knew Ufi was right, there was a bigger picture to look at. If they all stayed, the Trecons would be in serious trouble.

"Trinity squadrons, set course for our allies," announced Abbsnate. "Continue on our predestined route. Godspeed Commander Ufi."

"You as well, Abbsnate!"

After the Trinitys evacuated the area, the Titáns turned about and faced the Sharks. Without the Trinitys, it was more of an even battle with the pirates. After a few minutes, the Titáns proved superior once again. The Mihhidites forgot about the Trinitys, and retreated in record fashion in the face of the onrushing Titáns.

The tide turned quickly when the Raihan fleet arrived on the scene, however. Commander Ufi knew it was a desperate uphill fight for the Titáns. They presented a blockade for the Trinitys against the advancing Raihans for as long as they were able.

The Titáns bought the Trinitys enough time to maneuver around the advancing Raihan fleet, gain distance, and get the jump on meeting the Trecons.

Abbsnate was dejected. The allies needed the firepower of the Titáns in space. The Falcon gliders, energized webs, and spider paratroopers could've turned the tide for the Wanderers on the ground. Most of all, her heart ached that many good people had just given themselves to the cause.

CHAPTER 35

The Siege Begins

T he Raihans had a definite home-field advantage. They were afforded every edge, while the Trecons were going into battle with blinders on. The sinister Raihans hit the Trecons with every trick they had, even as the first Bruiser exited the event horizon of the portal.

Beyond their superior numbers, cyber warfare was the biggest advantage for the Raihans. Conflicting and false information thrown at them was nothing like the Trecons had experienced before! Everything from false coordinates to mayday abort messages flooded the Trecon databank. The invaders would run into serious trouble if they couldn't keep up pace with the Raihans in the cyber war! Commander Dach's Boxer crews sifted through data to map things out for the Trecons.

As each group struggled to adapt and fly clear of the rubble zone, it appeared they'd be easy pickings for the welcoming taskforce. The emerging Trecons were trapped between the portal and the Raihans, dodging meteorites as they oriented themselves to a new galactic dimension!

"Bearing 315 degrees port, slight angle of elevation, and half thrusters," bellowed CJ, as they narrowly avoided a massive space rock on the starboard side of the vessel!

Scraaaape, clank!

As they maneuvered, their shields shoved a substantial piece of jagged ice aside, juddering the ship violently! They had no choice but to push forward to avoid a traffic jam at the gateway of the portal.

Raihan war ships were attempting to make each group a roadblock for the next one. Krevety prodded CJ to find a way through.

"If you can't move us soon, we're in real danger of getting rammed in the back by the next group!"

"Working on it, sir! Milerous, set bearing to 30 degrees starboard, sharp angle of depression, and full thrusters!"

The unexpected tactic was like gliding down the drop on a supersonic roller coaster! They narrowly missed a massive meteorite, but made it below the field of fire for a moment of reprieve.

"Great job CJ," said General Krevety after his stomach caught up with him.

"Event horizon clear for the next group!"

As the Raihans rushed to close the gap, the area they'd just vacated would be a target for the next squad to aim for! Commander Dach shot an estimate of the coordinates through the portal.

CJ announced, "Slowing to idle, general."

"On your mark, CJ."

"Green to go!"

"Launch our fighters!"

The Raihan force was small at the choke point, but they held the advantage because the Trecons had to enter the portal five at a time and fight their way through the gauntlet before defending themselves or sending their Starlances into the fight. Raihan leadership were confident they could hold the exit zone and crush the Trecon arm of the coalition in the ergosphere of the portal.

Trecon Control knew it would be tough sledding, but the fighting capabilities of the Trecon fleet would be greatly increased with the Starlances buzzing around! As each group exited the portal zone and gained footing, their fighters would be launched to provide cover for their group and the next as the warships drove forward. The following crews would repeat the process over again, until the entire fleet was safely through the portal.

The Starlance pilots showcased great skill as they worked through the rubble and ripped an opening in the Raihan blockade!

Blast, clink, burst!

CJ saw a path into deep space. "Set course for the way-point ahead."

The Raihan fleet pounded the Trecons with great vigor as they attempted to speed through the gauntlet! CJ's surprise tactic worked well at first, but the gap closed fast. A Bruiser in the first group experienced heavy damage and listed toward them with dark smoke rolling from the bridge.

The Talons smelled blood and closed in!

Vzzt vzzt, boom!

Rupture, crash!

Control had briefed the danger of lingering *too long* and getting bogged down, but they quickly discovered that leaving the portal zone *too early* would leave the next group emerging naked without adequate cover. Each new squad would benefit from the big guns *and* the fighters.

Commander Dach contacted Krevety. "We can't continue to take losses like this, or we'll lose half the fleet here in the rocks!"

General Krevety ordered CJ to go back. "Cover that Boxer while we figure this out!"

Wham, gust!

The damaged Bruiser erupted into a blinding display of golden light!

The Trecons lost a Bruiser in each of the first two waves as they strove to change their tactics in impossible circumstances.

Each new batch would provide one circling sweep against the enemy before they rocketed away into deep space; they wouldn't ram straight through as originally planned. The tricky part was cutting through all the Raihan jargon so the next groups could follow the order!

As the Boxer crews tried to break a new Raihan code, Commander Dach used tried and tested light signals to communicate with the fleet. Dach sent out a simple message to the other Boxers. In all the noise, it didn't make sense to the portal defenders.

"Ground light signals for vehicles on tarmac, pass it on."

They were in space, not on a landing pad! The Raihans ignored the message.

Following the dispatch, Dach grabbed an LED flashlight and flashed a simple white light toward the portal.

"I hope this works!"

Flash. Flash. Flash.

Three flashing white lights cut through the fray. *Return to starting point!*

The tactic worked well for the Trecons in the heat of battle, and they employed their new tactics quickly! Two Bruisers and a Brawler circled back into the portal area and fired at the behemoth Raihan vessels with everything they had as the next group emerged! The results were palpable as the Raihans had to divide their focus to defend themselves against an enemy suddenly showing bite!

Krevety inspected the battle playing out before him and was satisfied they could leave when he noticed the warships from the forth group doing the same, all while flashing the signal from their bridge.

"Good work commander Dach," The general said. "Full thrusters CJ, straight ahead!"

The welcoming fleet's goal was to make the Trecons bleed energy and motivation as they passed through the gauntlet. Every hit sustained on the Trecon fleet lessened their ability to inflict damage on Raihan.

Most of the Talon pilots gained their first combat experience in typical Raihan fashion, outnumbering their electronically blinded enemies with an overwhelming force. It didn't take too much skill with all the advantages on their side! The Talons stayed in the comforting shadow of their carriers, not realizing the Starlances were providing defensive cover and not trying to destroy them. Through their limited military experience, the Talon pilots actually thought they were winning the battle!

For over three hours, the Trecons sent 95 groups through at two-minute intervals. As the final Bruiser disappeared from view, the Talons loaded back into the carriers and awaited their next orders. The Raihan welcoming taskforce stayed at the portal to ambush reinforcements coming through, and destroy the retreating Trecons as they tried to escape back through the event horizon.

Four Boxers, Five Bruisers, 12 Brawlers, and 17 Starlance fighters were lost during the battle, while the Raihans lost only one carrier and eight Talons. The welcoming fleet damaged 23 other ships, who were smoldering heavily as they limped along into deep space.

The Trecon warships continued to Raihan at their best pace, performing repairs and protecting themselves to the best of their ability along the way. Only 25 Starlance fighters stayed back to escort the battered ships to Raihan. Trecon had everything riding on the invasion, and they needed every gun available to them. Any assistance the rickety warships could offer when they arrived over Raihan would be valued by their comrades!

The healthy Trecon armada had no choice but to leave the others to continue to the meeting point with the Ryderson Omegans. Despite their losses, the battle-toughened Trecons made it to the coordinates with a high percentage of their fleet intact.

As they approached, the cosmos became tinted with a red haze of Raihan defenders.

"Red alert, battle positions. Launch all fighters," ordered General Krevety as they prepared for a major Raihan assault!

"Sir, another fleet is approaching fast," reported Major Tallik from his post.

They knew the gray cloud was either their RO ally, or Mihhidite Sharks arriving to outflank them. As the fleet approached closer, the Trecons were relieved to see the Trinity squadrons screaming toward them, eager to join in the fight!

"Glad to see you made it," said General Krevety.

Abbsnate bellowed, *"You as well, General!"* The sound of Krevety's voice raised her spirits.

"We've got some bumps and bruises from the portal, but our fleet is mostly intact."

"The Mihhidites didn't put up a fight for us! But then the Raihans showed up, and our Titáns fought them off."

"It's great to hear your voice, Abbsnate! Is Onsan with you?"

"I'm here, general?"

"Your dream is to be a fighter pilot, yet you'll be in the Trinity rather than a Starlance for the battle. If you'd like, we'll call a timeout so you can switch birds!"

Onsan laughed. *"Not necessary, general!"*

"Godspeed, see you both on the other side of the battle!"

*****

The encounter was like a lightweight boxer fighting a heavyweight for the championship. It was a long shot, but the lightweight was quicker and could win if everything went right. The coalition knew they had a vast advantage in skill, so they surprised the Raihan defenders when they drove straight into them in attack mode!

The diamond squadrons of Trinitys were virtually invincible, and when paired with the steadfast Starlances, they made for a formidable combination for the Raihans to deal with!

As the two opposing forces met in deep space, the coalition fighters immediately tore a hole into the immense Talon formation.

Blast, flash, baroom!

The cosmos lit up like a firework display as thousands of ships met head on!

The Raihan crews expected their foes to see their overwhelming numbers, turn tail and run. Raihan command had received reports from the portal and heard of an overwhelming victory, yet the Trecon faction appeared tough and ready to fight! The balloon of confidence the Talon pilots arrived with was easily burst when they were encountered so directly by the allies.

Facheew facheew, booom!

The Raihans were visibly flustered as they tried to gain their footing within the fray. There were hundreds of explosions as Talon pilots were baptized by strong-arm tactics of the invaders. Nobody had ever treated the Raihan bullies like this!

The coalition destroyed 20 Talons before they returned a laser shot at them!

Onsan was excited and blurted out, "Stick together. We have a chance to break them here!"

"It's just the beginning Onsan. Stay calm and conserve your energy. You're going to need to stay focused," cautioned Abbsnate.

"Right," he replied sheepishly.

Onsan realized he needed to keep his emotions in check because he was no more experienced than the Talon pilots that surrounded them. He retrieved his inner focus, but took a moment to admire the Starlances getting the better of the Talons. A determined smile formed on his face; Onsan was back in the game!

Facheew, flash!

Onsan shot down three Talons in the first 45 minutes of the battle, which didn't seem to matter because there were an unlimited amount coming at them.

Vzzt vzzt, clatter, quake!

The Trinity shields were superior, but their ships constantly shuddered as the Talon laser blasts deflected off them.

The Talon swarms seemed to have the goal of herding the invading ships toward the more powerful laser cannons of their warships, but the coalition pilots were too superior to be driven toward the Raihan anvil like dumb sheep!

Evidence of the underground resistance appeared as dozens of Talons tried to assist the coalition. Standard operating procedure was the ultimate rule within the Raihan pilots, and they were ordered to immediately fire upon any bird that broke rank.

Unfortunately for the coalition, the detractors were easy to spot. The Raihans couldn't afford another Abbsnate situation during a space battle.

The resistance contingent was quickly destroyed by the other Talon pilots. Over 50 were blasted into oblivion by other Talons within the first hour of the battle, then the resistance pilots weren't heard from again. Nameless heroes had sacrificed themselves to cause havoc, buying the allies time and distance as they drove forward!

After five hours of intense fighting, Abbsnate indicated that it was time for the special unit to make a run to the planet's surface to engage targets there and try to choke out the giant.

If it were a fight, the first round would've gone to the lightweight Trecon-RO alliance!

CHAPTER 36

Initial Assault on Com-Facility 12

A successful war relied on cooperative assistance from the ground, but it was an uphill battle. There were many surface skirmishes planned, but no way to coordinate them ahead of time. The underground resistance would have to band with the Wanderers on the fly.

The assault against the communication tower and diversionary riot on Base 13 were the only concrete plans. The two Wanderer factions had to be synchronized with a mixture of courage and blind faith toward a greater victory! They were in the gravest danger.

The allies knew of the risks taken by everyone involved, determined to contribute to their cause from the sky. The main goal of the air assault on Raihan was a concentrated focus on the capital city of Rochest, but they'd also send assistance to the limited resistance forces. It was imperative to arrive at both locations in time to prevent annihilation of the Wanderers!

Attacking the communication outpost was risky, but necessary to get the truth out to the victim planets and convince them to join the attack. Every morsel of information coming from the underground resistance indicated that if they succeeded, it would break the will of the Raihans and cause them to sue for peace. The Wanderers needed to disrupt the communication outpost for only an instant while their partners on the inside overcame the outward-focused defenders. Then the Integrator infiltrators would transmit a short impulse into deep space.

Once the allies received the communiqué, they'd send the vital information to the victim planets throughout the universe and enlist them for immediate help, (the Mihhidites were the only planet omitted from the list). The resistance Integrators knew they had only seconds to get the message out before the Raihan defenders retook the outpost.

The Raihans would react fast to shut down the rebellion, but it'd be spilled milk that couldn't be put back in the glass. Regardless of how President Grolegg tried to clean up the mess, the truth about the harvests would be on display for all to see! Integrator and Contributor defenders would see the evidence and have to decide what to do with it. The hope was that the underground would gain countless more fighters for the coalition in a major revolt!

The communication outpost was protected by a division of 550 soldiers and light infantry equipment. It was three-square kilometers in size, with a towering communication tower in the center of the base under maximum protection. The fortress was surrounded by 10-meter walls with laser cannon turrets every three meters on the front face, where the only two entrances were located.

There was no possible way for the Wanderers to make a dent in the communication facility without collaborators peppered within the troops. It was impossible to know how many allies were inside until the moment of truth!

*****

There was no turning back for the Wanderers as they amassed outside the outpost.

The Raihan guards took their positions when they saw the Wanderers arriving. "Prepare to open fire!" ordered an officer to the defenders.

Phase one completed: All the Raihan attention was focused outward to the Wanderer forces.

Thunder, crumble, spray!

A defense cannon roared, showering the Wanderers with cutting sand and rocks.

The Wanderers hit the ground! "The attackers know we're here. No use waiting around," yelled RRR.

"Attack!" The Wanderers began their assault.

A commotion appeared within the walls. It was encouraging evidence of Integrators joining the struggle.

Booom, blam!

Suddenly there were visible explosions within the stronghold as two cannon turrets burst into flames! There was mass confusion near the front gate as the underground Integrators attempted to help the Wanderers break in.

Inside the facility, the tower was overtaken and the impulse message transmitted!

Surge!

"I DOU LAU 1-06.75 AI 93 BT 20 MV 63 HU II WON LAU 2-13.5 EM 14 AX 09 PZ 24 OO III PIB LAU 3-20.25 DI 05 CN 26 BR 07 PV IV MIB LAU 4-27 LT 12 EQ 24 HS 03 UW V QUE MAG 5-33.75 IU 06 AS 08 DV 07 OL VI NIB LAU 6-40.5 FT 11 OX 03 EZ 07 CB VII WHO MAG 7-47.25 MR 87 KN 22 BQ 59 PW VIII STE LAU 8-54 DO 08 BT 25 QX 72 IX ROD MAG 9-60.75 RZ 05 OQ 18 CP 14 SO X BEU MAG 10-67.5 IL 04 AP 24 EU 12 XI SRO MAG 11-74.25 QT 01 WZ 09 KV 41 ON XII CIE MAG 12-81 BP 33 NR 05 DX 19 CS XIII BII LAU 13-87.75 DP 22 BM 01 NZ 10 CK XIV MIH LAU 14-94.5 -- -- -- -- -- -- -- XV R-O MAG 15-101.25 BN 17 MU 25 FY 20 RO XVI YIO MAG 16-108 KR 15 NF 23 CH 96 DZ XVII TIS MAG 17-114.75 AC 21 BL 10 OZ 06 EK XVIII LOE MAG 18-121.5 PI 16 NQ 84 CO 49 SW XIX TRE LAU 19-128.25 AJ 13 BK 76 TM 39 YI"

Dach addressed Krevety's Bruiser, *"They did it general!"*

"Decipher where the information needs to go and send it forward ASAP," ordered General Krevety. "Starting with the nearest planets!"

The coordinates of every victim planet were sent on an open frequency; eight through the portal into the Laurus dimension and 10 to the Magnus side. The signal broke down the location of the planets into super galactic, quadratic, ecliptic, and equatorial information. On the Laurus side of the portal, four Boxers waited to receive the data.

Commander Dach hailed Krevety from his Boxer ship, "General, the transmission was received by our Boxers!"

"Excellent! Lock on the originating location on Raihan. The Wanderers will be sitting ducks down there if we don't hurry."

"Done. I've forwarded the coordinates of the com center to our squad leaders."

There was a rush of jubilation on every Trecon and RO ship. The Allies had beaten the Raihans at their own game! General Krevety loaded the recorded distress message he and Abbsnate created earlier, and sent it out to the coordinates sent from Com-Facility 12. It was to be the turning point in the war! If dispatches came in from victims across the galaxy, Raihan would have to take a serious look at surrendering.

After only 30 seconds, the signal went down, meaning the Raihans had regained control of communication, and resistance Integrators had given their lives for the cause. Still, a treasure trove of information poured into the computers of the allied vessels, and *every* Raihan ship!

*****

In the Talon-filled skies above Base 13, the first wave of coalition fighters approached. Serlat and his shabby mob could only watch. He wisely ordered them to take cover.

Flash, bang!

The atmosphere exploded exuberantly like a fireworks celebration, as the contingent of allied fighters approached the planet. Starlances and Trinitys fought with the determination of knowing if they could get through to Rochest, they could put an irreversible crack in the confidence of the defenders!

Abbsnate hailed Krevety. "General, we've received the message impulse, authentication code 239812. I'm taking the Capital Fleet to our main target!"

"Keep your heads up," replied the general. A group of 50 Starlance fighters and 25 Trinitys broke away from the others and continued toward Rochest in attack formation. They were hoping to surprise the Raihans with a quick assault on the crowned jewel of their planet. If the allies could cut off the head of the beast, Raihan would fall!

The capital had advanced top-secret protection protocol that would make for an imposing target. Abbsnate had no idea of what they were getting into, despite all her years as a Contributor.

The capital city of Rochest was the only place on the planet populated by original Raihan inhabitants. Despite being a small demographic, they held all the political and economic puppet strings for everyone else! Seventy five percent of the vast riches on the planet were focused there. Raihan was so wealthy and industrious, that 25 percent of the trillelium wealth would appease the remaining population.

This seems too easy. Abbsnate expected an all-out effort by the Raihans to defend their capital city. To her surprise, a *minimal* number of Talons followed the allied fleet toward Rochest. The allied ships flew in and out, avoiding the ground defenses as they peppered the heavily shielded structures with laser fire and bombs, hoping to wear them down.

*****

On the ground, the com outpost attack was a signal taken by the resistance Integrators, some of whom revealed their true colors and started sabotage missions against ground targets and shields. Outside Base 13, hundreds of resistance Integrators made hectic attacks to inhibit defense, open the base, and provide weapons to the mass of Wanderers gathered outside. The lack of secure communication and a clear game plan leading to the attack was evident. The resistance forces looked frazzled in their efforts to aid the Wanderers.

Blast, rumble, kaboom!

As the sky buzzed with laser-blasting intensity, there were substantial clashes on the inside of the gates of main Base 13. A defense shield was destroyed in the ambush, but the resistance Integrators were quickly overtaken. Base 13 was the main billet used by the Raihans for the defense of the capital city; loyalty there was greater than anywhere else on the planet!

The allies erroneously thought the resistance would employ greater numbers upon hearing the impulse message, but it didn't happen. The gates of the base were held secure against the Wanderers. The quick defeat of the resistance fighters started a domino effect that spread into the atmosphere above!

*****

Outside the outpost, RRR focused on their next objective: To breach the compound and capture the weapons inside. It was an uphill battle from the start!

After the data surged into space, the attacking force used it to acquire the location of the distress signal and rushed in to help. The Wanderers were hopeful, with evidence of the allies filling the sky! Five Trinitys and seven Starlances broke from the upper atmosphere and raced to Com-Facility 12 to assist the Wanderers with the attack. The signal also attracted 50 Talons into the area.

Thunder, flash, glow!

The Talons blasted at the shabby army from the sky. They also proved to be stiff competition for the birds who'd arrived to provide air cover for the Wanderers.

The allied fighters skyrocketed down to the outpost base and noticed a weak spot in the wall where the Wanderer ground forces were trying to break through.

"You keep the Talons busy, and we'll engage the lasers on those walls," cried Tren Darvey, a veteran Starlance pilot. As the fighters approached, Darvey saw the wall cannons firing indiscriminately into the Wanderer masses. The Wanderers had no weapons powerful enough to reach the turret, so they were trapped! When they tried to dive for cover, the Raihans raised the intensity and pinned them down. There was no way for the Wanderers to escape the impending massacre!

Streak, bzzzzt bzzzzt, baroom!

Darvey dived, attacking a cannon position at full speed and destroying it, giving the Wanderers a momentary reprieve to fall back.

Every once in a while, a brawl would start as resistance Integrators tried to wrestle a turret away, only to be subdued by a larger force of Raihan loyalists. Darvey and his squad flew directly for the gun positions, occupying them while the Wanderers ran back for cover. Just as it appeared the allied pilots were making headway, more Talons zoomed in to fight them!

Vzzt vzzt, blast!

The Wanderers tried again to attack the weak spot, but to no avail. The Raihans were emboldened with the sudden surge of air support. They held their lines and pushed back the aggressors once again.

Darvey called command for backup, knowing the Wanderers couldn't last long. "We need more support directly, or there won't be anyone left down there to save!"

Commander Dach answered Darvey from his Boxer. *"Sending one Boulder down to your location, but we're spread dangerously thin up here. We can only afford to spare one Brawler escort. We'll try to get more troop transports through to you, but it may be a while."*

*****

Ranard Reud could appreciate the sporadic cover they were getting from the sky, but he knew it wasn't enough. The impulse message from Com-Facility 12 didn't have the desired effect on the Raihan ground or air forces; they simply didn't gain the number of resistance fighters they were hoping for. Years of brainwashing, restrictions, and surveillance had evidently paid off for the Raihans.

Minutes later, Reud's fears came to pass.

"Mayday, this is Boulder Transport 1. We're under heavy attack from every side. Our escort has been destroyed."

Crackle, sizzle!

"Mayda-."

Boom!

The Wanderers saw the Boulder troop transport fall to the ground like a blazing ton of bricks. Minutes earlier, it exited a Bruiser with high hopes of assisting the Wanderers at Com-Facility 12. Laser fire from the Raihan contingent proved too much. The Brawler escort was driven back and demolished, and the slow transport craft was left high and dry. Within a half-minute, its shields were gone.

Vreeeeew, crash!

The flaming ship was a testament it was too early to put Trecon marines on the ground. The transports were too sluggish to outrun or evade Raihan defenders, and the Trecons didn't have enough Brawler escorts to get them safely to the surface. After the first failed attempt, Krevety reluctantly contacted Commander Dach and put the land invasion on hold. He knew the Wanderers were desperate, but wouldn't send more Trecon plodders out where they couldn't defend themselves.

*****

RRR saw the writing on the wall after the crash. He yelled to his next in line, "We're on our own. If we can't breach the wall soon, we'll have to retreat."

Soon, Reud saw another batch of friendly fighters coming on the horizon, and for a moment his spirits were raised.

The warbirds appeared to make progress, pushing back the Raihans. Soon after, he noticed hundreds of Talons screaming into view to engage the alliance ships.

The coalition forces gave their every resource to the fight, yet the fortress wasn't breached. Raihan loyalists flooded to the weakened area of the wall with heavy weaponry. In the sky, the Talons were gaining the upper hand for Raihan once again. It was over.

RRR's fair skin was caked with blood and dirt, cemented with sweat. Small blue eyes squinted through the dust, searching for reinforcements. His valiant features turned bitter, and hope drained from his countenance as he read the writing on the wall. Reud had no choice and reluctantly gave the order, "Retreat. Retreat!"

CHAPTER 37

Wanderers Resistance Crushed

S oon the sheer number of Talons in the sky overwhelmed the invaders, driving them back where they could no longer provide cover for the resistance fighters on the ground in any location. The Wanderers had only one small weapon for every three people fighting, so their capability to defend themselves was very limited.

In the skies above, the Talons turned the tide against the superior skill of the invading forces. The rush to get to Rochest was slowed by heavy ground-to-air laser fusillades. Abbsnate knew that their main objective was to reach Rochest, but was visibly upset as she heard the evidence of Wanderer obliteration below them.

The Wanderers didn't have a chance, but there was little the pilots could do about it from the sky.

A wave of panic and guilt pressed its way into the stronghold of Abbsnate's mind. If the Wanderers were wiped out, it would be on her conscience for the rest of her life. Everything happening around them had started from her decision to defect from the Raihans, and it crashed in on her as victory was slipping away.

Onsan had seen her down before, but he sensed something different. "We can still reach Rochest and win this war," he awkwardly stated to provide support to her.

No response.

He sensed the guilt and frustration of miscalculation emanating from her. Abbsnate was strong, but not enough to hold in her feelings. "Why weren't there more defectors?"

It was Onsan's turn to keep her focused! He stated more directly, "I'm with you. We've been through a lot together, and none of it has been easy. Keep your head in the game and let's make it there!"

"Right, partner," Abbsnate seemed to snap from her daze. "Let's go then!"

Despite the evidence of devastation against the Wanderers, all the Trinity crew could do was keep moving toward Rochest and let the others provide ground support. They were still 50 kilometers out, slugging their way to the capital.

*****

RRR was filled with frustration and grief. He was torn apart, because he had to retreat for the safety of his Wanderer force; while the Integrator fighters were stuck inside being annihilated by brutal Raihan and Mihhidite tactics. The Raihan defenders took great pleasure in throwing the collaborators over the wall onto the hard desert ground, leaving many lame and crawling for safety across hundreds of meters of open ground.

The painful moans of the resistance Integrators joined in with the Wanderers lying wounded on the battlefield. Some Raihans took potshots at them as they tried to crawl away from the walls. Others were sympathetic to the helpless victims, causing more skirmishes.

Occasionally, Starlance and Trinity fighters were seen screaming back and forth, doing everything within their ability to protect the Wanderer masses with little effect. The best the Wanderers could do was spread out and stay low, to avoid the Raihan onslaught from the air and base cannons.

Around the battlefield, people were valiantly charging into the injured masses and attempting to pull them back from the walls. Many suffered the ultimate price as they tried to rescue their comrades.

In the middle of the Wanderers, Bodak Willstreak looked toward the fallen soldiers and turned to his brother. "We've got to get to the base of the wall, but how?"

"I don't know. We're pinned down," replied Rander.

Bodak's eyes flashed with anger. "We have to do something before we lose them all!"

"The order is to stay put and wait for reinforcements. The base is so fortified we'll never make it. Look at the cannons, they're trained on us," yelled Rander over the gun fire. "We'll die if we get any closer!"

Bodak yelled, "I say we help them!"

It was chaos all around!

"Stay back. They're baiting you," ordered Reud.

His orders fell largely on deaf ears. He'd lost control of his followers, through no fault of his own. RRR's words no longer affected the horrified Wanderers under his watch, as they rushed to the shadow of the walls to help.

Bodak Willstreak couldn't hold in his anger any longer; being a spectator wasn't in his DNA. "We have to do something for them!" As Willstreak stood up, RRR yelled another unheeded warning.

"No, Bodak!" yelled Rander Willstreak. "We can't make it there and back without cover."

"Aaarrrggghhh!"

Bodak Willstreak rushed toward the outpost, reaching one of the injured fighters lying at the base of the wall. Bodak was done listening, and Rander's hand was forced. He couldn't let his brother face the onslaught alone. Bodak grabbed a weapon lying beside a fallen combatant and fired toward the wall.

Pzew pzew!

They reached an injured man under heavy fire, using the terrain as best they could for cover.

"Take my hand. I'll get you out of here!" As Rander Willstreak pulled the resistance fighter to safety, Bodak aimed the laser pistol and fired an untrained volley toward a defender on the wall. Rander didn't look back but pulled for all he was worth to get the Integrator out of range.

Thunder!

Quake, spray!

Just as Rander reached the group, he looked over his shoulder and saw his brother crumble to the ground, hit by ground shrapnel from an explosion.

"Noooo!"

Bodak somehow got to his feet and stumbled the final 50 paces to the Wanderer assembly. Rander and others rushed out to retrieve the injured man, and pulled him back to adequate cover.

Similar scenes played out across the battlefield. Compassion wilted from inside the outpost as the Wanderers continued to take unnecessary casualties from coldhearted defenders.

With all the chaos around them, the Willstreak brothers only focused on the pain and sadness in each other's eyes. Rander looked at his brother with an obvious look of pride swelling along with the water, "That man would have died without you. I'm so proud of you right now."

As Rander looked closely at his younger brother, he realized he wouldn't make it. Bodak had been hit in the side and was losing blood rapidly.

"Medic!"

There were none.

Rander tore his shirt and used it for a bandage. Under different circumstances with proper medical attention, he'd have lived. There was nothing the elder brother could do but hold pressure on Bodak's bleeding wound, and try to comfort him.

Bodak looked up at his elder brother. "Find and take care of my family, Rander," he instructed with his final words.

"On my honor," answered Rander. As Rander held his brother close, Bodak slipped away.

Bodak Willstreak had been filled with hatred and revenge that ate away at his soul, but his final act displayed the compassion and self-sacrifice he'd be forever honored for!

Rander leaned over his brother and wept.

As he looked up through the tears, Rander's sadness turned into intense anger and determination. He picked up the weapon and continued his brother's final mission. Despite being severely pinned down, Rander Willstreak and his compatriots heroically saved 17 more Wanderers and Integrator allies during the next three hours!

*****

Outside main Base 13, the overwhelming numbers of the Raihan forces easily surrounded Serlat's mob and forced them to take cover further from the gates. Serlat knew that no matter what happened, the Raihans wouldn't allow them to leave the battle alive because each one of them showed a determination to overthrow the government!

Two thousand rebel Integrators were also driven from the gates of Base 13 and out into the open among the Wanderers. They'd fought with reckless abandon for the weary Wanderers, but their struggle going forward was for survival rather than defeating the Raihans!

Squeak nicker scrunch, squeak nicker scrunch!

Bully Mallet tanks advanced on the Wanderer crowd, pushing them back from cover and into the open terrain. The Raihans herded the aggressors into a horseshoe shape and pushed them to where they had no advantages left. Serlat knew it would be their last stand.

*****

The number of the resistance fighters wasn't what the coalition thought it would be. The allies' hope for Integrators being pulled to their cause was quickly dashed through the brutal display of retribution against defectors! Had they experienced more success early in battle, they would've pulled greater numbers for sure.

On top of everything else, evidence was surfacing that the impulse message failed. It was impossible to tell if the incoming reports were authentic, or more Raihan propaganda.

Despite their early triumphs, the allies' invasion flattened out.

It was more than the evil Raihans and Mihhidites that foiled the plot. Each person faced a choice, and most took the path of least resistance. Fear was the reason. Some grew afraid of injury in battle. However, the majority of the Integrators dreaded losing the good life, preferring comfort and indulgence over doing what was right. The Raihans had bought the loyalty of their captured prey.

It was a major flaw in Abbsnate's plan; a defect that was unpredictable. The coalition hoped for better results. Without numbers to even the sides, it became a hopeless mission.

CHAPTER 38

Raihan Air Power Unleashed

Talons were exploding and spiraling out of control at an incredible rate, yet they continued coming in relentless waves. It was unstoppable adrenaline mixed with intense focus for the coalition fighters in the colossal space battle! Thousands of Talons joined in the fight with the advantage of getting sustained mental breaks as they broke off and circled wide for their next surge.

For the coalition pilots, there were no mental breaks. They had to endure endless hours of maneuvering and life-or-death close-range fighting. Raihan warships targeted the fighters from an untouchable range, giving the pilots another obstacle to consider.

Flash, boosh!

"We need Bruiser backup right away to hold off those destroyers," shouted Starlance squad leader Dwre Onga as a Trecon fighter disintegrated in front of him from a powerfully accurate cannon blast!

Commander Dach contacted his escort Brawler. "The enemy has broken our ranks to your 3:00 on the Y-axis!"

"On it!" The Brawler turned and gave the carrier all she had, helping the Starlances fight off the giant for the moment.

After Dach sent away his destroyer sentry, he realized he was in serious trouble! Up to that point in the battle, Dach's

Boxer frigate came through in many clutch situations. He'd helped the allies stay virtually even with the Raihans. His ship stayed at the edge of the battle, where his crew of 100 call-out dispatchers were in constant contact with Starlance squad leaders. His communicators had many talents which included staying cool under pressure, talking fast, and being great explainers.

Commander Dach knew his Boxer was one of the most important ships in the armada. If he was destroyed, General Krevety would lose the best communication link to his fleet. Dach stood alone and vulnerable on the bridge, watching the battle rage on. He felt like something bad would happen. He wasn't disappointed!

Booom!

Suddenly, a big explosion rocked the ship! Commander Dach was thrown against a control panel. He struck his head against a corner. Dach felt for the lump, and blood covered his hand. Crimson flowed out from a gash under his red hair, into his green eyes, and down his freckled face. The commander simply didn't have time to be hurt. He wiped his brow and pulled on a hat to keep the blood from flowing into his eyes and obscuring his vision.

Bleat, bleat, bleat!

Alarms were buzzing amidst the flashing red lights; but everyone kept doing their jobs like before, trusting their comrades to help. Panicking wouldn't do any good! Dach looked up and saw a squad of Talons racing toward the ship. When the fighters picked out a target, they were like a swarm of killer bees. He knew soon dozens of Talons would be zooming in, intent on destruction!

Dach sent out a distress message. "Mayday, mayday, mayday, this is -."

Bang, shudder!

A second explosion rocked the ship, sending him and a few other cyber warriors into the wall, knocking them unconscious.

General Krevety was deeply concerned! "Save my escort!"

Three Starlances came to the defense of the Boxer and attacked the Raihans. "There's too many Talo-!"

Wham, flash!

The ship exploded before the pilot could finish his sentence.

Three more Starlances and a squadron of Trinitys engaged the growing cluster and drove them away from the Boxer.

Twenty Talons charged hard against the allied fighters!

Vzzt vzzt, flare, glow!

A Starlance succumbed to heavy fire.

A temporary reprieve came, as two battered Brawlers arrived on scene and clashed with the Raihan warships. The swarm left Dach's Boxer and found another target. Had the Raihans destroyed Dach's ship and divided the allied fleet, the battle would've turned quicker for the Raihans.

The coalition fleet couldn't make up for the difference much longer when fighting against a 20-1 Raihan advantage. The home team lost hundreds of ships, but there were *thousands* coming behind them to join the fight. When the invading forces destroyed a Talon, three more fighters drove into the formation to take its place!

There were widening breaches in the alliance defenses, forcing Trinity and Starlance fighters to mix their formations. The Raihans failed to take advantage like they should've. They weren't impulsive enough to take charge.

Under cover of the Starlance fighters, the Trinitys continued engaging the Talons during their flanking passes, and the Raihans were paying a heavy price with every round.

The coalition knew that their only hope to win the battle was to hold their own and hope Abbsnate reached Rochest soon. The Talons continually circled around for pass after endless pass, like a horde of gnats that didn't know when to quit!

*****

After two and a half days of heavy battling, a crack formed in the allied lines as the weight of the Raihan force was proving too much for them.

The most significant casualty was inflicted to a vaunted Trinity fighter as the hind-cannon was blasted in half. The damaged craft couldn't detach the bubble because the release mechanism had been damaged from the hit. The ship looked haunting to the other allied space fighters. The bloodstained uniform of the hind-gunner got caught in jagged metal, and floated in space like a sick flag!

The Trinity was left greatly incapacitated, and unable to protect the right flank of their formation. The gory visual was a *major* mental blow to the attacking fleet. Seeing the broken ship gave the allied fighters mixed signals. The warrior died heroically during a fight; but seeing the remains of their comrade was a constant reminder of their mortality. It was a bad omen glaring at them in the heat of battle!

Kaboom!

The next wave of Talons skyrocketed in and attacked the weakness, destroying the Trinity ship and the Starlance fighter attempting to protect it!

Similar scenes played out across the ether. In the skies above Raihan, the Talons were gaining the upper hand as they were gradually whittling down the formations of the Trinitys and engaging the Starlances with more confidence. Experience had played a heavy role in giving round one to the allies, but round two looked as though the Raihans were scoring uppercut haymakers that would quickly score a knockout win against the attackers!

Raihan leadership were bent on crushing the forces bent against them in the most decisive manner possible. There were many positive feelings within the higher offices in Rochest. The undisputed power of Raihan was on full display! They'd responded to the attack without mercy, and would leave no doubt to observing eyes throughout the universe that attacking them was unwise! Galactic domination would take root into the future!

The invasion would give Raihan leadership a true barometer for the size of the Contributor and Integrator insurgents threaded into their society. Raihan leaders felt they had all the resistance eggs in one neat little basket. Uncommitted rebel fighters would melt shamefully into the background after the war, and the revolution would be dead.

There was no way for the allies to regroup. They had to stick it out between thousands of Raihan ships blasting away at them mercilessly! General Krevety was in the command ship in the upper stratosphere and could see the epic battle turning upside down in front of him, yet he was powerless to do anything about it.

The best laid plans were going to waste. A significant part of the RO attack didn't work out for the allies. Titán cruisers would've helped the coalition smash their way to the surface sooner. Speedy Falcon gliders could've made it to Com-Facility 12 and Base 13 effortlessly, dropping their energy webs to aid the Wanderers and rebel Integrators. Spider troopers would've swiftly turned the tide on the ground. Commander Ufi and his fleet of Titáns were never heard from after they sent Abbsnate and the Trinitys ahead. Ufi and the Titán cruisers had sacrificed themselves to get the Trinitys to Raihan.

Krevety knew that dwelling on would've and could've was a waste of time. There was only one chance left. General Krevety knew they were gambling heavily by trying to overtake the capital city. He had to come to grips with it becoming a longer shot by the minute. As a leader, Krevety contemplated how the Raihans would accept their surrender if he was forced to sue for peace. The prospect didn't look good.

*****

Outside Base 13, the Raihans surrounded the resistance forces with 20,000 troops and 250 heavy ground-assault Mallet tanks. It was evident the battle was over! The Raihans called for all the leaders of the resistance to come out and surrender.

"Wanderer and resistance leadership, you have a chance to save those around you by surrendering yourselves," spat General Meka Ohibk into a bullhorn. Ohibk was a Mihhidite put in charge of escorting the leaders to Slae Nodk in the Base 13 Gallows.

Nobert Serlat's electric blue eyes had lost their spark, and were filled with hopelessness. He carried the weight of failure on tired shoulders. Serlat started to step forward, only to have his arm firmly held by his second-in-command, a Raihan nomad named Hio Figiop. Figiop gave him a stern look. "If you do this, it's all over for us!"

Serlat was their inspiration, and they needed to keep him safe until the end! They hadn't failed through any fault of his. Serlat held his ground with the others as the eyes of the Mihhidite scanned the crowd intensely.

To the surprise of General Ohibk, there was no movement within the ranks of the resistance as they appeared to dig in for the long haul. "Suit yourselves. We won't make it easy on you!"

It was an empty threat and everyone knew it. The Mihhidite general had to play a waiting game with the mob because there were strict orders from above not to openly maltreat prisoners. President Grolegg had given the order personally. He didn't want to entice immediate sympathy for the resistance within the Base 13 ranks. Most were planetary kin to the Wanderers and Integrator resistance forces. It was too risky to deal with them impatiently!

The Raihans had the initiative to take their time, separate the resistance, and make them pay later. It became apparent to the irritated Ohibk it would be a complicated operation. He volleyed another empty threat into the crowd. "Stand fast and prepare to defend yourselves!"

CHAPTER 39

A New Participant in the Game

The Raihan welcoming fleet awaited the Trecons outside the portal and prepared to obliterate them as they approached in retreat. They'd provided the first punch of the fight, and were waiting around to deliver the knockout blows in the final round!

The fleet had been inactive for a week, lethargic and waiting for their next order to come through. Fleet commander Nairb Sterlek had addressed his superiors with news that the impulse message had reached them, but that was it. He tried to block it, but was too slow. Sterlek delayed the update. No matter, because they were routing the Trecons anyway.

Sterlek knew he'd have the perfect opportunity to finish the terrified Trecons as they attempted to escape into the portal! Raihan official orders were to ensure the total destruction of the Trecon fleet in the bottleneck, and Sterlek dreamed of the accolades he'd receive after destroying the last Bruiser. He'd personally ensure the Trecons lost the intestinal fortitude to return to the Magnus system again!

After the battle, Sterlek never considered drilling to sharpen the skills of the Talon pilots. He only monitored the com and waited for news of the retreating Trecons.

Suddenly the Raihans' sleepy feeling of invincibility turned to one of collective terror and vulnerability! A fleet of five ghostly docking ships seemed to appear out of nowhere from the event horizon, almost invisible in space until they were right on top of the Raihan welcoming committee! Each Docker ship had four heavy fighters attached, two to each side. They sped up to a Vehemence carrier and unloaded an alternating high-low frequency-pulsing burst that fried the Raihan shields.

Eewlu-whoop-shriek-eewlu-whoop-shriek-eewlu-whoop-shriek-eewlu!

The Raihan carriers were equipped for high-frequency defense, but the alternating supersonic frequency burst was too much for the electronics of the vessel to compensate for. Along with the shields, their navigation and communication systems were thrown into a flux! Shortly after the cyber-attack, each docking vessel released four fierce spacecraft into the fight.

As 20 heavy fighters launched themselves intently against the Raihans, Sterlek sent an urgent message home, "Raihan Central Command, there are unidentified warships emerging from the portal and engaging us at this time! Mayday! Mayday! Mayd—."

Bzzeew, booom!

Sterlek's message was rudely cut off, as the bridge of the vessel took a direct hit from a Sonarian Docker.

"Classify the type of warship and confirm the identity of the aggressors," came the bemused reply from Raihan.

"Commander Sterlek do you copy? Over?"

Vweep, crash!

Another carrier shook so violently that two Talons hit the side of the bay during their exit from the ship and burst into flames, trapping the remaining fighters inside the firestorm with no outlet! Shortly afterward, the carrier exploded into ashes, providing the other Raihans a full view of the horror show!

The captain from a retreating destroyer answered Raihan Control, "Sir, these aren't Trecon or RO vessels. We can't identify them, I've never seen anything like them before. They came out of nowhere and knew just where to hit us!"

Leadership suspected that the impulse message got through, but it would've been impossible for the other planets to send reinforcements so soon! The startled Raihans engaged the mystery ships with a heavy barrage of laser fire from their Vengeance destroyers and Vehemence carriers, launching their Talons against them as best they could. Two Sonarian docking ships were destroyed by the heavy bombardment of Raihan firepower, but not before all their Crusader fighters were released for engagement.

Five more Dockers suddenly appeared through the event horizon.

Bzzeew bzzeew, spark, crash!

The cryptic ships opened fire on the Raihan vessels as five more Dockers advanced on their tails. Twenty more Sonarian Crusader fighters detached from their docking ships and joined the battle. They were relentless and accurate, inflicting significant damage on the Raihan fleet in a matter of seconds! After the vicious bombardment, 20 Crusaders re-docked on five ships. The Dockers set a course for Raihan at an ultrasonic speed!

There were quickly enough Sonarian ships to overwhelm the Raihan fleet. For the next three hours, the Sonarian Dockers continued until there were over 500 carrying 2,000 Crusader fighters through the portal!

Crusaders weren't fast or agile, but they didn't appear to embrace speed as an advantage in combat like typical fighters. Brute force was their game!

The Raihans wisely decided it was better to run for the cover of home rather than stay in the ergosphere and die. The lack of honor within the Raihan fleet further enraged the Sonarians against them. The Sonarians saw the Raihans evading through wreckage of Trecon warships. The Trecons had continued to fight and adhere to their mission despite great odds against them. The Sonarians instantly felt great respect for the Trecons, and the same level of disdain for the Raihans. Most of the Raihan fleet were destroyed as they attempted to escape the savage Crusaders!

"Prepare for the unidentified fleet to join the invasion force. They're rapidly heading in your direction," cautioned a Vengeance captain.

Baroom!

The captain had used his last words to report to Raihan command.

*****

The fierce fleet was from the planet Sonaria, through a third leg of the portal where the weakest point in the lining produced a tear because of the dimensional tug-of-war between Laurus and Magnus.

The Sonarians sped toward Raihan with reckless abandon, leaving destroyed and incapacitated warships in their wake! They were headed straight for a particular destination with a determined purpose. It appeared to the disabled Raihan ships that the Sonarians were employing the same tactic as them. They'd finish the Raihans off at their leisure on their way back to the portal.

Life-support systems were draining fast, and there was nothing the Raihans could do about it.

*****

Deep in the halls of Rochest, President Grolegg was beside himself looking for answers. They assumed the invading force was a third ally they hadn't accounted for. How could there be a third collaborator without them knowing about it? Being shielded from information was unprecedented in their history!

President Grolegg asked his com-tech, "Did the impulse message get through?"

"Yes, but it was scrambled," answered communications officer Dreck Lobart.

The Raihans had sent masking and follow-up communications following the impulse message. There wasn't time to act on the dispatch and send a rescue force, and the Sonarians weren't a vexed planet anyway. The prospects of being ambushed was incomprehensible, yet it was punching them in the face!

*****

Battered Trecon warships changed to offensive tactics as they joined their new partners in battle! The Sonarian fleet put on quite a show for the Trecons as they shattered the remaining Raihan ships around them, dispatching them in quick fashion! Crews of the Trecon fleet cheered with great vigor, as they watched the impressive display before them!

"Trecon fleet command, we have a new crop of allies joining our attack," announced Doh Knoth, commander of a damaged Bruiser. "The message impulse worked better than we'd anticipated!"

General Krevety responded with a distinct awe in his voice. *"The messages have just been deciphered and sent out hours ago. There'd be no time for anyone to respond yet. It should've taken weeks for them to answer. See if you can contact the fleet to get their origin planet."*

"They came through the portal, but I can't identify them!"

"Can you communicate with them?"

"Not yet." Knoth sent a hail to the surrounding Sonarian vessels, but there was no immediate response.

"Keep trying. Change the frequency of your messages," ordered General Krevety. *"And patch Commander Dach and I through as soon as you gain contact!"*

"Yes general," answered Captain Knoth.

The news gave the allies the will to fight on. Who was the new acquaintance who'd saved them just as hope seemed lost?

*****

305

Commander Ufi and his fleet of Titáns put up a fight to the last ship, but were ultimately crushed between the Raihans and Mihhidites. Boirt Zalbek's fleet of Sharks were whittled down fast in the fight. The ferocity of Ufi's fleet was evident to the last RO warship.

The mega-fleet was originally instructed to blockade the Royale system, but the introduction of the Sonarians into the war changed the plan.

Zalbek's fleet of 1500 sharks had a new assignment. They were to go maximum speed to the portal, and protect the Magnus dimension against anything coming through.

The Sharks approached the ergosphere in three days, and Zalbek couldn't believe his eyes. All was quiet. Burnt-out Vehemence carriers, Vengeance destroyers, and Talons cluttered the portal zone among the meteorites and Trecon warships. It was a lifeless scene; Zalbek could only imagine the devastation as the Sonarians bashed their way into the Magnus dimension.

Zalbek made a command decision based on the evidence. The Raihans were going to lose the war. He'd gained everything he could from them, and it was time for the Mihhidites to return to the Laurus side for good. When he reached the midway point of the portal, his Shark detected the exhaust path of the Dockers.

When the fleet was through to the Laurus ergosphere, Zalbek discovered that Mihhidite character had taken over. He was challenged for command of the fleet. The man was desperately outnumbered, but managed to escape into the portal. Zalbek knew he didn't want to face an onslaught in the Magnus dimension. His act of betrayal assured he was enemies with every major player in the war. His Shark and 52 others followed the wake into the Sonarian dimension. It was meant to be a short trip until the Shark fleet cleared the Laurus ergosphere.

Zalbek's desertion ensured the Mihhidites were taken out of the equation, further weakening the capabilities of the Raihans.

CHAPTER 40

The Sonarian Perspective

The allies didn't call the Sonarians to join their cause; their invitation was sealed by the Raihans!

Long before the Raihans discovered the portal, a Sonarian exploratory spacecraft passed through the newly discovered portal tear to explore the expanded universe on the other side. The crew were viewed as heroes as they headed through the wormhole into the great unknown!

The ship traveled through the portal and on through to Muudia during the summer season, when the gravitational pull was at its greatest. The unsuspecting vessel was pulled into the Muudia gravitational field and destroyed by the intense radiation bathing the planet! The remains of the Sonarian ship crashed into the planet's murky surface and embedded itself into a flow of molten trillelium as it descended toward the core of the planet.

The majority of the ship disintegrated on the planet's surface, but the dense strongbox transmitter survived intact. It was quickly swallowed up by Muudia and the beacon signal died instantaneously as it sank in the dense molten metal.

Sonarian scientists and government concluded the crew had entered a sun portal. They believed the ship was pulled in and destroyed by crashing into a star. Radiation levels sent back through, and the quick demise, left the Sonarians no reason to think differently!

When the autumn season approached, the molten trillelium flowed toward the core of the planet, taking the strongbox with it farther into the crust of Muudia. Sonarian exploration of the portal was terminated and never revisited, being deemed too dangerous. There were two sun portals known to them, and they were a dead end for resources.

Years later, when the relic was hit by the Trecon excavator, moisture conducted electrical power, transferring from the battery of the borer to the Sonarian unit. Electric current recharged the miser transmitter with enough dynamic juice to keep it going for 10 years!

When the Trecons pulled the transmitter to the surface, it was no longer sealed by the planet's thick trillelium-rich crust. The beacon was pulled free of the thick anechoic chamber, and sent its homing signal to the universe once again. As it called out to the Sonarians, the low frequency burst was magnified by radiation.

The Sonarians were drawn to Muudia once again, because the artifact called to them from the great beyond! They decided another exploratory mission was needed. Leadership selected an experienced crew, and commissioned a new Essence exploratory spacecraft for the important journey.

General Yoheim Seraden was the chief science officer in the Sonarian government. He wanted to personally investigate the signal. He was a man of quick action, knowing they had little time to waste securing the transmitter. There was a potential for the signal to go dark again, or be discovered by someone else.

Seraden and his crew left in the Essence three weeks after the signal alerted them. The active transmitter apprised them to its specific location through the portal, as if someone had turned on a flashlight and threw it down a well. They couldn't see the walls, but knew the way was clear of obstructions by following the light source on secure ground at the bottom.

The Sonarians didn't want to send a fleet into a waiting trap or chance a war with an enemy of unknown strength without first knowing what they were getting into. The Essence ship followed the ultrasonic pulsing signal of their strongbox to Muudia. The ship had basic weaponry, but speed and stealth were her best defenses.

As the Essence entered through the event horizon, the crew observed similar radiation levels to those recorded when their exploratory ship went missing. They exited the portal and entered the treacherous surroundings of the radiation zone of the Laurus solar system, and found plenty of activity as they narrowly avoided meteorites and debris in route to the planet.

The general detected no overt danger on Muudia despite the atmospheric conditions surrounding her. They found peaceful mining settlements, and felt safe to contact the Trecons to negotiate a return of their possession. There was every reason to believe the two parties could exchange ideas civilly, so the Sonarians could recover their transmitter.

Suddenly everything happening around Muudia played out in front of their eyes. The Essence detected the Mihhidite Sharks approaching MC1SA2 and retreated to a safe distance, where they observed the Raihan softening operation. They saw *Mule 357* perform the rescue mission and their attempt to outrun the Raihan carrier. They watched the dogfight and the Talon betrayal. Finally, they saw the Raihan ship take their strongbox transmitter from MC1SA2 and bolt off toward the portal.

After hostile actions were displayed by the Raihans, the Sonarian ship knew it was better to keep their distance from them. Seraden suspected it was a case of a mining colony who'd found the Sonarian transmitter by chance, just to have it stolen by criminals. Had the Trecons had the strongbox, an earnest attempt at negotiation would have taken place before any attack. However, a peaceful solution wouldn't be offered to the warmongering Raihans!

The Sonarians flew by the damaged Mule at close range and hailed the ship, but without success. As the Essence left the wounded cargo freighter behind, they viewed the *Mule 357* crew just as the Raihans had; like a small dying insect on a sidewalk that could be easily crushed if they had wished to. Seraden didn't have time to provide the Trecons with assistance because the situation was rapidly becoming a security risk for the Sonarians! The Essence left the '357 behind. Seraden was compelled to cut the distance between themselves and Knuddrul's *Rockwell III*.

It was apparent to the Sonarian crew that the Raihans wouldn't negotiate with them, based upon their actions against the Trecon mining camps. They observed the Raihans and prepared a full report on their capabilities, along with empirical evidence of dangers within the Laurus and Magnus solar systems.

The Raihans displayed many characteristics puzzling to the Sonarians. First, they attacked the camps for seemingly no reason except to steal the strongbox. They left the camps burning and the miners stranded with no recourse but to die defenseless with no means of escape. They savagely attacked the only ship who tried to rescue the stranded miners, a non-fighting and heavily damaged cargo freighter. The Raihans were heartless destroyers with no apparent motive for their assaults.

They weren't loyal to their brothers-in-arms. Seraden saw a Talon changing sides in a fight, and yet the Raihans just left the area. The Raihans didn't destroy the defector rat, which they could've done by terminating the Mule! Loyalty was the foundation of the Sonarian mindset. They were sure the Trecon crew were torturing the deserter as an enemy. A defector was seen with more contempt than an adversary. You could fight an enemy face-to-face, but a turncoat would stab you in the back unexpectedly. Retribution was brutal for traitors in the Sonarian culture!

What the general observed on and around planet Muudia confounded the Sonarians on many levels. A seed of hatred and contempt was planted deep in them for the Raihans. They were doubly concerned with the Raihan aggression they had observed on Muudia. As Seraden prepared his report, he outlined his observations and opinions. They'd take their property away from the Raihans and put it back safely in Sonarian hands. Seraden's top priority became keeping their homeland safe from such a sinister culture!

Sonaria was an enormous planet on the outer reaches of its galaxy, dark and persistently wet. Jagged slate mountains protruded everywhere on the surface, accentuating a gloomy landscape that lacked natural beauty. The Sonarians adapted well to their environment. Sonarians were towers of muscle averaging two meters tall. They were brawny, sleek, and powerful, just like their warships!

A fully loaded Sonarian Docker provided a well-equipped force for every stage of an attack. It held four Crusader attack ships and 40 soldiers for landing with other docking vessels, providing a hard-hitting terrestrial army! They had transmitter cannons that emitted a powerful range of light and sound frequencies designed to toy with enemy technology and render it useless, which was the case with the Raihan warships. The four Crusader fighters affixed to the exterior of the docking ships were heavy-duty and boxy, with laser blaster cannons protruding from all four wings.

Sonarian warbirds were the polar opposite of their Essence science spacecraft. It didn't matter to them they weren't the fastest ships in the battle, only that they were the meanest! Crusader fighters were built with heavy shielding to take a drubbing and keep coming back. Nothing in their design suggested mercy. The Crusaders were larger than typical fighters, similar in size to the RO's Trinitys. The outside was encrusted in a thin layer of the same dense metal as the frame of the strongbox transmitter, making their craft a hammering bully in a fight. They were just as content in ramming an enemy ship as they were blasting them into obliteration!

Crusader pilots were well trained. They flew in paired formations, with a crew leader using inventiveness to overcome real-time situations in battle. A study of their tactics would be impossible, because every pair acted differently based on their crew leader and the situation. The apparent randomness made the Crusaders intimidating to an enemy like the Raihans, who relied heavily on SOP's to guide them.

The Sonarian fleet was heading to Raihan, focused on destruction!

CHAPTER 41

Devastating Capital Siege and Raihan Surrender

As Abbsnate's Capital Fleet approached the outer edge of Rochest, they witnessed the Talons peeling away from their advance and leaving a clear path for the bombing strike of the government centers. To their amazement, an apparent Raihan retreat was happening before their eyes!

Several Starlance fighters broke off from their main fleet, to chase down and engage the escaping Talons. The Talons weren't interested in fighting any longer, and screamed away from them at their highest speed to find refuge in the upper atmosphere.

"Stick with the group. We have to stay focused on our goal of taking Rochest," Abbsnate called to her fellow attackers. "They're trying to separate us!" She couldn't believe that the tide had turned so quickly. Something was amiss.

Although she couldn't know it, the Talon flow stopped due to two unrelated events. First, all ships were being called back to a new battle location at an alarming rate, as Sonarian warships flooded the scene. Second, they were headed into a trap!

As the Starlances came back into formation, there was a palpable feeling of excitement within the group they were on the verge of victory. Abbsnate wisely warned them not to be too optimistic. "There's a surprise waiting for us in Rochest, so keep your head on a swivel!"

Booom streak fsheew, booom streak fsheew, booom streak fsheew, booom streak fsheew!

Blast, flash, glow!

An instant after the words escaped her mouth, a heavy barrage of surface fire lit up the sky around the capital. Two thousand ground-defense cannons fired into the sky at the Capital Fleet. With the first volley, seven allied fighters were blasted into dust!

Now it was clear to the Capital Fleet. The Talons had turned tail for their personal safety, because of the indiscriminate fire of the Rochest Defense Guardians!

A Trinity tried to dive below the laser fire, but had to pull up seconds before being destroyed. "There's a force field protecting the city. Retreat for now!"

Booom streak fsheew, booom streak fsheew, booom streak fsheew!

Flare, baroom!

The fleet immediately broke rank, and headed for the upper atmosphere as another barrage took out three more birds! The Capital Fleet was easily kept at bay and rendered useless to engage the defenders.

The ally fighters were unaware that they were playing into the Raihans' hands. The coalition had encountered the hammer of Rochest, and were about to experience the anvil of their warships!

*****

The emergence of the Sonarian fleet gave a shot of confidence to the invading forces; turning the tides quickly against the Raihans for the final time. President Grolegg was receiving an update from his commanders as he was hailed by General Krevety and given an ultimatum. The terms were simple: The Raihan government would accept their terms or the planet would continue to experience more attacks and the eventual ruin of their capital city.

As President Grolegg considered the terms, battles continued in the firmament above the planet. The atmosphere above Raihan indicated a clear reversal of power. Talons were breaking formation and flying for cover under the onslaught of the allied trio!

Tired Trinity and Starlance pilots were encouraged by their sudden success. They fought with a renewed sense of abandon alongside the Crusaders. With the surge of assistance from their new Sonarian allies, the birds could strike at the Raihan bases at will, and put a quick boot to the throat of the staggered giant. They'd put an end to the war before losing any more resources unnecessarily. Hundreds of Raihan warships left the stratosphere to engage the Sonarians in deep space, attempting to keep the Docker fleet at bay.

General Krevety saw victory arriving from the jaws of certain defeat, but he still didn't know the identity of the newcomers. He attempted to hail the Sonarian vessels again, but without success. "Keep trying until you get an answer," he ordered Commander Dach. "We have to know their origin."

"Yes general, we'll keep trying," replied the determined Boxer commander.

Pnoi Nbnok appeared on the bridge and interrupted their conversation, "Sir, we're attempting to contact them with standard high-frequency signals. This is very unusual, but I suggest we attempt our hails at lower antiquated frequencies instead."

"Give it a try," replied the general.

As they hit the right range of lower frequency, the Boxer commander discovered that the Sonarians had been attempting to contact them for some time.

Commander Dach patched the frequencies together, and inputted recorded voices of both into a translation device. *"Here you go general, see how this works!"*

Krevety broke the ice. "Welcome to the battle!"

General Krevety got a curious response. *"Greetings. I am General Yoheim Seraden. I, along with General Shrumann Shrog, are leading our fleet into battle. We're from the planet Sonaria. I have been acquainted with your Trecon race before, during the battle on the far side of the portal over the burning planet! We've come to retrieve our possession that was stolen by the Raihans."*

Seraden spoke with a heavy accent, but Dach had done well; the two men could understand each other well enough.

Krevety was perplexed. Sonaria wasn't included in the communication burst. The general knew of thousands of inhabited planets on the Laurus side of the portal, but had never heard of Planet Sonaria before. He'd get to the bottom of the mystery after the battle. Right then, he wouldn't look a gift horse in the mouth!

*****

Above the outer rings of Rochest, evidence of Raihan weakening wasn't visible yet. The Capital Fleet were too busy fighting for their lives to know what was happening elsewhere. The lighted 18-story Monument in the center of the city seemed to mock the fleet from the safety of the force field. As they turned away Abbsnate shook her fist at it, "I'll destroy that thing if it's the last thing I ever do!"

Booom streak fsheew, booom streak fsheew, booom streak fsheew, booom streak fsheew!

Shatter, bash, bright burst!

A Trinity and three Starlances were taken out!

The rising allies met their Talon foes once again, along with 100 Vengeance destroyers waiting to terminate them from above. In the allied haste to escape the surface-to-air defenses, they flew directly into the Raihan anvil trap! The Capital Fleet was suddenly in an impossible position. They tried to stay above the intense volley from below, while fighting against a gigantic fleet from above.

Seeing certain destruction flash before her eyes, Abbsnate hailed the Bruisers for help once again. The Raihans scrambled their signal, however; and for a moment it seemed they'd be stuck in limbo until there was no one left to fight!

Boom, boosh, bwoom!

Five Trinitys and two Starlances succumbed to the heavy barrage from above. Abbsnate's Capital Fleet had to choose their demise between the impossible Guardian defense below, and the vile fleet overhead. They were desperate.

"We have to withdraw and wait for more reinforcements. Our only shot is to band together in a cluster and give the destroyers everything we've got to break into the upper atmosphere!"

As Abbsnate was communicating her plan, Onsan looked for a weakness in the fleet above them. The destroyers seemed to form a perfect formation for hundreds of kilometers! "If we try to outflank the Vengeance ships, we'll be subjected to crossfire from all sides as we make a break for the opening. Our best option is to escape directly through the center of the fleet. We'll face the full effect of a head-on assault, but for a shorter duration."

Blast, shake, shudder!

Hundreds of Talons buzzed around them, trying to destroy the Capital Fleet!

"Prepare to ascend," was Abbsnate's order. "Stay in tight formation now!"

The heavily front-shielded Starlances led the way, with the Trinitys trailing close behind and fighting off the flanking Talons.

"Arghhhhh!"

Onsan yelled in defiance as they rose supersonically to meet the Raihan warships. If it was their last stand, they'd make a dent in the Raihan fleet before they died!

Baroom, blam!

Unexpectedly, the fire they were drawing from above was directed elsewhere as the Capital Fleet began the attack. Three destroyers burst into flames before their eyes, as 30 Sonarian Crusaders hurtled down to the rescue of the struggling Capital

Fleet. There were various cries of shock and confusion around them.

Abbsnate yelled, "What? How-who?" The stress and excitement around her turned Abbsnate's usual well-articulated speech into a child's garble. "We have to-. On through to the opening!"

Bottom line, they were saved!

*****

The Sonarian Dockers followed the signal of their long-lost transmitter, and worked their way through the fading Raihan defenses down to the Scientific Center. Upon landing, they made a ring with 30 ships surrounding the appropriate wing where their treasure was stored. Twelve hundred motivated soldiers promptly exited the Dockers, and provided a steely chokehold around the bay that housed their strongbox.

With everything happening around them, the Raihan scientists first thought it was best to shelter in place and employ a wait and see approach to the situation.

March, rataplan, tremor!

The Sonarian ground forces paraded forward and halted outside the bay that housed their transmitter. They were adorned in polished golden uniforms, trimmed with black high helmets, shiny combat boots, and thick leather belts. Each giant held a blaster in his hands, and a lethal look that seemed to beg non-compliance. They were itching for a fight!

Looking out into the faces of the fuming aliens, the scientists knew that opening the bay doors was the best decision to make!

Groan, screech, thud!

As the door slid open, the horde filed past the Raihans without fear of reprisal.

With the transmitter in hand, the Sonarian generals were relieved they'd met their first objective. The troops were ordered to stay in place, quarantine the bay, and await their superiors.

With Rochest threatened, the planet folded easily under the pressure, just as Abbsnate suggested. The mighty Raihan Empire was brought to her knees! President Yerb Grolegg had no other choice but to sue for peace.

CHAPTER 42

Restitution for the Wanderers

Throughout Raihan, everyone was experiencing apocalypse together as if they'd taken a time out during the battle. Sonarian show of force took the starch out of Raihan determination to defend smoldering ruins. Everyone's heads were pointed upward for hours, while they watched the Sonarians bashing the Raihan defenses.

Outside Com-Facility 12 and Base 13, the Raihan loyalists still had the Wanderer forces under guard, awaiting further orders. Everyone knew that the Raihans were defeated, but the balance of power still overwhelmingly favored the Raihans out there.

The Mihhidite contingent was itching for the Wanderers to make a false move so they could open fire upon them. Others within the Raihan defense force were no longer interested in warring against the Wanderer mob, but they also didn't want to just lay down their weapons to an angry insurrectionary crowd who'd been mistreated by their government for years!

Within the command centers, all the focus had been on a long, drawn-out battle going into the siege. Both sides were unprepared for such a short war with the Raihans losing in such a fashion! Rapid preparations for getting leaders together to discuss terms of surrender took time and resulted in confusion on the battlefields.

Ground forces outside the gates were forgotten about, to a point. Initial orders were given to the Raihan defense forces to cease fire but not to lay down their arms. Although the Wanderers were on the victorious side, they had to wait under the watch of the defeated Raihan forces who still had the weapons. A restlessness growing in the crowd indicated the situation could turn from bad to worse quickly.

The Wanderers kept their leaders well shielded from the Raihans because there wasn't an inkling of trust among them. The resistance fighters were becoming restless, feeling like a small forgotten detail in the big picture. It was growingly apparent to the Raihans that the Wanderers were no longer in the mood for being kept under close guard. Shouting turned into pushing matches where the lines of distinction came together.

Outside Base 13, coalition ground reinforcements arrived in two Boulder troop transports. The rescuers had a complex task ahead of them. They were instructed to confiscate weapons from everyone and separate them into two main groups: The Raihan loyalists on one side and the Wanderer and resistance forces on the other. Medical supplies and food were brought in to care for the weary and battle-wounded on both sides. The large mass of people was too much for the Trecons to handle.

"We need more assistance down here," said a Trecon Marine officer.

Abbsnate answered eagerly from her Trinity, *"On the way."*

Ten minutes later, Three Trinity fighters and another two Boulder transports landed on the edge of the crowd. As the ships landed, the RO birds kept their hind-cannons trained on the Mihhidites and Raihan defenders. If they tried to engage, the Trinitys would rain fire down upon them in an instant!

Abbsnate scuttled down the ladder on her craft oddly, almost tripping over the last rung as she hit the ground! Serlat broke free from the mob and limped toward the ships. The two ran toward each other, embracing tightly and sobbing as

Nobert Serlat picked up Abbsnate in his arms and twirled her in circles.

"I can't believe it daughter! Is this a dream?"

"Father, you look hurt. Are you alright?" She handed Serlat a canteen of water.

"Forget about me," he said holding Abbsnate in front of him. "I just want to look at you for a while!"

Onsan understood what was unfolding in front of him, and marveled as he saw the pilots and navigators from the other Trinitys' exit and greet the ragged-looking Wanderers. As Abbsnate and Serlat held their embrace, Onsan gathered from the surrounding conversation that Serlat was Abbsnate's father.

So long ago, she'd joined the mining mission against his wishes. A father would have enough on his mind regarding the mission, but adding his beautiful daughter on the trip with 1,000 young men added a whole new layer of stress. Little could he have known, keeping Abbsnate away from young science officers would be the easiest part of the expedition to Muudia! Abbsnate hadn't gone to be rebellious, only because she was one of her interest in science. She had one of the keenest minds in Ryderson Omega.

The next 24 years after Mission 15-101.25 would test her endurance. Being a solitary agent outside the tight Ryderson Omegan culture was more than the normal person could bear. There was a real possibility Abbsnate and Serlat would never see each other again, despite living less than 100 kilometers away on the same planet. Now they met, victorious!

After their passionate reunion, Abbsnate requested to Onsan that her father ride with her in the Trinity, and Onsan happily obliged.

"We have to go to the Wanderer settlements first," said Serlat as he buckled into the seat beside his daughter.

"Yes, father, show us where."

The Trinity lifted off and headed east into the rocky desert wilderness. After 10 minutes of flying low over the surface, they climbed over the foothills before dropping into what seemed to be an arid wasteland of dry, cracked desert. Abbsnate spotted a village on the horizon. The small huts appeared deserted as the Trinity eased down into the middle of the structures. The cockpit opened, and Serlat slowly descended down the vessel to the ground.

He yelled, "It's alright, you're safe to come out!"

Abbsnate watched faces populate in glassless windows. Older men and women slowly made their way out to the fighter craft. She recognized many as Ryderson Omegans, and they identified her too, coming up to excitedly greet her. Many had cursed her name, but suddenly the secretive plan made sense to them.

"How many are there here?" asked Abbsnate.

"There are 34 left in this settlement, but there are many other larger camps with older people than us."

"Everyone left behind were physically unable to march," explained Serlat.

"We need to get ground transports here to give them proper medical treatment." Abbsnate called for medical reinforcements.

Soon, medics arrived on the scene. The crews spent six hours visiting 14 settlements and rescuing 556 people. Abbsnate felt her heart melt with respect and admiration for the Wanderers.

The patients would thank Abbsnate or the medics gently loading them to be taken to proper nourishment and advanced medical care.

"No, thank you," was Abbsnate's only tear-filled response.

Abbsnate wasn't the only one in awe of the Wanderers. The medical crews, regardless of Raihan affiliation, looked at the Wanderers in wonderment. Many of the Integrator medics didn't know the full details of the settlements, and some even had planetary kin there. The air was ripe with a feeling of admiration and respect for the *former* Wanderers! They were the ones who'd given up a life of comfort to stand for the hope of seeing their homes again. They'd survived the worst the Raihans could dish out, and emerged victorious!

Great care was taken loading the resilient heroes. Serlat's heart swelled with pride, knowing that his daughter's sacrifice made it all possible in the first place!

*****

Onsan performed his own rescue operation. First, he led a small force to the purification factories to free the Trecon workers. The factory was running at full capacity. It hadn't been stopped yet because the Raihans expected a short decisive victory. Word slowly leaked through, but the factory hadn't halted production. The guards figured it was best to keep the workers sheltered and busy within its loud confines rather than have a revolt on their hands!

When Onsan and his force approached the factory entrance, the gig was up, however. The Mihhidite guards at the factory opened up the gates without a fight, and Onsan walked among Trecons in the ore purification process. As he walked down the smoky thoroughfare, Onsan admired the vastness of the workshop.

Ka-chink ka-chunk, ka-chink ka-chunk, whiiiir!

In the refinement plant, 18 large glowing pits were running deafeningly, straining to their full capacity. Nine machines on each side of the factory were separated by a thoroughfare through the middle, where heavy equipment was loading and unloading metal in its various stages of decontamination and purification. Each towering contraption was lurching and belching smoke heavily, as trillelium rose on conveyors up massive ramps before being dumped into the top of hoppers. The machines were crude and simple for a planet that prided itself in technology, but effectiveness kept the plant in service.

Hum kitscha thud, hum kitscha thud!

Gravity was the most important component used, as heavy metal rolled down and crashed into thick tumblers. Impurities were incinerated and exited the factory vertically

324

in huge smokestacks. After the metal was melted down and purified, it came out the bottom to be loaded as final product to be brought to storage.

Onsan ordered the machines to be stopped, and they stalled to a grinding halt around him.

Clatter, crank, screech, eerrt!

As the machinery quieted down, Curious Trecon workers formed a natural circle around Onsan, in a stoic fog about what was happening. The looks on their faces said it all. It was a fellow Trecon, but the uniform and rank of the young man indicated a freighter bridge officer, not a marine. They were puzzled, but there was also a collective sense of relief.

Colonel Honassen broke the silence, "So, we weren't forgotten after all!"

Onsan looked over the crowd and offered, "Hello, fellow Trecons, I'm Onsan Vorga. We're here to liberate you and bring you back home!"

Honassen moved closer and introduced himself. "I'm the officer in charge, Colonel Ferd Honassen." Rank wasn't outwardly worn. Everyone was wearing matching blue malodorous sweat-stained uniforms. The Trecons kept firm military structure, despite attempts to break it.

Onsan offered a salute to the exultant colonel. "General Krevety is hoping you're well, and is anxiously waiting to see you!"

The colonel returned his salute and stated, "After I get cleaned up."

Next, Onsan worked his way to the Base 13 Gallows, where 189 inmates were being held. Ninety-three were women who'd been classified by the Mihhidites as spies and lost contact with their children. Although they were broken physically, Onsan sensed a great deal of optimism and strength as he opened the cells to liberate them. There was suddenly a chance they'd see their children again, and hope burned visibly within them!

Onsan immediately contacted Major Tallik to initiate reunions. Thus, began a complicated process. Some would be grown soldiers, raised in the training orphanage. Others were still in the academy. The records would be studied, and every effort would be taken to reunite families.

When Onsan walked through the halls of the detention center, he passed by many bruised and broken prisoners in grateful awe of their liberators. They knew the powerful Raihan machine was beaten, but seemed to be in a state of suspended belief!

Dr. Hetle Orbne had been recently interrogated hard by Slae Nodk, and had trouble walking out under his own power. He was physically battered, but in relatively good spirits. As he limped along, the sight of others in need made the doc forget about his pain. Orbne's medical instincts took over, he ignored his injuries and attended to the other prisoners the best he could. He'd heal completely from his wounds soon enough.

Onsan was on the lookout for two prisoners mentioned to him by Abbsnate: Captain Yougsten Brell and Commander Steph Knuddrul. As instructed, Onsan had Captain Brell put into a solitary holding cell for his protection. Abbsnate wanted to make sure her former confidant was safe.

One liberator reported to Onsan, "Sir, there's no evidence of Commander Knuddrul."

Upon further inspection, a series of solitary cells were discovered behind a false wall. There was only one prisoner in the secluded stalls: Raihan public enemy number one, Prisoner 19-128.25!

Onsan entered the cell and noticed a frail Knuddrul hovering near death in dark solitary confinement. The damp cell was left unprotected from the outside elements. Dark water stains penetrated through the ceiling and down the walls of the dank cell. Onsan heard the man breathing heavily.

Wheeze, huff, pant.

Knuddrul squinted toward Onsan and asked weakly, "Come to finish the job?"

It was obvious Knuddrul didn't know whom he was talking to and assumed it was Slae Nodk. He was hanging on to his final thread of brashness, planning to go out on his own terms.

Onsan kept his military bearing and addressed the Raihan officer by his official title, "Commander Knuddrul, we're going to move you to a safer holding cell."

"Huh?"

Gasp, puff.

Knuddrul had started the whole ball rolling and made the invasion possible. Although he'd never own it; a far greater outcome than intended came from his self-serving arrogance. He deserved the dignity of being treated like a human again!

CHAPTER 43

Terms of Surrender

The swift allied victory complicated things greatly for everyone. General Krevety realized their first priority was to maintain control within the capital of Rochest. Those with knowledge and participation of corruption were put on strict schedules and house arrests. The restrictions were enforced for their protection and to limit their waning influence throughout the population. The full process of law would have to prevail, not one of vigilantism and chaos!

Abbsnate didn't get her wish to destroy the Monument on the city island. General Krevety had a different plan for it. The 18-story tower would serve as a memorial to the fallen who'd been sacrificed by Raihan along the way, rather than a testament of their power. In his mind, the Monument would symbolize the sacrifices of unknown heroes toward peace throughout the universe.

A closer look at the native Raihans inhabiting Rochest revealed an ugly sight behind the glamorous curtain. Although the community had all the wealth they could ever hope for, they could never beat the science of biology or steadiness of father time. Their population never recovered from the radiation effects of their early missions. Many family bloodlines were extinct, and others were struggling to hold steady.

The average age of the native Raihans in Rochest was 47 years. Their attempts at growing organic families were faltering. The Raihan nomads were not a viable option because they ran in small bands, and were elusive. They'd fight to the living soul and would yield nothing to the Rochest dwellers but permanently traumatized children! Efforts to repopulate with comparable biological races from other planets didn't yield positive results, either. The orphanage was a final grasp for them to restore a semblance of family. Wanderer children were adopted by Rochest families, but they could never control the burning rage within the orphanage kids.

After a child turned four, they were instituted into the academy where Raihan values were drilled into their minds. At 14, orphaned youth were transferred to the military academy, where their natural and technical skills were honed according to their strengths. despite all the advantages, some kids didn't feel right. Their heads were programed, but their hearts yearned for fraternity. There was a sixth sense inside, telling them they didn't belong there.

Such was the case with Strider Willstreak. He'd visited the Monument tower often. He knew he was from Yiohhaw, so he wore a path around the loop on floor 16. It was the only place on Raihan that felt like home, like his ancestors were calling out to him. There were 56 Willstreaks carved into the memorial stone, and no Willstreak Yiohhawans in the city. The kid couldn't believe all his relatives would've died when the Raihans saved them from the storms of Planet 6333.

Strider's formal education hailed the Raihans as humanitarians, performing 18 rescues in deep space on the far side of the portal. Something was off, information was missing. In the back of his mind, he saw all the holes and wondered how so many could be fooled. He learned about the lures of the lavish culture as he got older, and Strider understood the possibility that people didn't seek the truth because they didn't want to know it. The good life was too hard to pass on. As a result, Strider separated himself from everyone.

Rather than try to fit in, Strider engrossed himself in technology from a young age. Several attempts by adoptive parents fell apart. Strider wanted no part of immersing himself into a Raihan family. As he excelled through the technology program, Strider became more distant from those around him. He voluntarily pushed humans away for computers. Although Strider was an extreme example, other orphans showed similar attributes.

There was no viable solution for the imminent extinction of the Raihan race despite immense medical knowledge and resources. There was only frailty and regret hidden within the confines of the Raihan capital. Very few within the government knew what it looked like behind the scenes.

*****

President Grolegg was the person with the greatest access into the secret society of natural Raihans. Where he saw weakness within, he projected supremacy to the planet population to hole the status quo.

Grolegg got what he wanted politically through coercion, which went in both directions from his perch within the Rochest government center. The true Raihans were in no condition to surrender to the trio of allies because they no longer represented true influence there. President Grolegg was the puppet master who had all the power on Raihan. He was the person who surrendered to Krevety, as it should have been.

In Rochest, the main players arrived to discuss the terms of Raihan's immediate surrender and subsequent termination of war-time activities. As part of the agreement, a contingent was allowed full access to the main facilities of the Raihan government. All financial, military, and scientific zones would be carefully inspected. The group included General Krevety of the Trecons, Generals Shrog and Seraden of the Sonarians, Abbsnate Serlat of the Ryderson Omegans, Nobert Serlat of the Wanderer resistance forces, and President Grolegg.

Hio Figiop excused himself from the proceedings and returned to his roaming clan. He declared that the Raihan nomads wouldn't participate in the events. They were contented to return to the wilderness, free at last of government-endorsed harassment and persecution.

Major Tallik and a combined staff moderated and documented the proceedings. Each group had a smaller staff of three representatives. Long and complicated days were in store for everyone involved, and they wanted to do it right. Every leader had their own concerns and trepidations at the beginning of the meetings.

The main subjects of importance for the Trecons and Ryderson Omegans differed greatly from the Sonarians. The Trecons and RO's listed wealth distribution, the delicate process of possible relocation to home planets, and a newly structured Raihan government to rule the planet fairly. The Sonarians considered security and regulation of the gravitational portal as their top priority. They wanted to protect and limit access to their planet, and felt that a more authoritarian government was needed to accomplish their objective.

After their main concerns were voiced, an agenda was made and official meetings were planned to start in the morning on the following day. Each group were to produce an outline of their ideas, and they'd be brought forward for discussion and a vote. After a consensus on the issues by the three allies, a final draft would be put into transitionary law.

General Krevety wanted to return to Trecon but also knew he was needed during the transition. They were sitting on a powder keg that demanded his experience and attention. Raihan still held a massive amount of power in the galaxy, and any evidence of governmental collapse there would mean possible intergalactic war as planets lined up for their piece of the pie. They needed to keep up the appearance of a strong regime while they built up a foundation of a respectable government.

As Krevety drafted his proposal, he looked at "New Raihan" from many angles. New Raihan would be in flux far into the foreseeable future, with the biggest question being how they'd set up a fair government on the planet. Each individual should have a choice whether to return home or stay on New Raihan. Many galactic races thrived there! There were generations of people living there who wouldn't want to return to an unknown home across the universe. Some were too old and feeble to make a long journey back to their origin planet.

With the SOS dispatch that originated from Com-Facility 12, it was highly possible that New Raihan would have many visitors arriving in a constant flow. A peaceful communication and invitation was sent to the victim planets. All the societies would be represented within the council, except the felonious Mihhidites. Every member in the council would have equal say regarding the future of New Raihan.

The elected officials on New Raihan would have the same level of influence as a statesman on one's own planet, and would carry it with them throughout the universe. Wealth distribution would be fair among the victim planets. When an envoy arrived for the first time, they'd be greeted with a generous gift rather than sword rattling associated with war. Raihan was so prosperous, they could support the proposal with enough resources left over to sustain their economy.

The Sonarians were not interested in becoming a part of the process, but selected General Seraden to pacify the council. As for the security of the gravitational portal, the Sonarians took the lead role. A plan was devised by Shrog to have portal guardians, where the Trecons, RO's, and Sonarians would each play a part guarding their perspective entries from unregulated travel. Planetary kin arriving through would be registered to ensure that the fragile peace was preserved.

The plan quickly deteriorated for the Sonarians for several reasons. First, there were no planets close enough to the portal to provide a defense settlement for regulation of portal travel. They'd have to build space stations, or place permanent fleets in the ergosphere near the hazardous portal zones.

Second, they'd pay too heavy a price in maintenance. Constant radiation, SIDS, and meteorite showers would pound any vessels that orbited along the ergosphere or navigated through the portal. Deliberately sending people to serve near the ergosphere and exposing them to the subsequent radiation was unacceptable to the RO's and Trecons.

Last, if anything went wrong with the process of registration, feelings could quickly intensify to the point of another intergalactic war.

The more complicated the meetings got, the more agitated General Shrog became. He met secretly with his council. "I can see Sonarian wishes are always going to be vetoed by the other two! We won the war for them, but they've gained all the power!"

"Give it a little more time," pleaded General Seraden. "We're all still trying to figure each other out!"

In the mind of General Shrog, the world was black and white. One didn't sit at a table and discuss how to treat their conquered adversaries with dignity! Initially, they believed the meetings were to divide up the Raihan Empire among the three allies and punish the dishonorable. Shrog hated the process of a peaceful solution and wondered what was taking so long. The coalition should detail their demands and the Raihans accept their offer unconditionally, simple as that. The idea of a New Raihan was absurd to him!

As the process developed further, the Sonarian contingent had a feeling that their portal-security concerns were being put on the back burner compared to the provisional government and the division of riches proposed by the other two participants.

CHAPTER 44

Raihan Scientific Center

The ally representatives got a tour of the crown jewel of Raihan superiority, the Raihan Scientific Center. Despite their position as victors, the group felt privileged to tour the vast compound. It was like going on a guided tour to each victim planet.

The Scientific Center was where all the natural abilities and talents of victim Contributors came into focus to further Raihan influence. Imaginative inventions were on exhibition for the tour group. The work of visionary masters from every planet came to life around them. The flow of new blood and perspective had an effect of ensuring the Raihans would always be on the cutting edge of knowledge and technology.

The massive complex stretched over five square kilometers in a maximum-security area within Base 13. It was the most secretive and protected facility in the universe, where all the latest information was taken in, recorded, analyzed, and tested; keeping the Raihans on top of the technological mountain!

New alien technology passed through the facility before being integrated into Raihan society or sold throughout the universe. Because of their rigorous standards, the expertise coming out of the center gained Raihan a reputation as the best in the galaxy!

The Scientific Center had five main wings and one ambiguous annex, each headed by the top scientist in their field. The wing directors were independent from the others, answering only to the highest levels of the Raihan government. The facility was the second-most regarded place on the planet, behind only the capital city. From it flowed the true source of Raihan wealth and power. Everything began and ended there, where a meeting of minds from various extraterrestrial backgrounds melded into one.

The five wings within the Scientific Center included Terrestrial Research, Reaching Technology, Research and Development (R&D), Interplanetary Ecology, and Weaponry.

Trecon mining equipment, for example, was sent to the R&D wing so it could be studied to discover what had made them so effective in the deep exploration of Planet 6333. While the R&D wing was the undisputed end point for the Trecon mining equipment, finding a home for other incoming apparatus wasn't as cut and dry. The Scientific Center was the obvious destination for the Sonarian strongbox, but the prize had been in limbo as each leader fought to adopt it as their own!

Infighting was common. There'd been a history of contention from its inception, as the five wings battled one another for funding, space, and equipment. Because of the hyper-bureaucracy, the ambiguous Universal Tech Annex was created in the center of the facility. It provided equal access to all five entities while the government decided where its final home would be.

Upon realizing the relic was a transmitter, the Sonarian strongbox was moved from the Universal Tech Annex and awarded to the Reaching Technology wing. The head official in the Reaching Technology wing of the facility was General Dom Greudow.

The general gave Abbsnate a hateful glance as she walked by with the group, and the girl just smiled back at him.

"Nice to see you, General Greudow!"

"Humph," grumbled Greudow.

The tour was almost like going home for Abbsnate in a way.

There was a time when Abbsnate was a promising young scientist in the Reaching Technology wing under Greudow. As she worked her way up the ladder there, she realized that her plans of eventual escape could never be realized within the Reaching Technology wing. She needed a change of scenery to realize her long-term goals.

Abbsnate requested a transfer to the Weaponry wing. A move like that didn't foster suspicion, because they were made all the time. Ambitions had up-and-comers moving around the facility like pieces on a chessboard.

Once she got established in the Weaponry wing, Abbsnate moved to the pilot program to test and fly the prototype Talon II fighter craft. She gained a solid reputation there, as she had throughout her career. Those around her thought she was setting herself up for an elevated military position, and a political livelihood. Abbsnate realized that joining the Weaponry wing as a Talon pilot would help her gain traction for her ultimate escape plan.

Eventually, Abbsnate was named executive officer for the 19-128.25 softening operation. Her main purpose on the mission was to test and grade the new Talon II, along with fellow Weaponry wing research pilot Ljpoh HNoui.

An intimate view of Abbsnate's plan would reveal that her ultimate goal was to become commander of Mission 21-141.75. She could use her rank on the Rockwell to contact the miners on Muudia, warn them and enlist their help. As mission commander, she'd be in a better position to succeed against Raihan than the hero Yerb Hertag was as a com officer during the 16-108 Yiohhaw Mission. There were reservations attached to achieving mission commander, because competition for the position was steep.

Seeing the Trecon Mule fast-forwarded Abbsnate's plan because it was there for the taking. She wouldn't have to endure

13.5 years of uncertainty to start her true mission. However, Abbsnate would be taking calculated risks from the beginning.

Abbsnate's decision to let Ljpoh HNoui pilot the Talon II against the Mule was deliberate. She was no match for HNoui in the Talon II in an even fight, and she knew it. Had the Talon II been the stolen fighter, she'd have forced Brell's hand to recover the bird rather than leave her to face the treacherous hazard zone. She had one chance to get it right, and kicked off her mission outnumbered in an under-gunned ship.

*****

As the envoy continued their tour through the Scientific Center, they were amazed by their surroundings. The tour took eight hours, yet didn't scratch the surface! They zigzagged through well-lit corridors, down freight elevators 18 floors deep into the crust of the planet, and through enormous bays where alien technology was being meticulously taken apart and put back together.

The Terrestrial Research wing housed exhibits of plant and animal life from the far reaches of the universe. Bioengineered food and medical research were the main focus of the Interplanetary Ecology wing.

Everyone was civil, until the Raihans were discovered poring over frequencies to find a comparative to the strong-box transmitter. They were looking for the origin of the signal.

Major Tallik was confronted with a situation getting out of control fast. He hailed Krevety. *"General Krevety, you're needed in the Reaching Technology Wing as soon as you're able. We have a major issue brewing."*

"Copy, see you soon."

As the Sonarians were loading their strongbox transmitter in the Reaching Technology wing of the facility, they discovered that cryptographers were still hard at work in an adjoining laboratory researching the frequency spectrum and origin of the signal.

General Shrog was irate. "We were told to hold off loading while they decontaminated our transmitter of radiation, yet here they are, trying to track us."

"I'm sure there's a logical explanation for this. General Greudow?"

Greudow answered, "They're just doing their job. There's been a lot going on here lately. I forgot to terminate their activities, simple as that. They haven't touched it since you arrived."

General Shrog grew red in the face. "How do you expect me to believe that? As a matter of fact, why are you still in charge here, general?"

Krevety answered, "He's a scientific officer, Shrog, not affiliated with the military. His rank is a pay grade, simple as that. Similar to Seraden."

"I want all the research turned over to me now!"

General Krevety was irritated with the situation. He looked at General Greudow. "That's fair. Bring everything to us at once!"

Krevety's thoughts betrayed his countenance. *This is the last thing we need, tensions are already high!*

Stacks of data files and piles of computer equipment were brought out and turned over to Shrog. After he'd scoured the lab, the Sonarian looked satisfied.

It had been a long day, and the outing was cancelled for the evening. "We'll continue the tour tomorrow," said General Krevety.

Later that evening, Shrog had General Greudow and the encryption team taken prisoner so he could uncover what the Raihans knew about the return path to Sonaria. Word got back to General Krevety that the Sonarians had taken prisoners of war. He contacted General Shrog to assure they were being treated well, under the agreement with Raihan terms of surrender.

It was hard for Shrog to accept that not everyone on Raihan was guilty, some were brainwashed lab rats doing the bidding of the real masters.

Krevety explained to Shrog that if he mistreated the prisoners, then the Sonarians were not adhering to their end of the peace agreement. They'd cause unrest, and the planet would disintegrate into chaos!

Shrog assured General Krevety the prisoners were being treated well, and that he'd release them in a few days.

CHAPTER 45

The Reaper Initiative

The following day within the Weaponry wing of the Raihan Scientific Center, the allies found information that concerned them greatly! Abbsnate had warned Krevety about the possibilities of surprises within the wing. However, she didn't have full access until that day. Everyone's eyes were opened up to things that changed their opinion of the Raihan ability to wage war despite their weakened condition!

Burgeoning ideologies were growing within the walls of the wing, aggressive attitudes with fertile ground to grow. A message was found from President Grolegg to the Weaponry wing director, General Austin Reece. General Krevety cringed as he read it. Suddenly, hopes of a peaceful conclusion appeared to crumble, despite all they'd done to get things right.

Since Mission 14-94.5, the Mihhidites had gradually influenced leadership until their fingerprints tarnished the highest levels of Raihan ideology. The aggressive militants were gaining momentum in the government centers of Rochest and threatening to modify Raihan policy through persistence and attrition.

Outwardly, they'd claim that their advanced weapons were for protection, but realistically they craved only unfathomable power and wealth, beyond what Planet 6333 could bring them! Until recently, the Raihan government wasn't ready to push imperialism openly, but the war changed every-thing. The days of prospering from kidnapping a few thousand miners and stealing ore at a set time and place from Planet 6333 were over.

Due to Mihhidite influence, thought patterns had been gradually changing for years. The Raihans were in the devel-opment stage of many armaments and strategies that would make them a bigger threat throughout the universe. As the group was touring the Weaponry wing, they discovered new weapons and a communication memo of how the Raihans would use them. The discovery horrified the group because Raihan still had countless agents roaming the galaxy. It was possible they could use the ships to stage an invasion of their own to retake the planet!

The Talon II fighter was slated to replace the original bird within the year. Seventeen Talon II prototypes were being tested on and around Raihan. Five were based at the center, two were at different locales, and 10 were on the new *Vehemence XX* carrier. When the message was sent, testing on the new fighter was 85 percent completed. As soon as the bugs were worked out, they'd begin final production on the birds. They trusted Kufsiun to build the ships, and had a shipment of 700 arriving soon.

What made the new Talon II more dangerous were the newly advanced targeting systems, which made them twice as deadly as before. Retina-recognition technology married the ship in a biological way with its pilot, activating automated weapons systems infinitely faster than the finger-trigger can-nons of first-generation Talons. When flying into battle, the pilot would depress a bright blue button on the console. An illuminated screen would appear before the aeronaut, con-nected by frequency to their helmet, and synchronized with the eyes of the pilot through their retina.

The pilot could locate and destroy multiple targets by merely looking at them! As fast as they could pick out a tar-get, it would be fired upon. The cannons would also be more powerful plasma laser rays that could penetrate thick armor of enemy warships and disintegrate other fighters with a single shot! The newer plasma cannons didn't add too much size or weight to the Talon. The ship had a greater deep-space range than the original. Where the first-generation Talon could travel 483 kilometers for five hours safely from a carrier in deep space, the range of the new fighter was improved to venture 1046 kilometers for eight hours.

A squadron of Talon II fighters could be sent ahead of the main fleet to soften up a target before their following force showed up to clean up the mess. The Raihans already had overwhelming numbers in space, but the upgrade would be a game changer for them! If they expanded their role of conquest, an enhanced fighter like the Talon II would make them twice as formidable as before. The plan was to include flying squadrons of II's into their fleet and eventually replace the Talon I model over the next six years.

The crown jewel of the Reaper Initiative was the top-secret program which included nine ready-for-use gamma bombs, and the massive *Vehemence XX* carrier to house and deploy them. There were three carrier prototypes being tested, two on the surface and one out on a deep-space trial mission. Systems tests for the behemoth were 75 percent completed. The carrier was twice the size of her predecessor, with advanced systems and stores that allowed her to be deployed in space for five years without re-servicing! The ship housed two 24 Talon II squadrons within her massive hull.

When the carrier activated sensor blocking and automated suppression (SBAS or concealment mode), it was electronically undetectable to surrounding ships and equipment. The technology allowed it to disappear and travel discreetly to a far-off location and deploy the gamma bomb payload. Its ability to carry three gamma bombs made it the most dangerous, though. The gamma bombs were developed and tested three years prior on a remote (former) moon in the deserted Brevla solar system. The moon was obliterated by the bomb!

The *Vehemence XX* had advanced navigation and communication systems, along with increased rapidity travel that allowed her to journey between solar systems and the dimensional portal with ease. The news greatly concerned the allies.

General Shrog and his team dismissed themselves from the tour. The anger was evident as the goliaths left the room in a huff, like a raging river thundering toward a waterfall. General Seraden had no choice but to go along with the flow. He looked back and shot Krevety an expression of apology as the golden-clad Sonarians exited.

General Krevety looked at Abbsnate. "You worked here, but didn't know about this?"

Abbsnate looked awkwardly at the general. "I was away doing deep space trials in the Talon II until three months before the softening mission. I didn't have access to anything but the Talon II. Commander Brell knew, but he was sworn to secrecy. I was forbidden to tell Brell about the II, and he was forbidden to tell me about the *Vehemence XX.* Even though we were close, I couldn't afford to fully trust him."

They watched Shrog's contingent leave the bay in a huff.

"There's one of those ships out there somewhere. This really puts us behind the eight ball!"

Abbsnate shrugged. "If I'd have been poking around for information about a different program, I'd have been thrown into prison. They kept everything secretive in order to control the population. I flew blindly into the barrage over Rochest, remember!"

The general put his hand on Abbsnate's shoulder. "I'm not blaming you. The timing is just highly unfortunate!"

They looked through the records, and sent an investigation team to search for the bombs in their last known location.

*****

Vehemence XX testing went on as normal when the Raihans were planning for the war with the original two allies. The carrier was available for orders if needed, but the Raihans were expecting a short and decisive win. The ship flew out of range and continued their deep-space trials. They had to get the carrier ready for their travels to Trecon and Ryderson Omega.

When the Sonarian attack started, communication between Raihan Central Command and the *Vehemence XX* went black as the carrier went into SBAS concealment mode. The invisible ship was present throughout the remainder of the battle, doing what it could to help the Raihan cause. There weren't enough trained people left to man the other two prototype carriers. The *Vehemence XX* hadn't been heard from since Raihan's surrender.

General Reece was as elusive as the carrier. The investigators would get no answers from him!

*****

Three hours later, Onsan's crew found the bombs 50 meters underground in a secure compound at a remote desert location. *"Found 'em sir, we've located all nine gamma bombs!"*

"Great, put the bombs under guard until we decide what to do with them. We have to search the records and see where they ordered them from. The last thing we need is for the carrier to get ahold of three more from the origin planet!"

"Yes sir, my eyes will stay glued on them!"

"Quarantine everyone there. Did you find General Reece?"

"Negative general."

"Search the compound again, and ask around. The general could answer questions that would help keep us safe!" Based on the capture of Greudow, Krevety knew Reece would never give himself up.

The ship carried no gamma bombs for trials, but no one could be sure where the rogue *Vehemence XX* was except for the missing general! The carrier could be traveling among the Raihan atmosphere, or going through deep space to secure more bombs!

Krevety looked at the message again and shuddered. The letter from President Grolegg to General Reece indicated that colonization on Trecon and RO would be in play after they won the war. The critical memorandum was sent two weeks before the invasion:

> *General Austin Reece, we must defend ourselves against explicit hostility toward our peaceful planet. Our two-year timeline referring to the Talon II and next generation Vehemence XX programs have reached their final conclusion today! Those vessels are needed now as we strive to improve our galactic capabilities immediately! Because of the impending attack, our hand has been forced to expand our overt influence into neighboring galaxies and dimensions. We need to subjugate the antagonistic governments of Trecon and Ryderson Omega. Only through the unfortunate necessity of annexation, will we achieve peace. Our just colonization of the aggressive planets is the product of self-defense; protection of Raihan society and philosophies. Therefore, great urgency and focused attention are required to complete testing and render the Reaper Initiative a go straightaway.*

> *-P. Yerb Grolegg*

The language of the message precluded innocence and self-defense by the Raihans. If Grolegg took back Raihan, Trecon and RO would be painted as criminal regimes throughout the galaxy. It made General Krevety sick to his stomach!

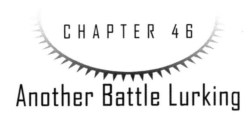

CHAPTER 46

Another Battle Lurking

As the meetings progressed, Sonarian leadership was visibly agitated with the process. It was abundantly clear that the Sonarians had no confidence that the provisional government could be trusted to overcome the void created as the old was transferred to the new.

General Shrog had a point to prove. "While we wait and trust the process, splintering factions will create a fertile environment for the planet to descend into civil war," stated Shrog bluntly. "Inside the lawless emptiness and lack of a controlling government, weapons and technology are ripe for the picking! We were lucky the bombs were recovered! There are too many here with inside information to break in and steal weaponry, in order to give their faction the upper hand."

Krevety tried to talk sense into the man. "You've seen for yourself, Abbsnate didn't know the full story here. Those who can put such pieces together have been detained."

Shrog's reddened neck turned three shades darker, and his murky blue eyes would have shot out lightening if looks could kill. "Then tell me Krevety, where is General Austin Reece?"

"Of course, general, I can't make promises, but it appears to be moving in a positive direction. We've reunited countless families together who've been apart for decades. Several victim planets have contacted us, and are sending representatives to contribute peacefully to the new assembly. Really, General Shrog, what more do you want?"

The paranoid Shrog wanted to be guaranteed the Raihans would never follow the Sonarians back through the portal and attack them with a built-up military force. At the top of his list of concerns was the missing general, followed by the new *Vehemence XX* carrier. "What of their super ship? No one has the ability to contact it or knows of its current location. The captain didn't follow terms of surrender and bring the ship into port," Shrog emphatically stated his case. "For all we know, the scoundrel captain is speeding to our planet with evil intentions."

"We've confirmed there are no bombs aboard the rogue vessel," replied Krevety. "There's an account for all nine gamma bombs within the Raihan arsenal. They've been put under the strictest security."

"I want a Sonarian guard there as well," Shrog quickly replied.

"Of course," replied General Krevety, putting on his best poker face.

The wise Trecon general had a sick feeling growing in the pit of his stomach he couldn't trust Shrog. Krevety realized that if he didn't act to protect New Raihan, others would soon be affected by the same paranoia as the Sonarian general. As soon as he could, General Krevety secretly ordered the bomb components be moved out of the compound to a safe location unknown to the Sonarians. Onsan would continue his mission guarding the "bombs." When the Sonarian patrol arrived, they'd be guarding only empty shells together.

Krevety and Serlat were getting the picture, despite Shrog's attempt to deceive them. General Shrog wanted to have access to everyone else on the Magnus and Laurus sides of the portal, but was paranoid about anyone entering the Sonarian side.

General Krevety spent long hours with Shrog during the next few days, and all he heard was talk about how the peace process was foreign to him. In the Sonarian dimension, going to war meant total annihilation of an enemy; survivors would be brought back to Sonaria as servants. Shrog couldn't comprehend warfare where a defeated foe was left to build up again. An enemy needed to be totally devastated so they couldn't conduct another attack.

The more Krevety listened, his instincts told him that Shrog eyed the resources on all sides of the portal. General Shrog was becoming a major threat. Based on his attitude and dominance in battle, no one would be safe if Sonarian expansionism spread throughout the galaxy! After all they'd been through, victory only gained them Sonarian imperialism over the Raihan variety.

Trecon and RO became guardians of New Raihan after the war. They stood in the way of Shrog's plans. Body language changed as each side realized they were sitting with an enemy. Krevety considered what the future looked like. How long until they were battling with Sonaria for their very existence, after Shrog was through with Raihan? Trecon and Ryderson Omega would face total devastation!

When the meetings hit another snag, General Shrog requested a recess so the Sonarians could convene.

"Let us confer to discuss our latest offer. We want to make sure we articulate our requests correctly," stated Shrog smugly.

After a two-and-a-half-hour recess, the general returned late in the day and gave everyone his ultimatum. Shrog worked himself into a foaming frenzy as he justified himself. "Planet Raihan is the ultimate evil in the universe, and we intend to destroy her. We'll give you two weeks to evacuate before we return to ensure the destruction of the planet!"

"You aren't serious," said Serlat in disbelief.

"We are justified to protect ourselves," bellowed the irate general. "Here on Raihan, the collaborated government is a weak government that will be overthrown by violent militants.

There are too many loose ends here to completely confirm the safety of our planet. The Raihans have a history steeped in deception and conquest. Things can't be changed by so few against so many in such a short period of time!"

The Sonarians appeared to circle their wagons behind their leader, and no amount of reasoning from General Krevety or Serlat seemed to matter.

Meetings were cancelled for the day, as Krevety called for a recess to catch their breath and take time to consider other options. Heated exchanges were common in treaty proceedings.

Serlat pleaded with General Shrog to reexamine their position and give the peace and reorganization process a chance to work.

Tumble, crash!

Shrog toppled over his chair in anger. "We won't be coming to another one of your meetings!" Angry emotions boiled over; he'd hit the end of his rope.

Allies became enemies in that moment. In a far corner of the room, Onsan silently unclipped the holster of his laser pistol in case something happened. Alongside him, the giant Sjlegen was tensing his muscles and preparing to charge into the Sonarian horde. Intensity spiked, and everyone on both sides prepared for a fight. Shrog waved to his followers to leave, suggesting that it wasn't the time for battle.

The agitated Sonarian council stood up and left abruptly.

Clink, clatter, clank!

The medals on Shrog's chest rattled as he stomped his way to the door. His golden uniform lost its luster, turning pale yellow as he tramped out in the tantrum.

The last one out made a final statement, and the door sounded like it would come off the hinges.

Slam!

As the rest of the council sat in shock and silence, a thought entered General Krevety's mind. The Sonarians were a dangerous and warring people. Had the Trecons successfully loaded the transmitter relic and brought it home, their planet would be under siege by the Sonarians at that very moment!

Later that evening, General Seraden contacted Krevety's stateroom and requested a meeting. The Trecon leader hoped that Seraden's request meant the Sonarians were coming to their senses and allowing reasonable sanctions to work. Perhaps if one Sonarian general could see the light, he could influence the other. Maybe they weren't an army of blood-thirsty conquerors after all.

Krevety's hopes were sunken when he saw Seraden's serious tone. "General Shrog is a warmonger. Believe me, we're not all like him. Many Sonarians value science and exploration. I'll try to appeal to the high council upon our return. The science community has equal representation there."

"Is there any chance you can change their mind?"

"The pendulum has swung in Shrog's favor since the Raihans have been a warring society. Shrog perceives a threat, so the consensus will be all in to eliminate the risk. I have a few friends in high places, though. I'll get to say my piece. It'll be an uphill battle, but I'll show them the evidence from the beginning."

"You must try your best General Seraden."

Seraden's brow rumpled over his blue eyes. The concerned man wanted Krevety to understand the full picture.

"There's something else."

"Yes, go on," said General Krevety earnestly.

"The portal is sour with radiation, but we'll still want it. In our dimension, those who control gateways gain unmatched power over the resources on both sides. You have to consider the possibility that even if we don't attack, we'll put a claim on the portal."

"I knew it!"

Before he left, Seraden informed Krevety that General Shrog ordered the Sonarians to leave Raihan within the next few hours.

Two hours later, Krevety heard the rumble of Shrog's fleet leaving Base 13. His hopes for a peaceful outcome were dashed. Once again, the clock was ticking!

*****

Ticktock ticktock ticktock, kaboom, baroom!
Two detonations tore the carriers apart in a brilliant display of kaleidoscopic colors against the starry night!
Strike, shatter, whomp!
Chunks of jagged metal ripped through the sky and crashed indiscriminately through spacecraft and dorm windows on the flight line of Base 13. Brilliant flames shot downward, as echoing explosions enveloped the docked *Vehemence XX* carriers.
Lurch, tumble, CRASH, BRIGHT BURST!
The carriers fell on top of the tarmac, taking out dozens of ships below them. Everything happened in a matter of seconds!

Tallik leaped into action and announced over the intercom, "Red alert, we're under attack!" Pilots rushed out to inspect their fighters. The fallen carriers had taken out most of the rapid-response fleet parked on the ramp. Lucky for them, there was no attack.

After the timebombs detonated, the skies were quiet. Dense black smoke blocked out the fading stars in the early morning light. Black soot and glowing embers rained down on the tarmac, covering the canopies of every spacecraft parked on the ramp.

"No enemy in sight," reported a ramp supervisor.

Mac Sjlegen and the firefighters jumped into action, and hailed tower control for their own protection as they neared the burning ships. They didn't want to be mistaken for attackers. "Crash 17 holding short at our station, requesting permission to enter the tarmac and fight the fires."

"Crash 17 and company, you're cleared to enter the tarmac!"
The fire trucks roared to action, sirens blaring!

Neeee-naw neeee-naw!
Boooshh!

Sirens added to the chaos of the fiery scene as crash fire trucks sped onto the ramp, projecting water and foam onto the fire, protecting the other vessels the best they could with their water cannons. They saved many ships, but the prototype carriers were a total loss.

Shrog's cronies had done well!

*****

Meanwhile, thousands of kilometers away, "General Shrog, the signals have died and the bombs have all detonated."

"How can you be sure they weren't moved beforehand?"

"They were equipped with anti-tampering devices. Any attempt to move the ground power units would have resulted in an instant explosion. Plus, they detonated precisely at the given time of 0400."

"Excellent! Let's turn our attention to the invasion!"

The Sonarian fleet had been underway for four hours, screaming through the cosmos after the ambush. Shrog left the devastation to the two concept *Vehemence XX* carriers docked at the base. They were the only weapons on the planet that threatened the Sonarians.

He could do nothing about the rogue carrier, but was confident the contingent on New Raihan couldn't get their act together in time to load the weapons of mass destruction and follow them to Sonaria. He'd wrecked all their data. Shrog was sure they couldn't find his home planet blinded as they were.

The general was sure they'd catch the ship with a tight-net blockade during the siege of Raihan. The Sonarians had ways. The carrier would show itself to their alternating frequency weapons. They'd bested Raihan technology before, they'd do it again.

Shrog was sure all his bases were covered. The transmitter was safely within his fleet, and those who'd studied it were gone. As far as the others on Raihan, there would've been no honor in destroying empty ships or bombing the barracks of sleeping soldiers. Shrog would save the carnage for the invasion!

*****

Tallik hailed his leader and asked, "General Krevety, shall we follow the Sonarian fleet?"

"No, they're long gone by now. They've obviously been playing us for fools and planning the attack for days. By the time we mobilize, they'd be at the portal. We're not going to follow them blindly through into their own backyard!"

Krevety's heart burned with anger and hatred. Had he not followed his instincts about Shrog, the nine gamma bombs would've also been targets for destruction!

Seraden's dependability was confirmed when the scientist was found in Shrog's quarters severely beaten and nearly dead. Bodies littered the room around him.

Shrog hadn't taken Seraden's council with Krevety lightly. General Seraden's junior officer, Colonel Landren Kaunfam, followed him closely, learning of his secret meeting with General Krevety. Kaunfam sold Seraden out to Shrog. Seraden was left alive only to deliver Krevety a message.

General Greudow and the cryptographers weren't so lucky. The gruesome scene in Shrog's stateroom would've made former Base 13 Gallows commandant Slae Nodk cringe! Shrog cruelly terminated the only links to the Sonarian transmitter in a brutal torture chamber. The grisly evidence suggested a slow interrogation process. Shrog ensured no one who'd touched the transmitter remained alive.

Seraden paid the ultimate price for his betrayal, even beyond the beatings. He was stripped of his honor by Shrog. In their culture, it was infinitely better to die with honor than be a colluder and outcast. He'd feel the wrath of the Sonarian juggernaut from the undesirable end of laser beams, but worse for Seraden was the thought of how his family would be dishonored!

General Seraden delivered the message from Shrog, "You must evacuate the innocent. Anyone who chooses to stay on Raihan will feel the full wrath of the Sonarians rained down upon them! You don't have much time. Shrog will return before you know it!"

Krevety offered a hand to lift Seraden off the gory floor. "Enough about that, let's get you to a doctor."

When General Shrog returned to Sonaria to give his report, he'd skew the evidence to convince them Raihan's imperialistic intentions. Leaving Seraden's voice of dissent behind worked greatly in Shrog's favor!

General Krevety's worst fears were coming to light before his eyes. Trecon and RO were committed to a bigger conflict than ever before!

CHAPTER 47

Difficult Choice for Volunteers

K revety called the *Mule 357* crew, General Seraden, and Nobert Serlat together for an impromptu meeting to discuss Shrog's declaration and their options before bringing it to the greater counsel. He wouldn't work so hard to free so many civilizations, to have it all come crashing down as they were about to reach their goals.

Glaring issues had to be addressed quickly.

Forming a super-fleet and waiting at the portal was discussed. They could stand up to the powerful Sonarians as a three-pronged defense force. However, joining would involve the unwanted components of Raihan aggression, namely President Grolegg and the Mihhidites. Krevety knew that enlisting them would be a gamble toward reinstating their power and validating Shrog's concerns of anarchy!

Also, it was impractical bringing so many together who'd fought against each other so recently. The Raihans might turn on the Trecons and RO's during their wait in the hazardous ergosphere.

An idea was brought to the floor by Onsan Vorga with a simple question.

"Can we destroy the portal and prevent *all sides* from re-entry?"

Onsan's judgement had gotten them through plenty of scrapes and undoubtedly saved the general's life more than once. He had a daring plan.

General Krevety was intrigued. "Go on."

"We'll relocate everyone to their desired side of the portal, then destroy it with a gamma bomb before the Sonarians return. Simple as that!"

"No one would return from such a mission," said Abbsnate.

"Are you kidding, a pilot with my skills could do it! We'd set a timer on the bomb, and I could come out the other side with my eyes closed!"

"Are you crazy Onsan? Be serious!"

"I'm serious as a heart attack!"

Onsan proposed his plan. After everyone was through the portal, he'd pilot a ship through and drop a gamma bomb as he entered the middle equalization point, where the three portal entries met. The gamma bombs were powerful enough to crack a planet in half, so realistically it could incapacitate the Sonarian tunnel for good and change the wormhole into an impassable sun portal. If it worked, the result would be a closed portal and safety on both sides of the galaxy. A carrier would offer the best speed and protection, but there was little hope of survival. Everyone knew it, but Onsan put on an optimistic face like he had a chance.

Abbsnate said, "That settles it! We have a lot of work to do!"

"We?"

"Yeah, you aren't doing this alone! The portal zone will be no picnic. Summer hasn't ended too long ago. The gateway will still be in Hazard-Class 8 conditions. The Raihan ships are built to handle the stress, but I can't say how the radiation and solar flares will affect the bomb. You'll need a second set of eyes."

*****

The plan of permanent separation saddened those who'd served aboard the *Mule 357* together, but everyone knew it was their best plan. Many would be permanently separated from their loved-ones.

As Onsan considered the risky portal mission, he realized he would likely never see his family again. His mind drifted to a particular summer trip they'd taken north of Tettegouche, where they camped in the great northern wilderness alongside Mic Mac Lake. Onsan and his father, Naed, arrived early to set up camp before his mother and sisters. It was supposed to be mild weather, but suddenly the sky opened up and turned into a pounding rainstorm, and the two were forced to set up camp in a downpour!

After pitching their tent in sideways rain, his father somehow got a fire going and they went for a walk to keep their blood flowing, while the camp stew warmed to a boil over the flames.

As they walked along, they came to the shore, where the storm was intensifying the waves as they crashed into the rocky shoreline and burst high into the frigid air. Despite all the chaos around them, his father remained calm.

"What an adventure! You'll remember tonight for the rest of your life!"

Later that evening, the rest of their family arrived: Rasah (Onsan's mother), Aurora, and Nyll (his sisters).

The rain didn't subside, but they made the best of it. They found shelter in a cave and made a fire. They ate and played games well into the night. His dad was right. The trip was his fondest family memory despite the horrible weather! They had many family trips under perfect conditions, yet the harsh elements of the rainy camping trip symbolized the resilient bonding of his family.

Onsan was in jeopardy of never seeing them again, nor camping along the shores of his favorite place in the universe.

He had a girl waiting for him back home. His impending engagement to Eella would end. They'd been friends since they were young. The thought of Eella eventually moving on from him and marrying another tore at his heart.

Not undertaking the daring mission meant putting everyone he cared for on Trecon in danger.

*****

Abbsnate knew she'd go on the mission, dispensing with the idea of governing Raihan with her father. Onsan needed her. Their experience working together gave the mission a higher chance of success. If the plan didn't work, there'd be no Raihan to help govern anyway!

The biggest thing that haunted Abbsnate, however, was her decision not to visit her mother upon returning to RO before the invasion. She'd felt it was better not to take advantage of her fortune, while others would die in battle without returning to Ryderson Omega.

Abbsnate met Serlat for a private dinner, their first in many years and most likely their last together. After a few hours of catching up, Abbsnate came to the choke point of the conversation. She explained to her father why she should go on the mission.

Serlat let her speak her mind, not interrupting once during her dialogue. He thought she was trying to convince herself as much as him.

"Tell mother I love her, but I had to go on the portal mission to protect her and all the inhabitants of Ryderson Omega."

Finally, Abbsnate left an opening for him to respond. Serlat took the opportunity any father would in the face of losing a daughter. The exhausted man rubbed his troubled blue eyes. His pointed chin quivered as he tried to speak.

"Abbsnate, you've done your duty well! Two dimensions are free from Raihan deceit because of your sacrifices and brave actions! It's not your obligation to contribute to the mission any longer. Your mother has already lost both of us once. I can't imagine her heartbreak at knowing that there was an opportunity to reunite and lose you a second time. I couldn't face her with such news. I-." Tears formed in Serlat's eyes as he struggled to continue, but he could force no words out.

Finally, he composed himself enough to choke out, "Won't you stay here with me?"

Seeing her father's tears opened a torrent in Abbsnate's eyes. She responded, "General Seraden says there are many portals in the Sonarian universe, some of them being connecting loops from one to another. Our whole mission once we're through is going to be finding our way back home."

Serlat scolded her. "Be realistic Abbsnate! What are the chances of ever making it back?"

"I've been away from Ryderson Omega for so long, it didn't feel like going home before the invasion because there was a mission to accomplish. If I went back to RO now, my mind would always be on a mission that isn't completed yet. I would be there in body, but my mind and soul would be in the distant corners of the universe with this family that I've grown to trust and love through our time spent together."

"Abbsnate, please reconsider."

"My mind is made up, I'm sorry!"

Abbsnate got up to leave, but felt the steady and loving hand of her father on her shoulder.

Serlat brought his face up to hers. "You're your father's daughter for sure! Please don't go so soon. Let's enjoy every hour together until preparations have to be made for your departure."

Abbsnate sat back down, and they finished their last meal together.

*****

All over Raihan, decisions were being weighed out in the hearts and minds of many qualified people. It wasn't just the mission crew who had to make difficult choices.

General Krevety decided he'd stay behind on New Raihan to help set up the transitional government, but his heart wasn't in the decision. He'd have to come to grips with never seeing his family again; rapidly approaching the age where portal travel wouldn't be possible anymore.

Abbsnate urged the general to go back to Trecon. Once the portal was destroyed, he'd be marooned forever. Serlat could move freely between New Raihan and Ryderson Omega. He'd have access to RO protection should anything go wrong with the portal mission or transitional government, God forbid. After considering the options, it was apparent to Krevety that the situation on the planet wouldn't be perfect no matter what he did. If the portal mission didn't work, the general would be needed on Trecon to prepare for a Sonarian invasion.

General Krevety opted to stay on Raihan as long as possible before departing for Trecon. He'd confer with representatives of the transitional government, and help prepare the portal crew until it was time for the last Bruiser to depart for the portal. Krevety knew there wouldn't be much sleep in the next few days, but there would be plenty of time for rest in deep space during his journey back to Trecon. Upon his return, Krevety would know if he could retire in the warmer climates of Southern Trecon with his wife. He'd even allow himself the excitement of meeting his first grandchild!

The assurances from Serlat gave Krevety strength, and the general felt revitalized as he prepared for the marathon days ahead. The first order of business for Krevety was to look at the list of volunteers for the portal bomb mission. From their ranks, his team would determine the experience and trustworthiness of each one. Others who weren't chosen for the mission would be the defenders of New Raihan.

Krevety and Serlat knew there were many holes in their plan, but it was all they could hope for in their situation.

CHAPTER 48

Crew Reunions

As mission volunteers trickled in, it was apparent to Krevety that the portal bomber mission would have a healthy crew going forward.

They proposed using a Bruiser or first-generation Vehemence carrier to complete the bombing mission.

"I'll get a team on it right away," said Milerous.

"Hold on," said Major Tallik. "Wiring a bomb-release module into the ship's systems is a complicated process. Having an army of workers wouldn't make a difference. There simply isn't time."

"The major is right," said General Krevety. "To rewire everything in that amount of time would be impossible. "Our goal is to activate and unload the bomb, then escape to a safe distance from the detonation. Without the proper housing for the bomb, it's a-." The general looked around.

Onsan finished his sentence. "A mission of no return!"

Abbsnate excused herself from the meeting, leaving the room with a determined step.

The new and improved Raihan instrument of destruction was the best option, having a custom-made bay for the gamma bomb module. The two docked at the Scientific Center were damaged beyond repair from the fleeting Sonarian attack.

"What a shame the carriers were destroyed," said Onsan. "They were made for the mission!"

The *Vehemence XX* was monstrous, with 12 decks rather than seven like the older carriers. Besides the gamma bomb, the behemoth ship would fit Starlance and Trinity fighters, exploratory crafts and probes; it had everything needed to safely complete the mission and possibly return safely.

Krevety shook his head, "General Shrog is no fool."

"We'd better move forward with the Bruiser. I'd rather have our Starlances protecting the route to the portal than Talons. Bruisers are being used for ark ships. If they suspect anything our birds will lead the way into the portal. Unfortunately, we'll have to leave the Trinitys behind. If they escort us, the Sonarians will know something's up."

CJ looked up from his seat with a determined face. "I'm in to navigate the ship."

Etan and Milerous stood up as well.

"Good. We'll bring the most talented and experienced pilots to bolster the chances of mission accomplishment."

"We'll, sir? I thought you were going back to Trecon."

"I'm not going to ask you to make sacrifices that I'm not willing to make myself."

Serlat reminded the general they must also prepare if the mission failed. Anything was possible, but it was a shaky plan at best. As the crew discussed the monumental task, feelings of doubt spread throughout the room.

*****

Abbsnate walked into Captain Brell's holding cell, and she was greeted with hateful and distrusting eyes. He'd have torn her apart if he could reach her! She was the reason he'd lost his command, and was sent to the Base 13 Gallows to rot. Captain Brell had the look of boundless hurt on his face that went far beyond the physical pain from the maltreatment he'd received in the Base 13 Gallows.

Brell's blue eyes watered, as emotion fought to get out. His brow showed a determination to not let her have the satisfaction of seeing him cry, although his quivering chin betrayed him. The man looked ragged. He was unshaven and his brown hair was long and unkempt. He'd lost weight. The faded blue prison uniform was shabby, and too large for his bony frame. The pungent smell of body odor was almost more than Abbsnate could take.

Captain Brell was the opposite of how Abbsnate knew him. Guilt and hate had taken a toll on the man. He'd let himself go.

In the distant past, Brell esteemed Abbsnate greatly. He'd patterned his career after her advice before being stabbed in the back. He was sure that everything Abbsnate ever said to him meant nothing to her.

Abbsnate knew the meeting would come sooner or later. She'd rehearsed her side of the discussion repeatedly in her head.

"I'd like to speak to Captain Brell alone."

The guards were surprised when she ordered his restraints loosened before they left the room. One offered, "We'll be right outside the door if he tries anything!"

"In his condition? Not likely," said the other.

Abbsnate knew she had but minutes to make Brell understand the plight of the Ryderson Omegan people, his similar history, and that the future was in their hands together once again.

She told the revolting man her personal story, and the pressure she was under to safely return her people home. Abbsnate didn't want to use Brell in the way she did, but felt it was her noble duty to complete her secret task. Abbsnate assured him that her words and feelings were real, but her duty to the Ryderson Omegan people outweighed their close relationship.

There were many aspects about the situation that didn't sit right with the former captain. Above all, he'd sent five of his subordinates directly out to their deaths.

"The oath I took as captain meant the world to me. Everyone on the ship looked to me to make educated decisions and keep them safe. I failed them!"

Abbsnate realized she had to use her intellect to change the direction of the conversation. There were plenty of things for them to work through, but it wasn't the time. Her eyes flashed with intense emotion as she began.

"May I remind you, we were on a warship, conducting combat operations against a damaged and under gunned cargo freighter! You weren't totally innocent in the situation, even though you suffered misfortune as a result of my plan. I was taking a huge risk as well, outnumbered five-to-one. It was a major gamble. You had the prerogative to chase me, or send another squadron out after me!"

After the mental splash of cold water in the face, Captain Brell came around.

Abbsnate began a pitch to him to share the new mission. "You now have a chance to improve your future by using your passion against new aggressors."

They both knew he'd be a valuable asset to their adventurous mission.

By the end, Brell was pleasantly astonished at the good fortune of getting released from prison and commanding a Raihan carrier once again! He stood up, looked Abbsnate in the eye and held out his hand. "Okay, I'm yours."

"Great, now let's go get our ship!"

Brell gave Abbsnate a puzzled look as they walked out of the cell together. They hurried to the nearest communication control room because there was no time to waste! The pair went to the com and hailed the undetectable *Vehemence XX* carrier soaring incognito over the planet. Abbsnate knew that her voice would only be received as a traitor, so she gave way for Captain Brell to contact the ship.

"This is going to be nearly impossible without an authentication code," Brell explained to Abbsnate.

"Give it your best shot!"

Captain Brell began, "*Vehemence XX*, are you out there and able to respond?"

No reply.

Brell repeated, "*Vehemence XX*, this is Captain Brell. Are you out there and able to respond?"

Still nothing.

"There's been an attack, but the Sonarian aggressors have left our atmosphere. We're depending on the Trecons and Ryderson Omegans as allies against the imminent return of the hostile Sonarians. It's important that you reply!"

Abbsnate was discouraged. "Keep trying to talk sense into him, we have no choice."

Suddenly General Krevety entered the room with a surprise guest in tow. President Grolegg followed Krevety into the room, flanked by two security officers. He offered a detestable glance toward Abbsnate and Brell at the com. They were the reason for this state of affairs in the first place!

Grolegg wasn't in the position of authority any longer, but he was still useful. As president of Raihan's crumbled government, he still held the responsibility and power to keep her citizens safe.

Reluctantly and in a forced tone, he began, "*Vehemence XX*, Captain Reg Piktkas, this is President Yerb Grolegg. Are you out there and able to respond? We need your ship docked on Raihan within the hour! Security authentication code 42OI5JH023."

To everyone's astonishment, Piktkas answered right away, "*We just don't want our carrier to get into the wrong hands.*"

Grolegg replied, "You'll be doing the right thing if you dock that ship. I know you've been monitoring everything down here closely since the Sonarians arrived. You know how much of a threat they are. Once again, security authentication code 42OI5JH023. Return to base straight away."

After about 30 seconds of conferring with his officers on the bridge and checking the verification code, Piktkas responded with evidence of situational knowledge. *"Yes, sir, but our dock was destroyed. Where shall we land?"*

Everyone, including the former president, breathed a collective sigh of relief! The crew could leave with the right ship for the job.

Onsan was astonished when Abbsnate returned with her guest. Her companion was the foremost expert on the weaponry and navigation systems of the state of-the-art Raihan *Vehemence XX* carrier.

Captain Brell had talked to Abbsnate about it while they served together, revealing only the basics for fear of saying too much and getting charged with treason. He'd studied the specifications and was set to become one of her first captains. It was to be the mega weapon used for wars such as the one they were involved with.

The Raihans could've made the Trecons and Ryderson Omegans surrender before the Sonarians arrived had they launched the carriers initially, but leadership disagreed. They thought they had the war won without them. The carriers had to be finished to initiate the Reaper Initiative after the battle. They were well on their way until the Sonarians got involved.

The captain addressed the crowd. He was short and to the point, "I'm willing to serve as captain for this deadly mission if you'll have me. It'll be a chance for redemption for me."

Brell's humility went a long way with the gathered officers. He was familiar with the ship's most intimate secrets, and his presence was a welcome addition to the crew. He was welcomed with open arms. Brell joined the portal crew, confident they could complete the first part of the mission if nothing else.

General Krevety smiled knowingly, sensing Abbsnate's intellect and charm brought Brell there so willingly.

To Krevety's pleasant surprise, the assembly area wasn't large enough to hold the crowd of volunteers! They had to turn people away, which he hoped would account for a strong defense force for New Raihan!

Notable volunteers included two Raihan experts on the new carrier, Captain Yougsten Brell and Captain Reg Piktkas; Colonel Ferd Honassen, Teb Tharly, Pnoi Nbnok, and fire-fighter/medic Mac Sjlegen from Trecon; the Sonarian science general Seraden; former resistance fighter and medical doctor Fana Tobor (along with her family which included a historian and a nurse), Tobor's partner Hetle Orbne; and mechanics Etan Esa-erg and Hebel Greten from Kufsiun.

The Trecon lynx was included on the ship, and was greatly disgusted that Etan was also part of the crew to vie for Abbsnate's affection. When Chase noticed Etan, he arched his back and growled under his breath. The cat sensed that he'd better behave or he might not be included, so he left his displeasure at that!

Over 4,800 volunteers came forward in all.

General Krevety explained the particulars of the mission. No one would be called out for not stepping forward, because there were limited roster spots and no guarantees they'd ever find their way back home again. No one left, they'd already decided to stick it out!

Seven Talon II's, 20 Talon's, 20 Starlance's, and 15 Trinity fighters were included in the mission. Besides primary and back-up fighter pilots, 18 maintenance personnel and 95 others were chosen for the daring mission. The mega-carrier could easily launch Starlance and Trinity fighters, as it was designed with different-sized bays to accommodate varying Raihan spacecraft.

Three empty bays included spare parts for the warships, one bay each for the Trinity, Starlance, and Talon fighters.

Their spacecraft inventory also included three medium-sized shuttles capable of extended deep-space travel. The crafts weren't meant for warfare, merely for cargo transfer and exploration.

Two shuttles would be a means to move people and equipment from point A to point B. They named the ships Bus 1 and Bus 2. The busses differed slightly from one another. Bus 1 was the smallest of the three shuttle-class spacecraft, and carried a crew of five. Bus 2 carried a crew of 15 with a moderate-sized cargo bay.

The Bus ships were almost removed from the inventory of the carrier for two more Trinitys, but the order was changed at the last minute. It wasn't entirely a war-time mission, and the crew would need a vehicle to send exploratory missions to the surface of planets. They didn't want to look aggressive to friendly planets in peaceful situations. It would be impractical to use fighters to replenish their supply stores; they'd have to break up supply shipments and take hundreds of trips back and forth!

The third shuttle wasn't meant to carry personnel or cargo, it was built merely for scientific investigation. It was slightly larger than the buses. The amply named Explorer 3 spacecraft included advanced NAV/COM and detection devices for deep scientific space exploration. It would be used only for investigation of the cosmos. The craft was too valuable to chance smashing supply crates into the equipment panels or putting the technology at the mercy of an unknown entity. They'd use the ship to discover accessible paths to portals, and map their way home.

They also included dozens of satellite probes, units the Raihans used to comb the universe for potential victim planets! The purpose of the probes was twofold; to be sent into unknown portals, and to provide a look ahead or behind the carrier to ensure their safety. It was imperative to know the viability of a portal path before going through it in a ship.

The crew's hope of returning home was bolstered by all the advancements aboard the new Raihan carrier, but the adventurous crew would provide the heart and soul for the mission.

CHAPTER 49

The Purpose and the Plan

General Krevety explained to the crew how the mission would start. They'd give the Trecon ark ships a head start, so they wouldn't be affected by the fireball supernova to come! Per the Sonarian agreement, those who wanted to travel safely back to Trecon would be granted immunity because they weren't considered enemies of Sonaria yet. After three days, the mission would begin.

General Seraden offered everyone a glimpse into his Sonarian universe, explaining it so they could understand. He was still in great pain from Shrog's attack, so he stayed seated and slumped over a table for support.

"We aren't as dominant within our dimension. There are many other planetary cultures known to us who hold more power and prestige because of their control of portals."

Within their dimension, portals were like rare currency, which granted certain privileges to those who controlled them. Some were simply guardians of their portal, cohabiting with the alien civilizations inhabiting the other side while ensuring peaceful travel through. Others used portals for total domination of the opposing galaxies. The Raihans were not unusual, just unique in their deceitful tactics against the miners of Planet 6333.

Seraden continued, "Sonarian attempts to gain control of the portal were halted when our transmitter signal went dead. Our interest was reborn again after it was revived by the Trecon miners on the burning planet."

General Seraden's theory was that the bomb explosion would create a vacuum, obliterating the gateway and sucking the stars together. Magnus and Laurus would collide at hypersonic speeds, pushing dynamic energy into the Sonarian dimension! If the mission succeeded, the stars would shoot the shielded carrier safely into the Sonarian universe. If not, they'd never know it. The carrier would be burned to a cinder in a fraction of a millisecond! Either way, the Muudia portal would become impassable.

Regardless of the outcome, Trecon, Ryderson Omega, and countless others would be saved from the Sonarian advance. They'd also be shut off from each other forever from the Muudia wormhole.

The portal entrance to the Sonarian universe was at the midpoint of the portal, where the gravitational pull from the Magnus and Laurus solar systems was equalized.

Seraden explained the unusual Sonarian event horizon. "Think of the portal sidewall as a "snare drum skin" made of strong neutron-laden fiber. The current passage into the Sonarian dimension is like a small pinhole in the drum skin." He looked around for effect, and everyone nodded that they understood.

"The bulk of the drum skin is stout enough to hold out the gravitational forces pushing on it at the moment, but the pinhole gets incrementally larger every year. If the gamma bomb were detonated at the midpoint of the portal, the size of the passageway into the Sonarian dimension would instantly go from a pin hole to that of a "baseball" being thrown through the skin at high speed! It would spider-web to the furthest edges of the drum. The Sonarian exit would instantly lose the strength to hold the forces back! The drum skin would be instantly disintegrated!"

"Fascinating," said Nbnok. "The only thing we don't know is the diameter of the "baseball" being thrown into the drumskin. Our survival depends on perfect placement and timing."

The general continued, "The resulting pressure created at the midpoint of the portal will cause excessive gravitational energy to burst through the hole, increasing it exponentially, like a shotgun shell of radiated energy and debris from the Magnus and Laurus dimensions bursting through the Sonarian event horizon and far beyond the ergosphere!

How'd we get from a baseball to a shotgun shell, wondered Nbnok.

"If we deposit the gamma bomb and high-tail it at maximum speed toward the Sonarian exit, the ship may burst out through to the Sonarian universe, leaving a new sun portal in our wake *before* we discover the diameter of the baseball!"

"Theoretically," said Nbnok scratching his head.

"The portal has been naturally ebbing away for some time. The same outcome would've happened in perhaps 100,000 years or so. Introduction of the gamma bomb, however, will do in a matter of nanoseconds what should have taken thousands of years to accomplish."

Captain Brell asked the next logical question. "If we make it, we'll be stuck in your dimension. How will we ever get back here!"

"Sonarian belief is that the universe is filled with a finite amount of matter and space. If we're correct, the situation will be like replenishing a lake. When water evaporates out, a spring refills it, or rainwater coming out of the sky keeps the lake at a certain level. Yet there's only so much water on a planet. Whenever something is expanding in one area, its shrinking in another, evidenced by the frequency and light of redshift and blueshift stars moving simultaneously in different directions. The portal had been leaking into the Sonarian dimension for a sometime, but on a smaller scale."

Onsan spoke up, "The Sonarian water theory makes perfect sense to me." He looked at the others who'd crossed through in the damaged Mule. "The outflow of gravitational energy at the midpoint was undeniable using the manual controls of the limping '357. We had to fight to get it back on course."

CJ nodded. "Right. All the automated masking systems were off-line, and we felt everything. The tired engines were barely enough to keep our momentum on course toward the Magnus gravitational field, and away from the Sonarian current pulling at us!"

According to the Sonarian theory, somewhere on the far side of the portal, a "trickling spring" was already leaking into the Magnus and Laurus dimensions. After the detonation, Seraden believed the springs would open up to reveal a new portal within both galaxies. General Seraden was confident there were many possible locations far from the Sonarian portal, where other passages could be discovered with a realistic chance of taking them back to their home dimensions.

"Portal loops are an existent phenomenon; recently proven after scientific investigation of the cosmic legends persisted on Sonaria. Finding the right path will take time. It'll be like attempting to decipher a combination lock with limited information. We already have some numbers to its grouping; cosmic data from both sides of the portal have been loaded into the database. The remaining numbers on the lock will have to be discovered, then articulated in the correct sequence. It will be difficult, but not impossible for a crew that's constantly reaching for the answers, and a ship with such advances as the *Vehemence XX*."

Returning home for the carrier crew would have to be a concerted effort of everyone involved, including scientists stationed on Trecon, Ryderson Omega, and Raihan. They were all to search for evidence of seismic events on the outer reaches of their particular galaxies, looking for connecting portals. Each newly-discovered portal might represent a window into the Sonarian universe, a possible path back home for the carrier crew.

Krevety addressed the *Vehemence XX* crew after the meeting. "You'll encounter many unforeseen dangers, beginning with the first stage of the mission. Every effort will be thoroughly exhausted within our home galaxies to help you complete your journey and return home safely. You all know that this mission is a long shot. Your greatest foes are time and the limitless expanse of space!"

CHAPTER 50

Journey Preparation

T he crew entered the Raihan *Vehemence XX* and got acquainted with one another. There were many reasons for distrust among them, and leadership would have its challenges during the first leg of their journey. Those with young families at home were strongly discouraged from applying for the unique mission; they'd done their part during the assault. The result was a young and adventurous, inexperienced crew. Two-thirds of the men and women were between the ages of 21 and 35. Older crew members would be highly valued for their wisdom and experience.

The crew was quite a sight in the assembly area. The gathering was a scene of self-segregation, with the former Raihans on one side of the room and the allied forces on the other. They were fidgety and untrusting of one another. When General Krevety's staff walked in, General Seraden became the white elephant in the room. As the Sonarian general looked around, he was thankful that looks couldn't kill. General Krevety took charge. He knew that survival was the unifying goal among them.

He looked around and waited for silence, then began his briefing.

"The Sonarians are a dangerous entity with a plan to conquer our dual dimensions. Although they give a guise that they are concerned for the safety of their planet, their true objective is to destroy, subjugate, and expand their influence to become the most powerful entity in all three dimensions. We can't and won't abide for this to happen. Each one of us must do our part to stand in their way and prevent their lethal plan!"

Whistle, applaud, shout!

The general paused, and waited for the crowd to quiet down.

"We've made every attempt to reunite families together. Yesterday we sent 42 ships out to return Wanderers to their home planets, some of them not seeing their homelands for decades, or never before."

The crowd cheered again, but Krevety held up his arms for silence. His face grew solemn.

"By volunteering for this mission, you're taking great risk of never returning to your home planet or seeing your families again. If you stay, you'll have to become one another's family! Each one of you has to be willing to lay it on the line for the other, regardless of the myriad of histories associated here. You'll never serve a greater purpose than what lies before you now. If you're having second thoughts, now is the time to step forward and leave this mission. No one will question your heart or will."

Rather than stepping forward, the entire crew stood up and gave the general a raucous applause.

Clap, foot stamp, howl!

Krevety knew the glue may not have set yet, but it had started to stabilize.

He continued, "General Seraden has assured me of his knowledge of various portal loops in his dimension. They may be the gateway home. All it takes is one, the right one! The vessel contains up-to-the-second technology, so there's a small chance you'll return home on the other side of this great adventure."

He ended his briefing trying his best to get the crew to meld into one, "We're gathered here because you're the bravest and best crew anyone could hope to assemble for such a mission. The state-of-the-art *Vehemence XX* is being loaded to the rafters with supplies, and retrofitted for fighters to be piloted by our best Trecon, Ryderson Omegan, and Raihan pilots."

The pilots stood up and cheered!

Krevety gestured to the crowd he was nearly finished. "The carrier will be ready to go in 48 hours. That means you'll need to be ready to work as a team in two days! Thus, I'm ordering a mandatory camaraderie event to last all day tomorrow, so you'll have at least met one another before you lift off into deep space together."

General Krevety ended his speech on a lighter note. "Finally, this ship is going to be christened with a new identity. It will from now on be called the V-357, in honor of a simple Trecon freighter named *Mule 357*. She had heart and guts to spare. The cargo ship provided her crew with refuge during turbulent times at the beginning of this adventure. Hopefully this ship will uphold her legacy. Enjoy yourselves tonight. Tomorrow, the mission begins!"

*****

After the crew left for the evening, General Krevety was called to the bridge of the V-357. A security guard doing his rounds in a supply bay found an infiltrator.

"General, we have a stowaway on board," announced CJ as Krevety entered the bridge.

General Krevety was deeply concerned. The brutal battle ended just days before. Sabotage was not out of the question at the infant stage of the mission. There were many who still didn't like one another, and it was obvious.

"Bring him here," replied an irritated Krevety.

After a few minutes, a sentry arrived with a lean teenager in tow. As the general looked him over, he presumed the scared youth meant no harm to the mission. Still, the kid represented a security breach.

Krevety lost his usual composure and rapidly fired questions at the kid, "Who are you? How'd you get through our security measures, and what's your business here?"

The young man looked up at the brooding general. "I want to be included on the mission."

General Krevety was taken aback as he looked at the fury in the kid's eyes; he gave a thoughtful response. "We have regulations that all crew are of fighting age, and you obviously don't fulfill our requirements. But I appreciate your willingness to be a part of this mission. Shouldn't you want to meet with your parents?"

The youth wasn't prepared to take no for an answer. "I'd be the best computer technician on this ship!"

Krevety smirked, he couldn't help it! He didn't have time to argue.

He retorted, "Can't babysit a kid in deep space, and that's final. Now, before you are taken off this ship, please tell me how you ducked around our advanced security systems."

The teen answered Krevety unapologetically, "I'm Strider Willstreak, and my planet Yiohhaw was taken hostage during the Raihan Mission 16-108. I've recently learned my mother died in childbirth 15 years ago, and my father died in the recent battle at the communication outpost."

Krevety appeared captivated by Willstreak.

Strider continued, "I've also learned that my uncle, Rander Willstreak, volunteered for this mission. I have no desire to return to Yiohhaw because there's nothing there for me now. I've no relatives left, except on this ship. I wish to be a part of this crew and serve with my uncle Rander Willstreak."

The general was amazed at the young man's candor. Yet he was concerned. There were obvious breaches in the security of the ship.

"How'd you get the top-secret manifest of the crew?" Krevety turned to Major Tallik. "Major, bring Rander Willstreak here right away!"

"Yes, general," replied Major Tallik as he exited the bridge.

"So, young Mr. Willstreak, you're becoming a greater security risk by the second. Is your uncle involved in this conspiracy as well?"

"No sir. No one else knew I was here."

"You're telling me you subverted our advanced security systems, viewed our manifest, and entered the vessel without the aid of an accomplice. I find that highly unlikely!"

Strider had gained the general's serious attention.

"What else do you know about our operation?"

The kid wasn't shy about reciting all the details about the mission, to include the armament and array of fighter and scientific craft on board. He knew more than most officers on the bridge!

After 10 minutes, Major Tallik returned. He was accompanied by Rander Willstreak and two guards. One look confirmed the family resemblance between the two.

Rander broke away and rushed to embrace the boastful youth. As he tried to hug Strider, it was evident the kid wasn't used to human contact. Rander backed away with his arms on Strider's shoulders.

"I searched for you in the academy, but no one knew where you were. I was told you were wandering the streets among Mihhidites during the Rochest raid, and likely hadn't made it. I've left messages with no reply, and I assumed the worst."

"According to the carvings on the walls of the Monument, you died years ago. I didn't believe it. I searched the Raihan databanks after the battle for fellow Willstreaks, and wasn't hopeful. When I looked at the manifest of this ship, I could hardly believe it. What happened to my father, how did he die?"

Rander got a far-away look in his eyes. It was evident it wasn't the time. "I'll tell you about your father later. He was a great hero."

With that, an irritated general Krevety broke in, "I like reunions as much as any person, but I aim to get to the bottom of how this kid has an intimate knowledge of our ship, its systems, and our mission!"

Major Tallik stepped in and briefed the general about the young stowaway. "Sir, I've checked out Raihan academy records. Here are the official particulars on Strider Willstreak."

Everything Krevety wondered about Strider was answered in his file. It detailed his advanced capability for technology and encryption, along with Raihan concerns about him being an outsider. Despite the kid's social awkwardness, his expertise with computer schematics was second to none.

He'd be a genuine asset to the mission if they took him along. After a long discussion with his uncle Rander and the command staff, it was decided that Strider would be accepted for the mission. When Strider was called back to the bridge and given the news, he accepted it unflinchingly.

"Okay." Strider was a serious kid who didn't outwardly express his emotions freely, but the general could tell he was contented with the verdict!

CHAPTER 51

Portal Clash

General Krevety's speech and mandatory camaraderie meal had positive effects on the newly assembled crew, but there was only so much bonding that would happen based upon the influence a superior officer!

Everyone would play nice with Krevety watching. He knew the truth. Only in the bowels of the V-357 lost in the vastness of deep space, would they inaugurate and nurture relationships that would see them through the tough times.

General Krevety promoted Brell to the rank of commander, because Captain Reg Piktkas was also on the mission. Abbsnate could vouch for Brell's character, but knew nothing about the other man. The move wasn't to diminish Piktkas's skills; he was to be a valued expert on the carrier. Krevety knew the crew needed a clear leader for such an undertaking, and Commander Brell was the best man for the job.

The time of departure arrived quickly. As the crew entered the V-357, a nervous excitement was palpable in the air. Everyone was on the spacecraft three hours before their departure time. General Krevety assured that the vessel wouldn't leave until its scheduled time. Checklists were looked over, and last-minute briefings were being conducted on every corner of the vessel. Three hours was nothing, compared to the years they'd be gone. They had to ensure everything was right before they left.

If the gamma bomb mission succeeded; the portal would be like a ripe, delicious apple torn out of Sonarian hands before they could taste its sweet flavor. Their anger would be at a fever pitch, leaving the '357 as the only outlet for their wrath!

Word came back from the portal that the Sonarians had a small fleet guarding the ergosphere. They'd kept their word and allowed the ark ships safe passage back to their home planets unharmed.

Dangerous Sonarian Dockers lurking around the portal meant a trial by fire from the get-go. It was a good thing in a way. Action sooner rather than later was better than waiting around in space for excuses to get irritated with one another!

The time came to part ways. General Krevety bid everyone good luck and safe travels until their return. He said goodbye to the Mule crew last, which was tough because of his great affection for them.

"We'll meet again," he choked. Krevety turned away from them, brushing tears from his dark brown eyes.

Abbsnate rushed up and threw her arms around the tall man. "Thank you for everything, General Tom!"

He smiled, thrown off by the new nickname. Krevety bent down and used his thumbs to dry the cheeks under Abbsnate's bright blue eyes. He kissed her forehead. "Words can't express my gratitude for all you've done. Godspeed on your journey. You'll always be in my heart. I'll miss you greatly."

Krevety turned away and walked up the ramp of the last Bruiser on Raihan.

The Willstreak incident stalled Krevety, causing him to stay an extra day to tie up security concerns. Time was an issue, but not an endgame for them. The Bruiser ark would go full-throttle to make up the needed distance before the V-357 arrived at the portal.

The Bruiser was filled to the brim with data and material from the Scientific Center. The most valuable information for the mission, however, were galactic facts from the Reaching Technology wing. They'd use the equipment and data to attempt to contact the carrier crew from the Trecon side of the universe. Krevety would do everything in his power to ensure the Trecons were looking into the stars for evidence of a usable portal loop.

*****

Commander Brell didn't wait too long for the cruise to get underway before initiating readiness drills. He knew the importance of crew familiarization. It was wise thinking. Every second counted, considering the potency of the Sonarian war-ships. The first time the fighters exited the V-357 together shouldn't be when they were flying into battle. They needed to establish themselves as a unified fighting force before they met the battle-hardened Sonarians.

The maneuvers served another important purpose. A slight delay would give Krevety more lead time to make it through the portal and around Laurus safely before the detonation. Brell turned to Colonel Honassen, "Do you think they're ready?"

"Only one way to find out," said Honassen.

"Red alert, red alert, red alert! Enemy ships approaching. Man your battle stations. Launch all fighters," called Commander Brell over the ship's intercom.

Bleeeaat, bleeeaat, bleeeaat!

The bridge flashed bright red for a moment, then to dim lighting as the red lights flashed in cadence with the steady announcement of red alert. It was a challenge to launch the fighters all at once, but it had to be done!

The crew seemed underprepared when Brell initiated the first drill.

Pilots tripped clumsily to their fighters, and turret gunners fared equally bad manning their battle stations. It took an eternity for the defense cannons to be operational, a full two minutes!

The first drill was slow; 1:45 out of the fighter bay door for the first ship, and last out at the 5:03 mark. Many minor mishaps occurred on the exercise, as the crews worked together for the first time. Thankfully, there were no accidents. The mistakes involved fluidity of the operation, and afterward, there was a debriefing to discuss ways to improve.

Onsan appreciated the preparation drills because he knew he needed stick time on the Starlance. He gained valuable combat experience aboard the Trinity, but piloting the Starlance would require a different skill set all together. He was familiar with the bird through books and simulators, but the maneuvers helped him become intimate with the complexities of his craft.

He was sluggish getting out of the gate for the first drill just like everyone else, and heard it from Abbsnate, "Let's see the skills you love to brag about, Onsan!"

The commander wasn't so lighthearted. He was brutally honest, "Not good enough, crew. We have to do better, because the Sonarians will be on us in seconds!"

It was apparent from the start that quality communication was at a premium, and it didn't take long for Commander Brell to gain everyone's confidence.

Brell called for seven more drills, until he was satisfied with the result. He wanted not only to ensure they could exit the ship efficiently, but also load rapidly after a battle. If they ran into an ambush against a superior force, they had to evacuate quickly without leaving their fighter pilots behind to fend for themselves.

By the end of the seventh maneuver, the crew had the first fighters out in less than a minute, and all fighters off the deck in 3:30. They could load up within five minutes, not bad considering they were loading 45 fighters! The crew grew in different ways; weary of the captain's drills, but mounting in confidence and experience as well!

When Commander Brell was satisfied with the results of their exercises, he ordered the vessel into SBAS concealment mode and set course for the portal at full speed.

*****

As they neared the ergosphere, they encountered five Sonarian docking ships, each loaded with four Crusaders. Commander Brell was thankful his fighter pilots were as good as they needed to be, battling together for the first time.

Bleeeaat, bleeeaat, bleeeaat!

The Klaxon sounded piercingly as the V-357 came out of concealment mode and surprised the Sonarians.

Commander Brell announced, "Red alert, red alert, red alert! Sonarian ships on the horizon. Battle stations. Launch all fighters and engage enemy."

The announcement over the ship's loudspeakers officially set the dangerous part of the mission into motion. The concealment mode of the V-357 gave them an advantage from the start. With Brell's announcement, the defense cannons were operational at an incredible 30 seconds, showering the Sonarians with rapid laser fire while the first fighters were exiting the carrier. All the squadrons were out and engaging the Sonarian ships before they had time to react!

Bzzzzt, bzzzzt, kaboom, bash!

Onsan felt he was gaining a mastery of the Starlance craft. His position was on the left flank of six Trinity fighters, a good place to be. As the fighters advanced, the Crusaders were intent on detaching from their docking ships for battle.

The Sonarians recently allowed Krevety's Bruiser through the portal without a conflict. They were unprepared for an ambush by an invisible carrier. They'd intimidated the inhabitants of the portal with their display of great power, but now were taken back by the aggressiveness of the V-357!

The Sonarians were caught with their pants down as the hammering squadron formations headed straight for the docking ships at top speed. The fighters had to take out the Docker frequency pulsars before the Sonarians could leach onto the '357, or the battle would turn quickly. Onsan's flank attacked and destroyed a docking ship before the last Crusader detached. A Trinity ended the Docker with the ferocious accuracy of their hind-cannon.

Bzzeew bzzeew, boom!

Suddenly a Crusader was on Onsan's tail, blasting away at him! He banked hard to the left, and the pursuer ran into another Trinity's blast. The Sonarian pilot let his emotions get in the way after seeing the Docker destroyed. It was a fatal mistake!

Laser fire and explosions filled the feverish rocky ergosphere!

"Enemy approaching on your left," roared Onsan to a fellow Starlance fighter. "Hold your course firm I've got him!"

Zzzrt zzzrt, bam, glow!

Right through the front wing! Although Onsan didn't destroy him in the pass, he damaged the Crusader and chased it away from his cohort.

"Thanks, I owe you one!" Onsan could have kicked himself for missing the direct shot as he rolled back into formation.

The Crusaders seemed awoken from their slumber and were fighting back with increased intensity! The remaining four Dockers were subjected to heavy V-357 cannon fire and Trinity onslaught, leaving the Crusaders with no cover as they were forced to defend themselves. Once their Dockers were destroyed, they'd be done for in deep space.

The V-357 crew still knew the wounded Sonarians were not to be taken lightly, regardless of their numerical disadvantage. They'd seen the destructive capabilities of the Dockers during the battles over Raihan. However, the V-357 ship included battle-tested Trinity and Starlance fighters, not inexperienced and terrified Talon pilots!

Bzzeew bzzeew, flash, baroom!

The diverse fleet engaged the Sonarians with a fierceness and vigor unmatched by the mindless attacks of the first Raihan fleets they'd fought. The Sonarian fleet was quickly overwhelmed. The Talons swarmed together like a school of fish, weaving between meteorites to draw Sonarian attention away from the carrier while the others attacked. The Talon IIs showed everyone their value as they blasted their targets with blazing rapid fire!

"Let's finish them," called Commander Brell as they directed their fire on the last two Dockers.

Eewlu-whoop-shriek-eewlu-whoop-shriek-eewlu-whoop-shriek-eewlu!

A Docker shot its frequency burst toward the carrier, but it was at the edge of its range, and ineffective as a single ship against the goliath. The carrier's powerful shields provided maximum protection against the leaching Docker under the expert guidance of Commander Brell.

Abbsnate's Trinity took out the attacker!

Boom, shatter!

Onsan encountered a Crusader turning aside and locking in on an approaching Talon fighter. He knew the Talon could hold it off for a second with its agility, but it was only a matter of time before the ship would be destroyed by the bellicose Crusader. He rolled quickly into attack position and noticed the pilot didn't bank off like before. The Crusader was determined to gain a kill for the Sonarians.

Bzzeew, spark, shudder!

The Crusader fired, and a penetrating laser burned off the left gun of the Talon. He'd destroy the startled bird with the next shot.

Without a second to spare, Onsan swooped down on the rear starboard side and fired a shot right into the cockpit of the Crusader.

Zzzrt zzzrt, smash, burst!

Onsan's first direct hit from the cockpit of his Starlance offered a spectacular view! There was a bright orange flash, as the laser cut through the shields and disabled the ship. A nanosecond later, the breach caused by the shot opened the Crusader to the radiation-filled ergosphere. It crumpled like a tin can, then luminously exploded into the black ether.

All Onsan could muster was, "Whoa, got him!"

Two Talons swooped in to escort their injured comrade home.

"About time you helped out! Nice shot," cried Abbsnate from her Trinity.

The Crusaders were a tough enemy, though, demonstrating they'd fight to their last breath. They showed no hint of dishonoring themselves through running from a superior force, although it was clear from early in the fight they were heavily outgunned and outmatched. The V-357 had no choice but to oblige the enemy quickly, and continue on with their important mission.

Bzzeew, flash, crush!

They dispatched the remaining Crusaders in short order, pressing them against the giant rocks moving riotously along the mouth of the portal! Many fighters boarded the '357 before the last Crusader was destroyed!

There was no time to celebrate their victory. A larger fleet was waiting on the other side for the V-357 carrier. There'd be more fighting when they passed through to the Sonarian dimension.

A damage assessment was completed, their only casualty was the gun shot off a Talon fighter. Crews got to work on it right away. They'd need every gun possible for the next phase of their mission.

"We've got a major problem," reported Pnoi Nbnok to Commander Brell. "The main fleet is trying to contact the ships on this side. Our technology has worked so far by playing back recorded loops to simulate no loss of contact. Once we enter the portal, however, our ability to send the simulations will likely be lost."

They'd used Raihan splicing as a necessity for self-defense and mission success. The V-357 had locked the Sonarian communications as they began their ambush, but didn't account for the fleet on the other side calling to receive regular status updates.

"We'll have deployed the bomb by then. What does that matter to us?"

Nbnok explained the situation to Brell, "Our calculated plan of 18 minutes inching away from the gamma bomb before initiating our full thrusters will be affected. We'll have to make it through in half the time, because the Docker fleet will respond instantly to investigate the loss of communication. If we encounter the Sonarians coming the other way, there's zero likelihood of escape."

CJ responded, "We'll have to enter the portal at higher speeds than normal to make up for the time. Prepare for a bumpy ride!"

"Bottom line is, our clock starts as soon as we enter the portal," Nbnok had a grave look on his face. "We can't control the quality of the message splice once we've entered the event horizon."

"Very well, we'll wait for the next call and answer just before we enter. What's the regularity of their calls?"

"They're asking for a PAR report every 15 minutes,"

Commander Brell did the math in his head and gave a grave answer. "If we're approached before we release the bomb, we'll have to make for the portal and detonate it right away to prevent them from destroying the ship but not the bomb."

Colonel Honassen asked, "Do you want to tell the crew, captain?"

Brell announced, "This may be much shorter of a mission than we originally planned. Fortunately, now that we're here, the mission will be completed either way. Billions of people are counting on us, and we won't let them down!"

CHAPTER 52

Threshold Closed for Business

A palpable feeling of tension flooded the carrier as the crew prepared the V-357 for her journey into the unknown. Once all the fighters were securely ratcheted down, the craft entered the event horizon.

Thunder, whoosh!

There was no going back on their mission of discharging the bomb and passing into the Sonarian universe. They rocketed through the portal and engaged their reverse thrusters when they entered the vacuum stillness in the center of the wormhole.

"Heeeree wee aaaree," said General Seraden.

CJ said, "Nooo cooompaany, thaaat'ss aa gooood staart!"

Commander Brell ordered, "Maakeee fiiinaal preeepaaraaatiioonss tooo reeleeaaasee theee gaaammaa booomb!"

Calculations were reassessed and confirmed.

"Reeeaady," said Nbnok with a thumbs-up.

"Nooo tiimeee tooo waaassteee, iinitiiiaatee!" Commander Brell and Colonel Honassen punched their synchronized controls, and the V-357 released the bomb into the vacuum with minimum thrust.

Schhwaff, roll!

The gamma bomb floated out into the vacuum.

Clunk, clack, click!

The bomb door closed and locked into place.

Everyone breathed easier, as the automated release system self-loaded and the airlock closed. It was like a deadly sliver had been extracted from their midst!

They had to gain enough distance away from the bomb to use their thrusters and not affect it. The bomb had a timer set for 18 minutes, which wouldn't give them much time to distance themselves from it at full speed to begin with. Now that the Sonarians were alerted, they'd have a mere nine minutes to escape! They preferred to inch away from the bomb with maximum discretion. They didn't have a choice but to cut corners and use maximum speed in three minutes, or when they detected Sonarians coming from the opposite direction.

The minimum thrust of the gamma bomb mechanism acted as it was designed to. The payload released and stayed in the vacuum behind the '357.

After one precarious minute inching away from the package, a squadron of five Sonarian ships suddenly appeared in range before them. The Dockers were on their way through the wormhole to investigate the loss of communication. They'd arrived sooner than Nbnok expected!

"Seeet shiiieeelllddss toooo fuuull poowwweer, anndd maaaxximmuuum thrruuusteeerss ahheeead," ordered Commander Brell, as the Sonarians closed range to two kilometers.

"Yeeess siiirrr," answered a queasy CJ.

They couldn't afford Nbnok's plan of three minutes idling from the bomb. If the Sonarians fired even one shot at them, it could be deflected by their shield and detonate the explosive! The super-responsiveness of the V-357 was their main advantage, but they had to distance themselves from the bomb before more Dockers jammed their route! It was a cosmic game of chicken, and no one moved aside!

Roar!

Smash, crunch!

The massive carrier breached a hole through the Sonarian formation like a bowling ball picking up a five-pin spare! The V-357 bullied past the determined blockade, sending the Dockers lurching around her as she raced through toward the exit. They were all in with the new plan now, there was no choice but to continue forward full-speed into the Sonarian universe. If the bomb detonated, they'd be dead before they knew it!

After a few seconds, they knew the bomb had handled the disruption caused by their maximum thrusters, and the crew could focus forward again. At full speed, they could distinguish no more Sonarians coming the other way. The ride through the portal was not what they expected.

Groan, blaze!

It was a supersonic ride through a tunnel that was dark and full of terror!

Pnoi Nbnok knew all bets were off as far as time was concerned. In the next few seconds, or minutes, they'd face the moment of truth!

Reeeeooooww, bellowed Chase, as if to say, *"Not again!"*

They hit the portal exit and passed the Sonarians too fast to notice the blur of vessels around them.

Their shields held firm, the crew couldn't distinguish if the rough ride was due to a turbulent ergosphere, or from ramming through the Sonarian fleet at supersonic speed!

MOOOOB, KABOOOOOM, VOOOMPPH!

The bomb detonated in the vacuum area of the portal and tore it wide open, just as General Seraden predicted. The initial explosion sucked everything back toward the event horizon for a moment, then shot them through into the Sonarian galaxy so intensely that a good part of the crew instantly blacked out. Due to the forces playing on their bodies, it was impossible to breathe! The temporary lack of oxygen put many into a sickened dreamlike state, including Onsan.

Those who stayed conscious felt the impossible forces of gravitational thrust pushing their organs into their bones as they were shot at an ultrasonic speed into the Sonarian universe! It would've been impossible for them to witness the gathering fleet disintegrating around them, because their speed was too great!

The Sonarians had felt invincible in their fleet of thousands. They hadn't bothered to raise their shields to enter the portal yet, so they didn't have a chance! Radiated debris shot out along with the V-357 into the Sonarian dimension, rendering the gathered Dockers heavily damaged and ineffective. Most of the Crusaders were violently ripped off the incapacitated Dockers from the force of the detonation! Crews of the less damaged ships thousands of kilometers away stared at the devastation in shell-shocked horror!

As the V-357 escaped through the fleet, coronal mass ejections flowed out of the orifice from the Magnus and Laurus suns. Each star tried intensely to right itself through magnetic reconnection, but as they attempted to enforce their mass, they were also ripping each other apart! The gamma bomb had created a colossal explosive effect of a smaller new third sun, releasing energy that followed the ship through the Sonarian invasion force!

The crew started to slowly awaken from their stupor. They noticed remnants of Sonarian vessels all around them. Incomprehensible compression waves had crushed against the ships, sending them spinning into the greater universe with untold intensity and velocity! The V-357 carrier carried the only healthy inhabitants around, surrounded for thousands of kilometers by a Sonarian boneyard scattered into the visible reaches of space. The carrier was but an insignificant fleck in the destruction. The unexplored universe unfolded in front of the '357 as the crew fought to gain its bearing in the turmoil of their surrounding milieu.

A new clock was ticking for them now. Commander Brell turned to CJ, "We've got to get out of here!" The result of the detonation was like an enormous neon sign announcing their arrival in the new galaxy, but they were powerless for minutes as they strove to acquaint themselves to the environment.

CJ tried to shake the cobwebs from his brain. "The ship's coming back on line, commander."

When Onsan finally awoke, he was experiencing vertigo so intense he felt out of body and light-headed, feeling he'd vomit if he tried to move. An hour later, he unbuckled from his seat, and stumbled down the corridor to inspect the damage. As he came upon Abbsnate, he noticed her sitting in a chair and staring out a port window. Chase was licking her face tenderly.

He asked her, "Abbsnate, how are you feeling?"

She smiled and responded groggily, "Here we go again, Onsan!"

Three hours after the gamma bomb detonation, the ship systems were returning to normal levels, thanks to Strider Willstreak and the advanced Raihan technology aboard. Life-sustaining medical systems, weapons, and basic ship navigation returned to full working order rapidly. There were no major injuries. All around the carrier, people were checking themselves, their shipmates, and equipment.

There was one major hurdle as they explored the new galaxy. Their galactic maps were useless, because there was no specific data of the Sonarian universe yet. General Seraden knew of the solar system, but the navigation port needed specific data to be effective. The ship would strive to map the cosmos for them, but it would take time until the reaching technology of the ship exposed and recorded the cosmos around them.

The mission heavily depended on the basic quadrant familiarity of a disheartened Sonarian general. Commander Brell didn't pull Seraden from his stateroom to see the devastation of his planetary kin. They couldn't know the entire fleet would be amassed at the portal so soon. The commander realized the detonation had saved the lives of countless people, but he'd keep his opinion to himself around General Seraden.

Commander Brell reported on the intercom. "We're safe for the time being, but we'll have to be on the move soon. The Sonarians have been incapacitated by the detonation for now, but they'll recover soon, with the goal of a swift revenge against us! Without the destruction of their fleet, we may have earned a compassionate ear from the scientific community on Sonaria, but we'll have no friends there anymore. We've helped General Shrog prove his point against us! Everything that he's said has come to fulfillment, or at least he'll spin it that way."

Brell continued, "We'll be in constant danger near the portal. Our goal within these first few days and weeks will be to navigate through the Sonarian nets that will be certainly laid out before us. We have many advancements on this ship to see us through, but you should all know that doing your job thoroughly is of the utmost importance! From here on out, the slightest oversight will put us all in grave danger going forward."

The commander let his words sink in before continuing, "As you know, we can stay in concealment mode for a while, but our mapping capabilities are greatly diminished during those times. For this mission to be successful, we'll soon need to branch out and send out our probes. All we have now is each other!"

The situation they'd just encountered brought unity to the crew through the sheer magnitude of their situation! In the rear observation deck, a crowd looked in awed silence at the newly formed sun portal sending its dark ginger and brilliant rubicund hues through the event horizon. The mission was a complete success on that account.

There was no going back; the successes and failures of their past lives were forever cauterized in the raging inferno behind them! From a distance, it looked stunning. It was too beautiful to have committed the unthinkable violence that resulted in the destruction surrounding them.

On the bridge, some were focusing on the unknown future rather than the past. Onsan and Abbsnate looked at each other with strange expressions. They were about to embark on their biggest adventure yet.

Commander Brell looked through the bridge shield and ordered CJ, "Proceed slowly. One-quarter speed."

The V-357 vanished into the vast new universe toward unknown adventures!

This book started out as a father-and-son lesson in self-expression as Anson was striving to improve his grades in 7th grade language arts. It began as a conversation about a good science fiction story, and we stretched the details from there, (to improve his writing skills). As Anson and Dean added plot and characters, the story improved to the point that it basically wrote itself!

Our family loves to go on camping excursions to Northern Minnesota. If you look close enough, references to Minnesota north shore campgrounds are evident. The camping story in chapter 47 is basically true, although it merges two parks together. The rainy campsite happened at Gooseberry Falls State Park. Anson and I pitched a tent in the rain. When Sarah and the girls arrived at our site, the family spent the wet evening playing board games in Lady Slipper Lodge instead of caves! Mic Mac lake is in Tettegouche State Park. We've enjoyed time spent at the cabins in Tettegouche Camp alongside the lake.

Dean has been married to Sarah for 19 years. They have three children, Anson (15), Natalie (13), and Abigail (10). (Abbsnate in our story is a combination of their nicknames).

Anson is a sophomore at Barnum High School in Minnesota. He loves all sports, but his passion is baseball. He's a stellar infielder, who used to watch Twins games on television wearing his glove! Anson and dad have spent countless hours on the ballfield in our back yard. He is gifted in music, playing the piano and singing in choir. He loves to spend time with his friends and take his dog, Finnigan, for walks through the woods near our home.

Natalie is an art aficionado, who's keen eye added important detail to the illustrations in this book. If you visit our home, evidence of her creativity abounds. Her imagination and enormous smile are a warm combination for everyone she has ever met!

CPSIA information can be obtained
at www.ICGtesting.com
Printed in the USA
BVHW09202523I019
561945BV00004B/7/P